ALAN E. NOURSE
RESURRECTED

The Works of Alan E. Nourse

By Alan E. Nourse
Edited by Greg Fowlkes

Includes the Special Bonus Story
AND NOW A MESSAGE . . .
By Greg Fowlkes

ALAN E. NOURSE
RESURRECTED

The Works of Alan E. Nourse

© 2011 Resurrected Press
www.ResurrectedPress.com

Published by Resurrected Press

This classic book was handcrafted by Resurrected Press. Resurrected Press is dedicated to bringing high quality classic books back to the readers who enjoy them. These are not scanned versions of the originals, but, rather, quality checked and edited books meant to be enjoyed!

Please visit ResurrectedPress.com to view our entire catalogue!

ISBN 13: 978-1-935774-87-7

Printed in the United States of America

FOREWORD

Alan E. Nourse was in many ways typical of the generation responsible for the "Golden Age of Science fiction." Born in the Midwest, he served in the Navy before entering college. He turned to writing to finance his education, and continued to write after obtaining his M.D. Most of his science fiction was written during the 50's. In later years he wrote a number of non-fiction books on both medical and scientific topics as well as a regular column on medicine for *Good Housekeeping*.

With his background, it is not surprising that much of his science fiction has a medical theme to it, whether in the humorous "The Coffin Cure" or the more serious "Martyr." In the story "Contamination Crew" he uses as a setting a time when Earth has become the physician to the Galaxy, a theme he was to explore in more detail in the novel *Star Surgeon*.

His approach to alien species was also influenced by his medical and scientific background, and falls squarely into the category of "hard" science fiction. "The Native Soil" and "PRoblem" are examples of this type of story. "Letter of the Law," while not centered around science, is also a story in the hard vein.

Nourse's interests were not limited to medicine and science. The 50's were a time of political turmoil. They had seen the aftermath of the collapse of one totalitarian scheme in fascism and the rise of another in communism. Even the United States had witnessed McCarthyism. Reflecting this environment, several of the stories in this collection have a distinctly political theme, notably "Bear Trap," "Martyr," "Infinite Intruder," and "Derelict."

The final eight stories in this volume were originally collected in *The Counterfeit Man* which was published in 1963 and represent a somewhat more mature phase of the author's career. There are satiric looks at both the medical profession and labor relations in "An Ounce of Cure" and "Meeting of the Board," as well as the humorous "Circus." Nourse's growing interest in psi powers and the paranormal is expressed in "My Friend Bobby" and "Second Sight" with the conclusion that such powers are at best a mixed blessing. Interstellar relations are the topics of "Image of the Gods" and "The Link." The final story, a journey into madness, is the subject of "The Dark Door." This group of stories, which was written in the late fifties and early sixties, are the products of a more experienced and confident writer, as evidenced by the improved style and subtler plots.

Alan E. Nourse was both a capable and intelligent writer, and his stories reflect a unique viewpoint during the period when he was most active as a science fiction writer. Because of this, Resurrected Press is proud to offer this collection of stories to you, the reader.

Greg Fowlkes
Editor-In-Chief
Resurrected Press
www.ResurrectedPress.com

Table Of Contents

DERELICT

ILLUSTRATED BY ED EMSH
ORIGINALLY PUBLISHED IN *IF: WORLDS OF SCIENCE FICTION*
MAY 1953

What was the mystery of this great ship from the dark, deep reaches of space? For, within its death-filled chambers— was the avenue of life!

DERELICT

John Sabo, second in command, sat bolt upright in his bunk, blinking wide-eyed at the darkness. The alarm was screaming through the Satellite Station, its harsh, nerve-jarring clang echoing and re-echoing down the metal corridors, penetrating every nook and crevice and cubicle of the lonely outpost, screaming incredibly through the dark sleeping period. Sabo shook the sleep from his eyes, and then a panic of fear burst into his mind. The alarm! Tumbling out of his bunk in the darkness, he crashed into the far bulkhead, staggering giddily in the impossible gravity as he pawed about for his magnaboots, his heart pounding fiercely in his ears. The *alarm*! Impossible, after so long, after these long months of bitter waiting— In the corridor he collided with Brownie, looking like a frightened gnome, and he growled profanity as he raced down the corridor for the Central Control.

Frightened eyes turned to him as he blinked at the bright lights of the room. The voices rose in a confused, anxious babble, and he shook his head and swore, and ploughed through them toward the screen. "Kill that damned alarm!" he roared, blinking as he counted faces. "Somebody get the Skipper out of his sack, pronto, and stop that clatter! What's the trouble?"

The radioman waved feebly at the view screen, shimmering on the great side panel. "We just picked it up—"

It was a ship, moving in from beyond Saturn's rings, a huge, gray-black blob in the silvery screen, moving in toward the Station with ponderous, clumsy grace, growing larger by the second as it sped toward them. Sabo felt the fear spill over in his mind, driving out all thought, and he sank into the control chair like a well-trained automaton. His gray eyes were wide, trained for long military years to miss nothing; his fingers moved over the panel with deft skill. "Get the men to stations," he growled, "and will somebody kindly get the Skipper down here, if he can manage to take a minute."

"I'm right here." The little graying man was at his elbow, staring at the screen with angry red eyes. "Who told you to shut off the alarm?"

"Nobody told me. Everyone was here, and it was getting on my nerves."

"What a shame." Captain Loomis' voice was icy. "I give orders on this Station," he said smoothly, "and you'll remember it." He scowled at the great gray ship, looming closer and closer. "What's its course?"

"Going to miss us by several thousand kilos at least. Look at that thing! It's *traveling*."

"Contact it! This is what we've been waiting for." The captain's voice was hoarse.

Sabo spun a dial, and cursed. "No luck. Can't get through. It's passing us—"

"Then *grapple* it, stupid! You want me to wipe your nose, too?"

Sabo's face darkened angrily. With slow precision he set the servo fixes on the huge gray hulk looming up in the viewer, and then snapped the switches sharply. Two small servos shoved their blunt noses from the landing port of the Station, and slipped silently into space alongside. Then, like a pair of trained dogs, they sped on their beams straight out from the Station toward the approaching ship. The intruder was dark, moving at tremendous velocity past the Station, as though unaware of its existence. The servos moved out, and suddenly diverged and reversed, twisting in long arcs to come alongside the strange ship, finally moving in at the same velocity on either side. There was a sharp flash of contact power; then, like a mammoth slow-motion monster, the ship jerked in midspace and turned a graceful end-for-end arc as the servo-grapplers gripped it like leeches and whined, glowing ruddy with the jolting power flowing through them. Sabo watched, hardly breathing, until the great ship spun and slowed and stopped. Then it reversed direction, and the servos led it triumphantly back toward the landing port of the Station.

Sabo glanced at the radioman, a frown creasing his forehead. "Still nothing?"

"Not a peep."

He stared out at the great ship, feeling a chill of wonder and fear crawl up his spine. "So this is the mysterious puzzle of Saturn," he muttered. "This is what we've been waiting for."

There was a curious eager light in Captain Loomis' eyes as he looked up. "Oh, no. Not this."

"What?"

"Not this. The ships we've seen before were tiny, flat." His little eyes turned toward the ship, and back to Sabo's heavy face. "This is something else, something quite different." A smile curved his lips, and he rubbed his hands together. "We go out for trout and come back with a whale. This ship's from space, deep space. Not from Saturn. This one's from the stars."

*   *   *   *   *

The strange ship hung at the side of the Satellite Station, silent as a tomb, still gently rotating as the Station slowly spun in its orbit around Saturn.

In the captain's cabin the men shifted restlessly, uneasily facing the eager eyes of their captain. The old man paced the floor of the cabin, his white hair mussed, his face red with excitement. Even his carefully calm face couldn't conceal the eagerness burning in his eyes as he faced the crew. "Still no contact?" he asked Sparks.

The radioman shook his head anxiously. "Not a sign. I've tried every signal I know at every wave frequency that could possibly reach them. I've even tried a dozen frequencies that couldn't possibly reach them, and I haven't stirred them up a bit. They just aren't answering."

Captain Loomis swung on the group of men. "All right, now, I want you to get this straight. This is our catch. We don't know what's aboard it, and we don't know where it came from, but it's our prize. That means not a word goes back home about it until we've learned all there is to learn. We're going to get the honors on this one, not some eager Admiral back home—"

The men stirred uneasily, worried eyes seeking Sabo's face in alarm. "What about the law?" growled Sabo. "The law says everything must be reported within two hours."

"Then we'll break the law," the captain snapped. "I'm captain of this Station, and those are your orders. You don't need to worry about the law—I'll see that you're protected, but this is too big to fumble. This ship is from the stars. That means it must have an Interstellar drive. You know what that means. The Government will fall all over itself to reward us—"

Sabo scowled, and the worry deepened in the men's faces. It was hard to imagine the Government falling all over itself for anybody. They knew too well how the Government worked. They had heard of the swift trials, the harsh imprisonments that awaited even the petty infringers. The Military Government had no time to waste on those who stepped out of line, they had no mercy to spare. And the men knew that their captain was not in favor in top Government circles. Crack patrol commanders were not shunted into remote, lifeless Satellite Stations if their stand in the Government was high. And deep in their minds, somehow, the men knew they couldn't trust this little, sharp-eyed, white-haired man. The credit for such a discovery as this might go to him, yes—but there would be little left for them.

"The law—" Sabo repeated stubbornly.

"Damn the law! We're stationed out here in this limbo to watch Saturn and report any activity we see coming from there. There's nothing in our orders about anything else. There have been ships from there, they think, but not this ship. The Government has spent billions trying to find an Interstellar, and never gotten to first base." The captain paused, his eyes narrowing. "We'll go aboard this ship," he said softly. "We'll find out what's aboard it, and where it's from, and we'll take its drive. There's been no resistance yet, but it could be dangerous. We can't assume anything. The boarding party will report everything they find to me. One of them will have to be a drive man. That's you, Brownie."

The little man with the sharp black eyes looked up eagerly. "I don't know if I could tell anything—"

"You can tell more than anyone else here. Nobody else knows space drive. I'll count on you. If you bring back a good report, perhaps we can cancel out certain—unfortunate items in your record. But one other should board with you—" His eyes turned toward John Sabo.

"Not me. This is your goat." The mate's eyes were sullen. "This is gross breach, and you know it. They'll have you in irons when we get back. I don't want anything to do with it."

"You're under orders, Sabo. You keep forgetting."

"They're illegal orders, sir!"

"I'll take responsibility for that."

Sabo looked the old man straight in the eye. "You mean you'd sell us down a rat hole to save your skin. That's what you mean."

Captain Loomis' eyes widened incredulously. Then his face darkened, and he stepped very close to the big man. "You'll watch your tongue, I think," he gritted. "Be careful what you say to me, Sabo. Be very careful. Because if you don't, *you'll* be in irons, and we'll see just how long you last when you get back home. Now you've got your orders. You'll board the ship with Brownie."

The big man's fists were clenched until the knuckles were white. "You don't know what's over there!" he burst out. "We could be slaughtered."

The captain's smile was unpleasant. "That would be such a pity," he murmured. "I'd really hate to see it happen—"

*   *   *   *   *

The ship hung dark and silent, like a shadowy ghost. No flicker of light could be seen aboard it; no sound nor faintest sign of life came from the tall, dark hull plates. It hung there, huge and imponderable, and swung around with the Station in its silent orbit.

The men huddled about Sabo and Brownie, helping them into their pressure suits, checking their equipment. They had watched the little scanning beetles crawl over the surface of the great ship, examining, probing every nook and crevice, reporting crystals, and metals, and irons, while the boarding party prepared. And still the radioman waited alertly for a flicker of life from the solemn giant.

Frightened as they were of their part in the illegal secrecy, the arrival of the ship had brought a change in the crew, lighting fires of excitement in their eyes. They moved faster, their voices were lighter, more cheerful. Long months on the Station had worn on their nerves—out of contact with their homes, on a mission that was secretly jeered as utter Governmental folly. Ships *had* been seen, years before, disappearing into the sullen bright atmospheric crust of Saturn, but there had been no sign of anything since. And out there, on the lonely guard Station, nerves had run ragged, always waiting, always watching, wearing away even the iron discipline of their military background. They grew bitterly weary of the same faces, the same routine, the constant repetition of inactivity. And through the months they had watched with increasing anxiety the conflict growing between the captain and his bitter, sullen-eyed second-in-command, John Sabo.

And then the ship had come, incredibly, from the depths of space, and the tensions of loneliness were forgotten in the flurry of activity. The locks whined and opened as the two men moved out of the Station on the little propulsion sleds, linked to the Station with light silk guy ropes. Sabo settled himself on the sled, cursing himself for falling so foolishly into the captain's scheme, cursing his tongue for wandering. And deep within him he felt a new sensation, a vague uneasiness and insecurity that he had not felt in all his years of military life. The strange ship was a variant, an imponderable factor thrown suddenly into his small world of hatred and bitterness, forcing him into unknown territory, throwing his mind into a welter of doubts and fears. He glanced uneasily across at Brownie, vaguely wishing that someone else were with him. Brownie was a troublemaker, Brownie talked too much, Brownie philosophized in a world that ridiculed philosophy. He'd known men like Brownie before, and he knew that they couldn't be trusted.

The gray hull gleamed at them as they moved toward it, a monstrous wall of polished metal. There were no dents, no surface scars from its passage through space. They found the entrance lock without difficulty, near the top of the ship's great hull, and Brownie probed the rim of the lock with a dozen instruments, his dark eyes burning eagerly. And then, with a squeal that grated in Sabo's ears, the oval port of the ship quivered, and slowly opened.

Silently, the sleds moved into the opening. They were in a small vault, quite dark, and the sleds settled slowly onto a metal deck. Sabo eased himself from the seat, tuning up his audios to their highest sensitivity, moving over to Brownie. Momentarily they touched helmets, and Brownie's excited voice came to him, muted, but breathless. "No trouble getting it open. It worked on the same principle as ours."

"Better get to work on the inner lock."

Brownie shot him a sharp glance. "But what about—inside? I mean, we can't just walk in on them—"

"Why not? We've tried to contact them."

Reluctantly, the little engineer began probing the inner lock with trembling fingers. Minutes later they were easing themselves through, moving slowly down the dark corridor, waiting with pounding hearts for a sound, a sign. The corridor joined another, and then still another, until they reached a great oval door. And then they were inside, in the heart of the ship, and their eyes widened as they stared at the thing in the center of the great vaulted chamber.

"My God!" Brownie's voice was a hoarse whisper in the stillness. "Look at them, Johnny!"

Sabo moved slowly across the room toward the frail, crushed form lying against the great, gleaming panel. Thin, almost boneless arms were pasted against the hard metal; an oval, humanoid skull was crushed like an eggshell into the knobs and levers of the control panel. Sudden horror shot through the big man as he looked around. At the far side of the room was another of the things, and still another, mashed, like lifeless jelly, into the floors and panels. Gently he peeled a bit of jelly away from the metal, then turned with a mixture of wonder and disgust. "All dead," he muttered.

Brownie looked up at him, his hands trembling. "No wonder there was no sign." He looked about helplessly. "It's a derelict, Johnny. A wanderer. How could it have happened? How long ago?"

Sabo shook his head, bewildered. "Then it was just chance that it came to us, that we saw it—"

"No pilot, no charts. It might have wandered for centuries." Brownie stared about the room, a frightened look on his face. And then he was leaning over the control panel, probing at the array of levers, his fingers working eagerly at the wiring. Sabo nodded approvingly. "We'll have to go over it with a comb," he said. "I'll see what I can find in the rest of the ship. You go ahead on the controls and drive." Without waiting for an answer he moved swiftly from the round chamber, out into the corridor again, his stomach almost sick.

It took them many hours. They moved silently, as if even a slight sound might disturb the sleeping alien forms, smashed against the dark metal panels. In another room were the charts, great, beautiful charts, totally unfamiliar, studded with star formations he had never seen, noted with curious, meaningless symbols. As Sabo worked he heard Brownie moving down into the depths of the ship, toward the giant engine rooms. And then, some silent alarm clicked into place in Sabo's mind, tightening his stomach, screaming to be heard. Heart pounding, he dashed down the corridor like a cat, seeing again in his mind the bright, eager eyes of the engineer. Suddenly the meaning of that eagerness dawned on him. He scampered down a ladder, along a corridor, and down another ladder, down to the engine room, almost colliding with Brownie as he crossed from one of the engines to a battery of generators on the far side of the room.

"Brownie!"

"What's the trouble?"

Sabo trembled, then turned away. "Nothing," he muttered. "Just a thought." But he watched as the little man snaked into the labyrinth of dynamos and coils and wires, peering eagerly, probing, searching, making notes in the little pad in his hand.

Finally, hours later, they moved again toward the lock where they had left their sleds. Not a word passed between them. The uneasiness was strong in Sabo's mind now, growing deeper, mingling with fear and a premonition of impending evil. A dead ship, a derelict, come to them by merest chance from some unthinkably remote star. He cursed, without knowing why, and suddenly he felt he hated

Brownie as much as he hated the captain waiting for them in the Station.

But as he stepped into the Station's lock, a new thought crossed his mind, almost dazzling him with its unexpectedness. He looked at the engineer's thin face, and his hands were trembling as he opened the pressure suit.

*   *   *   *   *

He deliberately took longer than was necessary to give his report to the captain, dwelling on unimportant details, watching with malicious amusement the captain's growing annoyance. Captain Loomis' eyes kept sliding to Brownie, as though trying to read the information he wanted from the engineer's face. Sabo rolled up the charts slowly, stowing them in a pile on the desk. "That's the picture, sir. Perhaps a qualified astronomer could make something of it; I haven't the knowledge or the instruments. The ship came from outside the system, beyond doubt. Probably from a planet with lighter gravity than our own, judging from the frailty of the creatures. Oxygen breathers, from the looks of their gas storage. If you ask me, I'd say—"

"All right, all right," the captain breathed impatiently. "You can write it up and hand it to me. It isn't really important where they came from, or whether they breathe oxygen or fluorine." He turned his eyes to the engineer, and lit a cigar with trembling fingers. "The important thing is *how* they got here. The drive, Brownie. You went over the engines carefully? What did you find?"

Brownie twitched uneasily, and looked at the floor. "Oh, yes, I examined them carefully. Wasn't too hard. I examined every piece of drive machinery on the ship, from stem to stern."

Sabo nodded, slowly, watching the little man with a carefully blank face. "That's right. You gave it a good going over."

Brownie licked his lips. "It's a derelict, like Johnny told you. They were dead. All of them. Probably had been dead for a long time. I couldn't tell, of course. Probably nobody could tell. But they must have been dead for centuries—"

The captain's eyes blinked as the implication sank in. "Wait a minute," he said. "What do you mean, *centuries?*"

Brownie stared at his shoes. "The atomic piles were almost dead," he muttered in an apologetic whine. "The ship wasn't going any place, captain. It was just wandering. Maybe it's wandered for thousands of years." He took a deep breath, and his eyes met the captain's for a brief agonized moment. "They don't have Interstellar, sir. Just plain, simple, slow atomics. Nothing different. They've been traveling for centuries, and it would have taken them just as long to get back."

The captain's voice was thin, choked. "Are you trying to tell me that their drive is no different from our own? That a ship has actually wandered into Interstellar space *without a space drive?*"

Brownie spread his hands helplessly. "Something must have gone wrong. They must have started off for another planet in their own system, and something went wrong. They broke into space, and they all died. And the ship just went on moving. They never intended an Interstellar hop. They couldn't have. They didn't have the drive for it."

The captain sat back numbly, his face pasty gray. The light had faded in his eyes now; he sat as though he'd been struck. "You—you couldn't be wrong? You couldn't have missed anything?"

Brownie's eyes shifted unhappily, and his voice was very faint. "No, sir."

The captain stared at them for a long moment, like a stricken child. Slowly he picked up one of the charts, his mouth working. Then, with a bitter roar, he threw it in Sabo's face. "Get out of here! Take this garbage and get out! And get the men to their stations. We're here to watch Saturn, and by god, we'll watch Saturn!" He turned away, a hand over his eyes, and they heard his choking breath as they left the cabin.

Slowly, Brownie walked out into the corridor, started down toward his cabin, with Sabo silent at his heels. He looked up once at the mate's heavy face, a look of pleading in his dark brown eyes, and then opened the door to his quarters. Like a cat, Sabo was in the room before him, dragging him in, slamming the door. He caught the little man by the neck with one savage hand, and shoved him unceremoniously against the door, his voice a vicious whisper. "*All right, talk! Let's have it now!*"

Brownie choked, his eyes bulging, his face turning gray in the dim light of the cabin. "Johnny! Let me down! What's the matter? You're choking me, Johnny—"

The mate's eyes were red, with heavy lines of disgust and bitterness running from his eyes and the corners of his mouth. "You stinking little liar! *Talk*, damn it! You're not messing with the captain now, you're messing with *me*, and I'll have the truth if I have to cave in your skull—"

"I told you the truth! I don't know what you mean—"

Sabo's palm smashed into his face, jerking his head about like an apple on a string. "That's the wrong answer," he grated. "I warn you, don't lie! The captain is an ambitious ass, he couldn't think his way through a multiplication table. He's a little child. But I'm not quite so dull." He threw the little man down in a heap, his eyes blazing. "You silly fool, your story is so full of holes you could drive a tank through it. They just up and died, did they? I'm supposed to believe that? Smashed up against the panels the way they were? Only one thing could crush them like that. Any fool could see it. Acceleration. And I don't mean atomic acceleration. Something else." He glared down at the man quivering on the floor. "They had Interstellar drive, didn't they, Brownie?"

Brownie nodded his head, weakly, almost sobbing, trying to pull himself erect. "Don't tell the captain," he sobbed. "Oh, Johnny, for god's sake, listen to me, don't let him know I lied. I was going to tell you anyway, Johnny, really I was. I've got a plan, a good plan, can't you see it?" The gleam of excitement came back into the sharp little eyes. "They had it, all right. Their trip probably took just a few months. They had a drive I've never seen before, non-atomic. I couldn't tell the principle, with the look I had, but I think I could work it." He sat up, his whole body trembling. "Don't give me away, Johnny, listen a minute—"

Sabo sat back against the bunk, staring at the little man. "You're out of your mind," he said softly. "You don't know what you're doing. What are you going to do when His Nibs goes over for a look himself? He's stupid, but not that stupid."

Brownie's voice choked, his words tumbling over each other in his eagerness. "He won't get a chance to see it, Johnny. He's got to take our word until he sees it, and we can stall him—"

Sabo blinked. "A day or so—maybe. But what then? Oh, how could you be so stupid? He's on the skids, he's out of favor and fighting for his life. That drive is the break that could put him on top. Can't you see he's selfish? He has to be, in this world, to get anything. Anything or anyone who blocks him, he'll destroy, if he can. Can't you see that? When he spots this, your life won't be worth spitting at."

Brownie was trembling as he sat down opposite the big man. His voice was harsh in the little cubicle, heavy with pain and hopelessness. "That's right," he said. "My life isn't worth a nickle. Neither is yours. Neither is anybody's, here or back home. Nobody's life is worth a nickle. Something's happened to us in the past hundred years, Johnny—something horrible. I've seen it creeping and growing up around us all my life. People don't matter any more, it's the Government, what the Government thinks that matters. It's a web, a cancer that grows in its own pattern, until it goes so far it can't be stopped. Men like Loomis could see the pattern, and adapt to it, throw away all the worthwhile things, the love and beauty and peace that we once had in our lives. Those men can get somewhere, they can turn this life into a climbing game, waiting their chance to get a little farther toward the top, a little closer to some semblance of security—"

"Everybody adapts to it," Sabo snapped. "They have to. You don't see me moving for anyone else, do you? I'm for *me*, and believe me I know it. I don't give a hang for you, or Loomis, or anyone else alive—just me. I want to stay alive, that's all. You're a dreamer, Brownie. But until you pull something like this, you can learn to stop dreaming if you want to—"

"No, no, you're wrong—oh, you're horribly wrong, Johnny. Some of us *can't* adapt, we haven't got what it takes, or else we have something else in us that won't let us go along. And right there we're beat before we start. There's no place for us now, and there never will be." He looked up at the mate's impassive face. "We're in a life where we don't belong, impounded into a senseless, never-ending series of fights and skirmishes and long, lonely waits, feeding this insane urge of the Government to expand, out to the planets, to the stars, farther and farther, bigger and bigger. We've got to go, seeking newer and greater worlds to conquer, with nothing to conquer them with, and nothing to conquer them for. There's life somewhere else in our solar system, so it must be sought out and conquered, no matter what or where it is. We live in a world of iron and fear, and there was no place for me, and others like me, *until this ship came*—"

Sabo looked at him strangely. "So I was right. I read it on your face when we were searching the ship. I knew what you were thinking...." His face darkened angrily. "You couldn't get away with it, Brownie. Where could you go, what could you expect to find? You're talking death, Brownie. Nothing else—"

"No, no. Listen, Johnny." Brownie leaned closer, his eyes bright and intent on the man's heavy face. "The captain has to take our word for it, until he sees the ship. Even then he couldn't tell for sure—I'm the only drive engineer on the Station. We have the charts, we could work with them, try to find out where the ship came from; I already have an idea of how the drive is operated. Another look and I could make it work. Think of it, Johnny! What difference does it make where we went, or what we found? You're a misfit, too, you know that—this coarseness and bitterness is a shell, if you could only see it, a sham. You don't really believe in this world we're in—who cares where, if only we could go, get away? Oh, it's a chance, the wildest, freak chance, but we could take it—"

"If only to get away from *him*," said Sabo in a muted voice. "Lord, how I hate him. I've seen smallness and ambition before— pettiness and treachery, plenty of it. But that man is our whole world knotted up in one little ball. I don't think I'd get home without killing him, just to stop that voice from talking, just to see fear cross his face one time. But if we took the ship, it would break him for good." A new light appeared in the big man's eyes. "He'd be through, Brownie. Washed up."

"And we'd be *free*—"

Sabo's eyes were sharp. "What about the acceleration? It killed those that came in the ship."

"But they were so frail, so weak. Light brittle bones and soft jelly. Our bodies are stronger, we could stand it."

Sabo sat for a long time, staring at Brownie. His mind was suddenly confused by the scope of the idea, racing in myriad twirling fantasies, parading before his eyes the long, bitter, frustrating years, the hopelessness of his own life, the dull aching feeling he felt deep in his stomach and bones each time he set back down on Earth, to join the teeming throngs of hungry people. He thought of the rows of drab apartments, the thin faces, the hollow, hunted eyes of the people he had seen. He knew that that was why he was a soldier—because soldiers ate well, they had time to sleep, they were never allowed long hours to think, and wonder, and grow dull and empty. But he knew his life had been barren. The life of a mindless automaton, moving from place to place, never thinking, never daring to think or speak, hoping only to work without pain each day, and sleep without nightmares.

And then, he thought of the nights in his childhood, when he had lain awake, sweating with fear, as the airships screamed across the dark sky above, bound he never knew where; and then, hearing in the far distance the booming explosion, he had played that horrible little game with himself, seeing how high he could count before he heard the weary, plodding footsteps of the people on the road, moving on to another place. He had known, even as a little boy, that the only safe place was in those bombers, that the place for survival was in the striking armies, and his life had followed the hard-learned pattern, twisting him into the cynical mold of the mercenary soldier, dulling the quick and clever mind, drilling into him the ways and responses of order and obey, stripping him of his heritage of love and humanity. Others less thoughtful had been happier; they had succeeded in forgetting the life they had known before, they had been able to learn easily and well the lessons of the repudiation of the rights of men which had crept like a blight through the world. But Sabo, too, was a misfit, wrenched into a mold he could not fit. He had sensed it vaguely, never really knowing when or how he had built the shell of toughness and cynicism, but also sensing vaguely that it was built, and that in it he could hide, somehow, and laugh at himself, and his leaders, and the whole world through which he plodded. He had laughed, but there had been long nights, in the narrow darkness of spaceship bunks, when his mind pounded at the shell, screaming out in nightmare, and he had wondered if he had really lost his mind.

His gray eyes narrowed as he looked at Brownie, and he felt his heart pounding in his chest, pounding with a fury that he could no longer deny. "It would have to be fast," he said softly. "Like lightning, tonight, tomorrow—very soon."

"Oh, yes, I know that. But we *can* do it—"

"Yes," said Sabo, with a hard, bitter glint in his eyes. "Maybe we can."

*   *   *   *   *

The preparation was tense. For the first time in his life, Sabo knew the meaning of real fear, felt the clinging aura of sudden death in every glance, every word of the men around him. It seemed incredible that the captain didn't notice the brief exchanges with the little engineer, or his own sudden appearances and disappearances about the Station. But the captain sat in his cabin with angry eyes, snapping answers without even looking up. Still, Sabo knew that the seeds of suspicion lay planted in his mind, ready to burst forth with awful violence at any slight provocation. As he worked, the escape assumed greater and greater proportions in Sabo's mind; he knew with increasing urgency and daring that nothing must stop him. The ship was there, the only bridge away from a life he could no longer endure, and his determination blinded him to caution.

Primarily, he pondered over the charts, while Brownie, growing hourly more nervous, poured his heart into a study of his notes and sketches. A second look at the engines was essential; the excuse he concocted for returning to the ship was recklessly slender, and Sabo spent a grueling five minutes dissuading the captain from accompanying him. But the captain's eyes were dull, and he walked his cabin, sunk in a gloomy, remorseful trance.

The hours passed, and the men saw, in despair, that more precious, dangerous hours would be necessary before the flight could be attempted. And then, abruptly, Sabo got the call to the captain's cabin. He found the old man at his desk, regarding him with cold eyes, and his heart sank. The captain motioned him to a seat, and then sat back, lighting a cigar with painful slowness. "I want you to tell me," he said in a lifeless voice, "exactly what Brownie thinks he's doing."

Sabo went cold. Carefully he kept his eyes on the captain's face. "I guess he's nervous," he said. "He doesn't belong on a

Satellite Station. He belongs at home. The place gets on his nerves."

"I didn't like his report."

"I know," said Sabo.

The captain's eyes narrowed. "It was hard to believe. Ships don't just happen out of space. They don't wander out interstellar by accident, either." An unpleasant smile curled his lips. "I'm not telling you anything new. I wouldn't want to accuse Brownie of lying, of course—or you either. But we'll know soon. A patrol craft will be here from the Triton supply base in an hour. I signaled as soon as I had your reports." The smile broadened maliciously. "The patrol craft will have experts aboard. Space drive experts. They'll review your report."

"An hour—"

The captain smiled. "That's what I said. In that hour, you could tell me the truth. I'm not a drive man, I'm an administrator, and organizer and director. You're the technicians. The truth now could save you much unhappiness— in the future."

Sabo stood up heavily. "You've got your information," he said with a bitter laugh. "The patrol craft will confirm it."

The captain's face went a shade grayer. "All right," he said. "Go ahead, laugh. I told you, anyway."

Sabo didn't realize how his hands were trembling until he reached the end of the corridor. In despair he saw the plan crumbling beneath his feet, and with the despair came the cold undercurrent of fear. The patrol would discover them, disclose the hoax. There was no choice left—ready or not, they'd *have* to leave.

Quickly he turned in to the central control room where Brownie was working. He sat down, repeating the captain's news in a soft voice.

"An *hour*! But how can we—"

"We've *got* to. We can't quit now, we're dead if we do."

Brownie's eyes were wide with fear. "But can't we stall them, somehow? Maybe if we turned on the captain—"

"The crew would back him. They wouldn't dare go along with us. We've got to run, nothing else." He took a deep breath. "Can you control the drive?"

Brownie stared at his hands. "I—I think so. I can only try."

"You've got to. It's now or never. Get down to the lock, and I'll get the charts. Get the sleds ready."

He scooped the charts from his bunk, folded them carefully and bound them swiftly with cord. Then he ran silently down the corridor to the landing port lock. Brownie was already there, in the darkness, closing the last clamps on his pressure suit. Sabo handed him the charts, and began the laborious task of climbing into his own suit, panting in the darkness.

And then the alarm was clanging in his ear, and the lock was flooded with brilliant light. Sabo stopped short, a cry on his lips, staring at the entrance to the control room.

The captain was grinning, a nasty, evil grin, his eyes hard and humorless as he stood there flanked by three crewmen. His hand gripped an ugly power gun tightly. He just stood there, grinning, and his voice was like fire in Sabo's ears. "Too bad," he said softly. "You almost made it, too. Trouble is, two can't keep a secret. Shame, Johnny, a smart fellow like you. I might have expected as much from Brownie, but I thought you had more sense—"

Something snapped in Sabo's mind, then. With a roar, he lunged at the captain's feet, screaming his bitterness and rage and frustration, catching the old man's calves with his powerful shoulders. The captain toppled, and Sabo was fighting for the power gun, straining with all his might to twist the gun from the thin hand, and he heard his voice shouting, "Run! *Go, Brownie, make it go!*"

The lock was open, and he saw Brownie's sled nose out into the blackness. The captain choked, his face purple. "Get him! Don't let him get away!"

The lock clanged, and the screens showed the tiny fragile sled jet out from the side of the Station, the small huddled figure clinging to it, heading straight for the open port of the gray ship. "Stop him! The guns, you fools, the guns!"

The alarm still clanged, and the control room was a flurry of activity. Three men snapped down behind the tracer-guns, firing without aiming, in a frenzied attempt to catch the fleeing sled. The sled began zig-zagging, twisting wildly as the shells popped on either side of it. The captain twisted away from Sabo's grip with a roar, and threw one of the crewmen to the deck, wrenching the gun controls from his hands. "Get the big ones on the ship! Blast it! If it gets away you'll all pay."

Suddenly the sled popped into the ship's port, and the hatch slowly closed behind it. Raving, the captain turned the gun on the sleek, polished hull plates, pressed the firing levels on the war-head servos. Three of them shot out from the Satellite, like deadly bugs, careening through the intervening space, until one of them struck the side of the gray ship, and exploded in purple fury against the impervious hull. And the others nosed into the flame, and passed on through, striking nothing.

Like the blinking of a light, the alien ship had throbbed, and jerked, and was gone.

With a roar the captain brought his fist down on the hard plastic and metal of the control panel, kicked at the sheet of knobs and levers with a heavy foot, his face purple with rage. His whole body shook as he turned on Sabo, his eyes wild. "You let him get away! It was your fault, yours! But *you* won't get away! I've got you, and you'll pay, do you hear that?" He pulled himself up until his face was bare inches from Sabo's, his teeth bared in a frenzy of hatred. "Now we'll see who'll laugh, my friend. You'll laugh in the death chamber, if you can still laugh by then!" He turned to the men around him. "Take him," he snarled. "Lock him in his quarters, and guard him well. And while you're doing it, take a good look at him. See how he laughs now."

They marched him down to his cabin, stunned, still wondering what had happened. Something had gone in his mind in that second, something that told him that the choice had to be made, instantly. Because he knew, with dull wonder, that in that instant when the lights went on he could have stopped Brownie, could have saved himself. He could have taken for himself a piece of the glory and promotion due to the discoverers of an Interstellar drive. But he had also known, somehow, in that short instant, that the only hope in the world lay in that one nervous, frightened man, and the ship which could take him away.

And the ship was gone. That meant the captain was through. He'd had his chance, the ship's coming had given him his chance, and he had muffed it. Now he, too, would pay. The Government would not be pleased that such a ship had leaked through his fingers. Captain Loomis was through.

And him? Somehow, it didn't seem to matter any more. He had made a stab at it, he had tried. He just hadn't had the luck. But he knew there was more to that. Something in his mind was singing, some deep feeling of happiness and hope had crept into his mind, and he couldn't worry about himself any more. There was nothing more for him; they had him cold. But deep in his mind he felt a curious satisfaction, transcending any fear and bitterness. Deep in his heart, he knew that *one* man had escaped.

And then he sat back and laughed.

INFINITE INTRUDER

ILLUSTRATED BY SMITH
ORIGINALLY PUBLISHED IN *PLANET SPACE SCIENCE FICTION,* JULY 1953

When Roger Strang found that someone was killing his son
— killing him horribly and often— he started investigating.
He wasn't prepared to find the results of another investigation
— this time about his own life.

Infinite Intruder

It was the second time they tried that Roger Strang realized someone was trying to kill his son.

The first time there had been no particular question. Accidents happen. Even in those days, with all the Base safety regulations and strict speed-way lane laws, young boys would occasionally try to gun their monowheels out of the slow lanes into the terribly swift traffic; when they did, accidents did occur. The first time, when they brought David home in the Base ambulance, shaken but unhurt, with the twisted smashed remains of his monowheel, Roger and Ann Strang had breathed weakly, and decided between themselves that the boy should be scolded within an inch of his young life. And the fact that David maintained tenaciously that he had never swerved from the slow monowheel lane didn't bother his parents a bit. They were acquainted with another small-boy frailty. Small boys, on occasion, are inclined to fib.

But the second time, David was not fibbing. Roger Strang *saw* the *accident* the second time. He saw all the circumstances involved. And he realized, with horrible clarity, that someone, somehow, was trying to kill his son.

It had been late on a Saturday afternoon. The free week-ends that the Barrier Base engineers had once enjoyed to take their families for picnics "outside," or to rest and relax, were things of the past, for the work on the Barrier was reaching a critical stage, demanding more and more of the technicians, scientists and engineers engaged in its development. Already diplomatic relations with the Eurasian Combine were becoming more and more impossible; the Barrier *had* to be built, and quickly, or another more terrible New York City would be the result. Roger had never cleared from his mind the flaming picture of that night of horror, just five years before, when the mighty metropolis had burst into radioactive flame, to announce the beginning of the first Atomic War. The year 2078 was engraved in millions of minds as the year of the most horrible—and the shortest—war in all history, for an armistice had been signed not four days after the first bomb had been dropped. An armistice, but an uneasy peace, for neither of the great nations had really known what atomic war would be like until it had happened. And once upon them, they found that atomic war was not practical, for both mighty opponents would have been gutted in a matter of weeks. The armistice had stopped the bombs, but hostilities continued, until the combined scientific forces of one nation could succeed in preparing a defense.

That particular Saturday afternoon had been busy in the Main Labs on the Barrier Base. The problem of erecting a continent-long electronic Barrier to cover the coast of North America was a staggering proposition. Roger Strang was nearly finished and ready for home as dusk was falling. Leaving his work at the desk, he was slipping on his jacket when David came into the lab. He was small for twelve years, with tousled sand-brown hair standing up at odd angles about a sharp, intelligent face. "I came to get you, Daddy," he said.

Roger smiled. "You rode all the way down here—just to go home with me?"

"Maybe we could get some Icy-pops for supper on the way home," David remarked innocently.

Roger grinned broadly and slapped the boy on the back. "You'd sell your soul for an Icy-pop," he grinned.

The corridor was dark. The man and boy walked down to the elevator, and in a moment were swishing down to the dark and deserted lobby below.

David stepped first from the elevator when the men struck. One stood on either side of the door in the shadow. The boy screamed and reeled from the blow across the neck. Suddenly Roger heard the sharp pistol reports. David dropped with a groan, and Roger staggered against the wall from a powerful blow in the face. He shook his head groggily, catching a glimpse of the two men running through the door into the street below, as three or four people ran into the lobby, flushed out by the shots.

*   *   *   *   *

Roger shouted, pointing to the door, but the people were looking at the boy. Roger sank down beside his son, deft fingers loosening the blouse. The boy's small face was deathly white, fearful sobs choking his breath as he closed his eyes and shivered. Roger searched under his blouse, trying to find the bullet holes—and found to his chagrin that there weren't any bullet holes.

"Where did you feel the gun?"

David pointed vaguely at his lower ribs. "Right there," he said. "It hurt when they shoved the gun at me."

"But they couldn't have pulled the trigger, if the gun was pointed there—" He examined the unbroken skin on the boy's chest, fear tearing through his mind.

A Security man was there suddenly, asking about the accident, taking Roger's name, checking over the boy. Roger resented the tall man in the gray uniform, felt his temper rise at the slightly sarcastic tone of the questions. Finally the trooper stood up, shaking his head. "The boy must have been mistaken," he said. "Kids always have wild stories to tell. Whoever it was may have been after *somebody*, but they weren't aiming for the boy."

Roger scowled. "This boy is no liar," he snapped. "I saw them shoot—"

The trooper shrugged. "Well, he isn't hurt. Why don't you go on home?"

Roger helped the boy up, angrily. "You're not going to do anything about this?"

"What can I do? Nobody saw who the men were."

Roger grabbed the boy's hand, helped him to his feet, and turned angrily to the door. In the failing light outside the improbability of the attack struck through him strongly. He turned to the boy, his face dark. "David," he said evenly, "you wouldn't be making up stories about feeling that gun in your ribs, would you?"

David shook his head vigorously, eyes still wide with fear. "Honest, dad. I told you the truth."

"But they *couldn't* have shot you in the chest without breaking the skin—" He glanced down at the boy's blouse and jacket, and stopped suddenly, seeing the blackened holes in the ripped cloth. He stooped down and sniffed the holes suspiciously, and shivered suddenly in the cold evening air.

The burned holes smelled like gunpowder.

*   *   *   *   *

"Strang, you must have been wrong." The large man settled back in his chair, his graying hair smoothed over a bald spot. "Someone trying to kill you I could see—there's plenty of espionage going on, and you're doing important work here. But your boy!" The chief of the Barrier Base Security shook his head. "You must have been mistaken."

"But I *wasn't* mistaken!" Roger Strang sat forward in his chair, his hands gripping the arms until his knuckles were white. "I told you exactly what happened. They got him as he came off the elevator, and shot at him. Not at me, Morrel, at my son. They just clubbed me in the face to get me out of the way—"

"What sort of men?" Morrel's eyes were sharp.

Roger scowled, running his hand through his hair. "It was too dark to see. They wore hats and field jackets. The gun could be identified by ballistics. But they were *fast*, Morrel. They knew who they were looking for."

Morrel rose suddenly, his face impatient. "Strang," he said. "You've been here at the Base for quite awhile. Ever since a month after the war, isn't that right? August, 2078? Somewhere around there, I know. But you've been working hard. I think maybe a rest would do you some good—"

"Rest!" Roger exploded. "Look, man—I'm not joking. This isn't the first time. The boy had a monowheel accident three weeks ago, and he swore he was riding in a safe lane where he belonged. It looked like an accident then—now it looks like a murder attempt. The slugs from the gun *must* be in the building—embedded in the plasterwork somewhere. Surely you could try to trace the gun." He glared at the man's impassive face bitterly, "Or maybe you don't want to trace the gun—"

Morrel scowled. "I've already checked on it. The gun wasn't registered in the Base. Security has a check on every firearm within a fifty-mile range. The attackers must have been outsiders."

Roger's face flushed. "That's not true, Morrel," he said softly, "and you know it's not true."

Morrel shrugged. "Have it your own way," he said, indifferently. "Take a rest, Strang. Go home. Get some rest. And don't bother me with any more of your fairy tales." He turned suddenly on Roger. "And be careful what *you* do with guns, Strang. The only thing about this that I *do* know is that somebody shot a pistol off and scared hell out of your son. You were the only one around, as far as I know. I don't know your game, but you'd better be careful—"

*   *   *   *   *

Strang left Security Headquarters, and crossed across to the Labs, frustrated and angry. His mind spun over the accident—incredulous, but more incredulous that Morrel would practically laugh at him. He stopped by the Labs building to watch the workmen putting up a large electronic projector in one of the test yards. Work was going ahead. But so slowly.

Roger was aware of the tall thin man who had joined him before he looked around. Martin Drengo put a hand on his shoulder. "Been avoiding me lately?"

"Martin!" Roger Strang turned, his face lighting up. "No, not avoiding you—I've been so busy my own wife hasn't seen me in four days. How are things in Maintenance?"

The thin man smiled sadly. "How are things ever in Maintenance? First a railroad breaks down, then there's a steel strike, then some paymaster doesn't make a payroll—the war knocked things for a loop, Roger. Even now things are still loopy. And how are things in Production?"

Roger scowled. "Let's have some coffee," he said.

They sat in a back corner booth of the Base Dispensary as Roger told about David. Martin Drengo listened without interruption. He was a thin man from top to bottom, a shock of unruly black hair topping an almost cadaverous face, blue eyes large behind thick lenses. His whole body was like a skeleton, his fingers long and bony as he lit a cigarette. But the blue eyes were quick, and the nods warm and understanding. He listened, and then he said, "It couldn't have been an outsider?"

Roger shrugged. "Anything is possible. But why? Why go after a kid?"

Drengo hunched his shoulders forward. "I don't get it," he said. "David has done nothing to give him enemies." He drew on his cigarette. "What did Morrel have to say?"

"He laughed at me! Wouldn't even listen to me. Told me to go home and go to bed, that I was all wet. I tell you, Martin, I *saw* it! You know I wouldn't lie, you know I don't see things that don't happen."

"Yes," said Martin, glumly. "I believe you, all right. But I can't see why your son should be the target. You'd be more likely." He stood up, stretching his long legs. "Look, old boy. Take Morrel's advice, at least temporarily. Go home and get some sleep now; you're all worked up. I'll go in and talk to Morrel. Maybe I can handle that old buzzard better than you can."

Roger watched his friend amble down the aisle and out of the store. He felt better now that he had talked to Drengo. Smiling to himself, he finished off his coffee. Many a scrape he and Martin had seen through together. He remembered that night of horror when the bomb fell on the city, his miraculous rescue, the tall thin figure, reflecting the red glare from his glasses, forcing his way through the burning timbers of the building, tearing Roger's leg loose from the rubble covering it; the frightful struggle through the rubbish, fighting off fear-crazed mobs that sought to stop them, rob them, kill them. They had made the long trek together, Martin and he, the Evacuation Road down to Maryland, the Road of Horrors, lined with the rotting corpses of the dead and the soon-dead, the dreadful refuse of that horrible night. Martin Drengo had been a stout friend to Roger; he'd been with Martin the night he'd met Ann; took the ring from Martin's finger when they stood at the altar on their wedding day; shared with Martin his closest confidence.

Roger sighed and paid for the coffee. What to do? The boy was home now, recovering from the shock of the attack. Roger caught an out-bound tri-wheel, and sped down the busy thoroughfare toward his home. If Martin could talk to Morrel, and get something done, perhaps they could get a line. Somehow, perhaps they could trace the attackers. In the morning he'd see Martin again, and they could figure out a scheme.

But he didn't have a chance to see Martin again. For at 11:30 that night, the marauders struck again. For the third time.

*   *   *   *   *

Through his sleep he heard a door close down below, and sat bolt upright in bed, his heart pounding wildly. Only a tiny sound, the click of a closing door—

Ann was sitting up beside him, brown hair close around her head, her body tense. "Roger!" she whispered. "Did you hear something?"

Roger was out of bed, bounding across the room, into the hall. Blood pounded in his ears as he rushed to David's room, stopped short before the open door.

The shots rang out like whip cracks, and he saw the yellow flame from the guns. There were two men in the dark room, standing at the bed where the boy lay rolled into a terrified knot. The guns cracked again and again, ripping the bedding, bursting the pillow into a shower of feathers, tearing the boy's pajamas from his thin body, a dozen blazing shots—

Roger let out a strangled cry, grabbed one of the men by the throat, in a savage effort to stop the murderous pistols. The other man caught him a coarse blow behind the ear, and he staggered hard against the wall. Dully he heard the door slam, heavy footsteps down the corridor, running down the stairs.

He struggled feebly to his feet, glancing at the still form on the bed. Choking back a sob he staggered down the hall, shouting to Ann as he went down the stairs, redoubling his speed as he heard the purr of autojets in the driveway. In a moment he was in his own car, frantically stamping on the starter. It started immediately, the motor booming, and the powerful jet engines forced the heavy car ahead dangerously, taking the corner on two of its three wheels. He knew that Ann would call Security, and he raced to gain on the tail lights that were disappearing down the winding residential road to the main highway. Throwing caution to the winds, Roger swerved the car across a front lawn, down between two houses, into an alley, and through another driveway, gaining three blocks. Ahead, at the junction with the main Base highway he saw the long black autojet turn right.

*   *   *   *   *

Roger snaked into traffic on the highway and bore down on the black car. Traffic was light because of the late hour, but the patrol was on the road and might stop him instead of the killers. The other car was traveling at top speed, swerving around the slower cars. Roger gained slowly. He fingered the spotlight, preparing to snap it in the driver's eyes. Taking a curve at 90, he crept up alongside the black car as he heard the siren of a patrol car behind him. Cursing, he edged over on the black car, snapped the spotlight full in the face of the driver—

The screaming siren forced him off the road, and he braked hard, his hands trembling. A patrolman came over to the car, gun drawn. He took a quick look at Roger, and his face tightened. "Mr. Strang," he said sharply. "We've been looking for you. You're wanted at Security."

"That car," Roger started weakly. "You've got to stop that car I was chasing—"

"Never mind that car," the patrolman snarled. "It's you they want. Hop out. We'll go in the patrol car."

"You've got to stop them—"

The patrolman fingered his gun. "Security wants to talk to you, Mr. Strang. Hop out."

Roger moved dazedly from his car. He didn't question the patrolman; he hardly even heard him. His mind raced in a welter of confusion, trying desperately to refute the brilliant picture in his mind from that split-second that the spotlight had rested on the driver of the black car, trying to fit the impossible pieces into their places. For the second man in the black autojet had been John Morrel, chief of Barrier Base Security, and the driver had been Martin Drengo—

*   *   *   *   *

The man at the desk was a stranger to Roger Strang. He was an elderly man, stooped, with graying hair and a small clipped mustache that seemed to stick out like antennae. He watched Roger impassively with steel gray eyes, motioning him to a chair.

"You led us a merry chase," he said flatly, his voice brittle. "A very merry chase. The alarm went out for you almost an hour ago."

Strang's cheeks were red with anger. "My son was shot tonight. I was trying to follow the killers—"

"Killers?" The man raised his eyebrows.

"Yes, killers!" Roger snapped. "Do I have to draw you a picture? They shot my son down in his bed."

The gray-haired man stared at him for a long time. "Well," he said finally in a baffled tone. "Now I've heard everything."

It was Roger's turn to stare. "Can't you understand what I've said? *My son was murdered.*"

The gray-haired man flipped a pencil down on the desk impatiently. "Mr. Strang," he said elaborately. "My name is Whitman. I flew down here from Washington tonight, after being called from my bed by the commanding officer of this base. I am the National Chief of the Federal Bureau of Security, Mr. Strang, and I am not interested in fairy tales. I would like you to come off it now, and answer some questions for me. And I don't want double-talk. I want answers. Do I make myself quite clear?"

Roger stared at him, finally nodded his head. "Quite," he said sourly.

Whitman hunched forward in his chair. "Mr. Strang, how long have you been working in the Barrier Base?"

"Five years. Ever since the bombing of New York."

Whitman nodded. "Oh, yes. The bombing of New York." He looked sharply at Roger. "And how old are you, Mr. Strang?"

Roger looked up, surprised. "Thirty-two, of course. You have my records. Why are you asking?"

The gray-haired man lit a cigarette. "Yes, we have your records," he said offhandedly. "Very interesting records, quite normal, quite in order. Nothing out of the ordinary." He stood up and looked out on the dark street. "Just one thing wrong with your records, Mr. Strang. They aren't true."

Roger stared. "This is ridiculous," he blurted. "What do you mean, they aren't true?"

Whitman took a deep breath, and pulled a sheet of paper out of a sheaf on his desk. "It says here," he said, "that you are Roger Strang, and that you were born in Indianola, Iowa, on the fourteenth of June, 2051. That your father was Jason Strang, born 11 August, 2023, in Chicago, Illinois. That you lived in Indianola until you were twelve, when your father moved to New York City, and was employed with the North American Electronics Laboratories. That you entered International Polytechnic Institute at the age of 21, studying physics and electronics, and graduated in June 2075 with the degree of Bachelor of Electronics. That you did further work, taking a Masters and Doctorate in Electronics at Polytech in 2077."

Whitman took a deep breath. "That's what it says here. A very ordinary record. But there is no record there of your birth in Indianola, Iowa, in 2051 or any other time. There is no record there of your father, the alleged Jason Strang, nor in Chicago. No one by the name of Jason Strang was ever employed by North American Electronics. No one by the name of Roger Strang ever attended Polytech." Whitman watched him with cold eyes. "To the best of our knowledge, and according to all available records, *there never was anyone named Roger Strang until after the bombing of New York.*"

Roger sat stock still, his mind racing. "This is silly," he said finally. "Perfectly idiotic. Those schools *must* have records—"

Whitman's face was tight. "They do have records. Complete records. But the name of Roger Strang is curiously missing from the roster of graduates in 2075. Or any other year." He snubbed his cigarette angrily. "I wish you would tell me, and save us both much unpleasantness. *Just who are you, Mr. Strang, and where do you come from?*"

Strang stared at the man, his pulse pounding in his head. Filtering into his mind was a vast confusion, some phrase, some word, some nebulous doubt that frightened him, made him almost believe that gray-haired man in the chair before him. He took a deep breath, clearing his mind of the nagging doubt. "Look here," he said, exasperated. "When I was drafted for the Barrier Base, they checked for my origin, for my education and credentials. If they had been false, I'd have been snapped up right then. Probably shot—they were shooting people for chewing their fingernails in those days. I wouldn't have stood a chance."

Whitman nodded his head vigorously. "Exactly!" he snapped. "You *should* have been picked up. But you weren't even suspected until we did a little checking after that accident in the Labs building yesterday. Somehow, false credentials got through for you. Security does not like false credentials. I don't know how you did it, but you did. I want to know how."

"But, I tell you—" Roger stood up, fear suddenly growing in his mind. He lit a cigarette, took two nervous puffs, and set it down, forgotten, on the ash-tray. "I have a wife," he said shakily. "I married her in New York City. We had a son, born in a hospital in New York City. He went to school there. Surely there must be some kind of record—"

Whitman smiled grimly, almost mockingly. "Good old New York City," he snarled. "Married there, you say? Wonderful! Son born there? In the one city in the country where that information *can never be checked*. That's very convenient, Mr. Strang. Or whoever you are. I think you'd better talk."

Roger snubbed out the cigarette viciously. "My son," he said after a long pause. "He was murdered tonight. Shot down in his bed—"

The Security Chief's face went white. "Garbage!" he snapped. "What kind of a fool do you think I am, Strang? Your son murdered—bah! When the alarm went out for you I personally drove to your home. Oddly enough this wife of yours wasn't at home, but your son was. Nice little chap. He made us some coffee, and explained that he didn't know where his parents were, because he'd been asleep all night. Quietly asleep in his bed—"

The words were clipped out, and rang in Roger's ears, incredibly. His hand shook violently as he puffed his cigarette, burning his fingers on the short butt. "I don't believe it," he muttered hollowly. "I saw it happen—"

Whitman sneered. "Are you going to talk or not?"

Roger looked up helplessly. "I don't—know—" he said, weakly. "I don't know."

The Security Chief threw up his hands in disgust. "Then we'll do it the hard way," he grated. Flipping an intercom switch, his voice snapped out cold in the still room. "Send in Psych squad," he growled. "We've got a job to do—"

*   *   *   *   *

Roger Strang lay back on the small bunk, his nerves yammering from the steady barrage, lights still flickering green and red in his eyes. His body was limp, his mind functioning slowly, sluggishly. His eyelids were still heavy from the drugs, his wrists and forehead burning and sore where the electrodes had been attached. His muscles hardly responded when he tried to move, his strength completely gone—washed out. He simply lay there, his shallow breathing returning to him from the dark stone walls.

The inquisition had been savage. The hot lights, the smooth-faced men firing questions, over and over, the drugs, the curious sensation of mouthing nonsense, of hearing his voice rambling on crazily, yet being unable in any way to control it; the hypnotic effect of Whitman's soft voice, the glitter in his steel-gray eyes, and the questions, questions, questions. The lie detector had been going by his side, jerking insanely at his answers, every time the same answers, every time setting the needle into wild gyrations. And finally the foggy, indistinct memory of Whitman mopping his forehead and stamping savagely on a cigarette, and muttering desperately, "It's no use! Lies! Nothing but lies, lies, lies! He *couldn't* be lying under this treatment, but he is. *And he knows he is!*"

Lies? Roger stretched his heavy limbs, his mind struggling up into a tardy rejection. Not lies! He hadn't lied—he had been answering the truth to the questions. He couldn't have been lying, for the answers were there, clear in his memory. And yet—the same nagging doubt crept through, the same feeling that had plagued him throughout the inquisition, the nagging, haunting, horrible conviction, somewhere in the depths of his numb brain that he *was* lying! Something was missing somewhere, some vast gap in his knowledge, something of which he simply was not aware. The incredible turnabout of Martin Drengo, the attack on David, who was killed, but somehow was not dead. He *had* to be lying—

But how could he lie, and still know that he was not lying? His sluggish mind wrestled, trying to choke back the incredible doubt. Somewhere in the morass, the picture of Martin Drengo came through—Drengo, the traitor, who was trying to kill his son—but the conviction swept through again, overpowering, the certain knowledge that Drengo was *not* a traitor, that he must trust Drengo. Drengo was his friend, his stalwart—

HIS AGENT!

Strang sat bolt upright on the cot, his head spinning. The thought had broken through crystal clear in the darkness, revealed itself for the briefest instant, then swirled down again into the foggy gulf. Agent? Why should he have an agent? What purpose? Frantically he scanned his memory for Drengo, down along the dark channels, searching. Drengo had come through the fire, into the burning building, carried him like a child through the flames into safety. Drengo had been best man at his wedding—but he'd been married before the bombing of the city. *Or had he?* Where did Drengo fit in? Was the fire the first time he had seen Drengo?

Something deep in his mind forced its way through, saying NO! YOU HAVE KNOWN HIM ALL YOUR LIFE! Roger fought it back, frantically. Never! Back in Iowa there had been no Drengo. Nor in Chicago. Nor in New York. He hadn't even known him in—IN NEW ALBANY!

*   *   *   *   *

Roger Strang was on his feet, shaking, cold fear running through his body, his nerves screaming. Had they ruined his mind? He couldn't think straight any more. Telling him things that weren't true, forcing lies into his mind—frightening him with the horrible conviction that his mind was really helpless, full of false data. What had happened to him? Where had the thought of "New Albany" come from? He shivered, now thoroughly frightened. There wasn't any "New Albany." Nowhere in the world. There just *wasn't* any such place.

Could he have two memories? Conflicting memories?

He walked shakily to the door, peered through the small peephole. In the morning they would try again, they had said. He shuddered, terribly afraid. He had felt his mind cracking under the last questioning; another would drive him completely insane. But Drengo would have the answers. Why had he shot little Davey? How did that fit in? Was this false-credential business part of some stupendous scheme against him? Impossible! But what else? He knew with sudden certain conviction that he must see Martin Drengo, immediately, before they questioned him again, before the fear and uncertainty drove him out of his mind. He called tentatively through the peephole, half-hoping to catch a guard's attention. And the call echoed through silent halls.

And then he heard Ann's voice, clear, cool, sharp in the prison darkness. Roger whirled, fear choking the shouts still ringing in his ears, gaped at the woman who stood in his cell—

She was lovelier than he had ever seen her, her tiny body clothed in a glowing fabric which clung to every curve, accenting her trim figure, her slender hips. Brown hair wreathed her lovely face, and Roger choked as the deep longing for her welled up in his throat. Speechlessly he took her in his arms, holding her close, burying his face in her hair, sobbing in joy and relief. And then he saw the glowing circle behind her, casting its eerie light into the far corners of the dark cell. In fiery greenness the ring shimmered in an aurora of violent power, but Ann paid no attention to it. She stepped back and smiled at him, her eyes bright. "Don't be frightened," she said softly, "and don't make any noise. I'm here to help you."

"But where did you come from?" The question forced itself out in a sort of strangled gasp.

"We have—means of going where we want to. And we want you to come with us." She pointed at the glowing ring. "We want to take you back to the time-area from which you came."

Roger goggled at her, confusion welling strong into his mind again. "Ann," he said weakly. "What kind of trick is this?"

She smiled again. "No trick," she said. "Don't ask questions, darling. I know you're confused, but there isn't much time. You'll just have to do what I say right now." She turned to the glowing ring. "We just step through here. Be careful that you don't touch the substance of the portal going through."

Roger Strang approached the glowing ring curiously, peered through, blinked, peered again. It was like staring at an inscrutable flat-black surface in the shadow. No light reflected through it; nothing could be seen. He heard a faint whining as he stood close to the ring, and he looked up at Ann, his eyes wide. "You can't see through it!" he exclaimed.

Ann was crouching on the floor near a small metallic box, gently turning knobs, checking the dial reading against a small chronometer on her wrist. "Steady, darling," she said. "Just follow me, carefully, and don't be afraid. We're going back home—to the time-area where we belong. You and I. I know— you don't remember. And you'll be puzzled, and confused, because the memory substitution job was very thorough. But you'll remember Martin Drengo, and John Morrel, and me. And I was your wife there, too—Are you ready?"

Roger stared at the ring for a moment. "Where are we going?" he asked. "How far ahead? Or behind—?"

"Ahead," she said. "Eighty years ahead—as far as we can go. That will bring us to the present time, the *real* present time, as far as we, and you, are concerned."

She turned abruptly, and stepped through the ring, and vanished as effectively as if she had disintegrated into vapor. Roger felt fear catch at his throat; then he followed her through.

They were standing in a ruins. The cell was gone, the prison, the Barrier Base. The dark sky above was bespeckled with a myriad of stars, and a cool night breeze swept over Roger's cheek. Far in the distance a low rumble came to his ears. "Sounds like a storm coming," he muttered to Ann, pulling his jacket closer around him.

"No storm," she said grimly. "Look!" She pointed a finger toward the northern horizon. Brazen against the blackness the yellow-orange of fire was rising, great spurts of multi-colored flames licking at the horizon. The rumble became a drone, a roar. Ann grasped Roger's arm and pulled him down to cover in the rubble as the invisible squadron swished across the sky, trailing jet streams of horrid orange behind them. Then to the south, in the direction of the flight, the drone of the engines gave way to the hollow boom-booming of bombing, and the southern horizon flared. Then, as suddenly as it had appeared, the rumble died away, leaving the flames licking the sky to the north and south.

Roger shivered. "War," he said. "Eurasia?"

She shook her head. "If only it were. There is no Eurasia now. The dictator took care of that. Nothing but gutted holes, and rubble." She stood up, helping Roger to his feet. Together they filed through the rubbish down to a roadway. Ann dialed a small wrist radio; in a few moments, out of the dark sky, the dim-out lights of a small 'copter came into view, and the machine settled delicately to the road. Two strange men were inside; they saluted Ann, and helped Roger aboard. Swiftly they clamped down the hatch tight, and the ship rose again silently into the air.

"Where are we going?" asked Roger Strang.

"We have a headquarters. Our data must be checked first. We can't reach a decision without checking. Then we can talk."

The 'copter swung high over the blazing inferno of a city far below. Strang glanced from the window, eyes widening at the holocaust. The crater holes were mammoth, huge spires of living flame rising to the sky, leaving mushroom columns of gray-black smoke that glowed an evil red from the furnace on the ground. "Not Eurasia?" Roger asked suddenly, his mind twisting in amazement. "But who? This is America, isn't it?"

"Yes. This is America. There is no Eurasia now. Soon there may not be an America. Nor even an Earth."

Roger looked up at Ann, eyes wide. "But those jet-planes— the bombing—*who is doing the bombing?*"

Ann Strang stared down at the sullen red fires of the city for a moment, her quiet eyes sad. "Those are Martian planes," she said.

*   *   *   *   *

The 'copter settled silently down into the heart of the city, glowing red from the flames and bombing. They hovered over the shining Palace, still tall, and superb, and intact, gleaming like a blood-streaked jewel in the glowing night. The 'copter settled on the roof of a low building across a large courtyard from the glittering Palace. Ann Strang stepped out, and motioned Roger to follow down a shaft and stairway into a small room below. She knocked at a door, and a strange man dressed in the curious glowing fabric opened it. His face lit up in a smile.

"Roger!" he cried. "We were afraid we couldn't locate you. We weren't expecting the Security to meddle. Someone got suspicious, somewhere, and began checking your references from their sources—and of course they were false. We were lucky to get you back at all, after Security got you." He clapped Roger on the back, and led him into the room.

John Morrel and Martin Drengo were standing near the rounded window, their faces thrown into grotesque relief against the red-orange glow outside. They turned and saluted, and Roger almost cried out, his mind spinning, a thousand questions cutting into his consciousness, demanding answers. But quite suddenly he was feeling a new power, a new effectiveness in his thinking, in his activity. He turned to Martin Drengo, his eyes questioning but no longer afraid. "What year is this?" he asked.

"This is 2165. March, 2165, and you're in New Albany, in the United States of North America. This is the city where you were born, the city you loved—and look at it!"

Roger walked to the window. The court below was full of people now, ragged people, some of them screaming, a disconsolate muttering rising from a thousand throats—burned people, mangled people. They milled about the mammoth courtyard before the glorious Palace, aimlessly, mindlessly. Far down the avenue leading from the Palace Roger could see the people evacuating the city, a long, desolate line of people, strange autos, carts, even animals, running down the broad avenue to escape from the flaming city.

"We're not in danger here," said Drengo, at his elbow. "No fire nor bomb can reach us here—that is the result of your mighty Atlantic Coast Barrier. Nothing more. It never was perfected in time, before the great Eastern Invasion and the second Atomic War. That was due to occur three years after the time-area where we visited. We were trying to stem it, to turn it aside. We don't know yet whether we succeeded or not."

He turned to the tall man standing at the door. "Markson, all the calculations are prepared. The Calc is evaluating the data against the Equation now, figuring all the variables. If our work did any good, we should know it soon." He sighed and pointed to the Palace. "But our fine Dictator is still alive, and the attack on Mars should be starting any minute—If we didn't succeed, nothing in all Time will stop him."

Roger lit a cigarette, his eyes questioning Drengo. "Dictator?"

Drengo sat down and stretched his legs. "The Dictator appeared four years ago, a nobody, a man from the masses of people on the planet. He rose into public favor like a sky-rocket, a remarkable man, an amazing man—a man who could talk to you, and control your thoughts in a single interview. There has never been a man with such personal magnetism and power, Roger, in all the history of Earth. A man who raised himself from nothing into absolute Dictatorship, and has handled the world according to his whim ever since.

"He is only a young man, Roger, just 32 years of age, but an irresistible man who can win anything from anybody. He writhed into the presidency first, and then deliberately set about rearranging the government to suit himself. And the people let him get away with it, followed him like sheep. And then he was Dictator, and he began turning the social and economic balance of the planet into a whirlwind. And then came Mars."

Martin stretched again, and lit a cigarette, his thin face grave in the darkened room. "The first landing was thirty years ago, and the possibilities for rich and peaceful commerce between Earth and Mars were clear from the first. Mars had what Earth lacked: the true civilization, the polished culture, the lasting socio-economic balance, the permanent peace. Mars could have taught us so much. She could have guided us out of the mire of war and hatred that we have been wallowing in for centuries. But the Dictator put an end to those possibilities." Drengo shrugged. "He was convinced that the Martians were weak, backward, decadent. He saw their uranium, their gold, their jewelry, their labor—and started on a vast impossible imperialism. If he had had his way, he would have stripped the planet in three years, but the Martians fought against us, turned from peace to suspicion, and finally to open revolt. And the Dictator could not see. He mobilized Earth for total war against Mars, draining our resources, decimating our population, building rockets, bombs, guns—" He stopped for a moment, breathing deeply. "But the Dictator didn't know what he was doing. He had never been on Mars. He has never seen Martians. He had no idea what they think, what they are capable of doing. He doesn't know what we know—that the Martians will win. He doesn't realize that the Martians can carry out a war for years without shaking their economy one iota, while he has drained our planet to such a degree that a war of more than two or three months will break us in half. He doesn't know that Mars can win, and that the Earth can't—"

Roger walked across the room, thoughtfully, his mind fitting pieces into place. "But where do I come in? David—Ann—I don't understand—"

Drengo looked Roger straight in the eye. "The Dictator's name," he said, "is Farrel Strang."

Roger stopped still. "Strang?" he echoed.

"Your son, Roger. Yours and Ann's."

"But—you said the Dictator was only 32—" Roger trailed off, regarding Ann in amazement.

Martin smiled. "People don't grow old so quickly nowadays," he said. "You are 57 years old, Roger. Ann is 53." He leaned back in his chair, his gaunt smile fading. "The Dictator has not been without opposition. You, his parents, opposed him at the very start, and he cast you off. People wiser than the crowds were able to rebuff his powerful personal appeal, to see through the robe of glory he had wrapped around himself. He has opposition, but he has built himself an impregnable fortress, and dealt swift death to any persons suspected of treason. A few have escaped— scientists, technologists, sociologists, physicists. The work of one group of men gave us a weapon which we hoped to use to destroy the Dictator. We found a way to move back in Time. We could leave the normal time-stream and move to any area of past time. So four of us went back, searching for the core of the economic and social upheaval on Earth, and trying to destroy the Dictator before he was born. Given Time travel, it should have been possible. So we went back—myself, John Morrel, Ann Strang, and you."

Roger shook his head, a horrible thought forming in his mind. "You were trying to kill David—my son—" he stopped short. "David *couldn't* have been my son!" He whirled on Martin Drengo. "*Who was that boy?*"

Martin looked away then, his face white. "The boy was your father," he said.

*   *   *   *   *

The drone of the jet bombers came again, whining into the still room. Roger Strang stood very still, staring at the gaunt man. Slowly the puzzle was beginning to fit together, and horror filtered into his mind. "My father—" he said. "Only twelve years old, but he was to be my father." He stared helplessly at the group in the room. "You were trying—to kill him!"

Martin Drengo stood up, his lean face grave. "We were faced with a terrific problem. Once we returned to a time-area, we had no way of knowing to what extent we could effect people and events that had already happened. We had to go back, to fit in, somehow, in an area where we never had been, to *make* things happen that had never happened before. We knew that if there was any way of doing it, we had to destroy Farrel Strang. But the patterns of history which had allowed him to rise had to be altered, too; destroying the man would not have been enough. So we tried to destroy him in the time-area where the leading time-patterns of *our* time had been formed. We had to kill his grandfather."

Roger shivered. "But if you had killed David—what would have happened *to me?*"

"Presumably the same thing that would have happened to the Dictator. In theory, *if we had succeeded* in killing your father, David, both you and the Dictator would have ceased to exist." Drengo took a deep breath. "The idea was yours, Roger. You knew the terrible damage your son was doing as Dictator. It was a last resort, and Ann and John and I pleaded with you to reconsider. But it was the obvious step."

Ann walked over to Roger, her face pale. "You insisted, Roger. So we did what we could to make it easy. We used the Dictator's favorite trick—a psycho-purge—to clear your mind of all conscious and subconscious memory of your true origin and environment, replacing it with a history and memory of the past-time area where we were going. We chose the contact-time carefully, so that we appeared in New York in the confusion of the bombing of 2078, making sure that your records would stand up under all but the closest examination. From then on, when Martin carried you out from the fire, you stored your own memory of that time-area and became a legitimate member of that society."

"But how could we pose as David's *parents*, if he was my father?"

Ann smiled. "Both David's parents were killed in the New York bombing; we knew that David survived, and we knew where he could be found. There was a close physical resemblance between you and the boy, though actually the resemblance was backwards, and he accepted you as a foster-father without question. With you equipped with a complete memory of your marriage to me in that time, of David's birth, and of your own history before and after the bombing of New York, you fit in well and played the part to perfection. Also, you acted as a control, to guide us, since you had no conscious knowledge beyond that time-area. Martin and Morrel were to be the assassins, the Intruders, and I was to keep tabs on you—"

"And the success of the attempt?"

Ann's face fell. "We don't know yet. We don't know what we accomplished, whether we stemmed the war or not—"

The tall man who had stepped into the room moved forward and threw a sheaf of papers on the floor, his face heavy with anger, his voice hoarse. "Yes, I'm afraid we do know," he said bitterly.

Martin Drengo whirled on him, his face white. "What do you mean, Markson?"

The tall man sank down in a chair tiredly. "We've lost, Martin. We don't need these calculations to tell. The word was just broadcast on the telecast. Farrel Strang's armada has just begun its attack on Mars—"

＊　　＊　　＊　　＊　　＊

For a moment the distant bombing was the only sound in the room. Then Martin Drengo said, "So he gave the order. And we've lost."

"We only had a theory to work on," said Morrel, staring gloomily at the curved window. "A theory and an equation. The theory said that a man returning through time could alter the social and technological trends of the people and times to which he returned, in order to change history that was already past. The theory said that if we could turn the social patterns and technological trends just slightly away from what they were, we could alter the entire makeup of society in our own time. And the Equation was the tool, the final check on any change. The Equation which evaluates the sum of social, psychological and energy factors in any situation, any city or nation or human society. The Equation has been proven, checked time and time again, but the theory didn't fit it. The theory was wrong."

Roger Strang sat up, suddenly alert. "That boy," he said, his voice sharp. "You nearly made a sieve of him, trying to shoot him. Why didn't he die?"

"Because he was on a high-order variable. Picture it this way: From any point in time, the possible future occurrences could be seen as vectors, an infinite number of possible vectors. Every activity that makes an alteration, or has any broad effect on the future is a high-order variable, but many activities have no grave implications for future time, and could be considered unimportant, or low-order variables. If a man turns a corner and sees something that stimulates him into writing a world-shaking manifesto, the high-order variable would have started when he decided to turn the corner instead of going the other way. But if he took one way home instead of another, and nothing of importance occurred as a result of the decision, a low-order variable would be set up.

"We found that the theory of alterations held quite well, for low-order variables. Wherever we appeared, whatever we did, we set up a definite friction in the normal time-stream, a distortion, like pulling a taut rubber band out. And we could produce changes—on low-order variables. But the elasticity of the distortion was so great as to warp the change back into the time-stream without causing any lasting alteration. When it came to high-order changes, *we simply couldn't make any*. We tried putting wrong data into the machines that were calculating specifications for the Barrier, and the false data went in, but the answers that came out were answers that *should* have appeared with the *right* data. We tried to commit a murder, to kill David Strang, and try as we would we couldn't do it. Because it would have altered a high-order variable, and they simply *wouldn't be altered*!"

"But you, Morrel," Roger exclaimed. "How about you? You were top man in the Barrier Base Security office. You must have made an impression."

Morrel smiled tiredly. "I really thought I had, time after time. I would start off a series of circumstances that should have had a grave alterative effect, and it would look for awhile as if a long-range change was going to be affected—and then it would straighten itself out again, with no important change occurring. It was maddening. We worked for five years trying to make even a small alteration—and brought back our data—" He pointed to the papers on the floor. "There are the calculations, applied on the Equation. Meaningless. We accomplished nothing. And the Dictator is still there."

Drengo slumped in his chair. "And he's started the war. The real attack. This bombardment outside is nothing. There are fifteen squadrons of space-destroyers already unloading atomic bombs on the surface of Mars, and that's the end, for us. Farrel Strang has started a war he can never finish—"

Roger Strang turned sharply to Drengo. "This Dictator," he said. "Where is he? Why can't he be reached now, and destroyed?"

"The Barrier. He can't be touched in the Palace. He has all his offices there, all his controls, and he won't let anyone in since the attempted assassination three months ago. He's safe there, and we can't touch him."

Roger scowled at the control panel on the wall. "How does this time-portal work?" he asked. "You say it can take us back— *why not forward?*"

"No good. The nature of Time itself makes that impossible. At the present instant of Time, everything that has happened has happened. The three-dimensional world in which we live has passed through the fourth temporal dimension, and nothing can alter it. But at this instant there are an infinite number of things that could happen next. The future is an infinite series of variables, and there's no conceivable way to predict which variable will actually be true."

Roger Strang sat up straight, staring at Drengo. "Will that portal work both ways?" he asked tensely.

Drengo stared at him blankly. "You mean, can it be reverse-wired? I suppose so. But—anyone trying to move into the future would necessarily become an *infinity* of people—he couldn't maintain his identity, because he'd have to have a body in every one of an infinite number of places he might be—"

"—*until the normal time stream caught up with him in the future!* And then he'd be in whatever place he fit!" Roger's voice rose excitedly. "Martin, can't you see the implications? Send me ahead—just a little ahead, an hour or so—and let me go into the Palace. If I moved my consciousness to the place where the Palace should be, where the Dictator should be, then when normal time caught up with me, *I could kill him!*"

Drengo was on his feet, staring at Roger with rising excitement. Suddenly he glanced at his watch. "By God!" he muttered. "*Maybe you could—*"

*   *   *   *   *

Blackness.

He had no body, no form. There was no light, no shape, nothing but eternal, dismal, unbroken blackness. This was the Void, the place where time had not yet come. Roger Strang shuddered, and felt the cold chill of the blackness creep into his marrow. He had to move. He wanted to move, to find the right place, moving with the infinity of possible bodies. A stream of consciousness was all he could grasp, for the blackness enclosed everything. A sort of death, but he knew he was not dead. Blackness was around him, and in him, and through him.

He could feel the timelessness, the total absence of anything. Suddenly he felt the loneliness, for he knew there was no going back. He had to transfer his consciousness, his mind, to the place where the Dictator was, hoping against hope that he could find the place before time caught him wedged in the substance of the stone walls of the Palace. He reached the place that *should* be right, and waited—

And waited. There was no time in this place, and he had to wait for the normal time stream. The blackness worked at his mind, filling him with fear, choking him, making him want to scream in frightened agony—waiting—

And suddenly, abruptly, he was standing in a brightly lighted room. The arched dome over his head sparkled with jewels, and through paneled windows the red glow of the city's fires flickered grimly. *He was in the Palace!*

He looked about swiftly, and crossed the room toward a huge door. In an instant he had thrown it open. The bright lights of the office nearly blinded him, and the man behind the desk rose angrily, caught Roger's eye full—

Roger gasped, his eyes widening. For a moment he thought he was staring into a mirror. For the man behind the desk, clothed in a rich glowing tunic was a living image of—*himself!*

The Dictator's face opened into startled surprise and fear as he recognized Roger, and a frightened cry came from his lips. There was no one else in the room, but his eyes ran swiftly to the visiphone. With careful precision Roger Strang brought the heat-pistol to eye level, and pulled the trigger. Farrel Strang crumpled slowly from the knees, a black hole scorched in his chest.

Roger ran to the fallen man, stared into his face incredulously. His son—and himself, as alike as twin dolls, for all the age difference. Drengo's words rose in Roger's mind: "Medicine is advanced, you know. People don't grow old so soon these days—"

Swiftly Roger slipped from his clothes, an impossibly bold idea translating itself into rapid action. He stripped the glowing tunic from the man's flaccid body, and slipped his arms into the sleeves, pulling the cape in close to cover the burned spot.

He heard a knock on the door. Frantically he forced the body under the heavy desk, and sat down in the chair behind it, eyes wide with fear. "Come in," he croaked.

A young deputy stepped through the door, approached the desk deferentially. "The first reports, sir," he said, looking straight at Roger. Not a flicker of suspicion crossed his face. "The attack is progressing as expected."

"Turn all reports over to my private teletype," Roger snapped. The man saluted. "Immediately, sir!" He turned and left the room, closing the door behind him.

Roger panted, closing his eyes in relief. He could pass! Turning to the file, he examined the detailed plans for the Martian attack; the numbers of ships, the squadron leaders, the zero hours—then he was at the teletype keyboard, passing on the message of peace, the message to stop the War with Mars, to make an armistice; ALL SQUADRONS AND SHIPS ATTENTION: CEASE AND DESIST IN ATTACK PLANS: RETURN TO TERRA IMMEDIATELY: BY ORDER OF FARREL STRANG.

Wildly he tore into the files, ripping out budget reports, stabilization plans, battle plans, evacuation plans. It would be simple to dispose of the Dictator's body as that of an imposter, an assassin—and simply take control himself in Farrel's place. They would carry on with *his* plans, *his* direction. And an era of peace, and stability and rich commerce would commence at long last. The sheaf of papers grew larger and larger as Roger emptied out the files: plans of war, plans of conquest, of slavery—he aimed the heat-pistol at the pile, saw it spring into yellow flame, and circle up to the vaulted ceiling in blue smoke.

*   *   *   *   *

And then he sat down, panting, and flipped the visiphone switch. "Send one man, unarmed, to the building across the courtyard. Have him bring Martin Drengo to me."

The deputy's eyes widened on the screen. "Unarmed, sir?"

"Unarmed," Roger repeated. "By order of your Dictator."

LETTER OF THE LAW

ORIGINALLY PUBLISHED IN *IF MAGAZINE*
JANUARY 1954

LETTER OF THE LAW

The place was dark and damp, and smelled like moldy leaves. Meyerhoff followed the huge, bear-like Altairian guard down the slippery flagstones of the corridor, sniffing the dead, musty air with distaste. He drew his carefully tailored Terran-styled jacket closer about his shoulders, shivering as his eyes avoided the black, yawning cell-holes they were passing. His foot slipped on the slimy flags from time to time, and finally he paused to wipe the caked mud from his trouser leg. "How much farther is it?" he shouted angrily.

The guard waved a heavy paw vaguely into the blackness ahead. Quite suddenly the corridor took a sharp bend, and the Altairian stopped, producing a huge key ring from some obscure fold of his hairy hide. "I still don't see any reason for all the fuss," he grumbled in a wounded tone. "We've treated him like a brother."

One of the huge steel doors clicked open. Meyerhoff peered into the blackness, catching a vaguely human outline against the back wall. "Harry?" he called sharply.

There was a startled gasp from within, and a skinny, gnarled little man suddenly appeared in the guard's light, like a grotesque, twisted ghost out of the blackness. Wide blue eyes regarded Meyerhoff from beneath uneven black eyebrows, and then the little man's face broke into a crafty grin. "Paul! So they sent *you*! I knew I could count on it!" He executed a deep, awkward bow, motioning Meyerhoff into the dark cubicle. "Not much to offer you," he said slyly, "but it's the best I can do under the circumstances."

Meyerhoff scowled, and turned abruptly to the guard. "We'll have some privacy now, if you please. Interplanetary ruling. And leave us the light."

The guard grumbled, and started for the door. "It's about time you showed up!" cried the little man in the cell. "Great day! Lucky they sent you, pal. Why, I've been in here for years—"

"Look, Zeckler, the name is Meyerhoff, and I'm not your pal," Meyerhoff snapped. "And you've been here for two weeks, three days, and approximately four hours. You're getting as bad as your gentle guards when it comes to bandying the truth around." He peered through the dim light at the gaunt face of the prisoner. Zeckler's face was dark with a week's beard, and his bloodshot eyes belied the cocky grin on his lips. His clothes were smeared and sodden, streaked with great splotches of mud and moss. Meyerhoff's face softened a little. "So Harry Zeckler's in a jam again," he said. "You *look* as if they'd treated you like a brother."

The little man snorted. "These overgrown teddy-bears don't know what brotherhood means, nor humanity, either. Bread and water I've been getting, nothing more, and then only if they feel like bringing it down." He sank wearily down on the rock bench along the wall. "I thought you'd never get here! I sent an appeal to the Terran Consulate the first day I was arrested. What happened? I mean, all they had to do was get a man over here, get the extradition papers signed, and provide transportation off the planet for me. Why so much time? I've been sitting here rotting—" He broke off in mid-sentence and stared at Meyerhoff. "You *brought* the papers, didn't you? I mean, we can leave now?"

Meyerhoff stared at the little man with a mixture of pity and disgust. "You are a prize fool," he said finally. "Did you know that?"

Zeckler's eyes widened. "What do you mean, fool? So I spend a couple of weeks in this pneumonia trap. The deal was worth it! I've got three million credits sitting in the Terran Consulate on Altair V, just waiting for me to walk in and pick them up. Three million credits—do you hear? That's enough to set me up for life!"

Meyerhoff nodded grimly. "*If* you live long enough to walk in and pick them up, that is."

"What do you mean, if?"

Meyerhoff sank down beside the man, his voice a tense whisper in the musty cell. "I mean that right now you are practically dead. You may not know it, but you are. You walk into a newly opened planet with your smart little bag of tricks, walk in here with a shaky passport and no permit, with no knowledge of the natives outside of two paragraphs of inaccuracies in the Explorer's Guide, and even then you're not content to come in and sell something legitimate, something the natives might conceivably be able to use. No, nothing so simple for you. You have to pull your usual high-pressure stuff. And this time, buddy, you're paying the piper."

"*You mean I'm not being extradited?*"

Meyerhoff grinned unpleasantly. "I mean precisely that. You've committed a crime here—a major crime. The Altairians are sore about it. And the Terran Consulate isn't willing to sell all the trading possibilities here down the river just to get you out of a mess. You're going to stand trial—and these natives are out to get you. Personally, I think they're *going* to get you."

Zeckler stood up shakily. "You can't believe anything the natives say," he said uneasily. "They're pathological liars. Why, you should see what they tried to sell *me*! You've never seen such a pack of liars as these critters." He glanced up at Meyerhoff. "They'll probably drop a little fine on me and let me go."

"A little fine of one Terran neck." Meyerhoff grinned nastily. "You've committed the most heinous crime these creatures can imagine, and they're going to get you for it if it's the last thing they do. I'm afraid, my friend, that your con-man days are over."

Zeckler fished in the other man's pocket, extracted a cigarette, and lighted it with trembling fingers. "It's bad, then," he said finally.

"It's bad, all right."

Some shadow of the sly, elfin grin crept over the little con-man's face. "Well, at any rate, I'm glad they sent you over," he said weakly. "Nothing like a good lawyer to handle a trial."

"*Lawyer?* Not me! Oh, no. Sorry, but no thanks." Meyerhoff chuckled. "I'm your advisor, old boy. Nothing else. I'm here to keep you from botching things up still worse for the Trading Commission, that's all. I wouldn't get tangled up in a mess with those creatures for anything!" He shook his head. "You're your own lawyer, Mr. Super-salesman. It's all your show. And you'd better get your head out of the sand, or you're going to lose a case like it's never been lost before!"

*   *   *   *   *

Meyerhoff watched the man's pale face, and shook his head. In a way, he thought, it was a pity to see such a change in the rosy-cheeked, dapper, cocksure little man who had talked his way glibly in and out of more jams than Meyerhoff could count. Trading brought scalpers; it was almost inevitable that where rich and unexploited trading ground was uncovered, it would first fall prey to the fast-trading boys. They spread out from Terra with the first wave of exploration—the slick, fast-talking con-men who could work new territories unfettered by the legal restrictions that soon closed down the more established planets. The first men in were the richest out, and through some curious quirk of the Terrestrial mind, they knew they could count on Terran protection, however crooked and underhand their methods.

But occasionally a situation arose where the civilization and social practices of the alien victims made it unwise to tamper with them. Altair I had been recognized at once by the Trading Commission as a commercial prize of tremendous value, but early reports had warned of the danger of wildcat trading on the little, musty, jungle-like planet with its shaggy, three-eyed inhabitants—warned specifically against the confidence tactics so frequently used—but there was always somebody, Meyerhoff reflected sourly, who just didn't get the word.

Zeckler puffed nervously on his cigarette, his narrow face a study in troubled concentration. "But I didn't *do* anything!" he exploded finally. "So I pulled an old con game. So what? Why should they get so excited? So I clipped a few thousand credits, pulled a little fast business." He shrugged eloquently, spreading his hands. "Everybody's doing it. They do it to each other without batting an eye. You should *see* these critters operate on each other. Why, my little scheme was peanuts by comparison."

Meyerhoff pulled a pipe from his pocket, and began stuffing the bowl with infinite patience. "And precisely what sort of con game was it?" he asked quietly.

Zeckler shrugged again. "The simplest, tiredest, moldiest old racket that ever made a quick nickel. Remember the old Terran gag about the Brooklyn Bridge? The same thing. Only these critters didn't want bridges. They wanted land—this gooey, slimy swamp they call 'farm land.' So I gave them what they wanted. I just sold them some land."

Meyerhoff nodded fiercely. "You sure did. A hundred square kilos at a swipe. Only you sold the same hundred square kilos to a dozen different natives." Suddenly he threw back his hands and roared. "Of all the things you *shouldn't* have done—"

"But what's a chunk of land?"

Meyerhoff shook his head hopelessly. "If you hadn't been so greedy, you'd have found out what a chunk of land was to these natives before you started peddling it. You'd have found out other things about them, too. You'd have learned that in spite of all their bumbling and fussing and squabbling they're not so dull. You'd have found out that they're marsupials, and that two out of five of them get thrown out of their mother's pouch before they're old enough to survive. You'd have realized that they have to start fighting for individual rights almost as soon as they're born. Anything goes, as long as it benefits them as individuals."

Meyerhoff grinned at the little man's horrified face. "Never heard of that, had you? And you've never heard of other things, too. You've probably never heard that there are just too many Altairians here for the food their planet can supply, and their diet is so finicky that they just can't live on anything that doesn't grow here. And consequently, land is the key factor in their economy, not money; nothing but land. To get land, it's every man for himself, and the loser starves, and their entire legal and monetary system revolves on that principle. They've built up the most confusing and impossible system of barter and trade imaginable, aimed at individual survival, with land as the value behind the credit. That explains the lying—of course they're liars, with an economy like that. They've completely missed the concept of truth. Pathological? You bet they're pathological! Only a fool would tell the truth when his life depended on his being a better liar than the next guy! Lying is the time-honored tradition, with their entire legal system built around it."

Zeckler snorted. "But how could they *possibly* have a legal system? I mean, if they don't recognize the truth when it slaps them in the face?"

Meyerhoff shrugged. "As we understand legal systems, I suppose they don't have one. They have only the haziest idea what truth represents, and they've shrugged off the idea as impossible and useless." He chuckled maliciously. "So you went out and found a chunk of ground in the uplands, and sold it to a dozen   separate,   self-centered,   half-starved   natives! Encroachment on private property is legal grounds for murder on this planet, and twelve of them descended on the same chunk of land at the same time, all armed with title-deeds." Meyerhoff sighed. "You've got twelve mad Altairians in your hair. You've got a mad planet in your hair. And in the meantime, Terra's most valuable uranium source in five centuries is threatening to cut off supply unless they see your blood splattered liberally all the way from here to the equator."

Zeckler was visibly shaken. "Look," he said weakly, "so I wasn't so smart. What am I going to do? I mean, are you going to sit quietly by and let them butcher me? How could I defend myself in a legal setup like *this*?"

Meyerhoff smiled coolly. "You're going to get your sly little con-man brain to working, I think," he said softly. "By Interplanetary Rules, they have to give you a trial in Terran legal form—judge, jury, court procedure, all that folderol. They think it's a big joke—after all, what could a judicial oath mean to them?—but they agreed. Only thing is, they're going to hang you, if they die trying. So you'd better get those stunted little wits of yours clicking—and if you try to implicate *me*, even a little bit, I'll be out of there so fast you won't know what happened."

With that Meyerhoff walked to the door. He jerked it inward sharply, and spilled two guards over on their faces. "Privacy," he grunted, and started back up the slippery corridor.

*   *   *   *   *

It certainly *looked* like a courtroom, at any rate. In the front of the long, damp stone room was a bench, with a seat behind it, and a small straight chair to the right. To the left was a stand with twelve chairs—larger chairs, with a railing running along the front. The rest of the room was filled almost to the door with seats facing the bench. Zeckler followed the shaggy-haired guard into the room, nodding approvingly. "Not such a bad arrangement," he said. "They must have gotten the idea fast."

Meyerhoff wiped the perspiration from his forehead, and shot the little con-man a stony glance. "At least you've got a courtroom, a judge, and a jury for this mess. Beyond that—" He shrugged eloquently. "I can't make any promises."

In the back of the room a door burst open with a bang. Loud, harsh voices were heard as half a dozen of the huge Altairians attempted to push through the door at once. Zeckler clamped on the headset to his translator unit, and watched the hubbub in the anteroom with growing alarm. Finally the question of precedent seemed to be settled, and a group of the Altairians filed in, in order of stature, stalking across the room in flowing black robes, pug-nosed faces glowering with self-importance. They descended upon the jury box, grunting and scrapping with each other for the first-row seats, and the judge took his place with obvious satisfaction behind the heavy wooden bench. Finally, the prosecuting attorney appeared, flanked by two clerks, who took their places beside him. The prosecutor eyed Zeckler with cold malevolence, then turned and delivered a sly wink at the judge.

In a moment the room was a hubbub as it filled with the huge, bumbling, bear-like creatures, jostling each other and fighting for seats, growling and complaining. Two small fights broke out in the rear, but were quickly subdued by the group of gendarmes guarding the entrance. Finally the judge glared down at Zeckler with all three eyes, and pounded the bench top with a wooden mallet until the roar of activity subsided. The jurymen wriggled uncomfortably in their seats, exchanging winks, and finally turned their attention to the front of the court.

"We are reading the case of the people of Altair I," the judge's voice roared out, "against one Harry Zeckler—" he paused for a long, impressive moment—"Terran." The courtroom immediately burst into an angry growl, until the judge pounded the bench five or six times more. "This—creature—is hereby accused of the following crimes," the judge bellowed. "Conspiracy to overthrow the government of Altair I. Brutal murder of seventeen law-abiding citizens of the village of Karzan at the third hour before dawn in the second period after his arrival. Desecration of the Temple of our beloved Goddess Zermat, Queen of the Harvest. Conspiracy with the lesser gods to cause the unprecedented drought in the Dermatti section of our fair globe. Obscene exposure of his pouch-marks in a public square. Four separate and distinct charges of jail-break and bribery—" The judge pounded the bench for order—"Espionage with the accursed scum of Altair II in preparation for interplanetary invasion."

The little con-man's jaw sagged lower and lower, the color draining from his face. He turned, wide-eyed, to Meyerhoff, then back to the judge.

"The Chairman of the Jury," said the Judge succinctly, "will read the verdict."

The little native in the front of the jury-box popped up like a puppet on a string. "Defendant found guilty on all counts," he said.

"Defendant is guilty! The court will pronounce sentence—"

"*Now wait a minute!*" Zeckler was on his feet, wild-eyed. "What kind of railroad job—"

The judge blinked disappointedly at Paul Meyerhoff. "Not yet?" he asked, unhappily.

"No." Meyerhoff's hands twitched nervously. "Not yet, Your Honor. Later, Your Honor. The trial comes *first*."

The judge looked as if his candy had been stolen. "But you *said* I should call for the verdict."

"Later. You have to have the trial before you can have the verdict."

The Altairian shrugged indifferently. "Now—later—" he muttered.

"Have the prosecutor call his first witness," said Meyerhoff.

Zeckler leaned over, his face ashen. "These charges," he whispered. "They're insane!"

"Of course they are," Meyerhoff whispered back.

"But what am I going to—"

"Sit tight. Let *them* set things up."

"But those *lies*. They're liars, the whole pack of them—" He broke off as the prosecutor roared a name.

The shaggy brute who took the stand was wearing a bright purple hat which sat rakishly over one ear. He grinned the Altairian equivalent of a hungry grin at the prosecutor. Then he cleared his throat and started. "This Terran riffraff—"

"The oath," muttered the judge. "We've got to have the oath."

The prosecutor nodded, and four natives moved forward, carrying huge inscribed marble slabs to the front of the court. One by one the chunks were reverently piled in a heap at the witness's feet. The witness placed a huge, hairy paw on the cairn, and the prosecutor said, "Do you swear to tell the truth, the whole truth, and nothing but the truth, so help you—" he paused to squint at the paper in his hand, and finished on a puzzled note, "—Goddess?"

The witness removed the paw from the rock pile long enough to scratch his ear. Then he replaced it, and replied, "Of course," in an injured tone.

"Then tell this court what you have seen of the activities of this abominable wretch."

The witness settled back into the chair, fixing one eye on Zeckler's face, another on the prosecutor, and closing the third as if in meditation. "I think it happened on the fourth night of the seventh crossing of Altair II (may the Goddess cast a drought upon it)—or was it the seventh night of the fourth crossing?—" he grinned apologetically at the judge—"when I was making my way back through town toward my blessed land-plot, minding my own business, Your Honor, after weeks of bargaining for the crop I was harvesting. Suddenly from the shadow of the building, this creature—" he waved a paw at Zeckler—"stopped me in my tracks with a vicious cry. He had a weapon I'd never seen before, and before I could find my voice he forced me back against the wall. I could see by the cruel glint in his eyes that there was no warmth, no sympathy in his heart, that I was—"

"Objection!" Zeckler squealed plaintively, jumping to his feet. "This witness can't even remember what night he's talking about!"

The judge looked startled. Then he pawed feverishly through his bundle of notes. "Overruled," he said abruptly. "Continue, please."

The witness glowered at Zeckler. "As I was saying before this loutish interruption," he muttered, "I could see that I was face to face with the most desperate of criminal types, even for Terrans. Note the shape of his head, the flabbiness of his ears. I was petrified with fear. And then, helpless as I was, this two-legged abomination began to shower me with threats of evil to my blessed home, dark threats of poisoning my land unless I would tell him where he could find the resting place of our blessed Goddess—"

"I never saw him before in my life," Zeckler moaned to Meyerhoff. "Listen to him! Why should I care where their Goddess—"

Meyerhoff gave him a stony look. "The Goddess runs things around here. She makes it rain. If it doesn't rain, somebody's insulted her. It's very simple."

"But how can I fight testimony like that?"

"I doubt if you *can* fight it."

"But they can't prove a word of it—" He looked at the jury, who were listening enraptured to the second witness on the stand. This one was testifying regarding the butcherous slaughter of eighteen (or was it twenty-three? Oh, yes, twenty-three) women and children in the suburban village of Karzan. The pogrom, it seemed, had been accomplished by an energy weapon which ate great, gaping holes in the sides of buildings. A third witness took the stand, continuing the drone as the room grew hotter and muggier. Zeckler grew paler and paler, his eyes turning glassy as the testimony piled up. "But it's not *true*," he whispered to Meyerhoff.

"Of course it isn't! Can't you understand? *These people have no regard for truth.* It's stupid, to them, silly, a mark of low intelligence. The only thing in the world they have any respect for is a liar bigger and more skillful than they are."

Zeckler jerked around abruptly as he heard his name bellowed out. "Does the defendant have anything to say before the jury delivers the verdict?"

"Do I have—" Zeckler was across the room in a flash, his pale cheeks suddenly taking on a feverish glow. He sat down gingerly on the witness chair, facing the judge, his eyes bright with fear and excitement. "Your—Your Honor, I—I have a statement to make which will have a most important bearing on this case. You must listen with the greatest care." He glanced quickly at Meyerhoff, and back to the judge. "Your Honor," he said in a hushed voice. "You are in gravest of danger. All of you. Your lives—your very land is at stake."

The judge blinked, and shuffled through his notes hurriedly as a murmur arose in the court. "Our land?"

"Your lives, your land, everything you hold dear," Zeckler said quickly, licking his lips nervously. "You must try to understand me—" he glanced apprehensively over his shoulder "now, because I may not live long enough to repeat what I am about to tell you—"

The murmur quieted down, all ears straining in their headsets to hear his words. "These charges," he continued, "all of them—they're perfectly true. At least, they *seem* to be perfectly true. But in every instance, I was working with heart and soul, risking my life, for the welfare of your beautiful planet."

There was a loud hiss from the back of the court. Zeckler frowned and rubbed his hands together. "It was my misfortune," he said, "to go to the wrong planet when I first came to Altair from my homeland on Terra. I—I landed on Altair II, a grave mistake, but as it turned out, a very fortunate error. Because in attempting to arrange trading in that frightful place, I made certain contacts." His voice trembled, and sank lower. "I learned the horrible thing which is about to happen to this planet, at the hands of those barbarians. The conspiracy is theirs, not mine. They have bribed your Goddess, flattered her and lied to her, coerced her all-powerful goodness to their own evil interests, preparing for the day when they could persuade her to cast your land into the fiery furnace of a ten-year-drought—"

Somebody in the middle of the court burst out laughing. One by one the natives nudged one another, and booed, and guffawed, until the rising tide of racket drowned out Zeckler's words. "The defendant is obviously lying," roared the prosecutor over the pandemonium. "Any fool knows that the Goddess can't be bribed. How could she be a Goddess if she could?"

Zeckler grew paler. "But—perhaps they were very clever—"

"And how could they flatter her, when she knows, beyond doubt, that she is the most exquisitely radiant creature in all the Universe? And *you* dare to insult her, drag her name in the dirt."

The hisses grew louder, more belligerent. Cries of "Butcher him!" and "Scald his bowels!" rose from the courtroom. The judge banged for silence, his eyes angry.

"Unless the defendant wishes to take up more of our precious time with these ridiculous lies, the jury—"

"Wait! Your Honor, I request a short recess before I present my final plea."

"Recess?"

"A few moments to collect my thoughts, to arrange my case."

The judge settled back with a disgusted snarl. "Do I have to?" he asked Meyerhoff.

Meyerhoff nodded. The judge shrugged, pointing over his shoulder to the anteroom. "You can go in there," he said.

Somehow, Zeckler managed to stumble from the witness stand, amid riotous boos and hisses, and tottered into the anteroom.

*   *   *   *   *

Zeckler puffed hungrily on a cigarette, and looked up at Meyerhoff with haunted eyes. "It—it doesn't look so good," he muttered.

Meyerhoff's eyes were worried, too. For some reason, he felt a surge of pity and admiration for the haggard con-man. "It's worse than I'd anticipated," he admitted glumly. "That was a good try, but you just don't know enough about them and their Goddess." He sat down wearily. "I don't see what you can do. They want your blood, and they're going to have it. They just won't believe you, no matter *how* big a lie you tell."

Zeckler sat in silence for a moment. "This lying business," he said finally, "exactly how does it work?"

"The biggest, most convincing liar wins. It's as simple as that. It doesn't matter how outlandish a whopper you tell. Unless, of course, they've made up their minds that you just naturally aren't as big a liar as they are. And it looks like that's just what they've done. It wouldn't make any difference to them *what* you say—unless, somehow, you could *make* them believe it."

Zeckler frowned. "And how do they regard the—the biggest liar? I mean, how do they feel toward him?"

Meyerhoff shifted uneasily. "It's hard to say. It's been my experience that they respect him highly—maybe even fear him a little. After all, the most convincing liar always wins in any transaction, so he gets more land, more food, more power. Yes, I think the biggest liar could go where he pleased without any interference."

Zeckler was on his feet, his eyes suddenly bright with excitement. "Wait a minute," he said tensely. "To tell them a lie that they'd have to believe—a lie they simply couldn't *help* but believe—" He turned on Meyerhoff, his hands trembling. "Do they *think* the way we do? I mean, with logic, cause and effect, examining evidence and drawing conclusions? Given certain evidence, would they have to draw the same conclusions that we have to draw?"

Meyerhoff blinked. "Well—yes. Oh, yes, they're perfectly logical."

Zeckler's eyes flashed, and a huge grin broke out on his sallow face. His thin body fairly shook. He started hopping up and down on one foot, staring idiotically into space. "If I could only think—" he muttered. "Somebody—somewhere—something I read."

"Whatever are you talking about?"

"It was a Greek, I think—"

Meyerhoff stared at him. "Oh, come now. Have you gone off your rocker completely? You've got a problem on your hands, man."

"No, no, I've got a problem in the bag!" Zeckler's cheeks flushed. "Let's go back in there—I think I've got an answer!"

The courtroom quieted the moment they opened the door, and the judge banged the gavel for silence. As soon as Zeckler had taken his seat on the witness stand, the judge turned to the head juryman. "Now, then," he said with happy finality. "The jury—"

"Hold on! Just one minute more."

The judge stared down at Zeckler as if he were a bug on a rock. "Oh, yes. You had something else to say. Well, go ahead and say it."

Zeckler looked sharply around the hushed room. "You want to convict me," he said softly, "in the worst sort of way. Isn't that right?"

Eyes swung toward him. The judge broke into an evil grin. "That's right."

"But you can't really convict me until you've considered carefully any statement I make in my own defense. Isn't that right?"

The judge looked uncomfortable. "If you've got something to say, go ahead and say it."

"I've got just one statement to make. Short and sweet. But you'd better listen to it, and think it out carefully before you decide that you really want to convict me." He paused, and glanced slyly at the judge. "You don't think much of those who tell the truth, it seems. Well, put *this* statement in your record, then." His voice was loud and clear in the still room. "*All Earthmen are absolutely incapable of telling the truth.*"

Puzzled frowns appeared on the jury's faces. One or two exchanged startled glances, and the room was still as death. The judge stared at him, and then at Meyerhoff, then back. "But you"—he stammered. "You're"—He stopped in mid-sentence, his jaw sagging.

One of the jurymen let out a little squeak, and fainted dead away. It took, all in all, about ten seconds for the statement to soak in.

And then pandemonium broke loose in the courtroom.

*   *   *   *   *

"Really," said Harry Zeckler loftily, "it was so obvious I'm amazed that it didn't occur to me first thing." He settled himself down comfortably in the control cabin of the Interplanetary Rocket and grinned at the outline of Altair IV looming larger in the view screen.

Paul Meyerhoff stared stonily at the controls, his lips compressed angrily. "You might at least have told me what you were planning."

"And take the chance of being overheard? Don't be silly. It had to come as a bombshell. I had to establish myself as a liar— the prize liar of them all, but I had to tell the sort of lie that they simply could not cope with. Something that would throw them into such utter confusion that they wouldn't *dare* convict me." He grinned impishly at Meyerhoff. "The paradox of Epimenides the Cretan. It really stopped them cold. They *knew* I was an Earthmen, which meant that my statement that Earthmen were liars was a lie, which meant that maybe I wasn't a liar, in which case—oh, it was tailor-made."

"It sure was." Meyerhoff's voice was a snarl.

"Well, it made me out a liar in a class they couldn't approach, didn't it?"

Meyerhoff's face was purple with anger. "Oh, indeed it did! And it put *all* Earthmen in exactly the same class, too."

"So what's honor among thieves? I got off, didn't I?"

Meyerhoff turned on him fiercely. "Oh, you got off just fine. You scared the living daylights out of them. And in an eon of lying they never have run up against a short-circuit like that. You've also completely botched any hope of ever setting up a trading alliance with Altair I, and that includes uranium, too. Smart people don't gamble with loaded dice. You scared them so badly they don't want anything to do with us."

Zeckler's grin broadened, and he leaned back luxuriously. "Ah, well. After all, the Trading Alliance was *your* outlook, wasn't it? What a pity!" He clucked his tongue sadly. "Me, I've got a fortune in credits sitting back at the consulate waiting for me—enough to keep me on silk for quite a while, I might say. I think I'll just take a nice, long vacation."

Meyerhoff turned to him, and a twinkle of malignant glee appeared in his eyes. "Yes, I think you will. I'm quite sure of it, in fact. Won't cost you a cent, either."

"Eh?"

Meyerhoff grinned unpleasantly. He brushed an imaginary lint fleck from his lapel, and looked up at Zeckler slyly. "That— uh—jury trial. The Altairians weren't any too happy to oblige. They wanted to execute you outright. Thought a trial was awfully silly—until they got their money back, of course. Not too much—just three million credits."

Zeckler went white. "But that money was in banking custody!"

"Is that right? My goodness. You don't suppose they could have lost those papers, do you?" Meyerhoff grinned at the little con-man. "And incidentally, you're under arrest, you know."

A choking sound came from Zeckler's throat. "*Arrest!*"

"Oh, yes. Didn't I tell you? Conspiring to undermine the authority of the Terran Trading Commission. Serious charge, you know. Yes, I think we'll take a nice long vacation together, straight back to Terra. And there I think you'll face a jury trial."

Zeckler spluttered. "There's no evidence—you've got nothing on me! What kind of a frame are you trying to pull?"

"A *lovely* frame. Airtight. A frame from the bottom up, and you're right square in the middle. And this time—" Meyerhoff tapped a cigarette on his thumb with happy finality—"this time I *don't* think you'll get off."

PRoblem

ORIGINALLY PUBLISHED IN *GALAXY*,
OCTOBER 1956

PRoblem

The letter came down the slot too early that morning to be the regular mail run. Pete Greenwood eyed the New Philly photocancel with a dreadful premonition. The letter said:

PETER:

Can you come East chop-chop, urgent? Grdznth problem getting to be a PRoblem, need expert icebox salesman to get gators out of hair fast. Yes? Math boys hot on this, citizens not so hot.   Please come.

TOMMY

Pete tossed the letter down the gulper with a sigh. He had lost a bet to himself because it had come three days later than he expected, but it had come all the same, just as it always did when Tommy Heinz got himself into a hole.

Not that he didn't like Tommy. Tommy was a good PR-man, as PR-men go. He just didn't know his own depth. PRoblem in a beady Grdznth eye! What Tommy needed right now was a Bazooka Battalion, not a PR-man. Pete settled back in the Eastbound Rocketjet with a sigh of resignation.

He was just dozing off when the fat lady up the aisle let out a scream. A huge reptilian head had materialized out of nowhere and was hanging in air, peering about uncertainly. A scaly green body followed, four feet away, complete with long razor talons, heavy hind legs, and a whiplash tail with a needle at the end. For a moment the creature floated upside down, legs thrashing. Then the head and body joined, executed a horizontal pirouette, and settled gently to the floor like an eight-foot circus balloon.

Two rows down a small boy let out a muffled howl and tried to bury himself in his mother's coat collar. An indignant wail arose from the fat lady. Someone behind Pete groaned aloud and quickly retired behind a newspaper.

The creature coughed apologetically. "Terribly sorry," he said in a coarse rumble. "So difficult to control, you know. Terribly sorry...." His voice trailed off as he lumbered down the aisle toward the empty seat next to Pete.

The fat lady gasped, and an angry murmur ran up and down the cabin. "Sit down," Pete said to the creature. "Relax. Cheerful reception these days, eh?"

"You don't mind?" said the creature.

"Not at all." Pete tossed his briefcase on the floor. At a distance the huge beast had looked like a nightmare combination of large alligator and small tyrannosaurus. Now, at close range Pete could see that the "scales" were actually tiny wrinkles of satiny green fur. He knew, of course, that the Grdznth were mammals—"docile, peace-loving mammals," Tommy's PR-blasts had declared emphatically—but with one of them sitting about a foot away Pete had to fight down a wave of horror and revulsion.

The creature was most incredibly ugly. Great yellow pouches hung down below flat reptilian eyes, and a double row of long curved teeth glittered sharply. In spite of himself Pete gripped the seat as the Grdznth breathed at him wetly through damp nostrils.

"Misgauged?" said Pete.

The Grdznth nodded sadly. "It's horrible of me, but I just can't help it. I *always* misgauge. Last time it was the chancel of St. John's Cathedral. I nearly stampeded morning prayer—" He paused to catch his breath. "What an effort. The energy barrier, you know. Frightfully hard to make the jump." He broke off sharply, staring out the window. "Dear me! Are we going *east*?"

"I'm afraid so, friend."

"Oh, dear. I wanted *Florida*."

"Well, you seem to have drifted through into the wrong airplane," said Pete. "Why Florida?"

The Grdznth looked at him reproachfully. "The Wives, of course. The climate is so much better, and they mustn't be disturbed, you know."

"Of course," said Pete. "In their condition. I'd forgotten."

"And I'm told that things have been somewhat unpleasant in the East just now," said the Grdznth.

Pete thought of Tommy, red-faced and frantic, beating off hordes of indignant citizens. "So I hear," he said. "How many more of you are coming through?"

"Oh, not many, not many at all. Only the Wives—half a million or so—and their spouses, of course." The creature clicked his talons nervously. "We haven't much more time, you know. Only a few more weeks, a few months at the most. If we couldn't have stopped over here, I just don't know *what* we'd have done."

"Think nothing of it," said Pete indulgently. "It's been great having you."

The passengers within earshot stiffened, glaring at Pete. The fat lady was whispering indignantly to her seat companion. Junior had half emerged from his mother's collar; he was busy sticking out his tongue at the Grdznth.

The creature shifted uneasily. "Really, I think—perhaps Florida would be better."

"Going to try it again right now? Don't rush off," said Pete.

"Oh, I don't mean to rush. It's been lovely, but—" Already the Grdznth was beginning to fade out.

"Try four miles down and a thousand miles southeast," said Pete.

The creature gave him a toothy smile, nodded once, and grew more indistinct. In another five seconds the seat was quite empty. Pete leaned back, grinning to himself as the angry rumble rose around him like a wave. He was a Public Relations man to the core—but right now he was off duty. He chuckled to himself, and the passengers avoided him like the plague all the way to New Philly.

But as he walked down the gangway to hail a cab, he wasn't smiling so much. He was wondering just how high Tommy was hanging him, this time.

* * * * *

The lobby of the Public Relations Bureau was swarming like an upturned anthill when Pete disembarked from the taxi. He could almost smell the desperate tension of the place. He fought his way past scurrying clerks and preoccupied poll-takers toward the executive elevators in the rear.

On the newly finished seventeenth floor, he found Tommy Heinz pacing the corridor like an expectant young father. Tommy had lost weight since Pete had last seen him. His ruddy face was paler, his hair thin and ragged as though chunks had been torn out from time to time. He saw Pete step off the elevator, and ran forward with open arms. "I thought you'd never get here!" he groaned. "When you didn't call, I was afraid you'd let me down."

"Me?" said Pete. "I'd never let down a pal."

The sarcasm didn't dent Tommy. He led Pete through the ante-room into the plush director's office, bouncing about excitedly, his words tumbling out like a waterfall. He looked as though one gentle shove might send him yodeling down Market Street in his underdrawers. "Hold it," said Pete. "Relax, I'm not going to leave for a while yet. Your girl screamed something about a senator as we came in. Did you hear her?"

Tommy gave a violent start. "Senator! Oh, dear." He flipped a desk switch. "What senator is that?"

"Senator Stokes," the girl said wearily. "He had an appointment. He's ready to have you fired."

"All I need now is a senator," Tommy said. "What does he want?"

"Guess," said the girl.

"Oh. That's what I was afraid of. Can you keep him there?"

"Don't worry about that," said the girl. "He's growing roots. They swept around him last night, and dusted him off this morning. His appointment was for *yesterday*, remember?"

"Remember! Of course I remember. Senator Stokes—something about a riot in Boston." He started to flip the switch, then added, "See if you can get Charlie down here with his giz."

He turned back to Pete with a frantic light in his eye. "Good old Pete. Just in time. Just. Eleventh-hour reprieve. Have a drink, have a cigar—do you want my job? It's yours. Just speak up."

"I fail to see," said Pete, "just why you had to drag me all the way from L.A. to have a cigar. I've got work to do."

"Selling movies, right?" said Tommy.

"Check."

"To people who don't want to buy them, right?"

"In a manner of speaking," said Pete testily.

"Exactly," said Tommy. "Considering some of the movies you've been selling, you should be able to sell anything to anybody, any time, at any price."

"Please. Movies are getting Better by the Day."

"Yes, I know. And the Grdznth are getting worse by the hour. They're coming through in battalions—a thousand a day! The more Grdznth come through, the more they act as though they own the place. Not nasty or anything—it's that infernal politeness that people hate most, I think. Can't get them mad, can't get them into a fight, but they do anything they please, and go anywhere they please, and if the people don't like it, the Grdznth just go right ahead anyway."

Pete pulled at his lip. "Any violence?"

Tommy gave him a long look. "So far we've kept it out of the papers, but there have been some incidents. Didn't hurt the Grdznth a bit—they have personal protective force fields around them, a little point they didn't bother to tell us about. Anybody who tries anything fancy gets thrown like a bolt of lightning hit him. Rumors are getting wild—people saying they can't be killed, that they're just moving in to stay."

Pete nodded slowly. "Are they?"

"I wish I knew. I mean, for sure. The psych-docs say no. The Grdznth agreed to leave at a specified time, and something in their cultural background makes them stick strictly to their agreements. But that's just what the psych-docs think, and they've been known to be wrong."

"And the appointed time?"

Tommy spread his hands helplessly. "If we knew, you'd still be in L.A. Roughly six months and four days, plus or minus a month for the time differential. That's strictly tentative, according to the math boys. It's a parallel universe, one of several thousand already explored, according to the Grdznth scientists working with Charlie Karns. Most of the parallels are analogous, and we happen to be analogous to the Grdznth, a point we've omitted from our PR-blasts. They have an eight-planet system around a hot sun, and it's going to get lots hotter any day now."

Pete's eyes widened. "Nova?"

"Apparently. Nobody knows how they predicted it, but they did. Spotted it coming several years ago, so they've been romping through parallel after parallel trying to find one they can migrate to. They found one, sort of a desperation choice. It's cold and arid and full of impassable mountain chains. With an uphill fight they can make it support a fraction of their population."

Tommy shook his head helplessly. "They picked a very sensible system for getting a good strong Grdznth population on the new parallel as fast as possible. The males were picked for brains, education, ability and adaptability; the females were chosen largely according to how pregnant they were."

Pete grinned. "Grdznth in utero. There's something poetic about it."

"Just one hitch," said Tommy. "The girls can't gestate in that climate, at least not until they've been there long enough to get their glands adjusted. Seems we have just the right climate here for gestating Grdznth, even better than at home. So they came begging for permission to stop here, on the way through, to rest and parturiate."

"So Earth becomes a glorified incubator." Pete got to his feet thoughtfully. "This is all very touching," he said, "but it just doesn't wash. If the Grdznth are so unpopular with the masses, why did we let them in here in the first place?" He looked narrowly at Tommy. "To be very blunt, what's the parking fee?"

"Plenty," said Tommy heavily. "That's the trouble, you see. The fee is so high, Earth just can't afford to lose it. Charlie Karns'll tell you why."

$$* \quad * \quad * \quad * \quad *$$

Charlie Karns from Math Section was an intense skeleton of a man with a long jaw and a long white coat drooping over his shoulders like a shroud. In his arms he clutched a small black box.

"It's the parallel universe business, of course," he said to Pete, with Tommy beaming over his shoulder. "The Grdznth can cross through. They've been able to do it for a long time. According to our figuring, this must involve complete control of mass, space and dimension, all three. And time comes into one of the three—we aren't sure which."

The mathematician set the black box on the desk top and released the lid. Like a jack-in-the-box, two small white plastic spheres popped out and began chasing each other about in the air six inches above the box. Presently a third sphere rose up from the box and joined the fun.

Pete watched it with his jaw sagging until his head began to spin. "No wires?"

"*Strictly* no wires," said Charlie glumly. "No nothing." He closed the box with a click. "This is one of their children's toys, and theoretically, it can't work. Among other things, it takes null-gravity to operate."

Pete sat down, rubbing his chin. "Yes," he said. "I'm beginning to see. They're teaching you this?"

Tommy said, "They're trying to. He's been working for weeks with their top mathematicians, him and a dozen others. How many computers have you burned out, Charlie?"

"Four. There's a differential factor, and we can't spot it. They have the equations, all right. It's a matter of translating them into constants that make sense. But we haven't cracked the differential."

"And if you do, then what?"

Charlie took a deep breath. "We'll have inter-dimensional control, a practical, utilizable transmatter. We'll have null-gravity, which means the greatest advance in power utilization since fire was discovered. It might give us the opening to a concept of time travel that makes some kind of sense. And power! If there's an energy differential of any magnitude—" He shook his head sadly.

"We'll also know the time-differential," said Tommy hopefully, "and how long the Grdznth gestation period will be."

"It's a fair exchange," said Charlie. "We keep them until the girls have their babies. They teach us the ABC's of space, mass and dimension."

Pete nodded. "That is, if you can make the people put up with them for another six months or so."

Tommy sighed. "In a word—yes. So far we've gotten nowhere at a thousand miles an hour."

*   *   *   *   *

"I can't do it!" the cosmetician wailed, hurling himself down on a chair and burying his face in his hands. "I've failed. Failed!"

The Grdznth sitting on the stool looked regretfully from the cosmetician to the Public Relations men. "I say—I *am* sorry...." His coarse voice trailed off as he peeled a long strip of cake makeup off his satiny green face.

Pete Greenwood stared at the cosmetician sobbing in the chair. "What's eating *him*?"

"Professional pride," said Tommy. "He can take twenty years off the face of any woman in Hollywood. But he's not getting to first base with Gorgeous over there. This is only one thing we've tried," he added as they moved on down the corridor. "You should see the field reports. We've tried selling the advances Earth will have, the wealth, the power. No dice. The man on the street reads our PR-blasts, and then looks up to see one of the nasty things staring over his shoulder at the newspaper."

"So you can't make them beautiful," said Pete. "Can't you make them cute?"

"With those teeth? Those eyes? Ugh."

"How about the 'jolly company' approach?"

"Tried it. There's nothing jolly about them. They pop out of nowhere, anywhere. In church, in bedrooms, in rush-hour traffic through Lincoln Tunnel—look!"

Pete peered out the window at the traffic jam below. Cars were snarled up for blocks on either side of the intersection. A squad of traffic cops were converging angrily on the center of the mess, where a stream of green reptilian figures seemed to be popping out of the street and lumbering through the jammed autos like General Sherman tanks.

"Ulcers," said Tommy. "City traffic isn't enough of a mess as it is. And they don't *do* anything about it. They apologize profusely, but they keep coming through." The two started on for the office. "Things are getting to the breaking point. The people are wearing thin from sheer annoyance—to say nothing of the nightmares the kids are having, and the trouble with women fainting."

The signal light on Tommy's desk was flashing scarlet. He dropped into a chair with a sigh and flipped a switch. "Okay, what is it now?"

"Just another senator," said a furious male voice. "Mr. Heinz, my arthritis is beginning to win this fight. Are you going to see me now, or aren't you?"

"Yes, yes, come right in!" Tommy turned white. "Senator Stokes," he muttered. "I'd completely forgotten—"

The senator didn't seem to like being forgotten. He walked into the office, looked disdainfully at the PR-men, and sank to the edge of a chair, leaning on his umbrella.

"You have just lost your job," he said to Tommy, with an icy edge to his voice. "You may not have heard about it yet, but you can take my word for it. I personally will be delighted to make the necessary arrangements, but I doubt if I'll need to. There are at least a hundred senators in Washington who are ready to press for your dismissal, Mr. Heinz—and there's been some off-the-record talk about a lynching. Nothing official, of course."

"Senator—"

"Senator be hanged! We want somebody in this office who can manage to *do* something."

"Do something! You think I'm a magician? I can just make them vanish? What do you want me to do?"

The senator raised his eyebrows. "You needn't shout, Mr. Heinz. I'm not the least interested in *what* you do. My interest is focused completely on a collection of five thousand letters, telegrams, and visiphone calls I've received in the past three days alone. My constituents, Mr. Heinz, are making themselves clear. If the Grdznth do not go, I go."

"That would never do, of course," murmured Pete.

The senator gave Pete a cold, clinical look. "Who is this person?" he asked Tommy.

"An assistant on the job," Tommy said quickly. "A very excellent PR-man."

The senator sniffed audibly. "Full of ideas, no doubt."

"Brimming," said Pete. "Enough ideas to get your constituents off your neck for a while, at least."

"Indeed."

"Indeed," said Pete. "Tommy, how fast can you get a PR-blast to penetrate? How much medium do you control?"

"Plenty," Tommy gulped.

"And how fast can you sample response and analyze it?"

"We can have prelims six hours after the PR-blast. Pete, if you have an idea, tell us!"

Pete stood up, facing the senator. "Everything else has been tried, but it seems to me one important factor has been missed. One that will take your constituents by the ears." He looked at Tommy pityingly. "You've tried to make them lovable, but they aren't lovable. They aren't even passably attractive. There's one thing they *are* though, at least half of them."

Tommy's jaw sagged. "Pregnant," he said.

"Now see here," said the senator. "If you're trying to make a fool out of me to my face—"

"Sit down and shut up," said Pete. "If there's one thing the man in the street reveres, my friend, it's motherhood. We've got several hundred thousand pregnant Grdznth just waiting for all the little Grdznth to arrive, and nobody's given them a side glance." He turned to Tommy. "Get some copywriters down here. Get a Grdznth obstetrician or two. We're going to put together a PR-blast that will twang the people's heart-strings like a billion harps."

The color was back in Tommy's cheeks, and the senator was forgotten as a dozen intercom switches began snapping. "We'll need TV hookups, and plenty of newscast space," he said eagerly. "Maybe a few photographs—do you suppose maybe *baby* Grdznth are lovable?"

"They probably look like salamanders," said Pete. "But tell the people anything you want. If we're going to get across the sanctity of Grdznth motherhood, my friend, anything goes."

"It's genius," chortled Tommy. "Sheer genius."

"If it sells," the senator added, dubiously.

"It'll sell," Pete said. "The question is: for how long?"

*   *   *   *   *

The planning revealed the mark of genius. Nothing sudden, harsh, or crude—but slowly, in a radio comment here or a newspaper story there, the emphasis began to shift from Grdznth in general to Grdznth as mothers. A Rutgers professor found his TV discussion on "Motherhood as an Experience" suddenly shifted from 6:30 Monday evening to 10:30 Saturday night. Copy rolled by the ream from Tommy's office, refined copy, hypersensitively edited copy, finding its way into the light of day through devious channels.

Three days later a Grdznth miscarriage threatened, and was averted. It was only a page 4 item, but it was a beginning.

Determined movements to expel the Grdznth faltered, trembled with indecision. The Grdznth were ugly, they frightened little children, they *were* a trifle overbearing in their insufferable stubborn politeness—but in a civilized world you just couldn't turn expectant mothers out in the rain.

Not even expectant Grdznth mothers.

By the second week the blast was going at full tilt.

In the Public Relations Bureau building, machines worked on into the night. As questionnaires came back, spot candid films and street-corner interview tapes ran through the projectors on a twenty-four-hour schedule. Tommy Heinz grew thinner and thinner, while Pete nursed sharp post-prandial stomach pains.

"Why don't people *respond*?" Tommy asked plaintively on the morning the third week started. "Haven't they got any feelings? The blast is washing over them like a wave and there they sit!" He punched the private wire to Analysis for the fourth time that morning. He got a man with a hag-ridden look in his eye. "How soon?"

"You want yesterday's rushes?"

"What do you think I want? Any sign of a lag?"

"Not a hint. Last night's panel drew like a magnet. The D-Date tag you suggested has them by the nose."

"How about the President's talk?"

The man from Analysis grinned. "He should be campaigning."

Tommy mopped his forehead with his shirtsleeve. "Okay. Now listen: we need a special run on all response data we have for tolerance levels. Got that? How soon can we have it?"

Analysis shook his head. "We could only make a guess with the data so far."

"Fine," said Tommy. "Make a guess."

"Give us three hours," said Analysis.

"You've got thirty minutes. Get going."

Turning back to Pete, Tommy rubbed his hands eagerly. "It's starting to sell, boy. I don't know how strong or how good, but it's starting to sell! With the tolerance levels to tell us how long we can expect this program to quiet things down, we can give Charlie a deadline to crack his differential factor, or it's the ax for Charlie." He chuckled to himself, and paced the room in an overflow of nervous energy. "I can see it now. Open shafts instead of elevators. A quick hop to Honolulu for an afternoon on the beach, and back in time for supper. A hundred miles to the gallon for the Sunday driver. When people begin *seeing* what the Grdznth are giving us, they'll welcome them with open arms."

"Hmmm," said Pete.

"Well, why won't they? The people just didn't trust us, that was all. What does the man in the street know about transmatters? Nothing. But give him one, and then try to take it away."

"Sure, sure," said Pete. "It sounds great. Just a little bit *too* great."

Tommy blinked at him. "Too great? Are you crazy?"

"Not crazy. Just getting nervous." Pete jammed his hands into his pockets. "Do you realize where *we're* standing in this thing? We're out on a limb—way out. We're fighting for time— time for Charlie and his gang to crack the puzzle, time for the Grdznth girls to gestate. But what are we hearing from Charlie?"

"Pete, Charlie can't just—"

"That's right," said Pete. "*Nothing* is what we're hearing from Charlie. We've got no transmatter, no null-G, no power, nothing except a whole lot of Grdznth and more coming through just as fast as they can. I'm beginning to wonder what the Grdznth *are* giving us."

"Well, they can't gestate forever."

"Maybe not, but I still have a burning desire to talk to Charlie. Something tells me they're going to be gestating a little too long."

They put through the call, but Charlie wasn't answering. "Sorry," the operator said. "Nobody's gotten through there for three days."

"Three days?" cried Tommy. "What's wrong? Is he dead?"

"Couldn't be. They burned out two more machines yesterday," said the operator. "Killed the switchboard for twenty minutes."

"Get him on the wire," Tommy said. "That's orders."

"Yes, sir. But first they want you in Analysis."

Analysis was a shambles. Paper and tape piled knee-deep on the floor. The machines clattered wildly, coughing out reams of paper to be gulped up by other machines. In a corner office they found the Analysis man, pale but jubilant.

"The Program," Tommy said. "How's it going?"

"You can count on the people staying happy for at least another five months." Analysis hesitated an instant. "If they see some baby Grdznth at the end of it all."

There was dead silence in the room. "Baby Grdznth," Tommy said finally.

"That's what I said. That's what the people are buying. That's what they'd better get."

Tommy swallowed hard. "And if it happens to be six months?"

Analysis drew a finger across his throat.

Tommy and Pete looked at each other, and Tommy's hands were shaking. "I think," he said, "we'd better find Charlie Karns right now."

*   *   *   *   *

Math Section was like a tomb. The machines were silent. In the office at the end of the room they found an unshaven Charlie gulping a cup of coffee with a very smug-looking Grdznth. The coffee pot was floating gently about six feet above the desk. So were the Grdznth and Charlie.

"Charlie!" Tommy howled. "We've been trying to get you for hours! The operator—"

"I know, I know." Charlie waved a hand disjointedly. "I told her to go away. I told the rest of the crew to go away, too."

"Then you cracked the differential?"

Charlie tipped an imaginary hat toward the Grdznth. "Spike cracked it," he said. "Spike is a sort of Grdznth genius." He tossed the coffee cup over his shoulder and it ricochetted in graceful slow motion against the far wall. "Now why don't you go away, too?"

Tommy turned purple. "We've got five months," he said hoarsely. "Do you hear me? If they aren't going to have their babies in five months, we're dead men."

Charlie chuckled. "Five months, he says. We figured the babies to come in about three months—right, Spike? Not that it'll make much difference to us." Charlie sank slowly down to the desk. He wasn't laughing any more. "We're never going to see any Grdznth babies. It's going to be a little too cold for that. The energy factor," he mumbled. "Nobody thought of that except in passing. Should have, though, long ago. Two completely independent universes, obviously two energy systems. Incompatible. We were dealing with mass, space and dimension—but the energy differential was the important one."

"What about the energy?"

"We're loaded with it. Super-charged. Packed to the breaking point and way beyond." Charlie scribbled frantically on the desk pad. "Look, it took energy for them to come through—immense quantities of energy. Every one that came through upset the balance, distorted our whole energy pattern. And they knew from the start that the differential was all on their side—a million of them unbalances four billion of us. All they needed to overload us completely was time for enough crossings."

"And we gave it to them." Pete sat down slowly, his face green. "Like a rubber ball with a dent in the side. Push in one side, the other side pops out. And we're the other side. When?"

"Any day now. Maybe any minute." Charlie spread his hands helplessly. "Oh, it won't be bad at all. Spike here was telling me. Mean temperature in only 39 below zero, lots of good clean snow, thousands of nice jagged mountain peaks. A lovely place, really. Just a little too cold for Grdznth. They thought Earth was much nicer."

"For them," whispered Tommy.

"For them," Charlie said.

MARTYR

ORIGINALLY PUBLISHED IN *FANTASTIC UNIVERSE*,
FEBRUARY 9, 2010

Rejuvenation for the millions—or rejuvenation for the five hundred lucky ones, the select ones, that can be treated each year? Tough, independent Senator Dan Fowler fights a one-man battle against the clique that seeks perpetual power and perpetual youth, in this hard-hitting novel by Alan E. Nourse. Why did it have to be his personal fight? The others fumble it—they'd foul it up, Fowler protested? But why was he in the fight and what was to happen to Senator Fowler's fight against this fantastic conspiracy? Who would win?

MARTYR

"I can break him, split his Criterion Committee wide open now while there's still a chance, and open rejuvenationup to everybody...."

*   *   *   *   *

Four and one half hours after Martian sunset, the last light in the Headquarters Building finally blinked out.

Carl Golden stamped his feet nervously against the cold, cupping his cigarette in his hand to suck up the tiny spark of warmth. The night air bit his nostrils and made the smoke tasteless in the darkness. Atmosphere screens kept the oxygen in, all right—but they never kept the biting cold out. As the light disappeared he dropped the cigarette, stamping it sharply into darkness. Boredom vanished, and warm blood prickled through his shivering legs.

He slid back tight against the coarse black building front, peering across the road in the gloom.

It was the girl. He had thought so, but hadn't been sure. She swung the heavy stone door shut after her, glanced both left and right, and started down the frosty road toward the lights of the colony.

Carl Golden waited until she was gone. He glanced at his wrist-chrono, and waited ten minutes more. He didn't realize that he was trembling until he ducked swiftly across the road. Through the window of the low, one-story building he could see the lobby call-board, with the little colored studs all dark. He smiled in unpleasant satisfaction—no one was left in the building. It was routine, just like everything else in this god-forsaken hole. Utter, abysmal, trancelike routine. The girl was a little later than usual, probably because of the ship coming in tomorrow. Reports to get ready, supply requisitions, personnel recommendations—

—and the final reports on Armstrong's death. Mustn't forget that. The *real* story, the absolute, factual truth, without any nonsense. The reports that would go, ultimately, to Rinehart and only Rinehart, as all other important reports from the Mars Colony had been doing for so many years.

Carl skirted the long, low building, falling into the black shadows of the side wall. Halfway around he came to the supply chute, covered with a heavy moulded-stone cover.

Now?

It had taken four months here to know that he would have to do it this way. Four months of ridiculous masquerade—made idiotic by the incredible fact that everyone took him for exactly what he pretended to be, and never challenged him—not even Terry Fisher, who drunk or sober always challenged everything and everybody! But the four months had told on his nerves, in his reactions, in the hollows under his quick brown eyes. There was always the spectre of a slip-up, an aroused suspicion. And until he had the reports before his eyes, he couldn't fall back on Dan Fowler's name to save him. He had shook Dan's hand the night he had left, and Dan had said, "Remember, son—I don't know you. Hate to do it this way, but we can't risk it now—" And they couldn't, of course. Not until they knew, for certain, who had murdered Kenneth Armstrong.

They already knew why.

*   *   *   *   *

The utter stillness of the place reassured him; he hoisted up the chute cover, threw it high, and shinned his long body into the chute. It was a steep slide; he held on for an instant, then let go. Blackness gulped him down as the cover snapped closed behind him.

He struck hard and rolled. The chute opened into the commissary in the third deep-level of the building, and the place was black as the inside of a pocket. He tested unbroken legs with a sigh of relief, and limped across to where the door should be.

In the corridor there was some light—dim phosphorescence from the Martian night-rock lining the walls and tiling the floor. He walked swiftly, cursing the clack-clack his heels made on the ringing stone. When he reached the end of the corridor he tried the heavy door.

It gave, complaining. Good, good! It had been a quick, imperfect job of jimmying the lock, so obviously poor that it had worried him a lot—but why should they test it? There was still another door.

He stepped into the blackness again, started across the room as the door swung shut behind him.

A shoe scraped, the faintest rustle of sound. Carl froze. His own trouser leg? A trick of acoustics? He didn't move a muscle.

Then: "Carl?"

His pocket light flickered around the room, a small secretary's ante-room. It stopped on a pair of legs, a body, slouched down in the soft plastifoam chair—a face, ruddy and bland, with a shock of sandy hair, with quixotic eyebrows. "Terry! For Christ sake, what—"

The man leaned forward, grinning up at him. "You're late, Carl." His voice was a muddy drawl. "Should have made it sooner than this, sheems—seems to me."

Carl's light moved past the man in the chair to the floor. The bottle was standing there, still half full. "My god, you're *drunk*!"

"Course I'm drunk. Whadj-ya think, I'd sober up after you left me tonight? No thanks, I'd rather be drunk." Terry Fisher hiccupped loudly. "I'd always rather be drunk, around this place."

"All right, you've got to get out of here—" Carl's voice rose with bitter anger. Of all times, of *all* times—he wanted to scream. "How did you get in here? You've *got* to get out—"

"So do you. They're on to you, Carl. I don't think you know that, but they are." He leaned forward precariously. "I had a talk with Barness this morning, one of his nice 'spontaneous' chats, and he pumped the hell out of me and thought I was too drunk to know it. They're expecting you to come here tonight—"

Carl heaved at the drunken man's arm, frantically in the darkness. "Get *out* of here, Terry, or so help me—"

Terry clutched at him. "Didn't you hear me? They *know* about you. Personell supervisor! They think you're spying for the Eastern boys—they're starting a Mars colony too, you know. Barness is sure you're selling them info—" The man hiccupped again. "Barness is an ass, just like all the other Retreads running this place, but I'm not an ass, and you didn't fool me for two days—"

Carl gritted his teeth. How could Terry Fisher know? "For the last time—"

Fisher lurched to his feet. "They'll get you, Carl. They can try you and shoot you right on the spot, and Barness will do it. I had to tell you, you've walked right into it, but you might still get away if—"

It was cruel. The drunken man's head jerked up at the blow, and he gave a little grunt, then slid back down on the chair. Carl stepped over his legs, worked swiftly at the door beyond. If they caught him now, Terry Fisher was right. But in five more minutes—

The lock squeaked, and the door fell open. Inside he tore through the file cases, wrenched at the locked drawers in frantic haste, ripping the weak aluminum sheeting like thick tinfoil. Then he found the folder marked KENNETH ARMSTRONG on the tab.

Somewhere above him an alarm went off, screaming a mournful note through the building. He threw on the light switch, flooding the room with whiteness, and started through the papers, one by one, in the folder. No time to read. Flash retinal photos were hard to superimpose and keep straight, but that was one reason why Carl Golden was on Mars instead of sitting in an office back on Earth—

He flipped the last page, and threw the folder onto the floor. As he went through the door, he flipped out the light, raced with clattering footsteps down the corridor.

Lights caught him from both sides, slicing the blackness like hot knives. "*All right, Golden. Stop right there.*"

Dark figures came out of the lights, ripped his clothing off without a word. Somebody wrenched open his mouth, shined a light in, rammed coarse cold fingers down into his throat. Then: "All right, you bastard, up stairs. Barness wants to see you."

They packed him naked into the street, hurried him into a three-wheeled ground car. Five minutes later he was wading through frosty dust into another building, and Barness was glaring at him across the room.

*   *   *   *   *

Odd things flashed through Carl's mind. You seldom saw a Repeater get really angry—but Barness was angry. The man's young-old face (the strange, utterly ageless amalgamation of sixty years of wisdom, superimposed by the youth of a twenty-year-old) had unaccustomed lines of wrath about the eyes and mouth. Barness didn't waste words. "What did you want down there?"

"Armstrong." Carl cut the word out almost gleefully. "And I got it, and there's nothing you or Rinehart or anybody else in between can do about it. I don't know *what* I saw yet, but I've got it in my eyes and in my cortex, and you can't touch it."

"You stupid fool, we can *peel* your cortex," Barness snarled.

"Well, you won't. You won't dare."

Barness glanced across at the officer who had brought him in. "Tommy—"

"Dan Fowler won't like it," said Carl.

Barness stopped short, blinking. He took a slow breath. Then he sank down into his chair. "Fowler" he said, as though dawn were just breaking.

"That's right. He sent me up here. I've found what he wants. Shoot me now, and when they probe you Dan will know I found it, and you won't be around for another rejuvenation."

Barness looked suddenly old. "What did he want?"

"The truth about Armstrong. Not the 'accident' story you fed to the teevies.... "*Tragic End for World Hero, Died With His Boots On*". Dan wanted the truth. Who killed him. Why this colony is grinding down from compound low to stop, and turning men like Terry Fisher into alcoholic bums. Why this colony is turning into a glorified, super-refined Birdie's Rest for old men. But mostly who killed Armstrong, how he was murdered, who gave the orders. And if you don't mind, I'm beginning to get cold."

"And you got all that," said Barness.

"That's right."

"You haven't read it, though."

"Not yet. Plenty of time for that on the way back."

Barness nodded wearily, and motioned the guard to give Carl his clothes. "I think you'd better read it tonight. Maybe it'll surprise you."

Golden's eyes widened. Something in the man's voice, some curious note of defeat and hopelessness, told him that Barness was not lying. "Oh?"

"Armstrong didn't have an accident, that's true. But nobody murdered him, either. Nobody gave any orders, to anybody, from anybody. Armstrong put a bullet through his head—quite of his own volition."

II

"All right, Senator," the young red-headed doctor said. "You say you want it straight—that's how you're going to get it." Moments before, Dr. Moss had been laughing. Now he wasn't laughing. "Six months, at the outside. Nine, if you went to bed tomorrow, retired from the Senate, and lived on tea and crackers. But where I'm sitting I wouldn't bet a plugged nickel that you'll be alive a month from now. If you think I'm joking, you just try to squeeze a bet out of me."

Senator Dan Fowler took the black cigar from his mouth, stared at the chewed-up end for a moment, and put it back in again. He had had something exceedingly witty all ready to say at this point in the examination; now it didn't seem to be too funny. If Moss had been a mealy-mouthed quack like the last Doc he had seen, okay. But Moss wasn't. Moss was obviously not impressed by the old man sitting across the desk from him, a fact which made Dan Fowler just a trifle uneasy. And Moss knew his turnips.

Dan Fowler looked at the doctor and said, "Garbage."

The red-headed doctor shrugged. "Look, Senator—sometimes a banana is a banana. I know heart disease, and I know how it acts. I know that it kills people if they wait too long. And when you're dead, no rejuvenation lab is going to bring you back to life again."

"Oh, hell! Who's dying?" Fowler's grey eyebrows knit in the old familiar scowl, and he bit down hard on the cigar. "Heart disease! So I get a little pain now and then—sure it won't last forever, and when it gets bad I'll come in and take the full treatment. But I can't do it now!" He spread his hands in a violent gesture. "I only came in here because my daughter dragged me. My heart's doing fine—I've been working an eighteen hour day for forty years now, and I can do it for another year or two—"

"But you have pain," said Dr. Moss.

"So? A little twinge, now and then."

"Whenever you lose your temper. Whenever anything upsets you."

"All right—a twinge."

"Which makes you sit down for ten or fifteen minutes. Which doesn't go away with one nitro-tablet any more, so you have to take two, and sometimes three—right?"

*　*　*　*　*

Dan Fowler blinked. "All right, sometimes it gets a little bad—"

"And it used to be only once or twice a month, but now it's almost every day. And once or twice you've blacked clean out for a while, and made your staff work like demons to cover for you and keep it off the teevies, right?"

"Say, who's been talking to you?"

"Jean has been talking to me."

"Can't even trust your own daughter to keep her trap shut." The Senator tossed the cigar butt down in disgust. "It happened once, yes. That god damned Rinehart is enough to make anybody black out." He thrust out his jaw and glowered at Dr. Moss as though it were all *his* fault. Then he grinned. "Oh, I know you're right, Doc. It's just that this is the wrong *time*. I can't take two months out now—there's too much to be done between now and the middle of next month."

"Oh, yes. The Hearings. Why not turn it over to your staff? They know what's going on."

"Nonsense. They know, but not like I know. After the Hearings, fine—I'll come along like a lamb. But now—"

Dr. Moss reddened, slammed his fist down on the desk. "Dammit, man, are you blind and deaf? Or just plain stupid? Didn't you hear me a moment ago? *You may not live through the Hearings.* You could *go*, just like that, any minute. But this is 2134 A.D., not the middle ages. It would be so utterly, hopelessly pointless to let that happen—"

Fowler champed his cigar and scowled. "After it was done I'd have to Free-Agent for a year, wouldn't I?" It was an accusation.

"You *should*. But that's a formality. If you want to go back to what you were doing the day you came from the Center—"

"Yes, *if*! But supposing I didn't? Supposing I was all changed?"

The young doctor looked at the old man shrewdly. Dan Fowler was 56 years old—and he looked forty. It seemed incredible even to Moss that the man could have done what he had done, and look almost as young and fighting-mad now as he had when he started. Clever old goat, too—but Dan Fowler's last remark opened the hidden door wide. Moss smiled to himself. "You're afraid of it, aren't you, Senator?"

"Of rejuvenation? Nonsense."

"But you are. You aren't the only one—it's a pretty frightening thing. Cash in the old model, take out a new one, just like a jet racer or a worn out talk-writer. Only it isn't machinery, it's your body, and your life." Dr. Moss grinned. "It scares a man. *Rejuvenation* isn't the right word, of course. Aside from the neurones, they take away every cell in your body, one way or another, and give you new ones. A hundred and fifty years ago Cancelmo and Klein did it on a dog, and called it *subtotal prosthesis*. A crude job—I've seen their papers and films. Vat-grown hearts and kidneys, revitalized vascular material, building up new organ systems like a patchwork quilt, coaxing new tissues to grow to replace old ones—but they got a living dog out of it, and that dog lived to the ripe old age of 37 years before he died."

*   *   *   *   *

Moss pushed back from his desk, watching Dan Fowler's face. "Then in 1992 Nimrock tried it on a man, and almost got himself hanged because the man died. That was a hundred and forty-two years ago. And then while he was still on trial, his workers completed the second job, and the man *lived*, and oh, how the jig changed for Nimrock!"

The doctor shrugged. As he talked, Dan Fowler sat silent, chewing his cigar furiously. But listening—he was listening, all right. "Well, it was crude, then," Moss said. "It's not so crude any more." He pointed to a large bronze plaque hanging on the office wall. "You've seen that before. Read it."

Dan Fowler's eyes went up to the plaque. A list of names. At the top words said, "*These ten gave life to Mankind.*"

Below it were the names:

Martin Aronson, Ph. D. Education

Thomas Bevalaqua Literature and Art

Chauncy Devlin Music

Frederick A. Kehler, M. S. Engineering

William B. Morse, L. L. D. Law

Rev. Hugh H. F. Norton Philosophy and Theology

Jacob Prowsnitz, Ph. D. History

Arthur L. Rodgers, M. D. Medicine

Carlotta Sokol, Ph. D. Sociopsychology

Harvey Tatum Business

"I know," said Dan Fowler. "June 1st, 2005. They were volunteers."

"Ten out of several dozen volunteers," Moss amended. "Those ten were chosen by lot. Already people were dreaming of what sub-total prosthesis could do. It could preserve the great minds, it could compound the accumulated wisdom of one lifetime with another lifetime—and maybe more. Those ten people— representing ten great fields of study—risked their lives. Not to live forever—just to see if rejuvenation could really preserve their minds in newly built bodies. All of them were old, older than you are, Senator, some were sicker than you, and all of them were afraid. But seven of the ten are *still alive today*, a hundred and thirty years later. Rodgers died in a jet crash. Tatum died of neuro-toxic virus, because we couldn't do anything to rebuild neurones in those days. Bevalaqua suicided. The rest are still alive, after two more rejuvenations."

"Fine," said Dan Fowler. "I still can't do it now."

"That was just ten people," Moss cut in. "It took five years to get ready for them. But now we can do five hundred a year—only five hundred select individuals, to live on instead of dying. And you've got the gall to sit there and tell me you don't have the time for it!"

*   *   *   *   *

The old man rose slowly, lighting another cigar. "It could be five thousand a year. That's why I don't have the time. Fifteen thousand, fifty thousand. We could do it—but we're not doing it. Walter Rinehart's been rejuvenated—twice already! *I'm* on the list because I shouted so loud they didn't dare leave me off. But *you're* not on it. Why not? You could be. Everybody could be."

Dr. Moss spread his hands. "The Criterion Committee does the choosing."

"*Rinehart's* criteria! Only five hundred a year. Use it for a weapon. Build power with it. Get a strangle-hold on it, and never, never let it go." The Senator leaned across the desk, his eyes bright with anger. "I haven't got time to stop what I'm doing now—because I can *stop* Rinehart, if I only live that long, I can break him, split his Criterion Committee wide open *now* while there's still a chance, and open rejuvenation up to everybody instead of five hundred lucky ones a year. I can stop him because I've dug at him and dug at him for twenty-nine years, and shouted and screamed and fought and made people listen. And if I fumble now, it'll all be down the drain, finished, washed up.

"If that happens, *nobody* will ever stop him."

There was silence in the room for a moment. Then Moss spread his hands. "The hearings are that critical, eh?"

"I'm afraid so."

"Why has it got to be *your* personal fight? Other people could do it."

"They'd fumble it. They'd foul it up. Senator Libby fouled it up once already, a long time ago. Rinehart's lived for a hundred and nineteen years, and he's learning new tricks every year. I've only lived fifty-six of them, but I know his tricks. I can beat him."

"But why *you*?"

"Somebody's got to do it. My card is on top."

A 'phone buzzer chirped. "Yes, he's here." Dr. Moss handed Dan the receiver. A moment later the Senator was grinning like a cat struggling into his overcoat and scarf. "Sorry, Doc—I know what you tell me is true, and I'm no fool. If I have to stop, I'll stop."

"Tomorrow, then."

"Not tomorrow. One of my lads is back from the Mars Colony. Tomorrow we pow-wow—but hard. After the hearings, Doc. And meanwhile, keep your eye on the teevies. I'll be seeing you."

The door clicked shut with a note of finality, and Dr. David Moss stared at it gloomily. "I hope so," he said. But nobody in particular heard him.

III

A Volta two-wheeler was waiting for him outside. Jean drove off down the drive with characteristic contempt for the laws of gravity when Dan had piled in, and Carl Golden was there, looking thinner, more gaunt and hawk-like than ever before, his brown eyes sharp under his shock of black hair, his long, thin aquiline nose ("If you weren't a Jew you'd be a discredit to the Gentiles," Dan Fowler had twitted him once, years before, and Carl had looked down his long, thin, aquiline nose, and sniffed, and let the matter drop, because until then he had never been sure whether his being a Jew had mattered to Dan Fowler or not, and now he knew, and was quite satisfied with the knowledge) and the ever-present cigarette between thin, sensitive fingers. Dan clapped him on the shoulder, and shot a black look at his daughter, relegating her to an indescribable Fowler limbo, which was where she belonged, and would reside until Dan got excited and forgot how she'd betrayed him to Dr. Moss, which would take about ten or fifteen minutes all told. Jean Fowler knew her father far too well to worry about it, and squinted out the window at the afternoon traffic as the car skidded the corner into the Boulevard Throughway, across the river toward home. "God damn it, boy, you could have *wired* me at least. One of Jean's crew spotted the passage list, so I knew you'd left, and got the hearing moved up to next month—"

Carl scowled. "I thought it was all set for February 15th."

Dan chuckled. "It was. But I was only waiting for you, and got the ball rolling as soon as I knew you were on your way. Dwight McKenzie is still writing the Committee's business calendar, of course, and he didn't like it a bit, but he couldn't find any solid reason why it *shouldn't* be set ahead. And I think our good friend Senator Rinehart is probably wriggling on the stick about now, just on the shock value of the switch. Always figure in the shock value of everything you do, my boy—it pays off more than you'd ever dream—"

Carl Golden shook his head. "I don't like it, Dan."

"What, the switch in dates?"

"The switch. I wish you hadn't done that."

"But why? Look, son, I know that with Ken Armstrong dead our whole approach has to be changed—it's going to be trickier, but it might even work out better. The Senate knows what's been going on between Rinehart and me, and so does the President. They know elections are due next June. They know I want a seat on his Criterion Committee before elections, and they know that to get on it I'll do my damnedest to unseat him. They know I've shaken him up, that he's scared of me. Okay, fine. With Armstrong there to tell how he was chosen for Retread back in '87, we'd have had Rinehart running for his life...."

"But you don't," Carl cut in flatly, "and that's that."

"What, are you crazy, son? *I needed Armstrong, bad.* Rinehart knew it, and had him taken care of. It was fishy—it stunk from here to Mars, but Rinehart covered it up fast and clean. But with the stuff you got up in the Colony, we can charge Rinehart with murder, and the whole Senate knows his motive already. He didn't *dare* to let Armstrong testify."

                    *   *   *   *   *

Carl was shaking his head sadly.

"Well, what's wrong?"

"You aren't going to like this, Dan. Rinehart's clean. Armstrong comitted suicide."

Fowler's mouth fell open, and he sat back hard. "Oh, no."

"Sorry."

"Ken Armstrong? Suicided?" He shook his head helplessly, groping for words. "I—I—oh, Jesus. I don't believe it. If Ken Armstrong suicided, I'm the Scarlet Whore of Babylon."

"Well, we'll try to keep *that* off the teevies."

"There's no chance that you're wrong," said the old man.

Carl shook his head. "There's plenty that's funny about that Mars Colony, but Armstrong's death was suicide. Period. Even Barness didn't understand it."

Sharp eyes went to Carl's face. "What's funny about the Colony?"

Carl shrugged, and lit a cigarette. "Hard to say. This was my first look, I had nothing to compare it with. But there's *something* wrong. I always thought the Mars Colony was a frontier, a real challenge—you know, Man against the Wilderness, and all that. Saloons jammed on Saturday nights with rough boys out to get some and babes that had it to give. A place that could take Earthbound softies and toughen them up in a week, working to tame down the desert—"

His voice trailed off. "They've got a saloon, all right—but everybody just comes in quietly and gets slobbery drunk. Met a guy named Fisher, thought the same thing I did when he came up five years ago. A real go-getter, leader type, lots of ideas and the guts to put them across. Now he's got a hob-nail liver and he came back here on the ship with me, hating Mars and everything up there, most of all himself. Something's wrong up there, Dan. Maybe that's why Armstrong bowed out."

The Senator took a deep breath. "Not a man like Ken Armstrong. Why, I used to worship him when I was a kid. I was ten when he came back to Earth for his second Retread." The old man shook his head. "I wanted to go back to Mars with him—I actually packed up to run away, until dear brother Paul caught me and squealed to Dad. Imagine."

"I'm sorry, Dan."

The car whizzed off the Throughway, and began weaving through the residential areas of Arlington. Jean swung under an arched gate, stopped in front of a large greystone house of the sort they hadn't built for a hundred years. Dan Fowler stared out at the grey November afternoon. "Well, then we're really on thin ice at the Hearings. We can still do it. It'll take some steam-rollering, but we can manage it." He turned to the girl. "Get Schirmer on the wire as soon as we get inside. I'll go over Carl's report for whatever I can find. Tell Schirmer if he wants to keep his job as Coordinator of the Medical Center next year, he'd better have all the statistics available on all rejuvenated persons past and present, in my office tomorrow morning."

Jean gave her father a queer look. "Schirmer's waiting for you inside right now."

"Oh? Why?"

"He wouldn't say. Nothing to do with politics, he said. Something about Paul."

*   *   *   *   *

Nathan Shirmer was waiting in the library, sipping a brandy and pretending to scan a Congressional Record in the viewer-box. He looked up, bird-like, as Dan Fowler strode in. "Well, Nate. Sit down, sit down. I see you're into my private stock already, so I won't offer you any. What's this about my brother?"

Schirmer coughed into his hand. "Why—Dan, I don't quite know how to tell you this. He was in Washington this afternoon—"

"Of course he was. He was supposed to go to the Center—" Dan broke off short, whirling on Schirmer. "Wait a minute! There wasn't a slip-up on this permit?"

"Permit?"

"For rejuvention, you ass! He's on the Starship Project, coordinating engineer of the whole works out there. He's got a fair place on the list coming to him three ways from Sunday. Follmer put the permit through months ago, and Paul has just been diddling around getting himself clear so he could come in—"

The little Coordinator's eyes widened. "Oh, there wasn't anything wrong on *our* side, if that's what you mean. The permit was perfectly clear, the doctors were waiting for him. It was nothing like that."

"Then what was it like?"

Nathan Schirmer wriggled, and tried to avoid Dan's eyes. "Your brother refused it. He laughed in our faces, and told us to go to hell, and took the next jet back to Nevada. All in one afternoon."

The vibration of the jet engines hung just at perception level, nagging and nagging at Dan Fowler, until he threw his papers aside with a snarl of disgust, and peered angrily out the window.

They were high, and moving fast. Far below was a tiny spot of light in the blackness. Pittsburgh. Maybe Cleveland. It didn't matter which. Jets traveled at such-and-such a rate of speed; they left at such-and-such a time and arrived elsewhere at such-and-such a time later. He could worry, or he could not-worry. The jet would bring him down in Las Vegas in exactly the same time, to the second, either way. Another half-hour taxi ride over dusty desert roads would bring him to the glorified quonset hut his brother called home. Nothing Dan Fowler could do would hurry the process of getting there.

Dan had called, and received no answer.

He had talked to the Las Vegas authorities, and even gotten Lijinsky at the Starship, and neither of them knew anything. The police said yes, they would check at Dr. Fowler's residence, if he wasn't out at the Ship, and check back. But they hadn't checked back, and that was two hours ago. Meanwhile, Carl had chartered him a plane.

God damn Paul to three kinds of hell. Of all miserable times to start playing games, acting like an imbecile child! And the work and sweat Dan had gone through to get that permit, to buy it beg it, steal it, gold-plate it. Of course the odds were good that Paul would have gotten it without a whisper from Dan—he was high on the list, he was critical to Starship, and certainly Starship was critical enough to rate. But Dan had gone out on a limb, way out—The Senator's fist clenched, and he drummed it helplessly on the empty seat, and felt a twinge of pain spread up his chest, down his arm. He cursed, fumbled for the bottle in his vest pocket. God damned heart and god damned brother and god damned Rinehart—did *everything* have to split the wrong way? Now? Of all times of all days of all his fifty-six years of life, *now*?

All right, Dan. Cool, boy. Relax. Shame on you. Can't you quit being selfish just for a little while? Dan didn't like the idea as it flickered through his mind, but then he didn't like anything too much right then, so he forced the thought back for a rerun.

Big Dan Fowler, *Senator* Dan Fowler, Selfish Dan Fowler loves Dan Fowler mostly.

Poor Paul.

* * * * *

The words had been going through his mind like a silly chant since the first moment he had seen Nate Schirmer in the library. Poor Paul. Dan did all right for himself, he did—made quite a name down in Washington, you know, a fighter, a real fighter. The Boy with the Golden Touch (joke, son, laugh now). Everything he ever did worked out with him on top, somehow. Paul was different. Smart enough, plenty of the old gazoo, but he never had Dan's drive. Bad breaks, right down the line. Kinda tough on a guy, with a comet like Dan in the family. Poor Paul.

He let his mind drift back slowly, remembering little things, trying to spot the time, the single instant in time, when he stopped fighting Paul and started feeling sorry for him. It had been different, years ago. Paul was the smart one, all right. Never had Dan's build but he could think rings around him. Dan was always a little slow—never forgot anything he learned, but he learned slow. Still, there were ways to get around that—

Dad and Mom always liked Paul the best (their first boy, you know) and babied him more, and that was decidedly tougher to get around—Still there were ways.

Like the night the prize money came from the lottery, when he and Paul had split a ticket down the middle. How old was he then—ten? Eleven? And Paul was fifteen. He'd grubbed up the dollar polishing cars, and met Paul's dollar halfway, never dreaming the thing would pay off. And when it did! Oh, he'd never forget that night. He wanted the jet-racer. The ticket paid two thousand, a hell of a lot of cash for a pair of boys—and the two thousand would buy the racer. He'd been so excited tears had poured down his face.... But Paul had said no. Split it even, just like the ticket, Paul had said. There were hot words, and pleading, and threats, and Paul had just laughed at him until he got so mad he wanted to kill him with only his fists. Bad mistake, that. Paul was skinny, not much muscle, read books all the time it looked like a cinch. But Paul had five years on him that he hadn't counted on. Important five years. Paul connected with just one—enough to lay Dan flat on his back with a concussion and a broken jaw, and that, my boy, was that.

Almost.

Dan had won the fight, of course. It was the broken jaw that did it, that night, later the fight Mom and Dad had, worse than usual, a cruel one, low blows, mean—But Dan got his racer, on the strength of the broken jaw. That jaw had done him a lot of good. Never grew quite right after that, got one of the centers of ossification, the doc had said, and Dan had been god's gift to the pen-and-brush men with that heavy, angular jaw—a fighter's jaw, they called it.

*   *   *   *   *

That started it, of course. He knew then that he could beat Paul. Good to know. But never *sure* of it, always having to prove it. The successes came, and always he let Paul know about them, watched Paul's face like a cat. And Paul would squirm, and sneer, and tell Dan that in the end it was brains that would pay off. Sour grapes, of course. If Paul had ever squared off to him again, man to man, they might have had it over with. But Paul just seemed content to sit and quietly hate him.

Like the night he broke the Universalists in New Chicago, at the hundred-dollar-a-plate dinner. He'd told them, that night. That was the night they'd cold-shouldered him, and put Libby up to run for Mayor. Oh, he'd raised a glorious stink that night—he'd never enjoyed himself so much in his life, turning their whole twisted machine right over to the public on a silver platter. Cutting loose from the old crowd, appointing himself a committee of one to nominate himself on an Independent Reform ticket, campaign himself, and elect himself. A whippersnapper of thirty-two. Paul had been amused by it all, almost indulgent. "You *do* get melodramatic, don't you, Dan? Well, if you want to cut your own throat, that's your affair." And Dan had burned, and told Paul to watch the teevies, he'd see a thing or two, and he did, all right. He remembered Paul's face a few months later, when Libby conceded at 11:45 PM on election night, and Dan rode into office with a new crowd of livewires who were ready to help him plow into New Chicago and clean up that burg like it'd never been cleaned up. And the sweetest part of the victory pie had been the look on Paul's face that night—

So they'd fought, and he'd won and rubbed it in, and Paul had lost, and hated him for it, until that mysterious day—when had it really happened?—when "that big-brained brother of mine" changed subtly into "Christ, man, quit floundering! Who wants engineers? They're all over the place, you'll starve to death" and then finally, to "poor Paul."

When had it happened? Why?

Dan wondered, suddenly, if he had ever really forgiven Paul that blow to the jaw—

Perhaps.

He shook himself, scowling into the plastiglass window blackness. Okay, they'd fought it out. Always jolly, always making it out to be a big friendly game, only it never was a game. He knew how much he owed to Paul. He'd known it with growing concern for a lot of years. And now if he had to drag him back to Washington by the hair, he'd drag the silly fool—

IV

They didn't look very much alike. There was a spareness about Paul—a tall, lean, hungry-looking man, with large soft eyes that hid their anger and a face that was lined with tiredness and resignation. A year ago, when Dan had seen him last, he had looked a young 60, closer to 45; now he looked an old, old 61. How much of this was the cancer Dan didn't know. The pathologist had said: "Not a very malignant tumor right now, but you can never tell when it'll blow up. He'd better be scheduled at the Center, if he's got a permit—"

But some of it was Paul, just Paul. The house was exactly as Dan had expected it would be (though he had never been inside this house since Paul had come to Starship Project fifteen years ago)—stuffy, severe, rather gloomy, rooms packed with bookshelves, drawing boards, odds and ends of papers and blueprints and inks, thick, ugly furniture from the early 2000's, a cluttered, improvised, helter-skelter barn of a testing-lab, with modern equipment that looked lost and alien scattered among the mouldering junk of two centuries.

"Get your coat," said Dan. "It's cold outside. We're going back to Washington."

"Have a drink." Paul waved him toward the sideboard. "Relax. Your pilot needs a rest."

"Paul, I didn't come here to play games. The games are over now."

Paul poured a brandy with deliberation. Handed Dan one, sipped his own. "Good brandy," he murmured. "Wish I could afford more of it."

"*Paul.* You're going with me."

The old man shrugged with a little tired smile. "I'll go with you if you insist, of course. But I'm not going."

"Do you know what you're saying?"

"Perfectly."

"Paul, you don't just say 'Thanks, but I don't believe I'll have any' when they give you a rejuvenation permit. *Nobody* refuses rejuvenation. Why, there are a million people out there begging for a place on the list. It's *life*, Paul. You can't just turn it down—"

"This *is* good brandy," said Paul. "Would you care to take a look at my lab, by the way? Not too well equipped, but sometimes I can work here better than—"

Dan swung on his brother viciously. "I will tell you what I'm going to do," he grated, hitting each word hard, like knuckles rapping the table. "I'm going to take you to the plane. If you won't come, my pilot and I will drag you. When we get to Washington, we'll take you to the Center. If you won't sign the necessary releases, I'll forge them. I'll bribe two witnesses who will swear in the face of death by torture that they saw you signing. I'll buy out the doctors that can do the job, and if they won't do it, I'll sweat them down until they *will*."

*   *   *   *   *

He slammed the glass down on the table, feeling his heart pounding in his throat, feeling the pain creep up. "I've got lots of things on lots of people, and I can get things done when I want them done. People don't fool with me in Washington any more, because when they do they get their fingers burned off at the knuckles. For Christ sake, Paul, I knew you were stubborn but I didn't think you were block-headed stupid!"

Paul shrugged, apologetically. "I'm impressed, Dan. Really."

"You don't think I can do it?" Dan roared.

"Oh, no doubt you *could*. But such a lot of trouble for an unwilling victim. And I'm your brother, Dan. Remember?"

Dan Fowler spread his hands in defeat, then sank down in the chair. "Paul, tell me *why*."

"I don't want to be rejuvenated." As though he were saying, "I don't want any sugar in my coffee."

"Why not? If I could only see why, if I knew what was going through your mind, maybe I could understand. But I can't."

Dan looked up at Paul, practically pleading. "You're *needed*. I had a tape from Lijinsky last month—do you know what he said? He said why couldn't you have come to Starship ten years earlier? Nobody knows that ship like you do, you're making it go. That ship can take men to the stars, now, with rejuvenation, and the same men can come back again to find the same people waiting for them when they get here. They can *live* that long, now. We've been tied down to seventy years of life, to a tight little universe of one sun and nine planets for thousands of years. Well, we can change that now. We can go out. That's what your work can do for us." He stared helplessly at his brother. "You could go out on that ship you're building, Paul. You've always wanted to. *Why not?*"

Paul looked across at him for a long moment. There was pity in his eyes. There was also hatred there, and victory, long awaited, bitterly won. "Do you really want me to tell you?"

"I want you to tell me."

Then Paul told him. It took about ten minutes. It was not tempered with mercy.

It split Dan Fowler's world wide open at the seams.

*   *   *   *   *

"You've been talking about the Starship," said Paul Fowler. "All right, that's as good a starting place as any. I came to Starship Project—what was it, fifteen years ago? Almost sixteen, I guess. This was my meat. I couldn't work well with people, I worked with *things*, processes, ideas. I dug in hard on Starship. I loved it, dreamed it, lived with it. I had dreams in those days. Work hard, make myself valuable here, maybe I'd *get* rejuvenation, so I could work more on Starship. I believed everything you just said. Alpha Centauri, Arcturus, Vega, anywhere we wanted to go—and I could go along! It wouldn't be long, either. We had Lijinsky back with us after his rejuvenation, directing the Project, we had Keller and Stark and Eddie Cochran—great men, the men who had pounded Starship Project into reality, took it out of the story books and made the people of this country want it bad enough to pay for it. Those men were back now—new men, rebuilt bodies, with all their knowledge and experience preserved. Only now they had something even more precious than life: *time.* And I was part of it, and I too could have time."

Paul shook his head, slowly, and sank back into the chair. His eyes were very tired. "A dream, nothing more. A fantasy. It took me fifteen years to learn what a dream it was. Not even a suspicion at first—only a vague puzzlement, things happening that I couldn't quite grasp. Easy to shrug off, until it got too obvious. Not a matter of wrong decisions, really. The decisions were right, but they were in the wrong places. Something about Starship Project shifting, changing somehow. Something being lost. Slowly. Nothing you could nail down, at first, but growing month by month.

"Then one night I saw what it was. That was when I equipped the lab here, and proved to myself that Starship Project was a dream."

* * * * *

He spread his hands and smiled at Dan like a benign old Chips to a third-form schoolboy. "The Starship isn't going to Alpha Centauri or anywhere else. It's not going to leave the ground. I thought I'd live long enough to launch that ship and be one of its crew. Well, I won't. That ship wouldn't leave the ground if I lived a million years."

"Garbage," said Dan Fowler succinctly.

"No, Dan. Not garbage. Unfortunately, we sometimes have to recognize our dreams as dreams, and look reality right square in the face. Starship Project is dying. Our whole civilization is dying. Nimrock drove the first nail into the coffin a hundred and thirty years ago—lord, if they'd only hanged him when his first rejuvenation failed! But that would only have delayed it. Now we're dying, slowly right now, but soon it will be fast, very fast. And do you know who's getting set to land the death-blow?" He smiled sadly across at his brother. "You are, Dan."

Dan Fowler sprang from his chair with a roar. "My god, Paul, you're *sick!* Of all the idiot's delights I ever heard, I—I—oh, Jesus." He stood shaking, groping for words, staring at his brother.

"You said you wanted me to tell you."

"Tell me! Tell me what?" Dan took a trembling breath, and sat down, visibly, gripping himself. "All right, all right, I heard what you said—you must mean something, but I don't know what. Let's be reasonable. Let's forget philosophy and semantics and concepts and all the frills for just a minute and talk about facts, huh? *Just facts.*"

"All right, facts," said Paul. "Kenneth Armstrong wrote MAN ON MARS in 2028—he was fifty-seven years old then, and he hadn't been rejuvenated yet. Fundamentally a good book, analyzing his first Mars Colony, taking it apart right down to the silk undies, to show why it had failed so miserably, and why the next one could succeed if he could ever get up there again. He had foresight; with rejuvenation just getting started, he had a whole flock of ideas about overpopulation and the need for a Mars Colony—he was all wet on the population angle, of course, but nobody knew that then. He kicked Keller and Lijinsky off on the Starship idea. They admit it—it was MAN ON MARS that first started them thinking. They were both young, with lots of fight in them. Okay?"

"Just stick to facts," said Dan coldly.

*   *   *   *   *

"Okay. Starship Project got started, and blossomed into the people's Baby. They started work on the basic blueprints about 60 years ago. Everybody knew it would be a long job—cost money, plenty of it, and there was so much to do before the building ever began. That was where I came in, fifteen years ago. Building. They were looking for engineers who weren't eager to get rich. It went fine. We started to build. Then Keller and Stark came back from rejuvenation. Lijinsky had been rejuvenated five years before."

"Look, I don't need a course in history," Dan exploded.

"Yes, you do," Paul snapped. "You need to sit down and listen for once, instead of shooting your big mouth off all the time. That's what you need real bad, Dan." Paul Fowler rubbed his chin. There were red spots in his cheeks. "Okay, there were some changes made. I didn't like the engine housing—I never had, so I went along with them a hundred percent on that. Even though I designed it—I'd learned a few things since. And there were bugs. It made perfectly good sense, talking to Lijinsky. Starship Project was pretty important to all of us. Dangerous to risk a fumble on the first play, even a tiny risk. We might never get another chance. Lijinsky knew we youngsters were driving along on adrenalin and nerves, and couldn't wait to get out there, but when you thought about it, what was the rush? Was it worth a chance of a fumble to get out there *this* year instead of *next*? Couldn't we take time to find a valid test for that engine at ultra-high acceleration before we put it back in? After all, we *had* time now—Keller and Stark just back with sixty more years to live—why the rush?

"Okay. I bought it. We worked out a valid test on paper. Took us four years of work on it to find out you couldn't build such a device on Earth, but never mind that. Other things were stalling all the while. The colony-plan for the ship. Choosing the crew— what criteria, what qualifications? There was plenty of time— why not make *sure* it's right? Don't leave anything crude, if we can refine it a little first—"

Paul sighed wearily. "It snowballed. Keller and Stark backed Lijinsky to the hilt. There was some trouble about money—I think you had your thumb in the pie there, getting it fixed for us, didn't you? More refining. Work it out. Detail. Get sidetracked on some aspect for a few years—so what? Lots of time. Rejuvenation, and all that, talk about the Universalists beating Rinehart out and throwing the Center open to everybody. Et cetera, et cetera. But somewhere along the line I began to see that it just wasn't true. The holdups, the changes, the digressions and snags and refinements were all excuses, all part of a big, beautiful, exquisitely reasonable facade built up to obscure the real truth. *Lijinsky and Keller and Stark had changed.*"

Dan Fowler snorted. "I know a very smart young doctor who told me that there *weren't* any changes."

"I don't mean anything physical—their bodies were fine. Nothing mental, either—they had the same sharp minds they always had. It was a change in values. They'd lost something that they'd had before. The *drive* that made them start Starship Project, the *urgency*, the vital importance of the thing—it was all gone. They just didn't have the push any more. They began to look for the easy way, and it was far easier to build and rebuild, and refine, and improve the Starship here on the ground than to throw that Starship out into space—"

*   *   *   *   *

There was a long, long silence. Dan Fowler sat grey-faced, staring at Paul, just shaking his head and staring. "I don't believe it," he said finally. "You do maybe, because you want to, but you're mixed up, Paul. I've seen Lijinsky's reports. There's been progress, regular progress, month by month. You've been too close to it, maybe. Of course there have been delays, but only when they were necessary. The progress has gone on—"

Paul stood up suddenly. "Come in here, Dan. Look." He threw open a door, strode rapidly down a corridor and a flight of stairs into the long, low barn of a laboratory. "Here, here, let me show you something." He pulled out drawers, dragged out rolls of blueprints. "These are my own. They're based on the working prints from Starship that we drew up ten years ago, scaled down to model size. I've tested them, I've run tolerances, I've checked the math five ways and back again. I've tested the parts, the engine—model size. The blueprints haven't got a flaw in them. They're perfect as they'll ever get. No, wait a minute, look—"

He strode fiercely across to slide back a floor panel, drew up the long, glittering thing from a well in the floor—sleek, beautiful, three feet long. Paul maneuvered a midget loading crane, guided the thing into launching position on the floor, then turned back to Dan. "There it is. Just a model, but it's perfect. Every detail is perfect. There's even fuel in it. No men, but there could be if there were any men small enough."

Anger was blazing in Paul's voice now, bitterness and frustration. "I built it, because I had to be sure. I've tested its thrust. I could launch this model for Alpha Centauri tonight— and *it would get there.* If there were little men who could get into it, *they'd* get there, too—alive. Starship Project is completed, it's been completed for ten years now, but do you know what happened to these blueprints, the originals? They were studied. They were improvements. They almost had the ship built, and then they took it apart again."

"But I've read the reports," Dan cried.

"Have you *seen* the Starship? Have you *talked* to them over there? It isn't just there, it's *everywhere*, Dan. There are only about 70,000 rejuvenated men alive in this hemisphere so far, but already the change is beginning to show. Go talk to the Advertising people—*there's* a delicate indicator of social change if there ever was one. See what they say. Who are they backing in the Government? You? Like hell. Rinehart? No, they're backing up 'Moses' Tyndall and his Abolitionist goon-squad who preach that rejuvenation is the work of Satan, and they're giving him enough strength that he's even getting *you* worried. How about Roderigo Aviado and his Solar Energy Project down in Antarctica? Do you know what he's been doing down there lately? You'd better find out, Dan. What's happening to the Mars Colony? Do you have any idea? You'd better find out. Have you gone to see any of the Noble Ten that are still rattling around? Oh, you ought to. How about all the suicides we've been having in the last ten years? What do the insurance people say about that?"

*   *   *   *   *

He stopped, from lack of breath. Dan just stared at him, shaking his head like Silly Willy on the teevies. "Find out what you're doing, Dan—before you push this universal rejuvenation idea of yours through. Find out—if you've got the guts to find out, that is. We've got a monster on our hands, and now you've got to be Big Dan Fowler playing God and turning him loose on the world. Well, be careful. Find out first, while you can. It's all here to see, if you'll open your eyes, but you're all so dead sure that you want life everlasting that nobody's even bothered to *look*. And now it's become such a political bludgeon that nobody *dares* to look."

The model ship seemed to gleam in the dim laboratory light. Dan Fowler walked over to it, ran a finger up the shiny side to the pinpoint tip. His face was old, and something was gone from his eyes when he turned back to Paul. "You've known this for so long, and you never told me. You never said a word." He shook his head slowly. "I didn't know you hated me so much. But I'm not going to let you win this one, either, Paul. You're wrong. I'm going to prove it if it kills me."

V

"Well, try his home number, then," Dan Fowler snarled into the speaker. He gnawed his cigar and fumed as long minutes spun off the wall clock. His fingers drummed the wall. "How's that? Dammit, I want to speak to Dwight McKenzie, his aide will *not* do—well, of course he's in town. I just saw him yesterday—"

He waited another five minutes, and then his half dollar clanked back in the return, with apologies. "All right, get his office when it opens, and call me back." He reeled off the number of the private booth.

Carl Golden looked up as he came back to the table and stirred sugar-cream into half-cold coffee. "No luck?"

"Son of a bitch has vanished." Dan leaned back against the wall, glowering at Carl and Jean. Through the transparent walls of the glassed-in booth, they could see the morning breakfast-seekers drifting into the place. "We should have him pretty soon." He bit off the end of a fresh cigar, and assaulted it with a match.

"Dad, you know what Dr. Moss said—"

"Look, little girl—if I'm going to die in ten minutes, I'm going to smoke for those ten minutes and enjoy them," Dan snapped. The coffee was like lukewarm dishwater. Both the young people sipped theirs with bleary early-morning resignation. Carl Golden needed a shave badly. He opened his second pack of cigarettes. "Did you sleep on the way back?"

Dan snorted. "What do you think?"

"I think Paul might be lying to you."

Dan shot him a sharp glance. "Maybe—but I don't think so. Paul has always been fussy about telling the truth. He's all wrong, of course—" (fresh coffee, sugar-cream)—"but I think *he* believes his tale. Does it sound like he's lying to you?"

Carl sighed and shook his head. "No. I don't like it. It sounds to me as though he's pretty sure he's right."

Dan clanked the cup down and swore. "He's demented, that's what he is! He's waited too long, his brain's starting to go. If that story of his were true, why has he waited so long to tell somebody about it?"

"Maybe he wanted to see you hang yourself."

"But I can only hang myself on facts, not on the paranoid ramblings of a sick old man. The horrible thing is that he probably believes it—he almost had me believing it, for a while. But it isn't true. He's wrong—good lord, he's *got* to be wrong." Dan broke off, staring across at Carl. He gulped the last of the coffee. "If he *isn't* wrong, then that's all, kiddies. The mountain sinks into the sea, with us just ten feet from the top of it."

"Well, would *you* walk into the Center for a Retread now without being sure he's wrong?"

"Of course I wouldn't," said Dan peevishly. "Paul has taken the game right out from under our noses. We've got to stop everything and find out *now*, before we do another damned thing." The Senator dragged a sheaf of yellow paper out of his breast pocket and spread it out on the table. "I worked it out on the way back. We've got a nasty job on our hands. More than we can possibly squeeze in before the Hearing come up on December 15th. So number one job is to shift the Hearings back again. I'll take care of that as soon as I can get McKenzie on the wire."

"What's your excuse going to be?" Jean wanted to know.

"Anything but the truth. McKenzie thinks I'm going to win the fight at the Hearings, and he wants to be on the right side of the toast when it's buttered. He'll shift the date back to February 15th. Okay, next step: we need a crew. A crowd that can do fast, accurate, hard work and not squeal if they don't sleep for a month or so. Tommy Sandborn should be in Washington—he can handle statistics for us. In addition, we need a couple of good sharp detectives. Jean?"

    *   *   *   *   *

The girl nodded. "I can handle that end. It'll take some time getting them together, though."

"How much time?"

"Couple of days."

"Fine, we can have lots of work for them in a couple of days." The Senator turned back to Carl. "I want you to hit Starship Project first thing."

Carl shook his head. "I've got a better man for that job. Saw him last night, and he's dying for something to do. You don't know him—Terry Fisher. He'll know how to dig out what we want. He was doing it for five years on Mars."

"The alky?" Dan didn't like it. "We can't risk a slip to the teevies. We just don't dare."

"There won't be any slip. Terry jumped in the bottle to get away from Mars, that's all. He'll stay cold when it counts."

"Okay, if you say so. I want to see the setup there, too, but I want it ready for a quick scan. Get him down there this morning to soften things up and get it all out on the table for me. You'd better tackle the ad-men, then. Let's see—Tenner's Agency in Philly is a good place to start. Then hit Metro Insurance. Don't waste time with underlings, go to the top and wave my name around like an orange flag. They won't like it a damned bit, but they know I have the finger on Kornwall in Communications. We'll take his scalp if they don't play ball. All you'll have to do is convince them of that."

"What's on Kornwall?"

"Kornwall has been fronting for 'Moses' Tyndall for years. That's why Tyndall never bothered me too much, because we could get him through Kornwall any time we wanted to. And the ad-men and Metro have everything they own sunk into Tyndall's plans." Carl's frown still lingered. "Don't worry about it, son. It's okay."

"I think maybe you're underestimating John Tyndall."

"Why?"

"I worked for him once, remember? He doesn't like you. He knows it's going to be you or him, in the long haul, with nobody else involved. And you realize what happens if 'Moses' gets wind of this mess? Finds out what your brother told you, or even finds out that you're worried about something?"

Dan chewed his lip. "He *could* be a pain, couldn't he?"

"He sure could. More than a pain, and Kornwall wouldn't be much help after the news got out."

"Well, we'll have to take the risk, that's all. We'll have to be fast and quiet." He pushed aside his coffee cup as the phone blinker started in. "I think that gets us started. Jean, you'll keep somebody on the switchboard, and keep track of us all. When I get through with McKenzie, I may be leaving the country for a while. You'll have to be my ears, and cover for me. *Yes*, yes. I was calling Dwight McKenzie—"

The phonebox squawked for a moment or two.

"Hello, Dwight?—What? Oh, thunder! Well, where is he? Timagami—Ontario? An island!" He covered the speaker and growled, "He's gone moose-hunting." Then: "Okay, get me Eastern Sea-Jet Charter Service."

Five minutes later they walked out onto the street and split up in three different directions.

*   *   *   *   *

A long series of grey, flickering pictures, then, for Dan Fowler. A fast meal in the car to the Charter Service landing field. Morning sun swallowed up, sky gray, then almost black, temperature dropping, a grey drizzling rain. Cold. Wind carrying it across the open field in waves, slashing his cheeks with icy blades of water. Grey shape of the ski-plane ("Eight feet of snow up there, according to the IWB reports. Lake's frozen three feet thick. Going to be a rough ride, Senator"). Jean's quick kiss before he climbed up, the sharp worry in her eyes ("Got your pills, Dad? Try to sleep. Take it easy. Give me a call about anything—") (But there aren't any phones, the operator said. Better not tell her that. Why scare her any more? Damned heart, anyway). A wobbly takeoff that almost dumped his stomach in his lap, sent the briefcase flying across the cabin. Then rain, and grey-black nothing out through the mid-day view ports, heading north. Faster, faster, why can't you get this crate to move? Sorry, Senator. Nasty currents up here. Maybe we can try going higher—

Time! Paul had called it more precious than life, and now time flew screaming by in great deadly sweeps, like a black-winged buzzard. And through it all, weariness, tiredness that he had never felt before. Not years, not work. Weary body, yes—and time was running out, he should have rejuvenated years ago. But now—*what if Paul were right?*

Can't do it now. Not until Paul is wrong, a thousand times wrong. That was it, of course, that was the weariness that wasn't time-weariness or body-weariness. Just mind-weariness. Weariness at the thought of wasted work, the wasted years—a wasted life. Unless Paul is very wrong.

A snarl of disgust, a toggle switch snapped, a flickering teevie screen. Wonderful pickup these days. News of the World

brought to you by Atomics International, the fuel to power the
Starship—the President returned to Washington today after
three-week vacation conference in Calcutta with Chinese and
Indian dignitaries—full accord and a cordial ending to the
meeting—American medical supplies to be made available—and
on the home front, appropriations renewed for Antarctica
Project, to bring solar energy into every home, Aviado was
quoted as saying—huge Abolitionist rally last night in New
Chicago as John 'Moses' Tyndall returned to that city to
celebrate the fifteenth birthday of the movement that started
there back in 2119—no violence reported as Tyndall lashed out
at Senator Daniel Fowler's universal rejuvenation program—
twenty-five hour work week hailed by Senator Rinehart of
Alaska as a great progressive step for the American people—
Senator Rinehart, chairman of the policy-making Criterion
Committee held forth hope last night that rejuvenation
techniques may increase the number of candidates to six
hundred a year within five years—and now, news from the
entertainment world—

Going down, then, into flurries of Northern snow, peering out
at the whiter gloom below, a long stretch of white with blobs of
black on either side, resolving into snow-laden black pines, a
long flat lake-top of ice and snow. Taxi-ing down, engines
roaring, sucking up snow into steam in the orange afterblast.
And ahead, up from the lake, a black blot of a house, with orange
window lights reflecting warmth and cheer against the
wilderness outside—

Then Dwight McKenzie, peering out into the gloom, eyes
widening in recognition, little mean eyes with streaks of fear
through them, widening and then smiling, pumping his hand.
"Dan! My god, I couldn't *imagine*—hardly ever see anybody up
here, you know. Come in, come in, you must be half frozen.
What's happened? Something torn loose down in Washington?"
And more questions, fast, tumbling over each other, no answers
wanted, talky-talk questions to cover surprise and fear and the
one large question of why Dan Fowler should be dropping down
out of the sky on *him*, which question he didn't think he wanted
answered just yet—

*   *   *   *   *

A huge, rugged room, blazing fire in a mammoth fireplace at the end, moose heads, a rug of thick black bear hide. "Like to come up here a day or two ahead of the party, you know," McKenzie was saying. "Does a man good to commune with his soul once in a while. Do you like to hunt? You should join us, Dan. Libby and Donaldson will be up tomorrow with a couple of guides. We could find you an extra gun. They say hunting should be good this year—"

One chair against the fireplace, a book hastily thrown down beside it, SEXTRA SPECIAL, Cartoons by Kulp. Great book for soul-searching Senators. Things were all out of focus after the sudden change from the cold, but now Dan was beginning to see. One book, one chair, but two half-filled sherry glasses at the sideboard—

"Can't wait, Dwight, I have to get back to the city, but I couldn't find you down there, and they didn't know when you were coming back. I just wanted to let you know that I put you to all that trouble for nothing—we don't need the Hearing date in December, after all."

Wariness suddenly in McKenzie's eyes. "Well! Nice of you to think of it, Dan—but it wasn't really any trouble. No trouble at all. December 15th is fine, as a matter of fact, better than the February date would have been. Give the Committee a chance to collect itself during the Holidays, ha, ha."

"Well, it now seems that it *wouldn't* be so good for me, Dwight. I'd much prefer it to be changed back to the February date."

"Well, now." Pause. "Dan, we *have* to settle these things sooner or later, you know. I don't know whether we can do that now—"

"Don't know! Why not?"

The moose-hunter licked both lips, couldn't keep his eyes on Dan's eyes, focused on his nose instead,—as if the nose were *really* the important part of the conversation. "It isn't just me that makes these decisions, Dan. Other people have to be consulted. It's pretty late to catch them now, you know. It might be pretty hard to do that—"

No more smiles from Dan. "Now look—you make the calendar, and you can change it." Face getting red, getting angry—careful, Dan, those two sherry glasses, watch what you say—"I want it changed back. And I've got to know right now."

"But you told me you'd be all ready to roll by December 15th—"

To hell with caution—he *had* to have time. "Look, there's no reason you can't do it if you want to, Dwight. I'd consider it a personal favor—I repeat, a very large personal favor—if you'd make the arrangements. I won't forget it—" What did the swine want, an arm off at the roots?

"Sorry," said a voice from the rear door of the room. Walter Rinehart walked across to the sideboard. "You don't mind if I finish this, Dwight?"

A deep breath from McKenzie, like a sigh of relief. "Go right ahead, Walt. Sherry, Dan?"

"No, I don't think so." It was Walter, all right. Tall, upright, dignified Walter, fine shock of wavy hair that was white as the snow outside. Young-old lines on his face. Some men looked finer after rejuvenation, much finer than before. There had been a chilly look about Walter Rinehart's eyes before his first Retread. Not now. A fine man, like somebody's dear old grandfather. Just give him a chunk of wood to whittle and a jack-blade to whittle it with—

But inside, the mind was the same. Inside, no changes. Author of the Rinehart Criteria, the royal road to a self-perpetuating "immortal elite."

*   *   *   *   *

Dan turned his back on Rinehart and said to McKenzie: "I want the date changed."

"I—I can't do it, Dan." An inquiring glance at Rinehart, a faint smiling nod in return.

He knew he'd blundered then, blundered badly. McKenzie was afraid. McKenzie wanted another lifetime, one of these days. He'd decided that Rinehart would be the one who could give it to him. But worse, far worse: Rinehart knew now that something had happened, something was wrong. "What's the matter, Dan?" he said smoothly. "You need more time? Why? You had it before, and you were pretty eager to toss it up. Well, what's happened, Dan?"

That was all. Back against the wall. The thought of bluffing it through, swallowing the December 15th date and telling them to shove it flashed through his mind. He threw it out violently, his heart sinking. That was only a few more days. They had weeks of work ahead of them. They needed more time, they *had* to have it—

Rinehart was grinning confidently. "Of course I'd like to cooperate, Dan. Only I have some plans for the Hearings, too. You've been getting on people's nerves, down in the city. There's even been talk of reconsidering your rejuvenation permit—"

Your move, Dan. God, what a blunder! Why did you ever come up here? And every minute you stand there with your jaw sagging just tells Rinehart how tight he's got you—*do* something, *anything*—

There was a way. Would Carl understand it? Carl had begged him never to use it, ever, under any circumstances. And Carl had trusted him when he had said he wouldn't—but if Carl were standing here now, he'd say yes, go ahead, use it, wouldn't he? He'd have to—

"I want the Hearings on February 15th," Dan said to Rinehart.

"Sorry, Dan. We can't be tossing dates around like that. Unless you'd care to tell me why."

"Okay." Dan grabbed his hat angrily. "I'll make a formal request for the change tomorrow morning, and read it on the teevies. Then I'll also announce a feature attraction that the people can look forward to when the Hearing date comes. We weren't planning to use it, but I guess you'd like to have both barrels right in the face, so that's what we'll give you."

Walter Rinehart roared with laughter. "*Another* feature attraction? You do dig them up, don't you? Ken Armstrong's dead, you know."

"Peter Golden's widow isn't."

*   *   *   *   *

The smile faded on Rinehart's face. He looked suddenly like a man carved out of grey stone. Dan trembled, let the words sink in. "You didn't think *anybody* knew about that, did you, Walt? Sorry. We've got the story on Peter Golden. Took us quite a while to piece it together, but we did with the help of his son. Carl remembers his father before the accident, you see, quite well. His widow remembers him even before that. And we have some fascinating recordings that Peter Golden made when he applied for rejuvenation, and when he appealed the Committee's decisions. Some of the private interviews, too, Walter."

"I gave Peter Golden forty more years of life," Rinehart said.

"You crucified him," said Dan, bluntly.

There was silence, long silence. Then: "Are you selling?"

"I'm selling." Cut out my tongue, Carl, but I'm selling.

"How do I know you won't break it anyway?"

"You don't know. Except that I'm telling you I won't."

Rinehart soaked that in with the last gulp of sherry. Then he smashed the glass on the stone floor. "Change the date," he said to McKenzie. "Then throw this vermin out of here."

Back in the snow and darkness Dan tried to breathe again, and couldn't quite make it. He had to stop and rest twice going down to the plane. Then he was sick all the way back.

VI

Early evening, as the plane dropped him off in New York Crater, and picked up another charter. Two cold eggs and some scalding coffee, eaten standing up at the airport counter. Great for the stomach, but there wasn't time to stop. Anyway, Dan's stomach wasn't in the mood for dim lights and pale wine, not just this minute. Questions howling through his mind. The knowledge that he had made the one Class A colossal blunder of his thirty years in politics, this last half-day. A miscalculation of a man! He should have known about McKenzie—at least suspected. McKenzie was getting old, he wanted a Retread, and wanted it badly. Before, he had planned to get it through Dan. Then something changed his mind, and he decided Rinehart would end up on top.

Why?

Armstrong's suicide, of course. Pretty good proof that even Rinehart hadn't known it was a suicide. If Carl had brought back evidence of murder, Dan would win, McKenzie thought. But evidence of suicide—it was shaky. Walt Rinehart has his hooks in too deep.

They piped down the fifteen minute warning for the Washington Jet. Dan gulped the last of his coffee, and found a visi-phone booth with a scrambler in working order. Two calls. The first one to Jean, to line up round-the-clock guards for Peter Golden's widow on Long Island. Jean couldn't keep surprise out of her voice. Dan grunted and didn't elaborate—just get them out there.

Then a call to locate Carl. He chewed his cigar nervously.

Two minutes of waiting while they called Carl from wherever he was. Then: "I just saw McKenzie. I found him hiding in Rhinehart's hip pocket."

"Jesus, Dan. We've got to have time."

"We've got it—but the price was very steep, son."

Silence then as Carl peered at him. Finally: "I see."

"If I hadn't been in such a hurry, if I'd only thought it out," Dan said miserably. "It was an awful error—and all mine, too."

"Well, don't go out and shoot yourself. I suppose it had to happen sooner or later. What about Mother?"

"She'll be perfectly safe. They won't get within a mile of her. Look, son—is Fisher doing all right?"

Carl nodded. "I talked to him an hour ago. He'll be ready for you by tomorrow night, he thinks."

"Sober?"

"Sober. And mad. He's the right guy for the job." Worried lines deepened on Golden's forehead. "Everything's O.K.? Rinehart won't dare—"

"I scared him. He'd almost forgotten. Everything's fine." Dan rang off, scowling. He wished he was as sure as he sounded. Rinehart's back was to the wall, now. Dan wasn't too sure he liked it that way.

An hour later he was in Washington, and Jean was dragging him into the Volta. "If you don't sleep now, I'll have you put to sleep. Now shut up while I drive you home."

A soft bed, darkness, escape. When had he slept last? It was heaven.

*　　*　　*　　*　　*

He slept the clock around, which he had not intended, and caught the next night-jet to Las Vegas, which he had intended. There was some delay with the passenger list after he had gone aboard, a fight of some sort, and the jet took off four minutes late. Dan slept again, fitfully.

Somebody slid into the adjoining seat. "Well! Good old Dan Fowler!"

A gaunt, frantic-looking man, with skin like cracked parchment across his high cheekbones, and a pair of Carradine eyes looking down at Dan. If Death should walk in human flesh, Dan thought, it would look like John Tyndall.

"What do you want, 'Moses'?"

"Just dropped by to chat," said Tyndall. "You're heading for Las Vegas, eh? Why?"

Dan jerked, fumbled for the upright-button. "I like the climate out there. If you want to talk, talk and get it over with."

Tyndall lifted a narrow foot and gave the recline-button a sharp jab, dumping the Senator back against the seat. "You're onto something. I can smell it cooking, and I want my share, right now."

Dan stared into the gaunt face, and burst out laughing. He had never actually been so close to John Tyndall before, and he did *not* like the smell, which had brought on the laugh, but he knew all about Tyndall. More than Tyndall himself knew, probably. He could even remember the early rallies Tyndall had led, feeding on the fears and suspicions and nasty rumors grown up in the early days. It was evil, they had said. This was not God's way, this was Man's way, as evil as Man was evil. If God had wanted Man to live a thousand years, he would have given him such a body—

Or:

They'll use it for a tool! Political football. They'll buy and sell with it. They'll make a cult of it, they're doing it right now! Look at Walter Rinehart. Did you hear about his scheme? To keep it down to five hundred a year? They'll make themselves a ruling class, an immortal elite, with Rinehart for their Black Pope. Better that *nobody* should have it—

Or:

Immortality, huh? But what kind? You hear what happened to Harvey Tatum? That's right, the jet-car man, big business. He was one of their 'Noble Ten' they're always bragging about. But they say he had to have special drugs every night, that he had *changed*. That's right, if he didn't get these drugs, see, he'd go mad and try to suck blood and butcher up children—oh, they didn't dare publish it, had to put him out of the way quietly, but my brother-in-law was down in Lancaster one night when—

*   *   *   *   *

All it really needed was the man, and one day there was 'Moses' Tyndall. Leader of the New Crusade for God. Small, at first. But the ad-men began supporting him, broadcasting his rallies, playing him up big. Abolish rejuvenation, it's a blot against Man's immortal soul. Amen. Then the insurance people came along, with money. (The ad-men and the insurance people weren't too concerned about Man's immortal soul—they'd take their share now, thanks—but this didn't bother Tyndall too much. Misguided, but they were on God's side. He prayed for them.) So they gave Tyndall the first Abolitionist seat in the Senate, in 2124, just nine years ago, and the fight between Rinehart and Dan Fowler that was brewing even then had turned into a three-cornered fight—

*   *   *   *   *

Dan grinned up at Tyndall and said, "Go away, John. Don't bother me."

"You've got something," Tyndall snarled. "What is that damn shadow of yours nosing around Tenner's for? Why the sudden leaping interest in Nevada? Two trips in three days—what are you trying to track down?"

"Why on Earth should I tell you anything, Holy Man?"

The parchment face wrinkled unpleasantly. "Because it would be very smart, that's why. Rinehart's out of it, now. Washed up, finished, thanks to you. Now it's just you or me, one or the other. You're in the way, and you're going to be gotten out of the way when you've finished up Rinehart, because I'm going to start rolling them. Go along with me now and you won't get smashed, Dan."

"Get out of here," Dan snarled, sitting bolt upright. "You gave it to Carl Golden, a long time ago when he was with you, remember? Carl's my boy now—do you think I'll swallow the same bait?"

"You'd be smart if you did." The man leaned forward. "I'll let you in on a secret. I've just recently had a—*vision*, you might say. There are going to be riots and fires and shouting, around the time of the Hearings. People will be killed. Lots of people— spontaneous outbursts of passion, of course, the great voice of the people rising against the Abomination. And against *you*, Dan. A few Repeaters may be taken out and hanged, and then when you have won against Rinehart, you'll find people thinking that you're really a traitor—"

"Nobody will swallow that," Dan snapped.

"Just watch and see. I can still call it off, if you say so." He stood up quickly as Dan's face went purple. "New Chicago," he said smoothly. "Have to see a man here, and then get back to the Capitol. Happy hunting, Dan. You know where to reach me."

He strode down the aisle of the ship, leaving Dan staring bleakly at an empty seat.

Paul, Paul—

*   *   *   *   *

He met Terry Fisher at the landing field in Las Vegas. A firm handshake, clear brown eyes looking at him the way a four-year-old looks at Santa Claus. "Glad you could come tonight, Senator. I've had a busy couple of days. I think you'll be interested." Remarkable restraint in the man's voice. His face was full of things unsaid. Dan caught it; he knew faces, read them like typescript. "What is it, son?"

"Wait until you see." Fisher laughed nervously. "I thought for a while that I was back on Mars."

"Cigar?"

"No thanks. I never use them."

The car broke through darkness across bumpy pavement. The men sat silently. Then a barbed-wire enclosure loomed up, and a guard walked over, peered at their credentials, and waved them through. Ahead lay a long, low row of buildings, and a tall something spearing up into the clear desert night. They stopped at the first building, and hurried up the steps.

Small, red-faced Lijinsky greeted them, all warm handshake and enthusiasm and unmistakable happiness and surprise. "A real pleasure, Senator! We haven't had a direct governmental look-see in quite a while. I'm glad I'm here to show you around."

"Everything is going right along, eh?"

"Oh, yes! She'll be a ship to be proud of. Now, I think we can arrange some quarters for you for the night, and in the morning we can sit down and have a nice, long talk."

Terry Fisher was shaking his head. "I think the Senator would like to see the ship now—isn't that right, Senator?"

Lijinsky's eyes opened wide, his head bobbed in surprise. Young-old creases on his face flickered. "Tonight? Oh, you can't really be serious. Why, it's almost two in the morning! We only have a skeleton crew working at night. Tomorrow you can see—"

"Tonight, if you don't mind." Dan tried to keep the sharp edge out of his voice. "Unless you have some specific objection, of course."

"Objection? None whatsoever." Lijinsky seemed puzzled, and a little hurt. But he bounced back: "Tonight it is, then. Let's go." There was no doubting the little man's honesty. He wasn't hiding anything, just surprised. But a moment later there was concern on his face as he led them out toward the factory compounds. "There's no question of appropriations, I hope, Senator?"

"No, no. Nothing of the sort."

"Well, I'm certainly glad to hear that. Sometimes our contacts from Washington are a little disappointed in the Ship, of course."

Dan's throat tightened. "Why?"

"No reason, really. We're making fine progress, it isn't that. Yes, things really buzz around here; just ask Mr. Fisher about *that*—he was here all day watching the workers. But there are always minor changes in plans, of course, as we recognize more of the problems."

Terry Fisher grimaced silently, and followed them into a small Whirlwind groundcar. The little gyro-car bumped down the road on its single wheel, down into a gorge, then out onto the flats. Dan strained his eyes, peering ahead at the spear of Starship gleaming in the distant night-lights. Pictures from the last Starship Progress Report flickered through his mind, and a frown gathered as they came closer to the ship. Then the car halted on the edge of the building-pit and they blinked down and up at the scaffolded monster.

Dan didn't even move from the car. He just stared. The report had featured photos, projected testing dates—even ventured a possible date for launching, with the building of the Starship so near to completion. That had been a month ago. Now Dan stared at the ship and shook his head, uncomprehending.

The hull-plates were off again, lying in heaps on the ground in a mammoth circle. The ship was a skeleton, a long, gawky structure of naked metal beams. Even now a dozen men were scampering around the scaffolding, before Dan's incredulous eyes, and he saw some of the beaming coming *off* the body of the ship, being dropped onto the crane, moving slowly to the ground.

Ten years ago the ship had looked the same. As he watched, he felt a wave of hopelessness sweep through him, a sense of desolate, empty bitterness. Ten years—

His eyes met Terry Fisher's in the gloom of the car, begging to be told it wasn't so. Fisher shook his head.

Then Dan said: "I think I've seen enough. Take me back to the air field."

*   *   *   *   *

"It was the same thing on Mars," Fisher was telling him as the return jet speared East into the dawn. "The refining and super-refining, the slowing down, the changes in viewpoint and planning. I went up there ready to beat the world barehanded, to work on the frontier, to build that colony, and maybe lead another one. I even worked out the plans for a break-away colony—we would need colony-builders when we went to the stars, I thought." He shrugged sadly. "Carl told you, I guess. They considered the break-away colony, carefully, and then Barness decided it was really too early. Too much work already, with just one colony. And there was, in a sense: frantic activity, noise, hubbub, hard work, fancy plans—all going nowhere. No drive, no real direction." He shrugged again. "I did a lot of drinking before they threw me off Mars."

"Nobody saw it happening?"

"It wasn't the sort of thing you see. You could only *feel* it. It started when Armstrong came to the colony, rejuvenated, to take over its development. And eventually, I think Armstrong did see it. That's why he suicided."

"But the Starship," Dan cried. "It was almost built, and they were *tearing it down*. I saw it with my own eyes."

"Ah, yes. For the twenty-seventh time, I think. A change in the engineering thinking, that's all. Keller and Lijinsky suddenly came to the conclusion that the whole thing might fall apart in midair at the launching. Can you imagine it? When rockets have been built for years, running to Mars every two months? But they could prove it on paper, and by the time they got through explaining it every damned soul on the project was saying yes, it might fall apart at the launching. Why, it's a standing joke with the workers. They call Keller "Old Jet Propulsion" and always have a good laugh. But then, Keller and Stark and Lijinsky should know what's what. They've all been rejuvenated, and working on the ship for years." Fisher's voice was heavy with anger.

Dan didn't answer. There didn't seem to be much *to* answer, and he just couldn't tell Fisher how it felt to have a cold blanket of fear wrapping around his heart, so dreadful and cold that he hardly dared look five minutes ahead right now. *We have a Monster on our hands—*

VII

He was sick when they reached Washington. The pain in his chest became acute as he walked down the gangway, and by the time he found a seat in the terminal and popped a nitro-tablet under his tongue he was breathing in deep, ragged gasps. He sat very still, trying to lean back against the seat, and quite suddenly he realized that he was very, very ill. The good red-headed Dr. Moss would smile in satisfaction, he thought bitterly. There was sweat on his forehead; it had never seemed very probable to him that he might one day die—he didn't *have* to die in this great, wonderful world of new bodies for old, he could live on, and on, and on. He could live to see the Golden Centuries of Man. A solar system teeming with life. Ships to challenge the stars, the barriers breaking, crumbling before their very eyes. Other changes, as short-lived Man became long-lived Man. Changes in teaching, in thinking, in feeling. Disease, the Enemy, was crushed. Famine, the Enemy, slinking back into the dim memory of history. War, the Enemy, pointless to extinction.

All based on one principle: Man must live. He need not die. If a man could live forty years instead of twenty, had it been wrong to fight the plagues that struck him down in his youth? If he could live sixty years instead of forty, had the great researchers of the 1940's and '50's and '60's been wrong? Was it any more wrong to want to live a thousand years? Who could say that it was?

He took a shuddering breath, and then nodded to Terry Fisher, and walked unsteadily to the cab stand. He would not believe what he had seen at Starship Project. It was not enough. Collect the evidence, *then* conclude. He gave Fisher an ashen smile. "It's nothing. The ticker kicks up once in a while, that's all. Let's go see what Carl and Jean and the boys have dug up." Fisher smiled grimly, an eager gleam in his eye.

Carl and Jean and the boys had dug up plenty. The floor of offices Dan rented for the work of his organization was going like Washington Terminal at rush hour. A dozen people were here and there, working with tapes, papers, program cards. Jean met them at the door, hustled them into the private offices in the back. "Carl just got here, too. He's down eating. The boys outside are trying to make sense out of his insurance and advertising figures."

"He got next to them okay?"

"Sure—but you were right, they didn't like it."

"What sort of reports?"

*   *   *   *   *

The girl sighed. "Only prelims. Almost all of the stuff is up in the air, which makes it hard to evaluate. The ad-men have to be figuring what they're going to do next half-century, so that they'll be there with the right thing when the time comes. But it seems they don't like what they see. People have to buy what the ad-men are selling, or the ad-men shrivel up, and already the trend seems to be showing up. People aren't in such a rush to buy. Don't have the same sense of urgency that they used to—" Her hands fluttered. "Well, as I say, it's all up in the air. Let the boys analyze for a while. The suicide business is a little more tangible. The rates are up, all over. But break it into first-generation and Repeaters, and it's pretty clear who's pushing it up."

"Like Armstrong," said Dan slowly.

Jean nodded. "Oh, here's Carl now."

He came in, rubbing his hands, and gave Dan a queer look. "Everything under control, Dan?"

Dan nodded. He told Carl about Tyndall's proposition. Carl gave a wry grin. "He hasn't changed a bit, has he?"

"Yes, he has. He's gotten lots stronger."

Carl scowled, and slapped the desk with his palm. "You should have stopped him, Dan. I told you that a long time ago—back when I first came in with you. He was aiming for your throat even then, trying to use me and what I knew about Dad to sell the country a pack of lies about you. He almost did, too. I hated your guts back then. I thought you were the rottenest man that ever came up in politics, until you got hold of me and pounded sense into my head. And Tyndall's never forgiven you that, either."

"All right—we're still ahead of him. Have you just finished with the ad-men?"

"Oh, no. I just got back from a trip south. My nose is still cold."

Dan's eyebrows went up. "And how was Dr. Aviado? I haven't seen a report from Antarctica Project for five years."

"Yes you have. You just couldn't read them. Aviado is quite a theoretician. That's how he got his money and his Project, down there, with plenty of room to build his reflectors and nobody around to get hurt if something goes wrong. Except a few penguins. And he's done a real job of development down there since his rejuvenation."

"Ah." Dan glanced up hopefully.

"Now there," said Carl, "is a real lively project. Solar energy into power on a utilitarian level. The man is fanatic, of course, but with his plans he could actually be producing in another five years." He lit a cigarette, drew on it as though it were bitter.

"Could?"

"Seems he's gotten sidetracked a bit," said Carl.

Dan glanced at Terry Fisher. "How?"

"Well, his equipment is working fine, and he can concentrate solar heat from ten square miles onto a spot the size of a manhole cover. But he hasn't gone too far converting it to useful power yet." Carl suddenly burst out laughing. "Dan, this'll kill you. Billions and billions of calories of solar heat concentrated down there, and what do you think he's doing with it? He's digging a hole in the ice two thousand feet deep and a mile wide. That's what."

"A hole in the ice!"

"Exactly. Conversion? Certainly—but first we want to be sure we're right. So right now his whole crew is very busy *trying to melt down Antarctica*. And if you give him another ten years, he'll have it done, by god."

*   *   *   *   *

This was the last, most painful trip of all.

Dan didn't even know why he was going, except that Paul had told him he should go, and no stone could be left unturned.

The landing in New York Crater had been rough, and Dan had cracked his elbow on the bulkhead; he nursed it now as he left the Volta on the deserted street of the crater city, and entered the low one-story lobby of the groundscraper. The clerk took his name impassively, and he sat down to wait.

An hour passed, then another.

Then: "Mr. Devlin will see you now, Senator."

Down in the elevator, four—five—six stories. Above him was the world; here, deep below, with subtly efficient ventilators and shafts and exotic cubby-holes for retreat, a man could forget that a world above existed.

Soft lighting in the corridor, a golden plastic door. The door swung open, and a tiny old man blinked out.

"Mr. Chauncey Devlin?"

"Senator Fowler!" The little old man beamed. "Come in, come in—my dear fellow, if I'd realized it was you, I'd never have dreamed of keeping you so long—" He smiled, obviously distressed. "Retreat has its disadvantages, too, you see. Nothing is perfect but life, as they say. When *you've* lived for a hundred and ninety years, you'll be glad to get away from people, and to be able to keep them out, from time to time."

In better light Dan stared openly at the man. A hundred and ninety years. It was incredible. He told the man so.

"Isn't it, though?" Chauncey Devlin chirped. "Well, I was a was-baby! Can you imagine? Born in London in 1945. But I don't even think about those horrid years any more. Imagine—people dropping bombs on each other!"

A tiny bird of a man—three times rejuvenated, and still the mind was sharp, the eyes were sharp. The face was a strange mixture of recent youth and very great age. It stirred something deep inside Dan—almost a feeling of loathing. An uncanny feeling.

"We've always known your music," he said. "We've always loved it. Just a week ago we heard the Washington Philharmonic doing—"

"The eighth." Chauncey Devlin cut him off disdainfully. "They always do the eighth."

"It's a great symphony," Dan protested.

Devlin chuckled, and bounced about the room like a little boy. "It was only half finished when they chose me for the big plunge," he said. "Of course I was doing a lot of conducting then, too. Now I'd much rather just write." He hurried across the long, softly-lit room to the piano, came back with a sheaf of papers. "Do you read music? This is just what I've been doing recently. Can't get it quite right, but it'll come, it'll come."

"Which will this be?" asked Dan.

"The tenth. The ninth was under contract, of course—strictly a pot-boiler, I'm afraid. Thought it was pretty good at the time, but *this* one—ah!" He fondled the smooth sheets of paper. "In this one I could *say* something. Always before it was hit and run, make a stab at it, then rush on to stab at something else. Not *this* one." He patted the manuscript happily. "With this one there will be *nothing* wrong."

"It's almost finished?"

"Oh, no. Oh, my goodness no! A fairly acceptable first movement, but not what I *will* do on it—as I go along."

"I see. I—understand. How long have you worked on it now?"

"Oh, I don't know—I must have it down here somewhere. Oh, yes. Started it in April of 2057. Seventy-seven years."

They talked on, until it became too painful. Then Dan rose, and thanked his host, and started back for the corridor and life again. He had never even mentioned his excuse for coming, and nobody had missed it.

Chauncey Devlin, a tiny, perfect wax-image of a man, so old, so wise, so excited and full of enthusiasm and energy and carefulness, working eagerly, happily—

Accomplishing nothing. Seventy-seven years. The picture of a man who had been great, and who had slowly ground to a standstill.

And now Dan knew that he hadn't really been looking at Chauncey Devlin at all. He had been looking at the whole human race.

VIII

February 15th, 2135.

The day of the Hearings, to consider the charges and petition formally placed by The Honorable Daniel Fowler, Independent Senator from the Great State of Illinois. The long oval hearing-room was filling early; the gallery above was packed by 9:05 in the morning. Teevie-boys all over the place. The Criterion Committee members, taking their places in twos and threes— some old, some young, some rejuvenated, some not, taking their places in the oval. Then the other Senators—not the President, of course, but he'll be well represented by Senator Rinehart himself, ah yes. Don't worry about the President.

*   *   *   *   *

Bad news in the papers. Trouble in New Chicago, where so much trouble seems to start these days. Bomb thrown in the Medical Center out there, a *bomb* of all things! Shades of Lenin. Couple of people killed, and one of the doctors nearly beaten to death on the street before the police arrived to clear the mob away. Dan Fowler's name popping up here and there, not pleasantly. Whispers and accusations, *sotto voce*. And 'Moses' Tyndall's network hookup last night—of course nobody with any sense listens to *him*, but did you hear that hall go wild?

Rinehart—yes, that's him. Well, he's got a right to look worried. If Dan can unseat him here and now, he's washed up. According to the rules of the Government, you know, Fowler can legally petition for Rinehart's chairmanship without risking it as a platform plank in the next election, and get a hearing here, and then if the Senate votes him in, he's got the election made. Dan's smart. They're scared to throw old Rinehart out, of course—after all, he's let them keep their thumbs on rejuvination all these years with his Criteria, and if they supported him they got named, and if they didn't, they didn't get named. Not quite as crude as that, of course, but that's what it boiled down to, let me tell you! But now, if they reject Dan's petition and the people give him the election over their heads, they're *really* in a spot. Out on the ice on their rosy red—

How's that? Can't be too long now. I see Tyndall has just come in, Bible and all. See if he's got any tomatoes in his pockets. Ol' Moses really gets you going—ever listen to him talk? Well, it's just as well. Damn, but it's hot in here—

In the rear chamber, Dan mopped his brow, popped a pill under his tongue, dragged savagely on the long black cigar. "You with me, son?"

Carl nodded.

"You know what it means."

"Of course. There's your buzzer. Better get in there." Carl went back to Jean and the others around the 80-inch screen, set deep in the wall. Dan put his cigar down, gently, as though he planned to be back to smoke it again before it went out, and walked through the tall oak doors.

*   *   *   *   *

The hubbub caught, rose up for a few moments, then dropped away. Dan took his seat, grinned across at Libby, leaned his head over to drop an aside into Parker's ear. Rinehart staring at the ceiling as the charges are read off in a droning voice—

—*Whereas the criteria for selection of candidates for sub-total prosthesis, first written by the Honorable Walter Rinehart of the Great State of Alaska, have been found to be inadequate, outdated, and utterly inappropriate to the use of sub-total prosthesis that is now possible—*

—*And whereas that same Honorable Walter Rinehart has repeatedly used the criteria, not in the just, honorable, and humble way in which such criteria must be regarded, but rather as a tool and weapon for his own furtherance and for that of his friends and associates—*

Dan waited, patiently. Was Rinehart's face whiter than it had been? Was the Hall quieter now? Maybe not—but wait for the petition—

—*The Senate of the United States of North America is formally petitioned that the Honorable Walter Rinehart should be displaced from his seat as Chairman in the Criterion Committee, and that his seat as Chairman of that committee should be resumed by the Honorable Daniel Fowler, author of this petition, who has hereby pledged himself before God to seek through this Committee in any and every way possible, the extention of the benefits of sub-total prosthesis techniques to all the people of this land and not to a chosen few—*

Screams, hoots, cat-calls, applause, all from the gallery. None below—Senatorial dignity forbade, and the anti-sound glass kept the noise out of the chamber below. Then Dan Fowler stood up, an older Dan Fowler than most of them seemed to remember. "You have heard the charges which have been read. I stand before you now, formally, to withdraw them—"

What, what? Jaws sagging, eyes wide; teevie camera frozen on the Senator's face, then jerking wildly around the room to catch the reaction—

"You have also heard the petition which has been read. I stand before you now, formally, to withdraw it—"

Slowly, measuring each word, he told them. He knew that words were not enough, but he told them. "Only 75,000 men and women have undergone the process, at this date, out of almost two hundred million people on this continent, yet it has already begun to sap our strength. We were told that no change was involved, and indeed we saw no change, but it was there, my friends. The suicides of men like Kenneth Armstrong did not just *occur*. There are many reasons that might lead a man to take his life in this world of ours—selfishness, self-pity, hatred of the world or of himself, bitterness, resentment—but it was none of these that motivated Kenneth Armstrong. *His death was the act of a bewildered, defeated mind*—for he saw what I am telling you now and knew that it was true. He saw Starships built and rebuilt, and never launched—colonies dying of lethargy, because there was no longer any drive behind them—brilliant minds losing sight of goals, and drifting into endless inconsequential digressions—lifetimes wasted in repetition, in re-doing and rewriting and re-living. He saw it: the downward spiral which could only lead to death for all of us in the last days.

"This is why I withdraw the charges and petition of this Hearing. This is why I reject rejuvenation, and declare that it is a monstrous thing *which we must not allow to continue*. This is why I now announce that I personally will nominate the Honorable John Tyndall for President in the elections next spring, and will promise him my pledged support, my political organization and experience, and my every personal effort to see that he is elected."

*   *   *   *   *

It seemed that there would be no end to it, when Dan Fowler had finished. 'Moses' Tyndall had sat staring as the blood drained out of his sallow face; his jaw gaped, and he half-rose from his chair, then sank back with a ragged cough, staring at the Senator as if he had been transformed into a snake. Carl and Terry were beside Dan in a moment, clearing a way back to the rear chambers, then down the steps of the building to a cab. Senator Libby intercepted them there, his face purple with rage, and McKenzie, bristling and indignant. "You've lost your mind, Dan."

"I have not. I am perfectly sane."

"But *Tyndall*! He'll turn Washington into a grand revival meeting, he'll—"

"Then we'll cut him down to size. He's *my* candidate, remember, not his own. He'll play my game if it pays him well enough. But I want an Abolitionist administration, and I'm going to get one."

In the cab he stared glumly out the window, his heart racing, his whole body shaking in reaction now. "You know what it means," he said to Carl for the tenth time.

"Yes, Dan, I know."

"It means no rejuvenation, for you or for any of us. It means proving something; to people that they just don't want to believe, and cramming it down their throats if we have to. It means taking away their right to keep on living."

"I know all that."

"Carl, if you want out—"

"Yesterday was the time."

"Okay then. We've got work to do."

IX

Up in the offices again, Dan was on the phone immediately. He knew politics, and people—like the jungle cat knows the whimpering creatures he stalks. He knew that it was the first impact, the first jolting blow that would win for them, or lose for them. Everything had to hit right. He had spent his life working with people, building friends, building power, banking his resources, investing himself. Now the time had come to cash in.

Carl and Jean and the others worked with him—a dreadful afternoon and evening, fighting off newsmen, blocking phone calls, trying to concentrate in the midst of bedlam. The campaign to elect Tyndall had to start *now*. They labored to record a work-schedule, listing names, outlining telegrams, drinking coffee, as Dan swore at his dead cigar like old times once again, and grinned like a madman as the plans slowly developed and blossomed out.

Then the phone jangled, and Dan reached out for it. It was that last small effort that did it. A sledge-hammer blow, from deep within him, sharp agonizing pain, a driving hunger for the air that he just couldn't drag into his lungs. He let out a small, sharp cry, and doubled over with pain. They found him seconds later, still clinging to the phone, his breath so faint as to be no breath at all.

*   *   *   *   *

He regained consciousness hours later. He stared about him at the straight lines of the ceiling, at the hospital bed and the hospital window. Dimly he saw Carl Golden, head dropping on his chest, dozing at the side of the bed.

There was a hissing sound, and he raised a hand, felt the tiny oxygen mask over his mouth and nose. But even with that help, every breath was an agony of pain and weariness.

He was so very tired. But slowly, through the fog, he remembered. Cold sweat broke out on his forehead, drenched his body. *He was alive.* Yet he remembered crystal clear the thought that had exploded in his mind in the instant the blow had come.

I'm dying. This is the end—it's too late now. And then, cruelly, *why did I wait so long?*

He struggled against the mask, sat bolt upright in bed. "I'm going to die," he whispered, then caught his breath. Carl sat up, smiled at him.

"Lie back, Dan. Get some rest."

Had he heard? Had Carl heard the fear he had whispered? Perhaps not. He lay back, panting, as Carl watched. Do you know what I'm thinking, Carl? I'm thinking how much I want to live. People don't *need* to die—wasn't that what Dr. Moss had said? It's such a terrible waste, he had said.

Too late, now. Dan's hands trembled. He remembered the Senators in the oval hall, hearing him speak his brave words; he remembered Rinehart's face, and Tyndall's, and Libby's. He was committed now. Yesterday, no. Now, yes.

Paul had been right, and Dan had proved it.

His eyes moved across to the bedside table. A telephone. He was still alive, Moss had said that sometimes it was possible *even when you were dying.* That was what they did with your father, wasn't it, Carl? Brave Peter Golden, who had fought Rinehart so hard, who had begged and pleaded for universal rejuvenation, waited and watched and finally caught Rinehart red-handed, to prove that he was corrupting the law and expose him. Simple, honest Peter Golden, applying so naively for his rightful place on the list, when his cancer was diagnosed. Peter Golden had been all but dead when he had finally whispered defeat, and given Rinehart his perpetual silence in return for life. They had snatched him from death, indeed. But he had been crucified all the same. They had torn away everything, and found a coward underneath.

Coward? Why? Was it wrong to want to live? Dan Fowler was dying. Why must it be him? He had committed himself to a fight, yes, but there were others, young men, who could fight. Men like Peter Golden's son.

But you are their leader, Dan. If you fail them, they will never win.

Carl was watching him silently, his lean dark face expressionless. Could the boy read his mind? Was it possible that he knew what Dan Fowler was thinking? Carl had always understood before. It had seemed that sometimes Carl had understood Dan far better than Dan did. He wanted to cry out to Carl now, spill over his dreadful thoughts.

There was no one to run to. He was facing himself now. No more cover-up, no deceit. Life or death, that was the choice. No compromise. Life or death, but decide *now*. Not tomorrow, not next week, not in five minutes—

He knew the answer then, the flaw, the one thing that even Paul hadn't known. That life is too dear, that a man loves life— not what he can *do* with life, but very life itself for its own sake—too much to die. It was no choice, not really. A man will *always* choose life, as long as the choice is really his. Dan Fowler knew that now.

It would be selling himself—like Peter Golden did. It would betray Carl, and Jean, and all the rest. It would mean derision, and scorn, and oblivion for Dan Fowler.

Carl Golden was standing by the bed when he reached out his arm for the telephone. The squeaking of a valve—what? Carl's hand, infinitely gentle, on his chest, bringing up the soft blankets, and his good clean oxygen dwindling, dwindling—

Carl!

How did you know?

*   *   *   *   *

She came in the room as he was reopening the valve on the oxygen tank. She stared at Dan, grey on the bed, and then at Carl. One look at Carl's face and she knew too.

Carl nodded, slowly. "I'm sorry, Jean."

She shook her head, tears welling up. "But you loved him so."

"More than my own father."

"Then *why?*"

"He wanted to be immortal. Always, that drove him. Greatness, power—all the same. Now he will be immortal, because we needed a martyr in order to win. Now we will win. The other way we would surely lose, and he would live on and on, and die every day." He turned slowly to the bed and brought the sheet up gently. "This is better. This way he will never die."

They left the quiet room.

THE COFFIN CURE

ORIGINALLY PUBLISHED IN *GALAXY*,
APRIL 1957

THE COFFIN CURE

When the discovery was announced, it was Dr. Chauncey Patrick Coffin who announced it. He had, of course, arranged with uncanny skill to take most of the credit for himself. If it turned out to be greater than he had hoped, so much the better. His presentation was scheduled for the last night of the American College of Clinical Practitioners' annual meeting, and Coffin had fully intended it to be a bombshell.

It was. Its explosion exceeded even Dr. Coffin's wilder expectations, which took quite a bit of doing. In the end he had waded through more newspaper reporters than medical doctors as he left the hall that night. It was a heady evening for Chauncey Patrick Coffin, M.D.

Certain others were not so delighted with Coffin's bombshell.

"It's idiocy!" young Dr. Phillip Dawson wailed in the laboratory conference room the next morning. "Blind, screaming idiocy. You've gone out of your mind—that's all there is to it. Can't you see what you've done? Aside from selling your colleagues down the river, that is?" He clenched the reprint of Coffin's address in his hand and brandished it like a broadsword. "'Report on a Vaccine for the Treatment and Cure of the Common Cold,' by C. P. Coffin, *et al.* That's what it says—*et al.* My idea in the first place. Jake and I both pounding our heads on the wall for eight solid months—and now you sneak it into publication a full year before we have any business publishing a word about it."

"Really, Phillip!" Dr. Chauncey Coffin ran a pudgy hand through his snowy hair. "How ungrateful! I thought for sure you'd be delighted. An excellent presentation, I must say—terse, succinct, unequivocal—" he raised his hand—"but *generously* unequivocal, you understand. You should have heard the ovation—they nearly went wild! And the look on Underwood's face! Worth waiting twenty years for."

"And the reporters," snapped Phillip. "Don't forget the reporters." He whirled on the small dark man sitting quietly in the corner. "How about that, Jake? Did you see the morning papers? This thief not only steals our work, he splashes it all over the countryside in red ink."

Dr. Jacob Miles coughed apologetically. "What Phillip is so stormed up about is the prematurity of it all," he said to Coffin. "After all, we've hardly had an acceptable period of clinical trial."

"Nonsense," said Coffin, glaring at Phillip. "Underwood and his men were ready to publish their discovery within another six weeks. Where would we be then? How much clinical testing do you want? Phillip, you had the worst cold of your life when you took the vaccine. Have you had any since?"

"No, of course not," said Phillip peevishly.

"Jacob, how about you? Any sniffles?"

"Oh, no. No colds."

"Well, what about those six hundred students from the University? Did I misread the reports on them?"

"No—98 per cent cured of active symptoms within twenty-four hours. Not a single recurrence. The results were just short of miraculous." Jake hesitated. "Of course, it's only been a month...."

"Month, year, century! Look at them! Six hundred of the world's most luxuriant colds, and now not even a sniffle." The chubby doctor sank down behind the desk, his ruddy face beaming. "Come, now, gentlemen, be reasonable. Think positively! There's work to be done, a great deal of work. They'll be wanting me in Washington, I imagine. Press conference in twenty minutes. Drug houses to consult with. How dare we stand in the path of Progress? We've won the greatest medical triumph of all times—the conquering of the Common Cold. We'll go down in history!"

And he was perfectly right on one point, at least.

They did go down in history.

*   *   *   *   *

The public response to the vaccine was little less than monumental. Of all the ailments that have tormented mankind through history none was ever more universal, more tenacious, more uniformly miserable than the common cold. It was a respecter of no barriers, boundaries, or classes; ambassadors and

chambermaids snuffled and sneezed in drippy-nosed unanimity.
The powers in the Kremlin sniffed and blew and wept genuine
tears on drafty days, while senatorial debates on earth-shaking
issues paused reverently upon the unplugging of a nose, the
clearing of a rhinorrheic throat. Other illnesses brought
disability, even death in their wake; the common cold merely
brought torment to the millions as it implacably resisted the
most superhuman of efforts to curb it.

Until that chill, rainy November day when the tidings broke
to the world in four-inch banner heads:

COFFIN NAILS LID ON COMMON COLD
"No More Coughin'" States Co-Finder of Cure
SNIFFLES SNIPED: SINGLE SHOT TO SAVE SNEEZERS

In medical circles it was called the Coffin Multicentric Upper
Respiratory Virus-Inhibiting Vaccine; but the papers could never
stand for such high-sounding names, and called it, simply, "The
Coffin Cure."

Below the banner heads, world-renowned feature writers
expounded in reverent terms the story of the leviathan struggle
of Dr. Chauncey Patrick Coffin (*et al.*) in solving this riddle of
the ages: how, after years of failure, they ultimately succeeded in
culturing the causative agent of the common cold, identifying it
not as a single virus or group of viruses, but as a multicentric
virus complex invading the soft mucous linings of the nose,
throat and eyes, capable of altering its basic molecular structure
at any time to resist efforts of the body from within, or the
physician from without, to attack and dispel it; how the
hypothesis was set forth by Dr. Phillip Dawson that the virus
could be destroyed only by an antibody which could "freeze" the
virus-complex in one form long enough for normal body defenses
to dispose of the offending invader; the exhausting search for
such a "crippling agent," and the final crowning success after
injecting untold gallons of cold-virus material into the hides of a
group of co-operative and forbearing dogs (a species which never
suffered from colds, and hence endured the whole business with
an air of affectionate boredom).

And finally, the testing. First, Coffin himself (who was
suffering a particularly horrendous case of the affliction he
sought to cure); then his assistants Phillip Dawson and Jacob
Miles; then a multitude of students from the University—

carefully chosen for the severity of their symptoms, the longevity of their colds, their tendency to acquire them on little or no provocation, and their utter inability to get rid of them with any known medical program.

They were a sorry spectacle, those students filing through the Coffin laboratory for three days in October: wheezing like steam shovels, snorting and sneezing and sniffling and blowing, coughing and squeaking, mute appeals glowing in their blood-shot eyes. The researchers dispensed the materials—a single shot in the right arm, a sensitivity control in the left.

With growing delight they then watched as the results came in. The sneezing stopped; the sniffling ceased. A great silence settled over the campus, in the classrooms, in the library, in classic halls. Dr. Coffin's voice returned (rather to the regret of his fellow workers) and he began bouncing about the laboratory like a small boy at a fair. Students by the dozen trooped in for checkups with noses dry and eyes bright.

In a matter of days there was no doubt left that the goal had been reached.

"But we have to be *sure*," Phillip Dawson had cried cautiously. "This was only a pilot test. We need mass testing now, on an entire community. We should go to the West Coast and run studies there—they have a different breed of cold out there, I hear. We'll have to see how long the immunity lasts, make sure there are no unexpected side effects...." And, muttering to himself, he fell to work with pad and pencil, calculating the program to be undertaken before publication.

But there were rumors. Underwood at Stanford, they said, had already completed his tests and was preparing a paper for publication in a matter of months. Surely with such dramatic results on the pilot tests *something* could be put into print. It would be tragic to lose the race for the sake of a little unnecessary caution....

Peter Dawson was adamant, but he was a voice crying in the wilderness. Chauncey Patrick Coffin was boss.

Within a week even Coffin was wondering if he had bitten off just a trifle too much. They had expected that demand for the vaccine would be great—but even the grisly memory of the early days of the Salk vaccine had not prepared them for the mobs of sneezing, wheezing red-eyed people bombarding them for the first fruits.

Clear-eyed young men from the Government Bureau pushed through crowds of local townspeople, lining the streets outside the Coffin laboratory, standing in pouring rain to raise insistent placards.

Seventeen pharmaceutical houses descended like vultures with production plans, cost-estimates, colorful graphs demonstrating proposed yield and distribution programs. Coffin was flown to Washington, where conferences labored far into the night as demands pounded their doors like a tidal wave.

One laboratory promised the vaccine in ten days; another said a week. The first actually appeared in three weeks and two days, to be soaked up in the space of three hours by the thirsty sponge of cold-weary humanity. Express planes were dispatched to Europe, to Asia, to Africa with the precious cargo, a million needles pierced a million hides, and with a huge, convulsive sneeze mankind stepped forth into a new era.

*   *   *   *   *

There were abstainers, of course. There always are.

"It doesn't bake eddy differets how much you talk," Ellie Dawson cried hoarsely, shaking her blonde curls. "I dod't wadt eddy cold shots."

"You're being totally unreasonable," Phillip said, glowering at his wife in annoyance. She wasn't the sweet young thing he had married, not this evening. Her eyes were puffy, her nose red and dripping. "You've had this cold for two solid months now, and there just isn't any sense to it. It's making you miserable. You can't eat, you can't breathe, you can't sleep."

"I dod't wadt eddy cold shots," she repeated stubbornly.

"But why not? Just one little needle, you'd hardly feel it."

"But I dod't like deedles!" she cried, bursting into tears. "Why dod't you leave be alode? Go take your dasty old deedles ad stick theb id people that wadt theb."

"Aw, Ellie—"

"I dod't care, *I dod't like deedles*!" she wailed, burying her face in his shirt.

He held her close, making comforting little noises. It was no use, he reflected sadly. Science just wasn't Ellie's long suit; she didn't know a cold vaccine from a case of smallpox, and no appeal to logic or common sense could surmount her irrational fear of hypodermics. "All right, nobody's going to make you do anything you don't want to," he said.

"Ad eddyway, thik of the poor tissue badufacturers," she sniffled, wiping her nose with a pink facial tissue. "All their little childred starvig to death."

"Say, you *have* got a cold," said Phillip, sniffing. "You've got on enough perfume to fell an ox." He wiped away tears and grinned at her. "Come on now, fix your face. Dinner at the Driftwood? I hear they have marvelous lamb chops."

It was a mellow evening. The lamb chops were delectable— the tastiest lamb chops he had ever eaten, he thought, even being blessed with as good a cook as Ellie for a spouse. Ellie dripped and blew continuously, but refused to go home until they had taken in a movie, and stopped by to dance a while. "I hardly ever gedt to see you eddy bore," she said. "All because of that dasty bedicide you're givig people."

It was true, of course. The work at the lab was endless. They danced, but came home early nevertheless. Phillip needed all the sleep he could get.

He awoke once during the night to a parade of sneezes from his wife, and rolled over, frowning sleepily to himself. It was ignominious, in a way—his own wife refusing the fruit of all those months of work.

And cold or no cold, she surely was using a whale of a lot of perfume.

*   *   *   *   *

He awoke, suddenly, began to stretch, and sat bolt upright in bed, staring wildly about the room. Pale morning sunlight drifted in the window. Downstairs he heard Ellie stirring in the kitchen.

For a moment he thought he was suffocating. He leaped out of bed, stared at the vanity table across the room. "*Somebody's spilled the whole damned bottle—*"

The heavy sick-sweet miasma hung like a cloud around him, drenching the room. With every breath it grew thicker. He searched the table top frantically, but there were no empty bottles. His head began to spin from the sickening effluvium.

He blinked in confusion, his hand trembling as he lit a cigarette. No need to panic, he thought. She probably knocked a bottle over when she was dressing. He took a deep puff, and burst into a paroxysm of coughing as acrid fumes burned down his throat to his lungs.

"Ellie!" He rushed into the hall, still coughing. The match smell had given way to the harsh, caustic stench of burning weeds. He stared at his cigarette in horror and threw it into the sink. The smell grew worse. He threw open the hall closet, expecting smoke to come billowing out. "Ellie! Somebody's burning down the house!"

"Whadtever are you talking about?" Ellie's voice came from the stair well. "It's just the toast I burned, silly."

He rushed down the stairs two at a time—and nearly gagged as he reached the bottom. The smell of hot, rancid grease struck him like a solid wall. It was intermingled with an oily smell of boiled and parboiled coffee, overpowering in its intensity. By the time he reached the kitchen he was holding his nose, tears pouring from his eyes. *"Ellie, what are you doing in here?"*

She stared at him. "I'b baking breakfast."

"But don't you *smell* it?"

"Sbell whadt?" said Ellie.

On the stove the automatic percolator was making small, promising noises. In the frying pan four sunnyside eggs were sizzling; half a dozen strips of bacon drained on a paper towel on the sideboard. It couldn't have looked more innocent.

Cautiously, Phillip released his nose, sniffed. The stench nearly choked him. "You mean you don't smell anything *strange?*"

"I did't sbell eddythig, period," said Ellie defensively.

"The coffee, the bacon—*come here a minute.*"

She reeked—of bacon, of coffee, of burned toast, but mostly of perfume. "Did you put on any fresh perfume this morning?"

"Before breakfast? Dod't be ridiculous."

"Not even a drop?" Phillip was turning very white.

"Dot a drop."

He shook his head. "Now, wait a minute. This must be all in my mind. I'm—just imagining things, that's all. Working too hard, hysterical reaction. In a minute it'll all go away." He poured a cup of coffee, added cream and sugar.

But he couldn't get it close enough to taste it. It smelled as if it had been boiling three weeks in a rancid pot. It was the smell of coffee, all right, but a smell that was fiendishly distorted, overpoweringly, nauseatingly magnified. It pervaded the room and burned his throat and brought tears gushing to his eyes.

Slowly, realization began to dawn. He spilled the coffee as he set the cup down. The perfume. The coffee. The cigarette....

"My hat," he choked. "Get me my hat. I've got to get to the laboratory."

*   *   *   *   *

It got worse all the way downtown. He fought down waves of nausea as the smell of damp, rotting earth rose from his front yard in a gray cloud. The neighbor's dog dashed out to greet him, exuding the great-grandfather of all doggy odors. As Phillip waited for the bus, every passing car fouled the air with noxious fumes, gagging him, doubling him up with coughing as he dabbed at his streaming eyes.

Nobody else seemed to notice anything wrong at all.

The bus ride was a nightmare. It was a damp, rainy day; the inside of the bus smelled like the men's locker room after a big game. A bleary-eyed man with three-days' stubble on his chin flopped down in the seat next to him, and Phillip reeled back with a jolt to the job he had held in his student days, cleaning vats in the brewery.

"It'sh a great morning," Bleary-eyes breathed at him, "huh, Doc?" Phillip blanched. To top it, the man had had a breakfast of salami. In the seat ahead, a fat man held a dead cigar clamped in his mouth like a rank growth. Phillip's stomach began rolling; he sank his face into his hand, trying unobtrusively to clamp his nostrils. With a groan of deliverance he lurched off the bus at the laboratory gate.

He met Jake Miles coming up the steps. Jake looked pale, too pale.

"Morning," Phillip said weakly. "Nice day. Looks like the sun might come through."

"Yeah," said Jake. "Nice day. You—uh—feel all right this morning?"

"Fine, fine." Phillip tossed his hat in the closet, opened the incubator on his culture tubes, trying to look busy. He slammed the door after one whiff and gripped the edge of the work table with whitening knuckles. "Why?"

"Oh, nothing. Thought you looked a little peaked, was all."

They stared at each other in silence. Then, as though by signal, their eyes turned to the office at the end of the lab.

"Coffin come in yet?"

Jake nodded. "He's in there. He's got the door locked."

"I think he's going to have to open it," said Phillip.

A gray-faced Dr. Coffin unlocked the door, backed quickly toward the wall. The room reeked of kitchen deodorant. "Stay right where you are," Coffin squeaked. "Don't come a step closer. I can't see you now. I'm—I'm busy, I've got work that has to be done—"

"You're telling *me*," growled Phillip. He motioned Jake into the office and locked the door carefully. Then he turned to Coffin. "When did it start for you?"

Coffin was trembling. "Right after supper last night. I thought I was going to suffocate. Got up and walked the streets all night. My God, what a stench!"

"Jake?"

Dr. Miles shook his head. "Sometime this morning, I don't know when. I woke up with it."

"That's when it hit me," said Phillip.

"But I don't understand," Coffin howled. "Nobody else seems to notice anything—"

"Yet," said Phillip, "we were the first three to take the Coffin Cure, remember? You, and me and Jake. Two months ago."

Coffin's forehead was beaded with sweat. He stared at the two men in growing horror. "*But what about the others?*" he whispered.

"I think," said Phillip, "that we'd better find something spectacular to do in a mighty big hurry. That's what I think."

*   *   *   *   *

Jake Miles said, "The most important thing right now is secrecy. We mustn't let a word get out, not until we're absolutely certain."

"But what's *happened*?" Coffin cried. "These foul smells, everywhere. You, Phillip, you had a cigarette this morning. I can smell it clear over here, and it's bringing tears to my eyes. And if I didn't know better I'd swear neither of you had had a bath in a week. Every odor in town has suddenly turned foul—"

"*Magnified*, you mean," said Jake. "Perfume still smells sweet—there's just too much of it. The same with cinnamon; I tried it. Cried for half an hour, but it still smelled like cinnamon. No, I don't think the *smells* have changed any."

"But what, then?"

"Our noses have changed, obviously." Jake paced the floor in excitement. "Look at our dogs! They've never had colds—and they practically live by their noses. Other animals—all dependent on their senses of smell for survival—and none of them ever have anything even vaguely reminiscent of a common cold. The multicentric virus hits primates only—*and it reaches its fullest parasitic powers in man alone!*"

Coffin shook his head miserably. "But why this horrible stench all of a sudden? I haven't had a cold in weeks—"

"Of course not! That's just what I'm trying to say," Jake cried. "Look, why do we have any sense of smell at all? Because we have tiny olfactory nerve endings buried in the mucous membrane of our noses and throats. But we have always had the virus living there, too, colds or no colds, throughout our entire lifetime. It's *always* been there, anchored in the same cells, parasitizing the same sensitive tissues that carry our olfactory nerve endings, numbing them and crippling them, making them practically useless as sensory organs. No wonder we never smelled anything before! Those poor little nerve endings never had a chance!"

"Until we came along in our shining armor and destroyed the virus," said Phillip.

"Oh, we didn't destroy it. We merely stripped it of a very slippery protective mechanism against normal body defences." Jake perched on the edge of the desk, his dark face intense. "These two months since we had our shots have witnessed a battle to the death between our bodies and the virus. With the help of the vaccine, our bodies have won, that's all—stripped away the last vestiges of an invader that has been almost a part of our normal physiology since the beginning of time. And now for the first time those crippled little nerve endings are just beginning to function."

"God help us," Coffin groaned. "You think it'll get worse?"

"And worse. And still worse," said Jake.

"I wonder," said Phillip slowly, "what the anthropologists will say."

"What do you mean?"

"Maybe it was just a single mutation somewhere back there. Just a tiny change of cell structure or metabolism that left one line of primates vulnerable to an invader no other would harbor. Why else should man have begun to flower and blossom intellectually—grow to depend so much on his brains instead of his brawn that he could rise above all others? What better reason than because somewhere along the line in the world of fang and claw *he suddenly lost his sense of smell*?"

They stared at each other. "Well, he's got it back again now," Coffin wailed, "and he's not going to like it a bit."

"No, he surely isn't," Jake agreed. "He's going to start looking very quickly for someone to blame, I think."

They both looked at Coffin.

"Now don't be ridiculous, boys," said Coffin, turning white. "We're in this together. Phillip, it was your idea in the first place—you said so yourself! You can't leave me now—"

The telephone jangled. They heard the frightened voice of the secretary clear across the room. "Dr. Coffin? There was a student on the line just a moment ago. He—he said he was coming up to see you. Now, he said, not later."

"I'm busy," Coffin sputtered. "I can't see anyone. And I can't take any calls."

"But he's already on his way up," the girl burst out. "He was saying something about tearing you apart with his bare hands."

Coffin slammed down the receiver. His face was the color of lead. "They'll crucify me!" he sobbed. "Jake—Phillip—you've got to help me."

Phillip sighed and unlocked the door. "Send a girl down to the freezer and have her bring up all the live cold virus she can find. Get us some inoculated monkeys and a few dozen dogs." He turned to Coffin. "And stop sniveling. You're the big publicity man around here; you're going to handle the screaming masses, whether you like it or not."

"But what are you going to do?"

"I haven't the faintest idea," said Phillip, "but whatever I do is going to cost you your shirt. We're going to find out how to catch cold again if we have to die."

*   *   *   *   *

It was an admirable struggle, and a futile one. They sprayed their noses and throats with enough pure culture of virulent live virus to have condemned an ordinary man to a lifetime of sneezing, watery-eyed misery. They didn't develop a sniffle among them. They mixed six different strains of virus and gargled the extract, spraying themselves and every inoculated monkey they could get their hands on with the vile-smelling stuff. Not a sneeze. They injected it hypodermically, intradermally, subcutaneously, intramuscularly, and intravenously. They drank it. They bathed in the stuff.

But they didn't catch a cold.

"Maybe it's the wrong approach," Jake said one morning. "Our body defenses are keyed up to top performance right now. Maybe if we break them down we can get somewhere."

They plunged down that alley with grim abandon. They starved themselves. They forced themselves to stay awake for days on end, until exhaustion forced their eyes closed in spite of all they could do. They carefully devised vitamin-free, protein-free, mineral-free diets that tasted like library paste and smelled worse. They wore wet clothes and sopping shoes to work, turned off the heat and threw windows open to the raw winter air. Then they resprayed themselves with the live cold virus and waited reverently for the sneezing to begin.

It didn't. They stared at each other in gathering gloom. They'd never felt better in their lives.

Except for the smells, of course. They'd hoped that they might, presently, get used to them. They didn't. Every day it grew a little worse. They began smelling smells they never dreamed existed—noxious smells, cloying smells, smells that drove them gagging to the sinks. Their nose-plugs were rapidly losing their effectiveness. Mealtimes were nightmarish ordeals; they lost weight with alarming speed.

But they didn't catch cold.

"*I* think you should all be locked up," Ellie Dawson said severely as she dragged her husband, blue-faced and shivering, out of an icy shower one bitter morning. "You've lost your wits. You need to be protected against yourselves, that's what you need."

"You don't understand," Phillip moaned. "We've *got* to catch cold."

"Why?" Ellie snapped angrily. "Suppose you don't—what's going to happen?"

"We had three hundred students march on the laboratory today," Phillip said patiently. "The smells were driving them crazy, they said. They couldn't even bear to be close to their best friends. They wanted something done about it, or else they wanted blood. Tomorrow we'll have them back and three hundred more. And they were just the pilot study! What's going to happen when fifteen million people find their noses going bad on them?" He shuddered. "Have you seen the papers? People are already going around sniffing like bloodhounds. And *now* we're finding out what a thorough job we did. We can't crack it, Ellie. We can't even get a toe hold. Those antibodies are just doing too good a job."

"Well, maybe you can find some unclebodies to take care of them," Ellie offered vaguely.

"Look, don't make bad jokes—"

"I'm not making jokes! All I want is a husband back who doesn't complain about how everything smells, and eats the dinners I cook, and doesn't stand around in cold showers at six in the morning."

"I know it's miserable," he said helplessly. "But I don't know how to stop it."

He found Jake and Coffin in tight-lipped conference when he reached the lab. "I can't do it any more," Coffin was saying. "I've begged them for time. I've threatened them. I've promised them everything but my upper plate. I can't face them again, I just can't."

"We only have a few days left," Jake said grimly. "If we don't come up with something, we're goners."

Phillip's jaw suddenly sagged as he stared at them. "You know what I think?" he said suddenly. "I think we've been prize idiots. We've gotten so rattled we haven't used our heads. And all the time it's been sitting there blinking at us!"

"What are you talking about?" snapped Jake.

"Unclebodies," said Phillip.

"Oh, great God!"

"No, I'm serious." Phillip's eyes were very bright. "How many of those students do you think you can corral to help us?"

Coffin gulped. "Six hundred. They're out there in the street right now, howling for a lynching."

"All right, I want them in here. And I want some monkeys. Monkeys with colds, the worse colds the better."

"Do you have any idea what you're doing?" asked Jake.

"None in the least," said Phillip happily, "except that it's never been done before. But maybe it's time we tried following our noses for a while."

                    *   *   *   *   *

The tidal wave began to break two days later ... only a few people here, a dozen there, but enough to confirm the direst newspaper predictions. The boomerang was completing its circle.

At the laboratory the doors were kept barred, the telephones disconnected. Within, there was a bustle of feverish—if odorous—activity. For the three researchers, the olfactory acuity had reached agonizing proportions. Even the small gas masks Phillip had devised could no longer shield them from the constant barrage of violent odors.

But the work went on in spite of the smell. Truckloads of monkeys arrived at the lab—cold-ridden monkeys, sneezing, coughing, weeping, wheezing monkeys by the dozen. Culture trays bulged with tubes, overflowed the incubators and work tables. Each day six hundred angry students paraded through the lab, arms exposed, mouths open, grumbling but co-operating.

At the end of the first week, half the monkeys were cured of their colds and were quite unable to catch them back; the other half had new colds and couldn't get rid of them. Phillip observed this fact with grim satisfaction, and went about the laboratory mumbling to himself.

Two days later he burst forth jubilantly, lugging a sad-looking puppy under his arm. It was like no other puppy in the world. This puppy was sneezing and snuffling with a perfect howler of a cold.

The day came when they injected a tiny droplet of milky fluid beneath the skin of Phillip's arm, and then got the virus spray and gave his nose and throat a liberal application. Then they sat back and waited.

They were still waiting three days later.

"It was a great idea," Jake said gloomily, flipping a bulging notebook closed with finality. "It just didn't work, was all."

Phillip nodded. Both men had grown thin, with pouches under their eyes. Jake's right eye had begun to twitch uncontrollably whenever anyone came within three yards of him. "We can't go on like this, you know. The people are going wild."

"Where's Coffin?"

"He collapsed three days ago. Nervous prostration. He kept having dreams about hangings."

Phillip sighed. "Well, I suppose we'd better just face it. Nice knowing you, Jake. Pity it had to be this way."

"It was a great try, old man. A great try."

"Ah, yes. Nothing like going down in a blaze of—"

Phillip stopped dead, his eyes widening. His nose began to twitch. He took a gasp, a larger gasp, as a long-dead reflex came sleepily to life, shook its head, reared back ...

Phillip sneezed.

He sneezed for ten minutes without a pause, until he lay on the floor blue-faced and gasping for air. He caught hold of Jake, wringing his hand as tears gushed from his eyes. He gave his nose an enormous blow, and headed shakily for the telephone.

*   *   *   *   *

"It was a sipple edough pridciple," he said later to Ellie as she spread mustard on his chest and poured more warm water into his foot bath. "The Cure itself depedded upod it—the adtiged-adtibody reactiod. We had the adtibody agaidst the virus, all ridght; what we had to find was sobe kide of adtibody agaidst the *adtibody*." He sneezed violently, and poured in nose drops with a happy grin.

"Will they be able to make it fast enough?"

"Just aboudt fast edough for people to get good ad eager to catch cold agaid," said Phillip. "There's odly wud little hitch...."

Ellie Dawson took the steaks from the grill and set them, still sizzling, on the dinner table. "Hitch?"

Phillip nodded as he chewed the steak with a pretence of enthusiasm. It tasted like slightly damp K-ration.

"This stuff we've bade does a real good job. Just a little too good." He wiped his nose and reached for a fresh tissue.

"I bay be wrog, but I thik I've got this cold for keeps," he said sadly. "Udless I cad fide ad adtibody agaidst the adtibody agaidst the adtibody—"

THE NATIVE SOIL

ORIGINALLY PUBLISHED IN *FANTASTIC UNIVERSE*,
JULY 1957

The Native Soil

Before the first ship from Earth made a landing on Venus, there was much speculation about what might be found beneath the cloud layers obscuring that planet's surface from the eyes of all observers.

One school of thought maintained that the surface of Venus was a jungle, rank with hot-house moisture, crawling with writhing fauna and man-eating flowers. Another group contended hotly that Venus was an arid desert of wind-carved sandstone, dry and cruel, whipping dust into clouds that sunlight could never penetrate. Others prognosticated an ocean planet with little or no solid ground at all, populated by enormous serpents waiting to greet the first Earthlings with jaws agape.

But nobody knew, of course. Venus was the planet of mystery.

When the first Earth ship finally landed there, all they found was a great quantity of mud.

There was enough mud on Venus to go all the way around twice, with some left over. It was warm, wet, soggy mud—clinging and tenacious. In some places it was gray, and in other places it was black. Elsewhere it was found to be varying shades of brown, yellow, green, blue and purple. But just the same, it was still mud. The sparse Venusian vegetation grew up out of it; the small Venusian natives lived down in it; the steam rose from it and the rain fell on it, and that, it seemed, was that. The planet of mystery was no longer mysterious. It was just messy. People didn't talk about it any more.

But technologists of the Piper Pharmaceuticals, Inc., R&D squad found a certain charm in the Venusian mud.

They began sending cautious and very secret reports back to the Home Office when they discovered just what, exactly was growing in that Venusian mud besides Venusian natives. The Home Office promptly bought up full exploratory and mining rights to the planet for a price that was a brazen steal, and then in high excitement began pouring millions of dollars into ships and machines bound for the muddy planet. The Board of Directors met hoots of derision with secret smiles as they rubbed their hands together softly. Special crews of psychologists were dispatched to Venus to contact the natives; they returned, exuberant, with test-results that proved the natives were friendly, intelligent, co-operative and resourceful, and the Board of Directors rubbed their hands more eagerly together, and poured more money into the Piper Venusian Installation.

It took money to make money, they thought. Let the fools laugh. They wouldn't be laughing long. After all, Piper Pharmaceuticals, Inc., could recognize a gold mine when they saw one.

They thought.

*   *   *   *   *

Robert Kielland, special investigator and trouble shooter for Piper Pharmaceuticals, Inc., made an abrupt and intimate acquaintance with the fabulous Venusian mud when the landing craft brought him down on that soggy planet. He had transferred from the great bubble-shaped orbital transport ship to the sleek landing craft an hour before, bored and impatient with the whole proposition. He had no desire whatever to go to Venus. He didn't like mud, and he didn't like frontier projects. There had been nothing in his contract with Piper demanding that he travel to other planets in pursuit of his duties, and he had balked at the assignment. He had even balked at the staggering bonus check they offered him to help him get used to the idea.

It was not until they had convinced him that only his own superior judgment, his razor-sharp mind and his extraordinarily shrewd powers of observation and insight could possibly pull Piper Pharmaceuticals, Inc., out of the mudhole they'd gotten themselves into, that he had reluctantly agreed to go. He wouldn't like a moment of it, but he'd go.

Things weren't going right on Venus, it seemed.

The trouble was that millions were going in and nothing was coming out. The early promise of high production figures had faltered, sagged, dwindled and vanished. Venus was getting to be an expensive project to have around, and nobody seemed to know just why.

Now the pilot dipped the landing craft in and out of the cloud blanket, braking the ship, falling closer and closer to the surface as Kielland watched gloomily from the after port. The lurching billows of clouds made him queasy; he opened his Piper samples case and popped a pill into his mouth. Then he gave his nose a squirt or two with his Piper Rhino-Vac nebulizer, just for good measure. Finally, far below them, the featureless gray surface skimmed by. A sparse scraggly forest of twisted gray foliage sprang up at them.

The pilot sighted the landing platform, checked with Control Tower, and eased up for the final descent. He was a skillful pilot, with many landings on Venus to his credit. He brought the ship up on its tail and sat it down on the landing platform for a perfect three-pointer as the jets rumbled to silence.

Then, abruptly, they sank—landing craft, platform and all.

The pilot buzzed Control Tower frantically as Kielland fought down panic. Sorry, said Control Tower. Something must have gone wrong. They'd have them out in a jiffy. Good lord, no, *don't* blast out again, there were a thousand natives in the vicinity. Just be patient, everything would be all right.

They waited. Presently there were thumps and bangs as grapplers clanged on the surface of the craft. Mud gurgled around them as they were hauled up and out with the sound of a giant sipping soup. A mud-encrusted hatchway flew open, and Kielland stepped down on a flimsy-looking platform below. Four small rodent-like creatures were attached to it by ropes; they heaved with a will and began paddling through the soupy mud dragging the platform and Kielland toward a row of low wooden buildings near some stunted trees.

As the creatures paused to puff and pant, the back half of the platform kept sinking into the mud. When they finally reached comparatively solid ground, Kielland was mud up to the hips, and mad enough to blast off without benefit of landing craft.

He surveyed the Piper Venusian Installation, hardly believing what he saw. He had heard the glowing descriptions of the Board of Directors. He had seen the architect's projections of fine modern buildings resting on water-proof buoys, neat boating channels to the mine sites, fine orange-painted dredge equipment (including the new Piper Axis-Traction Dredges that had been developed especially for the operation). It had sounded, in short, just the way a Piper Installation ought to sound.

But there was nothing here that resembled that. Kielland could see a group of little wooden shacks that looked as though they were ready at a moment's notice to sink with a gurgle into the mud. Off to the right across a mud flat one of the dredges apparently had done just that: a swarm of men and natives were hard at work dragging it up again. Control Tower was to the left, balanced precariously at a slight tilt in a sea of mud.

The Piper Venusian Installation didn't look too much like a going concern. It looked far more like a ghost town in the latter stages of decay.

Inside the Administration shack Kielland found a weary-looking man behind a desk, scribbling furiously at a pile of reports. Everything in the shack was splattered with mud. The crude desk and furniture was smeared; the papers had black speckles all over them. Even the man's face was splattered, his clothing encrusted with gobs of still-damp mud. In a corner a young man was industriously scrubbing down the wall with a large brush.

The man wiped mud off Kielland and jumped up with a gleam of hope in his tired eyes. "Ah! Wonderful!" he cried. "Great to see you, old man. You'll find all the papers and reports in order here, everything ready for you—" He brushed the papers away from him with a gesture of finality. "Louie, get the landing craft pilot and don't let him out of your sight. Tell him I'll be ready in twenty minutes—"

"Hold it," said Kielland. "Aren't you Simpson?"

The man wiped mud off his cheeks and spat. He was tall and graying. "That's right."

"Where do you think you're going?"

"Aren't you relieving me?"

"I am not!"

"Oh, my." The man crumbled behind the desk, as though his legs had just given way. "I don't understand it. They told me—"

"I don't care what they told you," said Kielland shortly. "I'm a trouble shooter, not an administrator. When production figures begin to drop, I find out why. The production figures from this place have never gotten high enough to drop."

"This is supposed to be news to me?" said Simpson.

"So you've got troubles."

"Friend, you're right about that."

"Well, we'll straighten them out," Kielland said smoothly. "But first I want to see the foreman who put that wretched landing platform together."

Simpson's eyes became wary. "Uh—you don't really want to see him?"

"Yes, I think I do. When there's such obvious evidence of incompetence, the time to correct it is now."

"Well—maybe we can go outside and see him."

"We'll see him right here." Kielland sank down on the bench near the wall. A tiny headache was developing; he found a capsule in his samples case and popped it in his mouth.

Simpson looked sad and nodded to the orderly who had stopped scrubbing down the wall. "Louie, you heard the man."

"But boss—"

Simpson scowled. Louie went to the door and whistled. Presently there was a splashing sound and a short, gray creature padded in. His hind feet were four-toed webbed paddles; his legs were long and powerful like a kangaroo's. He was covered with thick gray fur which dripped with thick black mud. He squeaked at Simpson, wriggling his nose. Simpson squeaked back sharply.

Suddenly the creature began shaking his head in a slow, rhythmic undulation. With a cry Simpson dropped behind the desk. The orderly fell flat on the floor, covering his face with his arm. Kielland's eyes widened; then he was sitting in a deluge of mud as the little Venusian shook himself until his fur stood straight out in all directions.

Simpson stood up again with a roar. "I've told them a thousand times if I've told them once—" He shook his head helplessly as Kielland wiped mud out of his eyes. "This is the one you wanted to see."

Kielland sputtered. "Can it talk to you?"

"It doesn't talk, it squeaks."

"Then ask it to explain why the platform it built didn't hold the landing craft."

Simpson began whistling and squeaking at length to the little creature. Its shaggy tail crept between its legs and it hung its head like a scolded puppy.

"He says he didn't know a landing craft was supposed to land on the platform," Simpson reported finally. "He's sorry, he says."

"But hasn't he seen a landing craft before?"

Squeak, squeak. "Oh, yes."

"Wasn't he told what the platform was being made for?"

Squeak, squeak. "Of course."

"Then why didn't the platform stand up?"

Simpson sighed. "Maybe he forgot what it was supposed to be used for in the course of building it. Maybe he never really did understand in the first place. I can't get questions like that across to him with this whistling, and I doubt that you'll ever find out which it was."

"Then fire him," said Kielland. "We'll find some other—"

"Oh, no! I mean, let's not be hasty," said Simpson. "I'd hate to have to fire this one—for a while yet, at any rate."

"Why?"

"Because we've finally gotten across to him—at least I *think* we have—just how to take down a dredge tube." Simpson's voice was almost tearful. "It's taken us months to teach him. If we fire him, we'll have to start all over again with another one."

Kielland stared at the Venusian, and then at Simpson. "So," he said finally, "I see."

"No, you don't," Simpson said with conviction. "You don't even begin to see yet. You have to fight it for a few months before you really see." He waved the Venusian out the door and turned to Kielland with burden of ten months' frustration in his voice. "They're *stupid*," he said slowly. "They are so incredibly stupid I could go screaming into the swamp every time I see one of them coming. Their stupidity is positively abysmal."

"Then why use them?" Kielland spluttered.

"Because if we ever hope to mine anything in this miserable mudhole, we've got to use them to do it. There just isn't any other way."

With Simpson leading, they donned waist-high waders with wide, flat silicone-coated pans strapped to the feet and started out to inspect the installation.

A crowd of a dozen or more Venusian natives swarmed happily around them like a pack of hounds. They were in and out of the steaming mud, circling and splashing, squeaking: and shaking. They seemed to be having a real field day.

"Of course," Simpson was saying, "since Number Four dredge sank last week there isn't a whale of a lot of Installation left for you to inspect. But you can see what there is, if you want."

"You mean Number Four dredge is the only one you've got to use?" Kielland asked peevishly. "According to my records you have five Axis-Traction dredges, plus a dozen or more of the old kind."

"Ah!" said Simpson. "Well, Number One had its vacuum chamber corroded out a week after we started using dredging. Ran into a vein of stuff with 15 per cent acid content, and it got chewed up something fierce. Number Two sank without a trace—over there in the swamp someplace." He pointed across the black mud flats to a patch of sickly vegetation. "The Mud-pups know where it is, they think, and I suppose they could go drag it up for us if we dared take the time, but it would lose us a month, and you know the production schedule we've been trying to meet."

"So what about Numbers Three and Five?"

"Oh, we still have them. They won't work without a major overhaul, though."

"Overhaul! They're brand new."

"They *were*. The Mud-pups didn't understand how to sluice them down properly after operations. When this guck gets out into the air it hardens like cement. You ever see a cement mixer that hasn't been cleaned out after use for a few dozen times? That's Numbers Three and Five."

"What about the old style models?"

"Half of them are out of commission, and the other half are holding the islands still."

"Islands?"

"Those chunks of semisolid ground we have Administration built on. The chunk that keeps Control Tower in one place."

"Well, what are they going to do—walk away?"

"That's just about right. The first week we were in operation we kept wondering why we had to travel farther every day to get to the dredges. Then we realized that solid ground on Venus isn't solid ground at all. It's just big chunks of denser stuff that floats on top of the mud like dumplings in a stew. But that was nothing compared to the other things—"

They had reached the vicinity of the salvage operation on Number Five dredge. To Kielland it looked like a huge cylinder-type vacuum cleaner with a number of flexible hoses sprouting from the top. The whole machine was three-quarters submerged in clinging mud. Off to the right a derrick floated hub-deep in slime; grapplers from it were clinging to the dredge and the derrick was heaving and splashing like a trapped hippopotamus. All about the submerged machine were Mud-pups, working like strange little beavers as the man supervising the operation wiped mud from his face and carried on a running line of shouts, curses, whistles and squeaks.

Suddenly one of the Mud-pups saw the newcomers. He let out a squeal, dropped his line in the mud and bounced up to the surface, dancing like a dervish on his broad webbed feet as he stared in unabashed curiosity. A dozen more followed his lead, squirming up and staring, shaking gobs of mud from their fur.

"No, *no!*" the man supervising the operation screamed. "*Pull,* you idiots. Come back here! Watch *out—*"

The derrick wobbled and let out a whine as steel cable sizzled out. Confused, the Mud-pups tore themselves away from the newcomers and turned back to their lines, but it was too late. Number Five dredge trembled, with a wet sucking sound, and settled back into the mud, blub—blub—blub.

The supervisor crawled down from his platform and sloshed across to where Simpson and Kielland were standing. He looked like a man who had suffered the torment of the damned for twenty minutes too long. "No more!" he screamed in Simpson's face. "That's all. I'm through. I'll pick up my pay any time you get it ready, and I'll finish off my contract at home, but I'm through here. One solid week I work to teach these idiots what I want them to do, and you have to come along at the one moment all week when I really need their concentration." He glared, his face purple. "Concentration! I should hope for so much! You got to have a brain to have concentration—"

"Barton, this is Kielland. He's here from the Home Office, to solve all our problems."

"You mean he brought us an evacuation ship?"

"No, he's going to tell us how to make this Installation pay. Right, Kielland?" Simpson's grin was something to see.

Kielland scowled. "What are you going to do with the dredge—just leave it there?" he asked angrily.

"No—I'm going to dig it out, again," said Barton, "after we take another week off to drum into those quarter-brained mudhens just what it is we want them to do—again—and then persuade them to do it—again—and then hope against hope that nothing happens along to distract them—again. Any suggestions?"

Simpson shook his head. "Take a rest, Barton. Things will look brighter in the morning."

"Nothing ever looks brighter in the morning," said Barton, and he sloshed angrily off toward the Administration island.

"You see?" said Simpson. "Or do you want to look around some more?"

*　　*　　*　　*　　*

Back in Administration shack, Kielland sprayed his throat with Piper Fortified Bio-Static and took two tetracycline capsules from his samples case as he stared gloomily down at the little gob of blue-gray mud on the desk before him.

The Venusian bonanza, the sole object of the multi-million-dollar Piper Venusian Installation, didn't look like much. It ran in veins deep beneath the surface. The R&D men had struck it quite by accident in the first place, sampled it along with a dozen other kinds of Venusian mud—and found they had their hands on the richest 'mycin-bearing bacterial growth since the days of the New Jersey mud flats.

The value of the stuff was incalculable. Twenty-first century Earth had not realized the degree to which it depended upon its effective antibiotic products for maintenance of its health until the mutating immune bacterial strains began to outpace the development of new antibacterials. Early penicillin killed 96 per cent of all organisms in its spectrum—at first—but time and natural selection undid its work in three generations. Even the broad-spectrum drugs were losing their effectiveness to a dangerous degree within decades of their introduction. And the new drugs grown from Earth-born bacteria, or synthesized in the laboratories, were too few and too weak to meet the burgeoning demands of humanity—

Until Venus. The bacteria indigenous to that planet were alien to Earth—every attempt to transplant them had failed—but they grew with abandon in the warm mud currents of Venus. Not all mud was of value: only the singular blue-gray stuff that lay before Kielland on the desk could produce the 'mycin-like tetracycline derivative that was more powerful than the best of Earth-grown wide spectrum antibiotics, with few if any of the unfortunate side-effects of the Earth products.

The problem seemed simple: find the mud in sufficient quantities for mining, dredge it up, and transport it back to Earth to extract the drug. It was the first two steps of the operation that depended so heavily on the mud-acclimated natives of Venus for success. They were as much at home in the mud as they were in the dank, humid air above. They could distinguish one type of mud from another deep beneath the surface, and could carry a dredge-tube down to a lode of the blue-gray muck with the unfailing accuracy of a homing pigeon.

If they could only be made to understand just what they were expected to do. And that was where production ground down to a slow walk.

The next few days were a nightmare of frustration for Kielland as he observed with mounting horror the standard operating procedure of the Installation.

Men and Mud-pups went to work once again to drag Number Five dredge out of the mud. It took five days of explaining, repeating, coaxing and threatening to do it, but finally up it came—with mud caked and hardened in its insides until it could never be used again.

So they ferried Number Six down piecemeal from the special orbital transport ship that had brought it. Only three landing craft sank during the process, and within two weeks Simpson and Barton set bravely off with their dull-witted cohorts to tackle the swamp with a spanking new piece of equipment. At last the delays were over—

Of course, it took another week to get the actual dredging started. The Mud-pups who had been taught the excavation procedure previously had either disappeared into the swamp or forgotten everything they'd ever been taught. Simpson had expected it, but it was enough to keep Kielland sleepless for three nights and drive his blood pressure to suicidal levels. At length, the blue-gray mud began billowing out of the dredge onto the platforms built to receive it, and the transport ship was notified to stand by for loading. But by the time the ferry had landed, the platform with the load had somehow drifted free of the island and required a week-long expedition into the hinterland to track it down. On the trip back they met a rainstorm that dissolved the blue-gray stuff into soup which ran out between the slats of the platform, and back into the mud again.

They did get the platform back, at any rate.

Meanwhile, the dredge began sucking up green stuff that smelled of sewage instead of the blue-gray clay they sought—so the natives dove mud-ward to explore the direction of the vein. One of them got caught in the suction tube, causing a three-day delay while engineers dismantled the dredge to get him out. In re-assembling, two of the dredge tubes got interlocked somehow, and the dredge burned out three generators trying to suck itself through itself, so to speak. That took another week to fix.

Kielland buried himself in the Administration shack, digging through the records, when the reign of confusion outside became too much to bear. He sent for Tarnier, the Installation physician, biologist, and erstwhile Venusian psychologist. Dr. Tarnier looked like the breathing soul of failure; Kielland had to steel himself to the wave of pity that swept through him at the sight of the man. "You're the one who tested these imbeciles originally?" he demanded.

Dr. Tarnier nodded. His face was seamed, his eyes lustreless. "I tested 'em. God help me, I tested 'em."

"How?"

"Standard procedures. Reaction times. Mazes. Conditioning. Language. Abstractions. Numbers. Associations. The works."

"Standard for Earthmen, I presume you mean."

"So what else? Piper didn't want to know if they were Einsteins or not. All they wanted was a passable level of intelligence. Give them natives with brains and they might have to pay them something. They thought they were getting a bargain."

"Some bargain."

"Yeah."

"Only your tests say they're intelligent. As intelligent, say, as a low-normal human being without benefit of any schooling or education. Right?"

"That's right," the doctor said wearily, as though he had been through this mill again and again. "Schooling and education don't enter into it at all, of course. All we measured was potential. But the results said they had it."

"Then how do you explain the mess we've got out there?"

"The tests were wrong. Or else they weren't applicable even on a basic level. Or something. I don't know. I don't even care much any more."

"Well I care, plenty. Do you realize how much those creatures are costing us? If we ever do get the finished product on the market, it'll cost too much for anybody to buy."

Dr. Tarnier spread his hands. "Don't blame me. Blame them."

"And then this so-called biological survey of yours," Kielland continued, warming to his subject. "From a scientific man, it's a prize. Anatomical description: limited because of absence of autopsy specimens. Apparently have endoskeleton, but organization of the internal organs remains obscure. Thought to be mammalianoid—there's a fence-sitter for you—but can't be certain of this because no young have been observed, nor any females in gestation. Extremely gregarious, curious, playful, irresponsible, etc., etc., etc. Habitat under natural conditions: uncertain. Diet: uncertain. Social organization: uncertain." Kielland threw down the paper with a snort. "In short, the only thing we're certain of is that they're here. Very helpful. Especially when every dime we have in this project depends on our teaching them how to count to three without help."

Dr. Tarnier spread his hands again. "Mr. Kielland, I'm a mere mortal. In order to measure something, it has to stay the same long enough to get it measured. In order to describe something, it has to hold still long enough to be observed. In order to form a logical opinion of a creature's mental capacity, it has to demonstrate some perceptible mental capacity to start with. You can't get very far studying a creature's habitat and social structure when most of its habitating goes on under twenty feet of mud."

"How about the language?"

"We get by with squeaks and whistles and sign language. A sort of pidgin-Venusian. They use a very complex system among themselves." The doctor paused, uncertainly. "Anyway, it's hard to get too tough with the Pups," he burst out finally. "They really seem to try hard—when they can just manage to keep their minds to it."

"Just stupid, carefree, happy-go-lucky kids, eh?"

Dr. Tarnier shrugged.

"Go away," said Kielland in disgust, and turned back to the reports with a sour taste in his mouth.

Later he called the Installation Comptroller. "What do you pay Mud-pups for their work?" he wanted to know.

"Nothing," said the Comptroller.

"*Nothing!*"

"We have nothing they can use. What would you give them—United Nations coin? They'd just try to eat it."

"How about something they *can* eat, then?"

"Everything we feed them they throw right back up. Planetary incompatibility."

"But there must be *something* you can use for wages," Kielland protested. "Something they want, something they'll work hard for."

"Well, they liked tobacco and pipes all right—but it interfered with their oxygen storage so they couldn't dive. That ruled out tobacco and pipes. They liked Turkish towels, too, but they spent all their time parading up and down in them and slaying the ladies and wouldn't work at all. That ruled out Turkish towels. They don't seem to care too much whether they're paid or not, though—as long as we're decent to them. They seem to like us, in a stupid sort of way."

"Just loving, affectionate, happy-go-lucky kids. I know. Go away." Kielland growled and turned back to the reports ... except that there weren't any more reports that he hadn't read a dozen times or more. Nothing that made sense, nothing that offered a lead. Millions of Piper dollars sunk into this project, and every one of them sitting there blinking at him expectantly.

For the first time he wondered if there really *was* any solution to the problem. Stumbling blocks had been met and removed before—that was Kielland's job, and he knew how to do it. But stupidity could be a stumbling block that was all but insurmountable.

Yet he couldn't throw off the nagging conviction that something more subtle than stupidity was involved....

Then Simpson came in, cursing and sputtering and bellowing for Louie. Louie came, and Simpson started dictating a message for relay to the transport ship. "Special order, rush, repeat, rush," Simpson grated. "For immediate delivery Piper Venusian Installation—one Piper Axis-Traction Dredge, previous specifications applicable—"

Kielland stared at him. "Again?"

Simpson gritted his teeth. "Again."

"Sunk?"

"Blub," said Simpson. "Blub, blub, blub."

Slowly, Kielland stood up, glaring first at Simpson, then at the little muddy creatures that were attempting to hide behind his waders, looking so forlorn and chastised and woebegone. "All right," Kielland said, after a pregnant pause. "That's all. You won't need to relay that order to the ship. Forget about Number Seven dredge. Just get your files in order and get a landing craft down here for me. The sooner the better."

Simpson's face lit up in pathetic eagerness. "You mean we're going to *leave?*"

"That's what I mean."

"The company's not going to like it—"

"The company ought to welcome us home with open arms," Kielland snarled. "They should shower us with kisses. They should do somersaults for joy that I'm not going to let them sink another half billion into the mud out here. They took a gamble and got cleaned, that's all. They'd be as stupid as your pals here if they kept coming back for more." He pulled on his waders, brushing penitent Mud-pups aside as he started for the door. "Send the natives back to their burrows or whatever they live in and get ready to close down. *I've* got to figure out some way to make a report to the Board that won't get us all fired."

He slammed out the door and started across to his quarters, waders going splat-splat in the mud. Half a dozen Mud-pups were following him. They seemed extraordinarily exuberant as they went diving and splashing in the mud. Kielland turned and roared at them, shaking his fist. They stopped short, then slunk off with their tails between their legs.

But even at that, their squeaking sounded strangely like laughter to Kielland....

In his quarters the light was so dim that he almost had his waders off before he saw the upheaval. The little room was splattered from top to bottom with mud. His bunk was coated with slime; the walls dripped blue-gray goo. Across the room his wardrobe doors hung open as three muddy creatures rooted industriously in the leather case on the floor.

Kielland let out a howl and threw himself across the room. *His samples case!* The Mud-pups scattered, squealing. Their hands were filled with capsules, and their muzzles were dripping with white powder. Two went between Kielland's legs and through the door. The third dove for the window with Kielland after him. The company man's hand closed on a slippery tail, and he fell headlong across the muddy bed as the culprit literally slipped through his fingers.

He sat up, wiping mud from his hair and surveying the damage. Bottles and boxes of medicaments were scattered all over the floor of the wardrobe, covered with mud but unopened. Only one large box had been torn apart, its contents ravaged.

Kielland stared at it as things began clicking into place in his mind. He walked to the door, stared out across the steaming gloomy mud flats toward the lighted windows of the Administration shack. Sometimes, he mused, a man can get so close to something that he can't see the obvious. He stared at the samples case again. Sometimes stupidity works both ways—and sometimes what looks like stupidity may really be something far more deadly.

He licked his lips and flipped the telephone-talker switch. After a misconnection or two he got Control Tower. Control Tower said yes, they had a small exploratory scooter on hand. Yes, it could be controlled on a beam and fitted with cameras. But of course it was special equipment, emergency use only—

He cut them off and buzzed Simpson excitedly. "Cancel all I said—about leaving. I mean. Change of plan. Something's come up. No, don't order anything—but get one of those natives that can understand your whistling and give him the word."

Simpson bellowed over the wire. "What word? What do you think you're doing?"

"I may just be saving our skins—we won't know for a while. But however you manage it, tell them we're definitely *not leaving Venus*. Tell them they're all fired—we don't want them around any more. The Installation is off limits to them from here on in. And tell them we've devised a way to mine the lode without them—got that? Tell them the equipment will be arriving as soon as we can bring it down from the transport."

"Oh, now look—"

"You want me to repeat it?"

Simpson sighed. "All right. Fine. I'll tell them. Then what?"

"Then just don't bother me for a while. I'm going to be busy. Watching TV."

An hour later Kielland was in Control Tower, watching the pale screen as the little remote-controlled explorer circled the installation. Three TV cameras were in operation as he settled down behind the screen. He told Sparks what he wanted to do, and the ship whizzed off in the direction the Mud-pup raiders had taken.

At first, there was nothing but dreary mud flats sliding past the cameras' watchful eyes. Then they picked up a flicker of movement, and the ship circled in lower for a better view. It was a group of natives—a large group. There must have been fifty of them working busily in the mud, five miles away from the Piper Installation. They didn't look so carefree and happy-go-lucky now. They looked very much like desperately busy Mud-pups with a job on their hands, and they were so absorbed they didn't even see the small craft circling above them.

They worked in teams. Some were diving with small containers; some were handling lines attached to the containers; still others were carrying and dumping. They came up full, went down empty, came up full. The produce was heaped in a growing pile on a small semisolid island with a few scraggly trees on it. As they worked the pile grew and grew.

It took only a moment for Kielland to tell what they were doing. The color of the stuff was unmistakable. They were mining piles of blue-gray mud, just as fast as they could mine it.

With a gleam of satisfaction in his eye, Kielland snapped off the screen and nodded at Sparks to bring the cameras back. Then he rang Simpson again.

"Did you tell them?"

Simpson's voice was uneasy. "Yeah—yeah, I told them. They left in a hurry. Quite a hurry."

"Yes, I imagine they did. Where are your men now?"

"Out working on Number Six, trying to get it up."

"Better get them together and pack them over to Control Tower, fast," said Kielland. "I mean everybody. Every man in the Installation. We may have this thing just about tied up, if we can get out of here soon enough—"

Kielland's chair gave a sudden lurch and sailed across the room, smashing into the wall. With a yelp he tried to struggle up the sloping floor; it reared and heaved over the other way, throwing Kielland and Sparks to the other wall amid a heap of instruments. Through the windows they could see the gray mud flats careening wildly below them. It took only an instant to realize what was happening. Kielland shouted, "Let's get out of here!" and headed down the stairs, clinging to the railing for dear life.

Control Tower was sinking in the mud. They had moved faster than he had anticipated, Kielland thought, and snarled at himself all the way down to the landing platform below. He had hoped at least to have time to parley, to stop and discuss the whys and wherefores of the situation with the natives. Now it was abundantly clear that any whys and wherefores that were likely to be discussed would be discussed later.

And very possibly under twenty feet of mud—

A stream of men were floundering out of Administration shack, plowing through the mud with waders only half strapped on as the line of low buildings began shaking and sinking into the morass. From the direction of Number Six dredge another crew was heading for the Tower. But the Tower was rapidly growing shorter as the buoys that sustained it broke loose with ear-shattering crashes.

Kielland caught Sparks by the shoulder, shouting to be heard above the racket. "The transport—did you get it?"

"I—I think so."

"They're sending us a ferry?"

"It should be on its way."

Simpson sloshed up, his face heavy with dismay. "The dredges! They've cut loose the dredges."

"Bother the dredges. Get your men collected and into the shelters. We'll have a ship here any minute."

"But what's happening?"

"We're leaving—if we can make it before these carefree, happy-go-lucky kids here sink us in the mud, dredges, Control Tower and all."

Out of the gloom above there was a roar and a streak of murky yellow as the landing craft eased down through the haze. Only the top of Control Tower was out of the mud now. The Administration shack gave a lurch, sagging, as a dozen indistinct gray forms pulled and tugged at the supporting structure beneath it. Already a circle of natives was converging on the Earthmen as they gathered near the landing platform shelters.

"They're cutting loose the landing platform!" somebody wailed. One of the lines broke with a resounding snap, and the platform lurched. Then a dozen men dived through the mud to pull away the slippery, writhing natives as they worked to cut through the remaining guys. Moments later the landing craft was directly overhead and men and natives alike scattered as she sank down.

The platform splintered and jolted under her weight, began skidding, then held firm to the two guy ropes remaining. A horde of gray creatures hurled themselves on those lines as a hatchway opened above and a ladder dropped down. The men scurried up the ropes just as the plastic dome of the Control Tower sank with a gurgle.

Kielland and Simpson paused at the bottom of the ladder, blinking at the scene of devastation around them.

"Stupid, you say," said Kielland heavily. "Better get up there, or we'll go where Control Tower went."

"But—everything—gone!"

"Wrong again. Everything saved." Kielland urged the administrator up the ladder and sighed with relief as the hatch clanged shut. The jets bloomed and sprayed boiling mud far and wide as the landing craft lifted soggily out of the mire and roared for the clouds above.

Kielland wiped sweat from his forehead and sank back on his cot with a shudder. "*We* should be so stupid," he said.

"I must admit," he said later to a weary and mystified Simpson, "that I didn't expect them to move so fast. But when you've decided in your mind that somebody's really pretty stupid, it's hard to adjust to the idea that maybe he *isn't*, all of a sudden. We should have been much more suspicious of Dr. Tarnier's tests. It's true they weren't designed for Venusians, but they were designed to assess intelligence, and intelligence isn't a quality that's influenced by environment or species. It's either there or it isn't, and the good Doctor told us unequivocally that it was there."

"But their behavior."

"Even that should have tipped us off. There is a very fine line dividing incredible stupidity and incredible *stubbornness*. It's often a tough differential to make. I didn't spot it until I found them wolfing down the tetracycline capsules in my samples case. Then I began to see the implications. Those Mud-pups were stubbornly and tenaciously determined to drive the Piper Venusian Installation off Venus permanently, by fair means or foul. They didn't care how it got off—they just wanted it off."

"But why? We weren't hurting them. There's plenty of mud on Venus."

"Ah—but not so much of the blue-gray stuff we were after, perhaps. Suppose a space ship settled down in a wheatfield in Kansas along about harvest time and started loading wheat into the hold? I suppose the farmer wouldn't mind too much. After all, there's plenty of vegetation on Earth—"

"They're *growing* the stuff?"

"For all they're worth," said Kielland. "Lord knows what sort of metabolism uses tetracycline for food—but they are growing mud that yields an incredibly rich concentration of antibiotic ... their native food. They grow it, harvest it, live on it. Even the way they shake whenever they come out of the mud is a giveaway—what better way to seed their crop far and wide? We were mining away their staff of life, my friend. You really couldn't blame them for objecting."

"Well, if they think they can drive us off that way, they're going to have to get that brilliant intelligence of theirs into action," Simpson said ominously. "We'll bring enough equipment down there to mine them out of house and home."

"Why?" said Kielland. "After all, they're mining it themselves a lot more efficiently than we could ever do it. And with Piper warehouses back on Earth full of old, useless antibiotics that they can't sell for peanuts? No, I don't think we'll mine anything when a simple trade arrangement will do just as well." He sank back in his cot, staring dreamily through the port as the huge orbital transport loomed large ahead of them. He found his throat spray and dosed himself liberally in preparation for his return to civilization. "Of course, the natives are going to be wondering what kind of idiots they're dealing with to sell them pure refined extract of Venusian beefsteak in return for raw chunks of unrefined native soil. But I think we can afford to just let them wonder for a while."

Bear Trap

Originally Published In *Fantastic Universe*,
December 1957

BEAR TRAP

The man's meteoric rise as a peacemaker in a nation tired by the long years of war made the truth even more shocking.

The huge troop transport plane eased down through the rainy drizzle enshrouding New York International Airport at about five o'clock in the evening. Tom Shandor glanced sourly through the port at the wet landing strip, saw the dim landing lights reflected in the steaming puddles. On an adjacent field he could see the rows and rows of jet fighters, wings up in the foggy rain, poised like ridiculous birds in the darkness. With a sigh he ripped the sheet of paper from the small, battered portable typewriter on his lap, and zipped the machine up in its slicker case.

Across the troop hold the soldiers were beginning to stir, yawning, shifting their packs, collecting their gear. Occasionally they stared at Shandor as if he were totally alien to their midst, and he shivered a little as he collected the sheets of paper scattered on the deck around him, checked the date, 27 September, 1982, and rolled them up to fit in the slim round mailing container. Ten minutes later he was shouldering his way through the crowd of khaki-clad men, scowling up at the sky, his nondescript fedora jammed down over his eyes to keep out the rain, slicker collar pulled up about his ears. At the gangway he stopped before a tired-looking lieutenant and flashed the small fluorescent card in his palm. "Public Information Board."

The officer nodded wearily and gave his coat and typewriter a cursory check, then motioned him on. He strode across the wet field, scowling at the fog, toward the dimmed-out waiting rooms.

He found a mailing chute, and popped the mailing tube down the slot as if he were glad to be rid of it. Into the speaker he said: "Special Delivery. PIB business. It goes to press tonight."

The female voice from the speaker said something, and the red "clear" signal blinked. Shandor slipped off his hat and shook it, then stopped at a coffee machine and extracted a cup of steaming stuff from the bottom after trying the coin three times.

Finally he walked across the room to an empty video booth, and sank down into the chair with an exhausted sigh. Flipping a switch, he waited several minutes for an operator to appear. He gave her a number, and then said, "Let's scramble it, please."

"Official?"

He showed her the card, and settled back, his whole body tired. He was a tall man, rather slender, with flat, bland features punctuated only by blond caret-shaped eyebrows. His grey eyes were heavy-lidded now, his mouth an expressionless line as he waited, sunk back into his coat with a long-cultivated air of lifeless boredom. He watched the screen without interest as it bleeped a time or two, then shifted into the familiar scrambled-image pattern. After a moment he muttered the Public Information Board audio-code words, and saw the screen even out into the clear image of a large, heavyset man at a desk.

"Hart," said Shandor. "Story's on its way. I just dropped it from the Airport a minute ago, with a rush tag on it. You should have it for the morning editions."

The big man in the screen blinked, and his heavy face lit up. "The story on the Rocket Project?"

Shandor nodded. "The whole scoop. I'm going home now." He started his hand for the cutoff switch.

"Wait a minute—" Hart picked up a pencil and fiddled with it for a moment. He glanced over his shoulder, and his voice dropped a little. "Is the line scrambled?"

Shandor nodded.

"What's the scoop, boy? How's the Rocket Project coming?"

Shandor grinned wryly. "Read the report, daddy. Everything's just ducky, of course—it's all ready for press. You've got the story, why should I repeat it?"

Hart scowled impatiently. "No, no— I mean the *scoop*. The real stuff. How's the Project going?"

"Not so hot." Shandor's face was weary. "Material cutoff is holding them up something awful. Among other things. The sabotage has really fouled up the west coast trains, and shipments haven't been coming through on schedule. You know—they ask for one thing, and get the wrong weight, or their supplier is out of material, or something goes wrong. And there's personnel trouble, too—too much direction and too little work. It's beginning to look as if they'll never get going. And now it looks like there's going to be another administration shakeup, and you know what that means—"

Hart nodded thoughtfully. "They'd better get hopping," he muttered. "The conference in Berlin is on the skids—it could be hours now." He looked up. "But you got the story rigged all right?"

Shandor's face flattened in distaste. "Sure, sure. You know me, Hart. Anything to keep the people happy. Everything's running as smooth as satin, work going fine, expect a test run in a month, and we should be on the moon in half a year, more or less, maybe, we hope—the usual swill. I'll be in to work out the war stories in the morning. Right now I'm for bed."

He snapped off the video before Hart could interrupt, and started for the door. The rain hit him, as he stepped out, with a wave of cold wet depression, but a cab slid up to the curb before him and he stepped in. Sinking back he tried to relax, to get his stomach to stop complaining, but he couldn't fight the feeling of almost physical illness sweeping over him. He closed his eyes and sank back, trying to drive the ever-plaguing thoughts from his mind, trying to focus on something pleasant, almost hoping that his long-starved conscience might give a final gasp or two and die altogether. But deep in his mind he knew that his screaming conscience was almost the only thing that held him together.

Lies, he thought to himself bitterly. White lies, black lies, whoppers—you could take your choice. There should be a flaming neon sign flashing across the sky, telling all people: "Public Information Board, Fabrication Corporation, fabricating of all lies neatly and expeditiously done." He squirmed, feeling the rebellion grow in his mind. Propaganda, they called it. A nice word, such a very handy word, covering a multitude of seething pots. PIB was the grand clearing house, the last censor of censors, and he, Tom Shandor, was the Chief Fabricator and Purveyor of Lies.

He shook his head, trying to get a breath of clean air in the damp cab. Sometimes he wondered where it was leading, where it would finally end up, what would happen if the people ever really learned, or ever listened to the clever ones who tried to sneak the truth into print somewhere. But people couldn't be told the truth, they had to be coddled, urged, pushed along. They had to be kept somehow happy, somehow hopeful, they had to be kept whipped up to fever pitch, because the long, long years of war and near war had exhausted them, wearied them beyond natural resiliency. No, they had to be spiked, urged and goaded—what would happen if they learned?

He sighed. No one, it seemed, could do it as well as he. No one could take a story of bitter diplomatic fighting in Berlin and simmer it down to a public-palatable "peaceful and progressive meeting;" no one could quite so skillfully reduce the bloody fighting in India to a mild "enemy losses topping American losses twenty to one, and our boys are fighting staunchly, bravely,"— No one could write out the lies quite so neatly, so smoothly as Tom Shandor—

The cab swung in to his house, and he stepped out, tipped the driver, and walked up the walk, eager for the warm dry room. Coffee helped sometimes when he felt this way, but other things helped even more. He didn't even take his coat off before mixing and downing a stiff rye-and-ginger, and he was almost forgetting his unhappy conscience by the time the video began blinking.

He flipped the receiver switch and sat down groggily, blinked at John Hart's heavy face as it materialized on the screen. Hart's eyes were wide, his voice tight and nervous as he leaned forward. "You'd better get into the office pronto," he said, his eyes bright. "You've *really* got a story to work on now—"

Shandor blinked. "The War—"

Hart took a deep breath. "Worse," he said. "David Ingersoll is dead."

*   *   *   *   *

Tom Shandor shouldered his way through the crowd of men in the anteroom, and went into the inner office. Closing the door behind him coolly, he faced the man at the desk, and threw a thumb over his shoulder. "Who're the goons?" he growled. "You haven't released a story yet—?"

John Hart sighed, his pinkish face drawn. "The press. I don't know how they got the word—there hasn't been a word released, but—" He shrugged and motioned Shandor to a seat. "You know how it goes."

Shandor sat down, his face blank, eyeing the Information chief woodenly. The room was silent for a moment, a tense, anticipatory silence. Then Hart said: "The Rocket story was great, Tommy. A real writing job. You've got the touch, when it comes to a ticklish news release—"

Shandor allowed an expression of distaste to cross his face. He looked at the chubby man across the desk and felt the distaste deepen and crystallize. John Hart's face was round, with little lines going up from the eyes, an almost grotesque, burlesque-comic face that belied the icy practical nature of the man behind it. A thoroughly distasteful face, Shandor thought. Finally he said, "The story, John. On Ingersoll. Let's have it, straight out."

Hart shrugged his stocky shoulders, spreading his hands. "Ingersoll's dead," he said. "That's all there is to it. He's stone-cold dead."

"But he can't be dead!" roared Shandor, his face flushed. "We just can't *afford* to have him dead—"

Hart looked up wearily. "Look, I didn't kill him. He went home from the White House this evening, apparently sound enough, after a long, stiff, nasty conference with the President. Ingersoll wanted to go to Berlin and call a showdown at the International conference there, and he had a policy brawl with the President, and the President wouldn't let him go, sent an undersecretary instead, and threatened to kick Ingersoll out of the cabinet unless he quieted down. Ingersoll got home at 4:30, collapsed at 5:00, and he was dead before the doctor arrived. Cerebral hemorrhage, pretty straightforward. Ingersoll's been killing himself for years—he knew it, and everyone else in Washington knew it. It was bound to happen sooner or later."

"He was trying to prevent a war," said Shandor dully, "and he was all by himself. Nobody else wanted to stop it, nobody that mattered, at any rate. Only the people didn't want war, and who ever listens to them? Ingersoll got the people behind him, so they gave him a couple of Nobel Peace Prizes, and made him Secretary of State, and then cut his throat every time he tried to do anything. No wonder he's dead—"

Hart shrugged again, eloquently indifferent. "So he was a nice guy, he wanted to prevent a war. As far as I'm concerned, he was a pain in the neck, the way he was forever jumping down

Information's throat, but he's dead now, he isn't around any more—" His eyes narrowed sharply. "The important thing, Tommy, is that the people won't like it that he's dead. They trusted him. He's been the people's Golden Boy, their last-ditch hope for peace. If they think their last chance is gone with his death, they're going to be mad. They won't like it, and there'll be hell to pay—"

Shandor lit a smoke with trembling fingers, his eyes smouldering. "So the people have to be eased out of the picture," he said flatly. "They've got to get the story so they won't be so angry—"

Hart nodded, grinning. "They've got to have a real story, Tommy. Big, blown up, what a great guy he was, defender of the peace, greatest, most influential man America has turned out since the half-century—you know what they lap up, the usual garbage, only on a slightly higher plane. They've got to think that he's really saved them, that he's turned over the reins to other hands just as trustworthy as his—you can give the president a big hand there—they've got to think his work is the basis of our present foreign policy—can't you see the implications? It's got to be spread on with a trowel, laid on skillfully—"

Shandor's face flushed deep red, and he ground the stub of his smoke out viciously. "I'm sick of this stuff, Hart," he exploded. "I'm sick of you, and I'm sick of this whole rotten setup, this business of writing reams and reams of lies just to keep things under control. Ingersoll was a great man, a *really* great man, and he was *wasted*, thrown away. He worked to make peace, and he got laughed at. He hasn't done a thing— because he couldn't. Everything he has tried has been useless, wasted. *That's* the truth—why not tell that to the people?"

Hart stared. "Get hold of yourself," he snapped. "You know your job. There's a story to write. The life of David Ingersoll. It has to go down smooth." His dark eyes shifted to his hands, and back sharply to Shandor. "A propagandist has to write it, Tommy—an ace propagandist. You're the only one I know that could do the job."

"Not me," said Shandor flatly, standing up. "Count me out. I'm through with this, as of now. Get yourself some other whipping boy. Ingersoll was one man the people could trust. And he was one man I could never face. I'm not good enough for him to spit on, and I'm not going to sell him down the river now that he's dead."

With a little sigh John Hart reached into the desk. "That's very odd," he said softly. "Because Ingersoll left a message for you—"

Shandor snapped about, eyes wide. "Message—?"

The chubby man handed him a small envelope. "Apparently he wrote that a long time ago. Told his daughter to send it to Public Information Board immediately in event of his death. Read it."

Shandor unfolded the thin paper, and blinked unbelieving:

In event of my death during the next few months, a certain amount of biographical writing will be inevitable. It is my express wish that this writing, in whatever form it may take, be done by Mr. Thomas L. Shandor, staff writer of the Federal Public Information Board.

I believe that man alone is qualified to handle this assignment.

(Signed)
David P. Ingersoll
Secretary of State,
United States of America.
4 June, 1981

Shandor read the message a second time, then folded it carefully and placed it in his pocket, his forehead creased. "I suppose you want the story to be big," he said dully.

Hart's eyes gleamed a moment of triumph. "As big as you can make it," he said eagerly. "Don't spare time or effort, Tommy. You'll be relieved of all assignments until you have it done—if you'll take it."

"Oh, yes," said Shandor softly. "I'll take it."

*   *   *   *   *

He landed the small PIB 'copter on an airstrip in the outskirts of Georgetown, haggled with Security officials for a few moments, and grabbed an old weatherbeaten cab, giving the address of the Ingersoll estate as he settled back in the cushions. A small radio was set inside the door; he snapped it on, fiddled with the dial until he found a PIB news report. And as he listened he felt his heart sink lower and lower, and the old familiar feeling of dirtiness swept over him, the feeling of being a part in an enormous, overpowering scheme of corruption and degradation. The Berlin conference was reaching a common meeting ground, the report said, with Russian, Chinese, and American officials making the first real progress in the week of talks. Hope rising for an early armistice on the Indian front. Suddenly he hunched forward, blinking in surprise as the announcer continued the broadcast: "The Secretary of State, David Ingersoll, was stricken with a slight head cold this evening on the eve of his departure for the Berlin Conference, and was advised to postpone the trip temporarily. John Harris Darby, first undersecretary, was dispatched in his place. Mr. Ingersoll expressed confidence that Mr. Darby would be able to handle the talks as well as himself, in view of the optimistic trend in Berlin last night—"

Shandor snapped the radio off viciously, a roar of disgust rising in his throat, cut off just in time. Lies, lies, lies. Some people *knew* they were lies—what could they really think? People like David Ingersoll's wife—

Carefully he reined in his thoughts, channelled them. He had called the Ingersoll home the night before, announcing his arrival this morning—

The taxi ground up a gravelled driveway, stopped before an Army jeep at the iron-grilled gateway. A Security Officer flipped a cigarette onto the ground, shaking his head. "Can't go in, Secretary's orders."

Shandor stepped from the cab, briefcase under his arm. He showed his card, scowled when the officer continued shaking his head. "Orders say *nobody*—"

"Look, blockhead," Shandor grated. "If you want to hang by your toes, I can put through a special check-line to Washington to confirm my appointment here. I'll also recommend you for the salt mines."

The officer growled, "Wise guy," and shuffled into the guard shack. Minutes later he appeared again, jerked his thumb toward the estate. "Take off," he said. "See that you check here at the gate before you leave."

He was admitted to the huge house by a stone-faced butler, who led him through a maze of corridors into a huge dining room. Morning sunlight gleamed through a glassed-in wall, and Shandor stopped at the door, almost speechless.

He knew he'd seen the girl somewhere. At one of the Washington parties, or in the newspapers. Her face was unmistakable; it was the sort of face that a man never forgets once he glimpses it—thin, puckish, with wide-set grey eyes that seemed both somber and secretly amused, a full, sensitive mouth, and blonde hair, exceedingly fine, cropped close about her ears. She was eating her breakfast, a rolled up newspaper by her plate, and as she looked up, her eyes were not warm. She just stared at Shandor angrily for a moment, then set down her coffee cup and threw the paper to the floor with a slam. "You're Shandor, I suppose."

Shandor looked at the paper, then back at her. "Yes, I'm Tom Shandor. But you're not Mrs. Ingersoll—"

"A profound observation. Mother isn't interested in seeing anyone this morning, particularly you." She motioned to a chair. "You can talk to me if you want to."

Shandor sank down in the proffered seat, struggling to readjust his thinking. "Well," he said finally. "I—I wasn't expecting you—" he broke into a grin—"but I should think you could help. You know what I'm trying to do—I mean, about your father. I want to write a story, and the logical place to start would be with his family—"

The girl blinked wide eyes innocently. "Why don't you start with the newspaper files?" she asked, her voice silky. "You'd find all sorts of information about daddy there. Pages and pages—"

"No, no— I don't want that kind of information. You're his daughter, Miss Ingersoll, you could tell me about him as a man. Something about his personal life, what sort of man he was—"

She shrugged indifferently, buttered a piece of toast, as Shandor felt most acutely the pangs of his own missed breakfast. "He got up at seven every morning," she said. "He brushed his teeth and ate breakfast. At nine o'clock the State Department called for him—"

Shandor shook his head unhappily. "No, no, that's not what I mean."

"Then perhaps you'd tell me precisely what you *do* mean?"
Her voice was clipped and hard.

Shandor sighed in exasperation. "The personal angle. His
likes and dislikes, how he came to formulate his views, his
relationship with his wife, with you—"

"He was a kind and loving father," she said, her voice
mocking. "He loved to read, he loved music—oh, yes, put that
down, he was a *great* lover of music. His wife was the apple of
his eye, and he tried, for all the duties of his position, to provide
us with a happy home life—"

"Miss Ingersoll."

She stopped in mid-sentence, her grey eyes veiled, and shook
her head slightly. "That's not what you want, either?"

Shandor stood up and walked to a window, looking out over
the wide veranda. Carefully he snubbed his cigarette in an
ashtray, then turned sharply to the girl. "Look. If you want to
play games, I can play games too. Either you're going to help me,
or you're not—it's up to you. But you forget one thing. I'm a
propagandist. I might say I'm a very expert propagandist. I can
tell a true story from a false one. You won't get anywhere lying
to me, or evading me, and if you choose to try, we can call it off
right now. You know exactly the type of information I need from
you. Your father was a great man, and he rates a fair shake in
the write-ups. I'm asking you to help me."

Her lips formed a sneer. "And *you're* going to give him a fair
shake, I'm supposed to believe." She pointed to the newspaper.
"With garbage like that? Head cold!" Her face flushed, and she
turned her back angrily. "I know your writing, Mr. Shandor. I've
been exposed to it for years. You've never written an honest, true
story in your life, but you always want the truth to start with,
don't you? I'm to give you the truth, and let you do what you
want with it, is that the idea? No dice, Mr. Shandor. And you
even have the gall to brag about it!"

Shandor flushed angrily. "You're not being fair. This story is
going to press straight and true, every word of it. This is one
story that won't be altered."

And then she was laughing, choking, holding her sides, as
the tears streamed down her cheeks. Shandor watched her,
reddening, anger growing up to choke him. "I'm not joking," he

snapped. "I'm breaking with the routine, do you understand? I'm through with the lies now, I'm writing this one straight."

She wiped her eyes and looked at him, bitter lines under her smile. "You couldn't do it," she said, still laughing. "You're a fool to think so. You could write it, and you'd be out of a job so fast you wouldn't know what hit you. But you'd never get it into print. And you know it. You'd never even get the story to the inside offices."

Shandor stared at her. "That's what you think," he said slowly. "This story will get to the press if it kills me."

The girl looked up at him, eyes wide, incredulous. "You *mean* that, don't you?"

"I never meant anything more in my life."

She looked at him, wonderingly, motioned him to the table, a faraway look in her eyes. "Have some coffee," she said, and then turned to him, her eyes wide with excitement. The sneer was gone from her face, the coldness and hostility, and her eyes were pleading. "If there were some way to do it, if you really meant what you said, if you'd really *do* it—give people a true story—"

Shandor's voice was low. "I told you, I'm sick of this mill. There's something wrong with this country, something wrong with the world. There's a rottenness in it, and your father was fighting to cut out the rottenness. This story is going to be straight, and it's going to be printed if I get shot for treason. And it could split things wide open at the seams."

She sat down at the table. Her lower lip trembled, and her voice was tense with excitement. "Let's get out of here," she said. "Let's go someplace where we can talk—"

*   *   *   *   *

They found a quiet place off the business section in Washington, one of the newer places with the small closed booths, catering to people weary of eavesdropping and overheard conversations. Shandor ordered beers, then lit a smoke and leaned back facing Ann Ingersoll. It occurred to him that she was exceptionally lovely, but he was almost frightened by the look on her face, the suppressed excitement, the cold, bitter lines about her mouth. Incongruously, the thought crossed his mind that he'd hate to have this woman against him. She looked as though she would be capable of more than he'd care to tangle with. For all her lovely face there was an edge of thin ice to her smile, a razor-sharp, dangerous quality that made him curiously uncomfortable. But now she was nervous, withdrawing a cigarette from his pack with trembling fingers, fumbling with his lighter until he struck a match for her. "Now," he said. "Why the secrecy?"

She glanced at the closed door to the booth. "Mother would kill me if she knew I was helping you. She hates you, and she hates the Public Information Board. I think dad hated you, too."

Shandor took the folded letter from his pocket. "Then what do you think of this?" he asked softly. "Doesn't this strike you a little odd?"

She read Ingersoll's letter carefully, then looked up at Tom, her eyes wide with surprise. "So this is what that note was. This doesn't wash, Tom."

"You're telling me it doesn't wash. Notice the wording. 'I believe that man alone is qualified to handle this assignment.' Why me? And of all things, why me *alone*? He knew my job, and he fought me and the PIB every step of his career. Why a note like this?"

She looked up at him. "Do you have any idea?"

"Sure, I've got an idea. A crazy one, but an idea. I don't think he wanted me because of the writing. I think he wanted me because I'm a propagandist."

She scowled. "It still doesn't wash. There are lots of propagandists—and why would he want a propagandist?"

Shandor's eyes narrowed. "Let's let it ride for a moment. How about his files?"

"In his office in the State Department."

"He didn't keep anything personal at home?"

Her eyes grew wide. "Oh, no, he wouldn't have dared. Not the sort of work he was doing. With his files under lock and key in the State Department nothing could be touched without his knowledge, but at home anybody might have walked in."

"Of course. How about enemies? Did he have any particular enemies?"

She laughed humorlessly. "Name anybody in the current administration. I think he had more enemies than anybody else in the cabinet." Her mouth turned down bitterly. "He was a stumbling block. He got in people's way, and they hated him for it. They killed him for it."

Shandor's eyes widened. "You mean you think he was murdered?"

"Oh, no, nothing so crude. They didn't have to be crude. They just let him butt his head against a stone wall. Everything he tried was blocked, or else it didn't lead anywhere. Like this Berlin Conference. It's a powder keg. Dad gambled everything on going there, forcing the delegates to face facts, to really put their cards on the table. Ever since the United Nations fell apart in '72 dad had been trying to get America and Russia to sit at the same table. But the President cut him out at the last minute. It was planned that way, to let him get up to the very brink of it, and then slap him down hard. They did it all along. This was just the last he could take."

Shandor was silent for a moment. "Any particular thorns in his side?"

Ann shrugged. "Munitions people, mostly. Dartmouth Bearing had a pressure lobby that was trying to throw him out of the cabinet. The President sided with them, but he didn't dare do it for fear the people would squawk. He was planning to blame the failure of the Berlin Conference on dad and get him ousted that way."

Shandor stared. "But if that conference fails, *we're in full-scale war!*"

"Of course. That's the whole point." She scowled at her glass, blinking back tears. "Dad could have stopped it, but they wouldn't let him. *It killed him,* Tom!"

Shandor watched the smoke curling up from his cigarette. "Look," he said. "I've got an idea, and it's going to take some fast work. That conference could blow up any minute, and then I think we're going to be in real trouble. I want you to go to your father's office and get the contents of his personal file. Not the business files, his personal files. Put them in a briefcase and subway-express them to your home. If you have any trouble, have them check with PIB—we have full authority, and I'm it right now. I'll call them and give them the word. Then meet me here again, with the files, at 7:30 this evening."

She looked up, her eyes wide. "What—what are you going to do?"

Shandor snubbed out his smoke, his eyes bright. "I've got an idea that we may be onto something—just something I want to check. But I think if we work it right, we can lay these boys that fought your father out by the toes—"

*   *   *   *   *

The Library of Congress had been moved when the threat of bombing in Washington had become acute. Shandor took a cab to the Georgetown airstrip, checked the fuel in the 'copter. Ten minutes later he started the motor, and headed upwind into the haze over the hills. In less than half an hour he settled to the Library landing field in western Maryland, and strode across to the rear entrance.

The electronic cross-index had been the last improvement in the Library since the war with China had started in 1958. Shandor found a reading booth in one of the alcoves on the second floor, and plugged in the index. The cold, metallic voice of the automatic chirped twice and said, "Your reference, pleeyuz."

Shandor thought a moment. "Give me your newspaper files on David Ingersoll, Secretary of State."

"Through which dates, pleeyuz."

"Start with the earliest reference, and carry through to current." The speaker burped, and he sat back, waiting. A small grate in the panel before him popped open, and a small spool plopped out onto a spindle. Another followed, and another. He turned to the reader, and reeled the first spool into the intake slot. The light snapped on, and he began reading.

Spools continued to plop down. He read for several hours, taking a dozen pages of notes. The references commenced in June, 1961, with a small notice that David Ingersoll, Republican from New Jersey, had been nominated to run for state senator. Before that date, nothing. Shandor scowled, searching for some item predating that one. He found nothing.

Scratching his head, he continued reading, outlining chronologically. Ingersoll's election to state senate, then to United States Senate. His rise to national prominence as economist for the post-war Administrator of President Drayton in 1966. His meteoric rise as a peacemaker in a nation tired from endless dreary years of fighting in China and India. His tremendous popularity as he tried to stall the re-intensifying cold-war with Russia. The first Nobel Peace Prize, in 1969, for the ill-fated Ingersoll Plan for World Sovereignty. Pages and pages and pages of newsprint. Shandor growled angrily, surveying the pile of notes with a sinking feeling of incredulity. The articles, the writing, the tone—it was all too familiar. Carefully he checked the newspaper sources. Some of the dispatches were Associated Press; many came direct desk from Public Information Board in New York; two other networks sponsored some of the wordage. But the tone was all the same.

Finally, disgusted, Tom stuffed the notes into his briefcase, and flipped down the librarian lever. "Sources, please."

A light blinked, and in a moment a buzzer sounded at his elbow. A female voice, quite human, spoke as he lifted the receiver. "Can I help you on sources?"

"Yes. I've been reading the newspaper files on David Ingersoll. I'd like the by-lines on this copy."

There was a moment of silence. "Which dates, please?"

Shandor read off his list, giving dates. The silence continued for several minutes as he waited impatiently. He was about to hang up and leave when the voice spoke up again. "I'm sorry, sir. Most of that material has no by-line. Except for one or two items it's all staff-written."

"By whom?"

"I'm sorry, no source is available. Perhaps the PIB offices could help you—"

"All right, ring them for me, please." He waited another five minutes, saw the PIB cross-index clerk appear on the video screen. "Hello, Mr. Shandor. Can I help you?"

"I'm trying to trace down the names of the Associated Press and PIB writers who covered stories on David Ingersoll over a period from June 1961 to the present date—"

The girl disappeared for several moments. When she reappeared, her face was puzzled. "Why, Mr. Shandor, you've been doing the work on Ingersoll from August, 1978 to Sept. 1982. We haven't closed the files on this last month yet—"

He scowled in annoyance. "Yes, yes, I know that. I want the writers before I came."

The clerk paused. "Until you started your work there was no definite assignment. The information just isn't here. But the man you replaced in PIB was named Frank Mariel."

Shandor turned the name over in his mind, decided that it was familiar, but that he couldn't quite place it. "What's this man doing now?"

The girl shrugged. "I don't know, just now, and have no sources. But according to our files he left Public Information Board to go to work in some capacity for Dartmouth Bearing Corporation."

Shandor flipped the switch, and settled back in the reading chair. Once again he fingered through his notes, frowning, a doubt gnawing through his mind into certainty. He took up a dozen of the stories, analyzed them carefully, word for word, sentence by sentence. Then he sat back, his body tired, eyes closed in concentration, an incredible idea twisting and writhing and solidifying in his mind.

It takes one to catch one. That was his job—telling lies. Writing stories that weren't true, and making them believable. Making people think one thing when the truth was something else. It wasn't so strange that he could detect exactly the same sort of thing when he ran into it. He thought it through again and again, and every time he came up with the same answer. There was no doubt.

Reading the newspaper files had accomplished only one thing. He had spent the afternoon reading a voluminous, neat, smoothly written, extremely convincing batch of bold-faced lies. Lies about David Ingersoll. Somewhere, at the bottom of those lies was a shred or two of truth, a shred hard to analyze, impossible to segregate from the garbage surrounding it. But somebody had written the lies. That meant that somebody knew the truths behind them.

Suddenly he galvanized into action. The video blinked protestingly at his urgent summons, and the Washington visiphone operator answered. "Somewhere in those listings of yours," Shandor said, "you've got a man named Frank Mariel. I want his number."

*   *   *   *   *

He reached the downtown restaurant half an hour early, and ducked into a nearby visiphone station to ring Hart. The PIB director's chubby face materialized on the screen after a moment's confusion, and Shandor said: "John—what are your plans for releasing the Ingersoll story? The morning papers left him with a slight head cold, if I remember right—" Try as he would, he couldn't conceal the edge of sarcasm in his voice.

Hart scowled. "How's the biography coming?"

"The biography's coming along fine. I want to know what kind of quicksand I'm wading through, that's all."

Hart shrugged and spread his hands. "We can't break the story proper until you're ready with your buffer story. Current plans say that he gets pneumonia tomorrow, and goes to Walter Reed tomorrow night. We're giving it as little emphasis as possible, running the Berlin Conference stories for right-hand column stuff. That'll give you all day tomorrow and half the next day for the preliminary stories on his death. Okay?"

"That's not enough time." Shandor's voice was tight.

"It's enough for a buffer-release." Hart scowled at him, his round face red and annoyed. "Look, Tom, you get that story in, and never mind what you like or don't like. This is dynamite you're playing with—the Conference is going to be on the rocks in a matter of hours—that's straight from the Undersecretary— and on top of it all, there's trouble down in Arizona—"

Shandor's eyes widened. "The Rocket Project—?"

Hart's mouth twisted. "Sabotage. They picked up a whole ring that's been operating for over a year. Caught them red- handed, but not before they burnt out half a calculator wing. They'll have to move in new machines now before they can go on—set the Project back another week, and that could lose the war for us right there. Now *get that story in*." He snapped the switch down, leaving Shandor blinking at the darkened screen.

Ten minutes later Ann Ingersoll joined him in the restaurant booth. She was wearing a chic white linen outfit, with her hair fresh, like a blonde halo around her head in the fading evening light. Her freshness contrasted painfully with Tom's curling collar and dirty tie, and he suddenly wished he'd picked up a shave. He looked up and grunted when he saw the fat briefcase under the girl's arm, and she dropped it on the table between them and sank down opposite him, studying his face. "The reading didn't go so well," she said.

"The reading went lousy," he admitted sheepishly. "This the personal file?"

She nodded shortly and lit a cigarette. "The works. They didn't even bother me. But I can't see why all the precaution— I mean, the express and all that—"

Shandor looked at her sharply. "If what you said this morning was true, that file is a gold mine, for us, but more particularly, for your father's enemies. I'll go over it closely when I get out of here. Meantime, there are one or two other things I want to talk over with you."

She settled herself, and grinned. "Okay, boss. Fire away."

He took a deep breath, and tiredness lined his face. "First off: what did your father do before he went into politics?"

Her eyes widened, and she arrested the cigarette halfway to her mouth, put it back on the ashtray, with a puzzled frown on her face. "That's funny," she said softly. "I thought I knew, but I guess I don't. He was an industrialist—way, far back, years and years ago, when I was just a little brat—and then we got into the war with China, and I don't know what he did. He was always making business trips; I can remember going to the airport with mother to meet him, but I don't know what he did. Mother always avoided talking about him, and I never got to see him enough to talk—"

Shandor sat forward, his eyes bright. "Did he ever entertain any business friends during that time—any that you can remember?"

She shook her head. "I can't remember. Seems to me a man or two came home with him on a couple of occasions, but I don't know who. I don't remember much before the night he came home and said he was going to run for Congress. Then there were people galore—have been ever since."

"And what about his work at the end of the China war? After he was elected, while he was doing all that work to try to smooth things out with Russia—can you remember him saying anything, to you, or to your mother, about *what* he was doing, and how?"

She shook her head again. "Oh, yes, he'd talk—he and mother would talk—sometimes argue. I had the feeling that things weren't too well with mother and dad many times. But I can't remember anything specific, except that he used to say over and over how he hated the thought of another war. He was afraid it was going to come—"

Shandor looked up sharply. "But he hated it—"

"Yes." Her eyes widened. "Oh, yes, he hated it. Dad was a good man, Tom. He believed with all his heart that the people of the world wanted peace, and that they were being dragged to war because they couldn't find any purpose to keep them from it. He believed that if the people of the world had a cause, a purpose, a driving force, that there wouldn't be any more wars. Some men fought him for preaching peace, but he wouldn't be swayed. Especially he hated the pure-profit lobbies, the patriotic drum-beaters who stood to get rich in a war. But dad had to die, and there aren't many men like him left now, I guess."

"I know." Shandor fell silent, stirring his coffee glumly. "Tell me," he said, "did your father have anything to do with a man named Mariel?"

Ann's eyes narrowed. "Frank Mariel? He was the newspaper man. Yes, dad had plenty to do with him. He hated dad's guts, because dad fought his writing so much. Mariel was one of the 'fight now and get rich' school that were continually plaguing dad."

"Would you say that they were enemies?"

She bit her lip, wrinkling her brow in thought. "Not at first. More like a big dog with a little flea, at first. Mariel pestered dad, and dad tried to scratch him away. But Mariel got into PIB, and then I suppose you could call them enemies—"

Shandor sat back, frowning, his face dark with fatigue. He stared at the table top for a long moment, and when he looked up at the girl his eyes were troubled. "There's something wrong with this," he said softly. "I can't quite make it out, but it just doesn't look right. Those newspaper stories I read—pure bushwa, from beginning to end. I'm dead certain of it. And yet—" he paused, searching for words. "Look. It's like I'm looking at a jigsaw puzzle that *looks* like it's all completed and lying out on the table. But there's something that tells me I'm being foxed, that it isn't a complete puzzle at all, just an illusion, yet somehow I can't even tell for sure where pieces are missing—"

The girl leaned over the table, her grey eyes deep with concern. "Tom," she said, almost in a whisper. "Suppose there *is* something, Tom. Something big, what's it going to do to *you*, Tom? You can't fight anything as powerful as PIB, and these men that hated dad could break you."

Tom grinned tiredly, his eyes far away. "I know," he said softly. "But a man can only swallow so much. Somewhere, I guess, I've still got a conscience—it's a nuisance, but it's still there." He looked closely at the lovely girl across from him. "Maybe it's just that I'm tired of being sick of myself. I'd like to *like* myself for a change. I haven't liked myself for years." He looked straight at her, his voice very small in the still booth. "I'd like some other people to like me, too. So I've got to keep going—"

Her hand was in his, then, grasping his fingers tightly, and her voice was trembling. "I didn't think there was anybody left like that," she said. "Tom, you aren't by yourself—remember that. No matter what happens, I'm with you all the way. I'm— I'm afraid, but I'm with you."

He looked up at her then, and his voice was tight. "Listen, Ann. Your father planned to go to Berlin before he died. What was he going to *do* if he went to the Berlin Conference?"

She shrugged helplessly. "The usual diplomatic fol-de-rol, I suppose. He always—"

"No, no—that's not right. He wanted to go so badly that he died when he wasn't allowed to, Ann. He must have had something in mind, something concrete, something tremendous. Something that would have changed the picture a great deal."

And then she was staring at Shandor, her face white, grey eyes wide. "Of course he had something," she exclaimed. "He *must* have—oh, I don't know what, he wouldn't say what was in his mind, but when he came home after that meeting with the President he was furious— I've never seen him so furious, Tom, he was almost out of his mind with anger, and he paced the floor, and, swore and nearly tore the room apart. He wouldn't speak to anyone, just stamped around and threw things. And then we heard him cry out, and when we got to him he was unconscious on the floor, and he was dead when the doctor came—" She set her glass down with trembling fingers. "He had something big, Tom, I'm sure of it. He had some information that he planned to drop on the conference table with such a bang it would stop the whole world cold. *He knew something* that the conference doesn't know—"

Tom Shandor stood up, trembling, and took the briefcase. "It should be here," he said. "If not the whole story, at least the missing pieces." He started for the booth door. "Go home," he said. "I'm going where I can examine these files without any interference. Then I'll call you." And then he was out the door, shouldering his way through the crowded restaurant, frantically weaving his way to the street. He didn't hear Ann's voice as she called after him to stop, didn't see her stop at the booth door, watch in a confusion of fear and tenderness, and collapse into the booth, sobbing as if her heart would break. Because a crazy, twisted, impossible idea was in his mind, an idea that had plagued him since he had started reading that morning, an idea with an answer, an acid test, folded in the briefcase under his arm. He bumped into a fat man at the bar, grunted angrily, and finally reached the street, whistled at the cab that lingered nearby.

The car swung up before him, the door springing open automatically. He had one foot on the running board before he saw the trap, saw the tight yellowish face and the glittering eyes inside the cab. Suddenly there was an explosion of bright purple brilliance, and he was screaming, twisting and screaming and reeling backward onto the sidewalk, doubled over with the agonizing fire that burned through his side and down one leg, forcing scream after scream from his throat as he blindly staggered to the wall of the building, pounded it with his fists for relief from the searing pain. And then he was on his side on the sidewalk, sobbing, blubbering incoherently to the uniformed policeman who was dragging him gently to his feet, seeing through burning eyes the group of curious people gathering around. Suddenly realization dawned through the pain, and he let out a cry of anger and bolted for the curb, knocking the policeman aside, his eyes wild, searching the receding stream of traffic for the cab, a picture of the occupant burned indelibly into his mind, a face he had seen, recognized. The cab was gone, he knew, gone like a breath of wind. The briefcase was also gone—

*   *   *   *   *

He gave the address of the Essex University Hospital to the cabby, and settled back in the seat, gripping the hand-guard tightly to fight down the returning pain in his side and leg. His mind was whirling, fighting in a welter of confusion, trying to find some avenue of approach, some way to make sense of the mess. The face in the cab recurred again and again before his eyes, the gaunt, putty-colored cheeks, the sharp glittering eyes. His acquaintance with Frank Mariel had been brief and unpleasant, in the past, but that was a face he would never forget. But how could Mariel have known where he would be, and when? There was precision in that attack, far too smooth precision ever to have been left to chance, or even to independent planning. His mind skirted the obvious a dozen times, and each time rejected it angrily. Finally he knew he could no longer reject the thought, the only possible answer. Mariel had known where he would be, and at what time. Therefore, someone must have told him.

He stiffened in the seat, the pain momentarily forgotten. Only one person could have told Mariel. Only one person knew where the file was, and where it would be after he left the restaurant—he felt cold bitterness creep down his spine. She had known, and sat there making eyes at him, and telling him how wonderful he was, how she was with him no matter what happened—and she'd already sold him down the river. He shook his head angrily, trying to keep his thoughts on a rational plane. *Why?* Why had she strung him along, why had she even started to help him? And why, above all, turn against her own father?

The Hospital driveway crunched under the cab, and he hopped out, wincing with every step, and walked into a phone booth off the lobby. He gave a name, and in a moment heard the P.A. system echoing it: "Dr. Prex; calling Dr. Prex." In a moment he heard a receiver click off, and a familiar voice said, "Prex speaking."

"Prex, this is Shandor. Got a minute?"

The voice was cordial. "Dozens of them. Where are you?"

"I'll be up in your quarters." Shandor slammed down the receiver and started for the elevator to the Resident Physicians' wing.

He let himself in by a key, and settled down in the darkened room to wait an eternity before a tall, gaunt man walked in, snapped on a light, and loosened the white jacket at his neck. He was a young man, no more than thirty, with a tired, sober face and jet black hair falling over his forehead. His eyes lighted as he saw Shandor, and he grinned. "You look like you've been through the mill. What happened?"

Shandor stripped off his clothes, exposing the angry red of the seared skin. The tall man whistled softly, the smile fading. Carefully he examined the burned area, his fingers gentle on the tender surface, then he turned troubled eyes to Shandor. "You've been messing around with dirty guys, Tom. Nobody but a real dog would turn a scalder on a man." He went to a cupboard, returned with a jar of salve and bandages.

"Is it serious?" Shandor's face was deathly white. "I've been fighting shock with thiamin for the last hour, but I don't think I can hold out much longer."

Prex shrugged. "You didn't get enough to do any permanent damage, if that's what you mean. Just fried the pain-receptors in your skin to a crisp, is all. A little dose is so painful you can't do anything but holler for a while, but it won't hurt you permanently unless you get it all over you. Enough can kill you." He dressed the burned areas carefully, then bared Shandor's arm and used a pressure syringe for a moment. "Who's using one of those things?"

Shandor was silent for a moment. Then he said, "Look, Prex. I need some help, badly." His eyes looked up in dull anger. "I'm going to see a man tonight, and I want him to talk, hard and fast. I don't care right now if he nearly dies from pain, but I want him to talk. I need somebody along who knows how to make things painful."

Prex scowled, and pointed to the burn. "This the man?"

"That's the man."

Prex put away the salve. "I suppose I'll help you, then. Is this official, or grudge?"

"A little of both. Look, Prex, I know this is a big favor to ask, but it's on the level. Believe me, it's square, nothing shady about it. The method may not be legal, but the means are justified. I can't tell you what's up, but I'm asking you to trust me."

Prex grinned. "You say it's all right, it's all right. When?"

Shandor glanced at his watch. "About 3:00 this morning, I think. We can take your car."

They talked for a while, and a call took the doctor away. Shandor slept a little, then made some black coffee. Shortly before three the two men left the Hospital by the Physicians' entrance, and Prex's little beat-up Dartmouth slid smoothly into the desultory traffic for the suburbs.

*   *   *   *   *

The apartment was small and neatly furnished. Shandor and the Doctor had been admitted by a sleepy doorman who had been jolted to sudden attention by Tom's PIB card, and after five minutes pounding on the apartment door, a sleepy-eyed man opened the door a crack. "Say, what's the idea pounding on a man's door at this time of night? Haven't you—"

Shandor gave the door a shove with his shoulder, driving it open into the room. "Shut up," he said bluntly. He turned so the light struck his face, and the little man's jaw dropped in astonishment. "Shandor!" he whispered.

Frank Mariel looked like a weasel—sallow, sunken-cheeked, with a yellowish cast to his skin that contrasted unpleasantly with the coal black hair. "That's right," said Shandor. "We've come for a little talk. Meet the doctor."

Mariel's eyes shifted momentarily to Prex's stoney face, then back to Shandor, ghosts of fear creeping across his face. "What do you want?"

"I've come for the files."

The little man scowled. "You've come to the wrong man. I don't have any files."

Prex carefully took a small black case from his pocket, unsnapped a hinge, and a small, shiny instrument fell out in his hand. "The files," said Shandor. "Who has them?"

"I—I don't know—"

Shandor smashed a fist into the man's face, viciously, knocking him reeling to the floor. "You tried to kill me tonight," he snarled. "You should have done it up right. You should stick to magazine editing and keep your nose out of dirty games, Mariel. Who has the files?"

Mariel picked himself up, trembling, met Shandor's fist, and sprawled again, a trickle of blood appearing at his mouth. "Harry Dartmouth has the files," he groaned. "They're probably in Chicago now."

"What do you know about Harry Dartmouth?"

Mariel gained a chair this time before Shandor hit him. "I've only met him a couple of times. He's the president of Dartmouth Bearing Corporation and he's my boss—Dartmouth Bearing publishes '*Fighting World*.' I do what he tells me."

Shandor's eyes flared. "Including murder, is that right?" Mariel's eyes were sullen. "Come on, talk! Why did Dartmouth want Ingersoll's personal files?"

The man just stared sullenly at the floor. Prex pressed a stud on the side of the shiny instrument, and a purple flash caught Mariel's little finger. Mariel jerked and squealed with pain. "Speak up," said Shandor. "I didn't hear you."

"Probably about the bonds," Mariel whimpered. His face was ashen, and he eyed Prex with undisguised pleading. "Look, tell him to put that thing away—"

Shandor grinned without humor. "You don't like scalders, eh? Get a big enough dose, and you're dead, Mariel—but I guess you know that, don't you? Think about it. But don't think too long. What about the bonds?"

"Ingersoll has been trying to get Dartmouth Bearing Corporation on legal grounds for years. Something about the government bonds they held, bought during the China wars. You know, surplus profits—Dartmouth Bearing could beat the taxes by buying bonds. Harry Dartmouth thought Ingersoll's files had some legal dope against them—he was afraid you'd try to make trouble for the company—"

"So he hired his little pixie, eh? Seems to me you'd have enough on your hands editing that rag—"

Mariel shot him an injured look. "'*Fighting World*' has the second largest magazine circulation in the country. It's a good magazine."

"It's a warmonger propaganda rag," snapped Shandor. He glared at the little man. "What's your relation to Ingersoll?"

"I hated his guts. He was carrying his lily-livered pacifism right to the White House, and I couldn't see it. So I fought him every inch of the way. I'll fight what he stands for now he's dead—"

Shandor's eyes narrowed. "That was a mistake, Mariel. You weren't supposed to know he is dead." He walked over to the little man, whose face was a shade whiter yet. "Funny," said Shandor quietly. "You say you hated him, but I didn't get that impression at all."

Mariel's eyes opened wide. "What do you mean?"

"Everything you wrote for PIB seems to have treated him kindly."

A shadow of deep concern crossed Mariel's face, as though for the first time he found himself in deep water. "PIB told me what to write, and I wrote it. You know how they work."

"Yes, I know how they work. I also know that most of your writing, while you were doing Public Information Board work, was never ordered by PIB. Ever hear of Ben Chamberlain, Mariel? Or Frank Eberhardt? Or Jon Harding? Ever hear of them, Mariel?" Shandor's voice cut sharply through the room. "Ben Chamberlain wrote for every large circulation magazine in the country, after the Chinese war. Frank Eberhardt was the man behind Associated Press during those years. Jon Harding was the silent publisher of three newspapers in Washington, two in New York, and one in Chicago. Ever hear of those men, Mariel?"

"No, no—"

"You know damned well you've heard of them. Because *those men were all you.* Every single one of them—" Shandor was standing close to him, now, and Mariel sat like he had seen a ghost, his lower lip quivering, forehead wet. "No, no, you're wrong—"

"No, no, I'm right," mocked Shandor. "I've been in the newspaper racket for a long time, Mariel. I've got friends in PIB—real friends, not the shamus crowd you're acquainted with that'll take you for your last nickel and then leave you to starve. Never mind how I found out. You hated Ingersoll so much you handed him bouquets all the time. How about it, Mariel? All that writing—you couldn't praise him enough. Boosting him, beating the drum for him and his policies—every trick and gimmick known in the propaganda game to give him a boost, make him the people's darling—how about it?"

Mariel was shaking his head, his little eyes nearly popping with fright. "It wasn't him," he choked. "Ingersoll had nothing to do with it. It was Dartmouth Bearing. They bought me into the spots. Got me the newspapers, supported me. Dartmouth Bearing ran the whole works, and they told me what to write—"

"Garbage! Dartmouth Bearing—the biggest munitions people in America, and I'm supposed to believe that they told you to go to bat for the country's strongest pacifist! What kind of sap do you take me for?"

"It's true! Ingersoll had nothing to do with it, nothing at all." Mariel's voice was almost pleading. "Look, I don't know what Dartmouth Bearing had in mind. Who was I to ask questions? You don't realize their power, Shandor. Those bonds I spoke of— they hold millions of dollars worth of bonds! They hold enough bonds to topple the economy of the nation, they've got bonds in the names of ten thousand subsidiary companies. They've been telling Federal Economics Commission what to do for the past ten years! And they're getting us into this war, Shandor—lock, stock and barrel. They pushed for everything they could get, and they had the money, the power, the men to do whatever they wanted. You couldn't fight them, because they had everything sewed up so tight nobody could approach them—"

Shandor's mind was racing, the missing pieces beginning, suddenly, to come out of the haze. The incredible, twisted idea broke through again, staggering him, driving through his mind like icy steel. "Listen, Mariel. I swear I'll kill you if you lie to me, so you'd better tell the truth. Who put you on my trail? Who told you Ingersoll was dead, and that I was scraping up Ingersoll's past?"

The little man twisted his hands, almost in tears. "Harry Dartmouth told me—"

"And who told Harry Dartmouth?"

Mariel's voice was so weak it could hardly be heard. "The girl," he said.

Shandor felt the chill deepen. "And where are the files now?"

"Dartmouth has them. Probably in Chicago—I expressed them. The girl didn't dare send them direct, for fear you would check, or that she was being watched. I was supposed to pick them up from you, and see to it that you didn't remember—"

Shandor clenched his fist. "Where are Dartmouth's plants located?"

"The main plants are in Chicago and Newark. They've got a smaller one in Nevada."

"And what do they make?"

"In peacetime—cars. In wartime they make tanks and shells."

"And their records? Inventories? Shipping orders, and files? Where do they keep them?"

"I—I don't know. You aren't thinking of—"

"Never mind what I'm thinking of, just answer up. Where are they?"

"All the administration offices are in Chicago. But they'd kill you, Shandor—you wouldn't stand a chance. They can't be fought, I tell you."

Shandor nodded to Prex, and started for the door. "Keep him here until dawn, then go on home, and forget what you heard. If anything happens, give me a ring at my home." He glared at Mariel. "Don't worry about me, bud—they won't be doing anything to me when I get through with them. They just won't be doing anything at all."

*   *   *   *   *

The idea had crystallized as he talked to Mariel. Shandor's mind was whirling as he walked down toward the thoroughfare. Incredulously, he tried to piece the picture together. He had known Dartmouth Bearing was big—but that big? Mariel might have been talking nonsense, or he might have been reading the Gospel. Shandor hailed a cab, sat back in the seat scratching his head. How big could Dartmouth Bearing be? Could *any* corporation be that big? He thought back, remembering the rash of post-war scandals and profit-gouging trials, the anti-trust trials. In wartime, bars are let down, *no one* can look with disfavor on the factories making the weapons. And if one corporation could buy, and expand, and buy some more—it might be too powerful to be prosecuted after the war—

Shandor shook his head, realizing that he was skirting the big issue. Dartmouth Bearing connected up, in some absurd fashion, but there was a missing link. Mariel fit into one side of the puzzle, interlocking with Dartmouth. The stolen files might even fit, for that matter. But the idea grew stronger. A great, jagged piece in the middle of the puzzle was missing—the key piece which would tie everything together. He felt his skin prickle as he thought. An impossible idea—and yet, he realized, if it were true, everything else would fall clearly into place—

He sat bolt upright. It *had* to be true—

He leaned forward and gave the cabby the landing field address, then sat back, feeling his pulse pounding through his arms and legs. Nervously he switched on the radio. The dial fell to some jazz music, which he tolerated for a moment or two, then flipped to a news broadcast. Not that news broadcasts really meant much, but he wanted to hear the Ingersoll story release for the day. He listened impatiently to a roundup of local news: David Ingersoll stricken with pneumonia, three Senators protesting the current tax bill—he brought his attention around sharply at the sound of a familiar name—

"—disappeared from his Chicago home early this morning. Mr. Dartmouth is president of Dartmouth Bearing Corporation, currently engaged in the manufacture of munitions for Defense, and producing much of the machinery being used in the Moon-rocket in Arizona. Police are following all possible leads, and are confident that there has been no foul play.

"On the international scene, the Kremlin is still blocking—" Shandor snapped off the radio abruptly, his forehead damp. Dartmouth disappeared, and with him the files—why? And where to go now to find them? If the idea that was plaguing him was true, sound, valid—he'd *have* to have the files. His whole body was wet with perspiration as he reached the landing field.

The trip to the Library of Congress seemed endless, yet he knew that the Library wouldn't be open until 8:00 anyway. Suddenly he felt a wave of extreme weariness sweep over him— when had he last slept? Bored, he snapped the telephone switch and rang PIB offices for his mail. To his surprise, John Hart took the wire, and exploded in his ear, "Where in hell have you been? I've been trying to get you all night. Listen, Tom, drop the Ingersoll story cold, and get in here. The faster the better."

Shandor blinked. "Drop the story? You're crazy!"

"*Get in here!*" roared Hart. "From now on you've *really* got a job. The Berlin Conference blew up tonight, Tom—high as a kite. *We're at war with Russia*—"

Carefully, Shandor plopped the receiver down on its hook, his hands like ice. Just one item first, he thought, just one thing I've got to know. *Then* back to PIB, maybe.

He found a booth in the Library, and began hunting, time pressing him into frantic speed. The idea was incredible, but it *had* to be true. He searched the micro-film files for three hours before he found it, in a "Who's Who" dating back to 1958, three years before the war with China. A simple, innocuous listing, which froze him to his seat. He read it, unbelievingly, yet knowing that it was the only possible link. Finally he read it again.

David P. Ingersoll. Born 1922, married 1947. Educated at Rutgers University and MIT. Worked as administrator for International Harvester until 1955. Taught Harvard University from 1955 to 1957.

David P. Ingersoll, becoming, in 1958, the executive president of Dartmouth Bearing Corporation....

*   *   *   *   *

He found a small, wooded glade not far from the Library, and set the 'copter down skillfully, his mind numbed, fighting to see through the haze to the core of incredible truth he had uncovered. The great, jagged piece, so long missing, was suddenly plopped right down into the middle of the puzzle, and now it didn't fit. There were still holes, holes that obscured the picture and twisted it into a nightmarish impossibility. He snapped the telephone switch, tried three numbers without any success, and finally reached the fourth. He heard Dr. Prex's sharp voice on the wire.

"Anything happen since I left, Prex?"

"Nothing remarkable." The doctor's voice sounded tired. "Somebody tried to call Mariel on the visiphone about an hour after you had gone, and then signed off in a hurry when he saw somebody else around. Don't know who it was, but he sounded mighty agitated." The doctor's voice paused. "Anything new, Tom?"

"Plenty," growled Shandor bitterly. "But you'll have to read it in the newspapers." He flipped off the connection before Prex could reply.

Then Shandor sank back and slept, the sleep of total exhaustion, hoping that a rest would make the shimmering, indefinite picture hold still long enough for him to study it. And as he drifted into troubled sleep a greater and more pressing question wormed upward into his mind.

He woke with a jolt, just as the sun was going down, and he knew then with perfect clarity what he had to do. He checked quickly to see that he had been undisturbed, and then manipulated the controls of the 'copter. Easing the ship into the sky toward Washington, he searched out a news report on the radio, listened with a dull feeling in the pit of his stomach as the story came through about the breakdown of the Berlin Conference, the declaration of war, the President's meeting with Congress that morning, his formal request for full wartime power, the granting of permission by a wide-eyed, frightened legislature. Shandor settled back, staring dully at the ground moving below him, the whisps of evening haze rising over the darkening land. There was only one thing to do. He had to have Ingersoll's files. He knew only one way to get them.

Half an hour later he was settling the ship down, under cover of darkness, on the vast grounds behind the Ingersoll estate, cutting the motors to effect a quiet landing. Tramping down the ravine toward the huge house, he saw it was dark; down by the gate he could see the Security Guard, standing in a haze of blue cigarette smoke under the dim-out lights. Cautiously he slipped across the back terrace, crossing behind the house, and jangled a bell on a side porch.

Ann Ingersoll opened the door, and gasped as Shandor forced his way in. "Keep quiet," he hissed, slipping the door shut behind him. Then he sighed, and walked through the entrance into the large front room.

"Tom! Oh, Tom, I was afraid— Oh, *Tom*!" Suddenly she was in his arms sobbing, pressing her face against his shirt front. "Oh, I'm so glad to see you, Tom—"

He disengaged her, turning from her and walking across the room. "Let's turn it off, Ann," he said disgustedly. "It's not very impressive."

"Tom—I—I *wanted* to tell you. I just didn't know what to do. I didn't believe them when they said you wouldn't be harmed, I was afraid. Oh, Tom, I wanted to tell you, believe me—"

"You didn't tell me," he snapped. "They were nervous, they slipped up. That's the only reason I'm alive. They planned to kill me."

She stared at him tearfully, shaking her head from side to side, searching for words. "I—I didn't want that—"

He whirled, his eyes blazing. "You silly fool, what do you think you're doing when you play games with a mob like this? Do you think they're going to play fair? You're no clod, you know better than that—" He leaned over her, trembling with anger. "You set me up for a sucker, but the plan fell through. And now I'm running around loose, and if you thought I was dangerous before, you haven't seen anything like how dangerous I am now. You're going to tell me some things, now, and you're going to tell them straight. You're going to tell me where Harry Dartmouth went with those files, where they are right now. Understand that? *I want those files.* Because when I have them I'm going to do exactly what I started out to do. I'm going to write a story, the whole rotten story about your precious father and his two-faced life. I'm going to write about Dartmouth Bearing Corporation and all its flunky outfits, and tell what they've done to this country and the people of this country." He paused, breathing heavily, and sank down on a chair, staring at her. "I've learned things in the past twenty-four hours I never dreamed could be true. I should be able to believe anything, I suppose, but these things knocked my stilts out from under me. This country has been had—right straight down the line, for a dozen years. We've been sold down the river like a pack of slaves, and now we're going to get a look at the cold ugly truth, for once."

She stared at him. "What do you mean—about my precious father—?"

"Your precious father was at the bottom of the whole slimy mess."

"No, no—not dad." She shook her head, her face chalky. "Harry Dartmouth, maybe, but not dad. Listen a minute. I didn't set you up for anything. I didn't know what Dartmouth and Mariel were up to. Dad left instructions for me to contact Harry Dartmouth immediately, in case he died. He told me that—oh, a year ago. Told me that before I did anything else, I should contact Dartmouth, and do as he said. So when he died, I contacted Harry, and kept in contact with him. He told me you were out to burn my father, to heap garbage on him after he was dead before the people who loved him, and he said the first thing you would want would be his personal files. Tom, I didn't know you, then—I knew Harry, and knew that dad trusted him, for some reason, so I believed him. But I began to realize that what he said wasn't true. I got the files, and he said to give them to you, to string you along, and he'd pick them up from you before you had a chance to do any harm with them. He said he wouldn't hurt you, but I—I didn't believe him, Tom. I believed you, that you wanted to give dad a fair shake—"

Shandor was on his feet, his eyes blazing. "So you turned them over to Dartmouth anyway? And what do you think he's done with them? Can you tell me that? Where has he gone? Has he burnt them? If not, what's he going to do with them?"

Her voice was weak, and she looked as if she were about to faint. "That's what I'm trying to tell you," she said, shakily. "He doesn't have them. I have them."

Shandor's jaw dropped. "Now, wait a minute," he said softly. "You gave me the briefcase, Mariel snatched it and nearly killed me—"

"A dummy, Tom. I didn't know who to trust, but I knew I believed you more than I believed Harry. Things happened so fast, and I was so confused—" She looked straight at him. "I gave you a dummy, Tom."

His knees walked out from under him, then, and he sank into a chair. "You've got them here, then," he said weakly.

"Yes. I have them here."

*   *   *   *   *

The room was in the back of the house, a small, crowded study, with a green-shaded desk lamp. Shandor dumped the contents of the briefcase onto the desk, and settled down, his heart pounding in his throat. He started at the top of the pile, sifting, ripping out huge sheafs of papers, receipts, notes, journals, clippings. He hardly noticed when the girl slipped out of the room, and he was deep in study when she returned half an hour later with steaming black coffee. With a grunt of thanks he drank it, never shifting his attention from the scatter of papers, papers from the personal file of a dead man. And slowly, the picture unfolded.

An ugly picture. A picture of deceit, a picture full of lies, full of secret promises, a picture of scheming, of plotting, planning, influencing, coercing, cheating, propagandizing—all with one single-minded aim, with a single terrible goal.

Shandor read, numbly, his mind twisting in protest as the picture unfolded. David Ingersoll's control of Dartmouth Bearing Corporation and its growing horde of subsidiaries under the figurehead of his protege, Harry Dartmouth. The huge profits from the Chinese war, the relaxation of control laws, the millions of war-won dollars ploughed back into government bonds, in a thousand different names, all controlled by Dartmouth Bearing Corporation—

And Ingersoll's own work in the diplomatic field—an incredibly skillful, incredibly evil channeling of power and pressure toward the inevitable goal, hidden under the cloak of peaceful respectability and popular support. The careful treaties, quietly disorganizing a dozen national economics, antagonizing the great nation to the East under the all too acceptable guise of "peace through strength." Reciprocal trade agreements bitterly antagonistic to Russian economic development. The continual bickering, the skillful manipulation hidden under the powerful propaganda cloak of a hundred publications, all coursing to one ultimate, terrible goal, all with one purpose, one aim—

War. War with anybody, war in the field and war on the diplomatic front. Traces even remained of the work done within the enemy nations, bitter anti-Ingersoll propaganda from within the ranks of Russia herself, manipulated to strengthen Ingersoll in America, to build him up, to drive the nations farther apart, while presenting Ingersoll as the pathetic prince of world peace, fighting desperately to stop the ponderous wheels of the irresistible juggernaut—

And in America, the constant, unremitting literary and editorial drumbeating, pressuring greater war preparation, distilling hatreds in a thousand circles, focussing them into a single channel. Tremendous propaganda pressure to build armies, to build weapons, to get the Moon-rocket project underway—

Shandor sat back, eyes drooping, fighting to keep his eyes open. His mind was numb, his body trembling. A sheaf of papers in a separate folder caught his eye, production records of the Dartmouth Bearing Corporation, almost up to the date of Ingersoll's death. Shandor frowned, a snag in the chain drawing his attention. He peered at the papers, vaguely puzzled. Invoices from the Chicago plant, materials for tanks, and guns, and shells. Steel, chemicals. The same for the New Jersey plant, the same with a dozen subsidiary plants. Shipments of magnesium and silver wire to the Rocket Project in Arizona, carried through several subsidiary offices. The construction of a huge calculator for the Project in Arizona. Motors and materials, all for Arizona—something caught his mind, brought a frown to his large bland face, some off-key note in the monstrous symphony of production and intrigue that threw up a red flag in his mind, screamed for attention—

And then he sipped the fresh coffee at his elbow and sighed, and looked up at the girl standing there, saw her hand tremble as she steadied herself against the desk, and sat down beside him. He felt a great confusion, suddenly, a vast sympathy for this girl, and he wanted to take her in his arms, hold her close, *protect* her, somehow. She didn't know, she *couldn't* know about this horrible thing. She couldn't have been a party to it, a part of it. He knew the evidence said yes, she knows the whole story, she *helped* them, but he also knew that the evidence, somehow, was wrong, that somehow, he still didn't have the whole picture—

She looked at him, her voice trembling. "You're wrong, Tom," she said.

He shook his head, helplessly. "I'm sorry. It's horrible, I know. But I'm not wrong. This war was planned. We've been puppets on strings, and one man engineered it, from the very start. Your father."

Her eyes were filled with tears, and she shook her head, running a tired hand across her forehead. "You didn't know him, Tom. If you did, you'd know how wrong you are. He was a great man, fine man, but above all he was a *good* man. Only a monster could have done what you're thinking. Dad hated war, he fought it all his life. He couldn't be the monster you think."

Tom's voice was soft in the darkened room, his eyes catching the downcast face of the trembling girl, fighting to believe in a phantom, and his hatred for the power that could trample a faith like that suddenly swelled up in bitter hopeless rage. "It's here, on paper, it can't be denied. It's hateful, but it's here, it's what I set out to learn. It's not a lie this time, Ann, it's the truth, and this time it's *got to be told*. I've written my last false story. This one is going to the people the way it is. This one is going to be the truth."

He stopped, staring at her. The puzzling, twisted hole in the puzzle was suddenly there, staring him in the face, falling down into place in his mind with blazing clarity. Staring, he dived into the pile of papers again, searching, frantically searching for the missing piece, something he had seen, and passed over, the one single piece in the story that didn't make sense. And he found it, on the lists of materials shipped to the Nevada plant. Pig Iron. Raw magnesium. Raw copper. Steel, electron tubes, plastics, from all parts of the country, all being shipped to the Dartmouth Plant in Nevada—

Where they made only shells—

At first he thought it was only a rumble in his mind, the shocking realization storming through. Then he saw Ann jump up suddenly, white-faced and race to the window, and he heard the small scream in her throat. And then the rumbling grew louder, stronger, and the house trembled. He heard the whine of jet planes scream over the house as he joined her at the window, heard the screaming whines mingled with the rumbling thunder. And far away, on the horizon, the red glare was glowing, rising, burning up to a roaring conflagration in the black night sky—

"Washington!" Her voice was small, infinitely frightened.

"Yes. That's Washington."

"Then it really *has* started." She turned to him with eyes wide with horror, and snuggled up to his chest like a frightened child. "Oh, Tom—"

"It's here. What we've been waiting for. What your father started could never be stopped any other way than this—"

The roar was louder now, rising to a whining scream as another squad of dark ships roared overhead, moving East and

South, jets whistling in the night. "This is what your father wanted."

She was crying, great sobs shaking her shoulders. "You're wrong, you're wrong—oh, Tom, you must be wrong—"

His voice was low, almost inaudible in the thundering roar of the bombardment. "Ann, I've got to go ahead. I've got to go tonight. To Nevada, to the Dartmouth plant there. I know I'm right, but I have to go, to check something—to make sure of something." He paused, looking down at her. "I'll be back, Ann. But I'm afraid of what I'll find out there. I need you behind me. Especially with what I have to do, I need you. You've got to decide. Are you for me? Or against me?"

She shook her head sadly, and sank into a chair, gently removing his hands from her waist. "I loved my father, Tom," she said in a beaten voice. "I can't help what he's done—I loved him. I—I can't be with you, Tom."

*   *   *   *   *

Far below him he could see the cars jamming the roads leaving Washington. He could almost hear the noise, the screeching of brakes, the fistfights, the shouts, the blatting of horns. He moved south over open country, hoping to avoid the places where the 'copter might be spotted and stopped for questioning. He knew that Hart would have an alarm out for him by now, and he didn't dare risk being stopped until he reached his destination, the place where the last piece to the puzzle could be found, the answer to the question that was burning through his mind. Shells were made of steel and chemicals. The tools that made them were also made of steel. Not manganese. Not copper. Not electron relays, nor plastic, nor liquid oxygen. Just steel.

The 'copter relayed south and then turned west over Kentucky. Shandor checked the auxiliary tanks which he had filled at the Library landing field that morning; then he turned the ship to robot controls and sank back in the seat to rest. His whole body clamored for sleep, but he knew he dare not sleep. Any slip, any contact with Army aircraft or Security patrol could throw everything into the fire— For hours he sat, gazing hypnotically at the black expanse of land below, flying high over the pitch-black countryside. Not a light showed, not a sign of life.

Bored, he flipped the radio button, located a news broadcast. "—the bombed area did not extend west of the Appalachians. Washington DC was badly hit, as were New York and Philadelphia, and further raids are expected to originate from Siberia, coming across the great circle to the West coast or the Middle west. So far the Enemy appears to have lived up to its agreement in the Ingersoll pact to outlaw use of atomic bombs, for no atomic weapons have been used so far, but the damage with block-busters has been heavy. All citizens are urged to maintain strictest blackout regulations, and to report as called upon in local work and civil defense pools as they are set up. The attack began—"

Shandor sighed, checked his instrument readings. Far in the East the horizon was beginning to lighten, a healthy, white-grey light. His calculations placed him over Eastern Nebraska, and a few moments later he nosed down cautiously and verified his location. Lincoln Airbase was in a flurry of activity; the field was alive with men, like little black ants, preparing the reserve fighters and pursuits for use in a fever of urgent speed. Suddenly the 'copter radio bleeped, and Tom threw the switch. "Over."

An angry voice snarled, "You up there, whoever you are, where'd you leave your brains? No civilian craft are allowed in the air, and that's orders straight from Washington. Don't you know there's a war on? Now get down here, before you're shot down—"

Shandor thought quickly. "This is a Federal Security ship," he snapped. "I'm just on a reconnaissance—"

The voice was cautious. "Security? What's your corroboration number?"

Shandor cursed. "JF223R-864. Name is Jerry Chandler. Give it a check if you want to." He flipped the switch, and accelerated for the ridge of hills that marked the Colorado border as the radio signal continued to bleep angrily, and a trio of pursuit planes on the ground began warming up. Shandor sighed, hoping they would check before they sent ships after him. It might at least delay them until he reached his destination.

Another hour carried him to the heart of the Rockies, and across the great salt fields of Utah. His fuel tanks were low, being emptied one by one as the tiny ship sped through the bright morning sky, and Tom was growing uneasy, until suddenly, far to the west and slightly to the north he spotted the plant, nestling in the mountain foothills. It lay far below, sprawling like some sort of giant spider across the rugged terrain. Several hundred cars spread out to the south of the plant, and he could see others speeding in from the temporary village across the ridge. Everything was quiet, orderly. He could see the shipments, crated, sitting in freight cars to the north. And then he saw the drill line running over to the right of the plant. He followed it, quickly checking a topographical map in the cockpit, and his heart started pounding. The railroad branch ran between two low peaks and curved out toward the desert. Moving over it, he saw the curve, saw it as it cut off to the left— and seemed to stop dead in the middle of the desert sand—

Shandor circled even lower, keeping one ear cocked on the radio, and settled the ship on the railroad line. And just as he cut the motors, he heard the shrill whine of three pursuit ships screaming in from the Eastern horizon—

He was out of the 'copter almost as soon as it had touched, throwing a jacket over his arm, and racing for the place where the drill line ended. Because he had seen as he slid in for a landing, just what he had suspected from the topographical map. The drill didn't end in the middle of a desert at all. It went right on into the mountainside.

The excavation was quite large, the entrance covered and camouflaged neatly to give the very impression that he had gotten from the air. Under the camouflage the space was crowded, stacked with crates, boxes, materials, stacked all along the walls of the tunnel. He followed the rails in, lighting his way with a small pocket flashlight when the tunnel turned a corner, cutting off the daylight. Suddenly the tunnel widened, opening out into a much wider room. He sensed, rather than saw, the immense size of the vault, smelt the odd, bitter odor in the air. With the flashlight he probed the darkness, spotting the high, vaulted ceiling above him. And below him—

At first he couldn't see, probing the vast excavation before him, and then, strangely, he saw but couldn't realize what he saw. He stared for a solid minute, uncomprehending, then, stifling a gasp, he *knew what he was looking at—*

Lights. He had to have lights, to see clearly what he couldn't believe. Frantically, he spun the flashlight, seeking a light panel, and then, fascinated, he turned the little oval of light back to the pit. And then he heard the barest whisper of sound, the faintest intake of breath, and he ducked, frozen, as a blow whistled past his ear. A second blow from the side caught him solidly in the blackness, grunting, flailing out into a tangle of legs and arms, cursing, catching a foot in his face, striking up into soft, yielding flesh—

And his head suddenly exploded into a million dazzling lights as he sank unconscious to the ground—

                    *   *   *   *   *

It was a tiny room, completely without windows, the artificial light filtering through from ventilation slits near the top. Shandor sat up, shaking as the chill in the room became painfully evident. A small electric heater sat in the corner beaming valiantly, but the heat hardly reached his numbed toes. He stood up, shaking himself, slapping his arms against his sides to drive off the coldness—and he heard a noise through the door as soon as he had made a sound.

Muted footsteps stopped outside the door, and a huge man stepped inside. He looked at Shandor carefully, then closed the door behind him, without locking it. "I'm Baker," he rasped cheerfully. "How are you feeling?"

Shandor rubbed his head, suddenly and acutely aware of a very sore nose and a bruised rib cage. "Not so hot," he muttered. "How long have I been out?"

"Long enough." The man pulled out a plug of tobacco, ripped off a chunk with his teeth. "Chew?"

"I smoke." Shandor fished for cigarettes in an empty pocket.

"Not in here you don't," said Baker. He shrugged his huge shoulders and settled affably down on a bench near the wall. "You feel like talking?"

Shandor eyed the unlocked door, and turned his eyes to the huge man. "Sure," he said. "What do you want to talk about?"

"I don't want to talk about nothin'," the big man replied, indifferently. "Thought you might, though."

"Are you the one that roughed me up?"

"Yuh." Baker grinned. "Hope I didn't hurt you much. Boss said to keep you in one piece, but we had to hurry up, and take care of those Army guys you brought in on your tail. That was dumb. You almost upset everything."

Memory flooded back, and Shandor's eyes widened. "Yes—they followed me all the way from Lincoln—what happened to them?"

Baker grinned and chomped his tobacco. "They're a long way away now. Don't worry about them."

Shandor eyed the door uneasily. The latch hadn't caught, and the door had swung open an inch or two. "Where am I?" he asked, inching toward the door. "What—what are you planning to do to me?"

Baker watched him edging away. "You're safe," he said. "The boss'll talk to you pretty soon if you feel like it—" He squinted at Tom in surprise, pointing an indolent thumb toward the door. "You planning to go out or something?"

Tom stopped short, his face red. The big man shrugged. "Go ahead. I ain't going to stop you." He grinned. "Go as far as you can."

Without a word Shandor threw open the door, looked out into the concrete corridor. At the end was a large, bright room. Cautiously he started down, then suddenly let out a cry and broke into a run, his eyes wide—

He reached the room, a large room, with heavy plastic windows. He ran to one of the windows, pulse pounding, and stared, a cry choking in his throat. The blackness of the crags contrasted dimly with the inky blackness of the sky beyond. Mile upon mile of jagged, rocky crags, black rock, ageless, unaged rock. And it struck him with a jolt how easily he had been able to run, how lightning-swift his movements. He stared again, and then he saw what he had seen in the pit, standing high outside the building on a rocky flat, standing bright and silvery, like a phantom finger pointing to the inky heavens, sleek, smooth, resting on polished tailfins, like an other-worldly bird poised for flight—

A voice behind him said, "You aren't really going anyplace, you know. Why run?" It was a soft voice, a kindly voice, cultured, not rough and biting like Baker's voice. It came from directly behind Shandor, and he felt his skin crawl. He had heard that voice before—many times before. Even in his dreams he had heard that voice. "You see, it's pretty cold out there. And there isn't any air. You're on the Moon, Mr. Shandor—"

He whirled, his face twisted and white. And he stared at the small figure standing at the door, a stoop-shouldered man, white hair slightly untidy, crow's-feet about his tired eyes. An old man, with eyes that carried a sparkle of youth and kindliness. The eyes of David P. Ingersoll.

*   *   *   *   *

Shandor stared for a long moment, shaking his head like a man seeing a phantom. When he found words, his voice was choked, the words wrenched out as if by force. "You're—you're alive."

"Yes. I'm alive."

"Then—" Shandor shook his head violently, turning to the window, and back to the small, white-haired man. "Then your death was just a fake."

The old man nodded tiredly. "That's right. Just a fake."

Shandor stumbled to a chair, sat down woodenly. "I don't get it," he said dully. "I just don't get it. The war—that—that I can see. I can see how you worked it, how you engineered it, but this—" he gestured feebly at the window, at the black, impossible landscape outside. "This I can't see. They're bombing us to pieces, they're bombing out Washington, probably your own home, your own family—last night—" he stopped, frowning in confusion—"no, it couldn't have been last night—two days ago?—well, whatever day it was, they were bombing us to pieces, and you're up here—*why*? What's it going to get you? This war, this whole rotten intrigue mess, and then *this*?"

The old man walked across the room and stared for a moment at the silent ship outside. "I hope I can make you understand. We had to come here. We had no choice. We couldn't do what we wanted any other way than to come here—*first*. Before anybody else."

"But why *here*? They're building a rocket there in Arizona. They'll be up here in a few days, maybe a few weeks—"

"Approximately forty-eight hours," corrected Ingersoll quietly. "Within forty-eight hours the Arizona rocket will be here. If the Russian rocket doesn't get here first."

"It doesn't make sense. It won't do you any good to be here if the Earth is blasted to bits. Why come here? And why bring *me* here, of all people? What do you want with me?"

Ingersoll smiled and sat down opposite Shandor. "Take it easy," he said gently. "You're here, you're safe, and you're going to get the whole story. I realize that this is a bit of a jolt—but you had to be jolted. With you I think the jolt will be very beneficial, since we want you with us. That's why we brought you here. We need your help, and we need it very badly. It's as simple as that."

Shandor was on his feet, his eyes blazing. "No dice. This is your game, not mine. I don't want anything to do with it—"

"But you don't know the game—"

"I know plenty of the game. I followed the trail, right from the start. I know the whole rotten mess. The trail led me all the way around Robin Hood's barn, but it told me things—oh, it told me plenty! It told me about you, and this war. And now you want me to help you! What do you want me to do? Go down and tell the people it isn't really so bad being pounded to shreds? Should I tell them they aren't really being bombed, it's all in their minds? Shall I tell them this is a war to defend their freedoms, that it's a great crusade against the evil forces of the world? What kind of a sap do you think I am?" He walked to the window, his whole body trembling with anger. "I followed this trail down to the end, I scraped my way down into the dirtiest, slimiest depths of the barrel, and I've found you down there, and your rotten corporations, and your crowd of heelers. And on the other side are three hundred million people taking the lash end of the whip on Earth, helping to feed you. And you ask me to help you!"

"Once upon a time," Ingersoll interrupted quietly, "there was a fox."

Shandor stopped and stared at him.

"—and the fox got caught in a trap. A big bear trap, with steel jaws, that clamped down on him and held him fast by the leg. He wrenched and he pulled, but he couldn't break that trap open, no matter what he did. And the fox knew that the farmer would come along almost any time to open that bear trap, and the fox knew the farmer would kill him. He knew that if he didn't get out of that trap, he'd be finished, sure as sin. But he was a clever fox, and he found a way to get out of the bear trap." Ingersoll's voice was low, tense in the still room. "Do you know what he did?"

Shandor shook his head silently.

"It was a very simple solution," said Ingersoll. "Drastic, but simple. *He gnawed off his leg.*"

Another man had entered the room, a small, weasel-faced man with sallow cheeks and slick black hair. Ingersoll looked up with a smile, but Mariel waved him on, and took a seat nearby.

"So he chewed off his leg," Shandor repeated dully. "I don't get it."

"The world is in a trap," said Ingersoll, watching Shandor with quiet eyes. "A great big bear trap. It's been in that trap for decades—ever since the first World War. The world has come to a wall it can't climb, a trap it can't get out of, a vicious, painful, torturous trap, and the world has been struggling for seven decades to get out. It hasn't succeeded. And the time is drawing rapidly nigh for the farmer to come. Something had to be done, and done fast, before it was too late. The fox had to chew off its leg. And I had to bring the world to the brink of a major war."

Shandor shook his head, his mind buzzing. "I don't see what you mean. We never had a chance for peace, we never had a chance to get our feet on the ground from one round to the next. No time to do anything worthwhile in the past seventy years—I don't see what you mean about a trap."

Ingersoll settled back in his chair, the light catching his face in sharp profile. "It's been a century of almost continuous war," he said. "You've pointed out the whole trouble. We haven't had time to catch our breath, to make a real peace. The first World War was a sorry affair, by our standards—almost a relic of earlier European wars. Trench fighting, poor rifles, soap-box aircraft—nothing to distinguish it from earlier wars but its scope. But twenty uneasy years went by, and another war began, a very different sort of war. This one had fast aircraft, fast mechanized forces, heavy bombing, and finally, to cap the climax, atomics. That second World War could hold up its head as a real, strapping, fighting war in any society of wars. It was a stiff war, and a terrible one. Quite a bit of progress, for twenty years. But essentially, it was a war of ideologies, just as the previous one had been. A war of intolerance, of unmixable ideas—"

The old man paused, and drew a sip of water from the canister in the corner. "Somewhere, somehow, the world had missed the boat. Those wars didn't solve anything, they didn't even make a very strong pretense. They just made things worse. Somewhere, human society had gotten into a trap, a vicious circle. It had reached the end of its progressive tether, it had no place to go, no place to expand, to great common goal. So ideologies arose to try to solve the dilemma of a basically static society, and they fought wars. And they reached a point, finally, where they could destroy themselves unless they broke the vicious circle, somehow."

Shandor looked up, a deep frown on his face. "You're trying to say that they needed a new frontier."

"Exactly! They desperately needed it. There was only one more frontier they could reach for. A frontier which, once attained, has no real end." He gestured toward the black landscape outside. "There's the frontier. Space. The one thing that could bring human wars to an end. A vast, limitless frontier which could drive men's spirits upward and outward for the rest of time. And that frontier seemed unattainable. It was blocked off by a wall, by the jaws of a trap. Oh, they tried. After the first war the work began. The second war contributed unimaginably to the technical knowledge. But after the second war, they could go no further. Because it cost money, it required a tremendous effort on the part of the people of a great nation to do it, and they couldn't see why they should spend the money to get to space. After all, they had to work up the atomics and new weapons for the next war—it was a trap, as strong and treacherous as any the people of the world had ever encountered.

"The answer, of course, was obvious. Each war brought a great surge of technological development, to build better weapons, to fight bigger wars. Some developments led to extremely beneficial ends, too—if it hadn't been for the second war, a certain British biologist might still be piddling around his understaffed, underpaid laboratory, wishing he had more money, and wondering why it was that that dirty patch of mold on his petri dish seemed to keep bacteria from growing—but the second war created a sudden, frantic, urgent demand for something, anything, that would *stop infection—fast.* And in no time, penicillin was in mass production, saving untold thousands of lives. There was no question of money. Look at the Manhattan project. How many millions went into that? It gave us atomic power, for war, and for peace. For peaceful purposes, the money would never have been spent. But if it was for the sake of war—"

Ingersoll smiled tiredly. "Sounds insane, doesn't it? But look at the record. I looked at the record, way back at the end of the war with China. Other men looked at the record, too. We got together, and talked. We knew that the military advantage of a rocket base on the moon could be a deciding factor in another major war. Military experts had recognized that fact back in the 1950's. Another war could give men the technological kick they needed to get them to space—possibly *in time.* If men got to space before they destroyed themselves, the trap would be broken, the frontier would be opened, and men could turn their energies away from destruction toward something infinitely greater and more important. With space on his hands men could get along without wars. But if we waited for peacetime to go to space, we might never make it. It might be too late.

"It was a dreadful undertaking. I saw the wealth in the company I directed and controlled at the end of the Chinese war, and the idea grew strong. I saw that a huge industrial amalgamation could be undertaken, and succeed. We had a weapon in our favor, the most dangerous weapon ever devised, a thousand times more potent than atomics. Hitler used it, with terrible success. Stalin used it. Haro-Tsing used it. Why couldn't Ingersoll use it? Propaganda—a terrible weapon. It could make people think the right way—it could make them think almost *any* way. It made them think war. From the end of the last war we started, with propaganda, with politics, with money. The group grew stronger as our power became more clearly understood. Mariel handled propaganda through the newspapers, and PIB, and magazines—a clever man—and Harry Dartmouth handled production. I handled the politics and diplomacy. We had but one aim in mind—to bring about a threat of major war that would drive men to space. To the moon, to a man-made satellite, *somewhere or anywhere* to break through the Earth's gravity and get to space. And we aimed at a controlled war. We had the power to do it, we had the money and the plants. We just had to be certain it wasn't the *ultimate* war. It wasn't easy to make sure that atomic weapons wouldn't be used this time—but they will not. Both nations are too much afraid, thanks to our propaganda program. They both leaped at a chance to make a face-saving agreement. And we hoped that the war could be held off until we got to the moon, and until the Arizona rocket project could get a ship launched for the moon. The wheels we had started just moved too fast. I saw at the beginning of the Berlin Conference that it would explode into war, so I decided the time for my 'death' had arrived. I had to come here, to make sure the war doesn't go on any longer than necessary."

Shandor looked up at the old man, his eyes tired. "I still don't see where I'm supposed to fit in. I don't see why you came here at all. Was that a wild-goose chase I ran down there, learning about this?"

"Not a wild goose chase. The important work can't start, you see, until the rocket gets here. It wouldn't do much good if the Arizona rocket got here, to fight the war. It may come for war, but it must go back for peace. We built this rocket to get us here first—built it from government specifications, though they didn't know it. We had the plant to build it in, and we were able to hire technologists *not* to find the right answers in Arizona until we were finished. Because the whole value of the war-threat depended solely and completely upon our getting here *first*. When the Arizona rocket gets to the moon, the war must be stopped. Only then can we start the real 'operation Bear Trap.' That ship, whether American or Russian, will meet with a great surprise when it reaches the Moon. We haven't been spotted here. We left in darkness and solitude, and if we were seen, it was chalked off as a guided missile. We're well camouflaged, and although we don't have any sort of elaborate base—just a couple of sealed rooms—we have a ship and we have weapons. When the first ship comes up here, the control of the situation will be in our hands. Because when it comes, it will be sent back with an ultimatum to *all* nations—to cease warfare, or suffer the most terrible, nonpartisan bombardment the world has ever seen. A pinpoint bombardment, from our ship, here on the Moon. There won't be too much bickering I think. The war will stop. All eyes will turn to us. And then the big work begins."

He smiled, his thin face showing tired lines in the bright light. "I may die before the work is done. I don't know, nor care. I have no successor, nor have we any plans to perpetuate our power once the work is done. As soon as the people themselves will take over the work, the job is theirs, because no group can hope to ultimately control space. But first people must be sold on space, from the bottom up. They must be forced to realize the implications of a ship on the moon. They must realize that the first ship was the hardest, that the trap is sprung. The amputation is a painful one, there wasn't any known anaesthetic, but it will heal, and from here there is no further need for war. But the people must see that, understand its importance. They've got to have the whole story, in terms that they can't mistake. And that means a propagandist—"

"You have Mariel," said Shandor. "He's had the work, the experience—"

"He's getting tired. He'll tell you himself his ideas are slow, he isn't on his toes any longer. He needs a new man, a helper, to take his place. When the first ship comes, his job is done." The old man smiled. "I've watched you, of course, for years. Mariel saw that you were given his job when he left PIB to edit *'Fighting World.'* He didn't think you were the man, he didn't trust you—thought you had been raised too strongly on the sort of gibberish you were writing. I thought you were the only man we could use. So we let you follow the trail, and watched to see how you'd handle it. And when you came to the Nevada plant, we *knew* you were the man we had to have—"

Shandor scowled, looking first at Ingersoll, then at Mariel's impassive face. "What about Ann?" he asked, and his voice was unsteady. "She knew about it all the time?"

"No. She didn't know anything about it. We were afraid she had upset things when she didn't turn my files over to Dartmouth as he'd told her. We were afraid you'd go ahead and write the story as you saw it then, which would have wrecked our plan completely. As it was, she helped us sidestep the danger in the long run, but she didn't know what she was really doing." He grinned. "The error was ours, of course. We simply underestimated our man. We didn't know you were that tenacious."

Shandor's face was haggard. "Look. I—I don't know what to think. This ship in Arizona—how long? When will it come? How do you know it'll ever come?"

"We waited until our agents there gave us a final report. The ship may be leaving at any time. But there's no doubt that it'll come. If it doesn't, one from Russia will. It won't be long." He looked at Shandor closely. "You'll have to decide by then, Tom."

"And if I don't go along with you?"

"We could lose. It's as simple as that. Without a spokesman, the plan could fall through completely. There's only one thing you need to make your decision, Tom—faith in men, and a sure conviction that man was made for the stars, and not for an endless circle of useless wars. Think of it, Tom. That's what your decision means."

Shandor walked to the window, stared out at the bleak landscape, watched the great bluish globe of earth, hanging like a huge balloon in the black sky. He saw the myriad pinpoints of light in the blackness on all sides of it, and shook his head, trying to think. So many things to think of, so very many things—

"I don't know," he muttered. "I just don't know—"

*   *   *   *   *

It was a long night. Ideas are cruel, they become a part of a man's brain, an inner part of his chemistry, they carve grooves deep in his mind which aren't easily wiped away. He knew he'd been living a lie, a bitter, hopeless, endless lie, all his life, but a liar grows to believe his own lies. Even to the point of destruction, he believes them. It was so hard to see the picture, now that he had the last piece in place.

A fox, and a bear trap. Such a simple analogy. War was a hellish proposition, it was cruel, it was evil. It could be lost, so very easily. And it seemed so completely, utterly senseless to cut off one's own leg—

And then he thought, somewhere, sometime, he'd see her again. Perhaps they'd be old by then, but perhaps not—perhaps they'd still be young, and perhaps she wouldn't know the true story yet. Perhaps he could be the first to tell her, to let her know that he had been wrong— Maybe there could be a chance to be happy, on Earth, sometime. They might marry, even, there might be children. To be raised for what? Wars and wars and more wars? Or was there another alternative? Perhaps the stars were winking brighter—

*   *   *   *   *

A hoarse shout rang through the quiet rooms. Ingersoll sat bolt upright, turned his bright eyes to Mariel, and looked down the passageway. And then they were crowding to the window as one of the men snapped off the lights in the room, and they were staring up at the pale bluish globe that hung in the sky, squinting, breathless—

And they saw the tiny, tiny burst of brightness on one side of that globe, saw a tiny whisp of yellow, cutting an arc from the edge, moving farther and farther into the black circle of space around the Earth, slicing like a thin scimitar, moving higher and higher, and then, magically, winking out, leaving a tiny, evaporating trail behind it.

"You saw it?" whispered Mariel in the darkness. "You saw it, David?"

"Yes. I saw it." Ingersoll breathed deeply, staring into the blackness, searching for a glimmer, a glint, some faint reassurance that it had not been a mirage they had seen. And then Ingersoll felt a hand in his, Tom Shandor's hand, gripping his tightly, wringing it, and when the lights snapped on again, he was staring at Shandor, tears of happiness streaming from his pale, tired eyes. "You saw it?" he whispered.

Shandor nodded, his heart suddenly too large for his chest, a peace settling down on him greater than any he had ever known in his life.

"They're coming," he said.

CONTAMINATION CREW

ILLUSTRATED BY ED EMSHWILLER
ORIGINALLY PUBLISHED IN *IF: WORLDS OF SCIENCE FICTION,*
FEBRUARY 1958

Orders were orders! The creature had to be killed.
But just how does one destroy the indestructible?

Contamination Crew

(*The following is taken from the files of the Medical Disciplinary Board, Hospital Earth, from the preliminary hearings in re: The Profession vs. Samuel B. Jenkins, Physician; First Court of Medical Affairs, final action pending.*)

COM COD S221VB73 VOROCHISLOV SECTOR; 4th GALACTIC PERIOD 22, 2341
GENERAL SURVEY SHIP MERCY TO HOSPITAL EARTH
VIA: FASTEST POSSIBLE ROUTING, PRIORITY UNASSIGNED
TO: Lucius Darby, Physician Grade I, Black Service Director of Galactic   Periphery Services, Hospital Earth
FROM: Samuel B. Jenkins, Physician Grade VI, Red Service General
Practice Patrol Ship *Lancet* (Attached GSS *Mercy* pro tem)

SIR: The following communication is directed to your attention in hopes that it may anticipate various charges which are certain to be placed against me as a Physician of the Red Service upon the return of the General Survey Ship *Mercy* to Hospital Earth (expected arrival four months from above date).

These charges will undoubtedly be preferred by one Turvold Neelsen, Physician Grade II of the Black Service, and Commander of the *Mercy* on its current survey mission into the Vorochislov Sector. Exactly what the charges will be I cannot say, since the Black Doctor in question refuses either audience or communication with me at the present time; however, it seems likely that treason, incompetence and mutinous insubordination will be among the milder complaints registered.

It is possible that even Malpractice might be added, so you can readily understand the reasons for this statement—

The following will also clarify my attached request that the GSS *Mercy*, upon arrival in orbit around Hospital Earth, be met immediately by a decontamination ship carrying a vat of hydrochloric acid, concentration 3.7%, measuring no less than twenty by thirty by fifty feet, and that Quarantine officials be prepared to place the entire crew of the *Mercy* under physical and psychiatric observation for a period of no less than six weeks upon disembarkation.

The facts, in brief, are as follows:

Three months ago, as crew of the General Practice Patrol Ship *Lancet*, my colleague Green Doctor Wallace Stone and myself began investigating certain peculiar conditions existing on the fourth planet of Mauki, Vorochislov Sector (Class I Medical Service Contract.) The entire population of that planet was found to be suffering from a mass psychotic delusion of rather spectacular proportions: namely, that they and their entire planet were in imminent danger of being devoured, in toto, by an indestructible non-humanoid creature which they called a *hlorg*. The Maukivi were insistent that a *hlorg* had already totally consumed a non-existent outer planet in their system, and was now hard at work on neighboring Mauki V. It was their morbid fear that Mauki IV was next on its list. No amount of reassurance could convince them of the foolishness of these fears, although we exhausted our energy, our patience, and our food and medical supplies in the effort. Ultimately we referred the matter to the Grey Service, feeling confident that it was a psychiatric problem rather than medical or surgical. We applied to the GSS *Mercy* to take us aboard to replenish our ship's supplies, and provide us a much-needed recovery period. The Black Doctor in command approved our request and brought us aboard.

The trouble began two days later....

*   *   *   *   *

There were three classes of dirty words in use by the men who travelled the spaceways back and forth from Hospital Earth.

There were the words you seldom used in public, but which were colorful and descriptive in private use.

Then there were the words which you seldom used even in private, but which effectively relieved feelings when directed at mirrors, inanimate objects, and people who had just left the room.

Finally, there were the words that you just didn't use, period. You knew they existed; you'd heard them used at one time or another, but to hear them spoken out in plain Earth-English was enough to rock the most space-hardened of the Galactic Pill Peddlers back on his well-worn heels.

Black Doctor Turvold Neelsen's Earth-English was spotty at best, but the word came through without any possibility of misinterpretation. Red Doctor Sam Jenkins stared at the little man and felt his face turning as scarlet as the lining of his uniform cape.

"But that's ridiculous!" he finally stammered. "Quite aside from the language you use to suggest it."

"Ah! So the word still has some punch left, eh? At least you puppies bring something away from your Medical Training, even if it's only taboos." The Black Doctor scowled across the desk at Jenkins' lanky figure. "But sometimes, my good Doctor, it is better to face a fact than to wait for the fact to face you. Sometimes we have to crawl out of our ivory towers for a minute or two—you know?"

Jenkins reddened again. He had never had any great love for physicians of the Black Service—who did?—but he found himself disliking this short, blunt-spoken man even more cordially than most. "Why implicate the *Lancet*?" he burst out. "You've landed the *Mercy* on plenty of planets before we brought the *Lancet* aboard her—"

"But we did not have it with us before the *Lancet* came aboard, and we do have it now. The implication is obvious. You have brought aboard a contaminant."

He'd said it again.

Red Doctor Jenkins' face darkened. "The Green Doctor and I have maintained the *Lancet* in perfect conformity with the Sterility Code. We've taken every precaution on both landing and disembarking procedures. What's more, we've spent the last three months on a planet with *no* mutually compatible flora or fauna. From Hospital Earth viewpoint, Mauki IV is sterile. We made only the briefest check-stop on Mauki V before joining you. It was a barren rock, but we decontaminated again after leaving. If you have a—a *contaminant* on board your ship, sir, it didn't come from the *Lancet*. And I won't be held responsible."

It was strong language to use to a Black Doctor, and Sam Jenkins knew it. There were doctors of the Green and Red Services who had spent their professional lives on some god-forsaken planetoid at the edge of the Galaxy for saying less. Red Doctor Sam Jenkins was too near the end of his Internship, too nearly ready for his first Permanent Planetary Appointment with the rank, honor, and responsibility it carried to lightly risk throwing it to the wind at this stage—

But a Red Doctor does not bring a contaminant aboard a survey ship, he thought doggedly, no matter what the Black Doctor says—

Neelsen looked at the young man slowly. Then he shrugged. "Of course, I'm merely a pathologist. I realize that we know nothing of medicine, nor of disease, nor of the manner in which disease is spread. All this is beyond our scope. But perhaps you'll permit one simple question from a dull old man, just to humor him."

Jenkins looked at the floor. "I'm sorry, sir."

"Just so. You've had a very successful cruise this year with the *Lancet*, I understand."

Jenkins nodded.

"A most successful cruise. Four planets elevated from Class IV to Class II contracts, they tell me. Morua II elevated from Class VI to Class I, with certain special riders. A plague-panic averted on Setman I, and a very complex virus-bacteria symbiosis unravelled on Orb III. An illustrious record. You and your colleague from the Green Service are hoping for a year's exemption from training, I imagine—" The Black Doctor looked up sharply. "You searched your holds after leaving the Mauki planets, I presume?"

Jenkins blinked. "Why—no, sir. That is, we decontaminated according to—"

"I see. You didn't search your holds. I suppose you didn't notice your food supplies dwindling at an alarming rate?"

"No—" The Red Doctor hesitated. "Not really."

"Ah." The Black Doctor closed his eyes wearily and flipped an activator switch. The scanner on the far wall buzzed into activity. It focussed on the rear storage hold of the *Mercy* where the little *Lancet* was resting on its landing rack. "Look closely, Doctor."

At first Jenkins saw nothing. Then his eye caught a long, pink glistening strand lying across the floor of the hold. The scanner picked up the strand, followed it to the place where it emerged from a neat pencil-sized hole in the hull of the *Lancet*. The strand snaked completely across the room and disappeared through another neat hole in the wall into the next storage hold.

Jenkins shook his head as the scanner flipped back to the hole in the *Lancet's* hull. Even as he watched, the hole enlarged and a pink blob began to emerge. The blob kept coming and coming until it rested soggily on the edge of the hole. Then it teetered and fell *splat* on the floor.

"Friend of yours?" the Black Doctor asked casually.

It was a pink heap of jelly just big enough to fill a scrub bucket. It sat on the floor, quivering noxiously. Then it sent out pseudopods in several directions, probing the metal floor. After a few moments it began oozing along the strand of itself that lay on the floor, and squeezed through the hole into the next hold.

"Ugh," said Sam Jenkins, feeling suddenly sick.

"The hydroponic tanks are in there," the Black Doctor said. "You've seen one of those before?"

"Not in person." Jenkins shook his head weakly. "Only pictures. It's a *hlorg*. We thought it was only a Maukivi persecution fantasy."

"This thing is growing pretty fast for a persecution fantasy. We spotted it eight hours ago, demolishing what was left of your food supply. It's twice as big now as it was then."

"Well, we've got to get rid of it," said Jenkins, suddenly coming to life.

"Amen, Doctor."

"I'll get the survey crew alerted right away. We won't waste a minute. And my apologies." Jenkins was hurrying for the door. "I'll get it cleared out of here fast."

"I do hope so," said the Black Doctor. "The thing makes me ill just to think about."

"I'll give you a clean-ship report in twenty-four hours," the Red Doctor said as confidently as he could and beat a hasty retreat down the corridor. He was wishing fervently that he felt as confident as he sounded.

The Maukivi had described the *hlorg* in excruciating detail. He and Green Doctor Stone had listened, and smiled sadly at each other, day after day, marvelling at the fanciful delusion. *Hlorgs*, indeed! And such creatures to dream up—eating, growing, devouring plant, animal and mineral without discrimination—

And the Maukivi had stoutly maintained that this *hlorg* of theirs was indestructible—

*   *   *   *   *

Green Doctor Wally Stone, true to his surgical calling, was a man of action.

"You mean there *is* such a thing?" he exploded when his partner confronted him with the news. "For real? Not just somebody's pipe dream?"

"There is," said Jenkins, "and we've got it. Here. On board the *Mercy*. It's eating like hell-and-gone and doubling its size every eight hours."

"Well what are you waiting for? Toss it overboard!"

"Fine! And what happens to the next party it happens to land on? We're supposed to be altruists, remember? We're supposed to worry about the health of the Galaxy." Jenkins shook his head. "Whatever we do with it, we have to find out just what we're tossing before we toss."

The creature had made itself at home aboard the *Mercy*. In the spirit of uninvited guests since time immemorial, it had established a toehold with remarkable asperity, and now was digging in for the long winter. Drawn to the hydroponic tanks like a flea to a dog, the *hlorg* had settled its bulbous pink body down in their murky depths with a contented gurgle. As it grew larger the tank-levels grew lower, the broth clearer.

The fact that the twenty-five crewmen of the *Mercy* depended on those tanks for their food supply on the four-month run back to Hospital Earth didn't seem to bother the *hlorg* a bit. It just sank down wetly and began to eat.

Under Jenkins' whip hand, and with Green Doctor Stone's assistance, the Survey Crew snapped into action. Survey was the soul and lifeblood of the medical services supplied by Hospital Earth to the inhabited planets of the Galaxy. Centuries before, during the era of exploration, every Earth ship had carried a rudimentary Survey Crew—a physiologist, a biochemist, an immunologist, a physician—to determine the safety of landings on unknown planets. Other races were more advanced in technological and physical sciences, in sales or in merchandising—but in the biological sciences men of Earth stood unexcelled in the Galaxy. It was not surprising that their casual offerings of medical services wherever their ships touched had led to a growing demand for those services, until the first Medical Service Contract with Deneb III had formalized the planetary specialty. Earth had become Hospital Earth, physician to a Galaxy, surgeon to a thousand worlds, midwife to those susceptible to midwifery and psychiatrist to those whose inner lives zigged when their outer lives zagged.

In the early days it had been a haphazard arrangement; but gradually distinct Services appeared to handle problems of medicine, surgery, radiology, psychiatry and all the other functions of a well-appointed medical service. Under the direction of the Black Service of Pathology, Hospital ships and Survey ships were dispatched to serve as bases for the tiny General Practice Patrol ships that answered the calls of the planets under Contract.

But it was the Survey ships that did the basic dirty-work on any new planet taken under Contract—outlining the physiological and biochemical aspects of the races involved, studying their disease patterns, their immunological types, their susceptibility to medical, surgical, or psychiatric treatment. It was an exacting service to perform, and Survey did an exacting job.

Now, with their own home base invaded by a hungry pink jelly-blob, the Survey Crew of the *Mercy* dug in with all fours to find a way to exorcise it.

The early returns were not encouraging.

Bowman, the anatomist, spent six hours with the creature. He'd go after the functional anatomy first, he thought, as he approached the task with gusto. Special organs, vital organ systems—after all, every Achilles had his heel. Functional would spot it if anything would—

Six hours later he rendered a preliminary report. It consisted of a blank sheet of paper and an expression of wild frustration.

"What's this supposed to mean?" Jenkins asked.

"Just what it says."

"But it says nothing!"

"That's exactly what it means." Bowman was a thin, wistful-looking man with a hawk nose and a little brown mustache. He subbed as ship's cook when things were slow in his specialty. He wasn't a very good cook, but what could anyone do with the sludge from the harvest shelf of a hydroponic tank? Now, with the *hlorg* incumbent, there wasn't even any sludge.

"I drained off a tank and got a good look at it before it crawled over into the next one," Bowman said. "Ugly bastard. But from a strictly anatomical standpoint I can't help you a bit."

Green Doctor Stone glowered over Jenkins' shoulder at the man. "But surely you can give us *something*."

Bowman shrugged. "You want it technical?"

"Any way you like."

"Your *hlorg* is an ideal anamorph. A nothing. Protoplasm, just protoplasm."

Jenkins looked up sharply. "What about his cellular organization?"

"No cells," said Bowman. "Unless they're sub-microscopic, and I'd need an electron-peeker to tell you that."

"No organ systems?"

"Not even an integument. You saw how slippery he looked? That's why. There's nothing holding him in but energy."

"Now, look," said Stone. "He eats, doesn't he? He must have waste materials of some sort."

Bowman shook his head unhappily. "Sorry. No urates. No nitrates. No CO_2. Anyway, he doesn't eat because he has nothing to eat with. He absorbs. And that includes the lining of the tanks, which he seems to like as much as the contents. He doesn't *bore* those holes he makes—he *dissolves* them."

They sent Bowman back to quarters for a hot bath and a shot of Happy-O and looked up Hrunta, the biochemist.

Hrunta was glaring at paper electrophoretic patterns and pulling out chunks of hair around his bald spot. He gave them a snarl and shoved a sheaf of papers into their hands.

"Metabolic survey?" Jenkins asked.

"Plus," said Hrunta. "You're not going to like it, either."

"Why not? If it grows, it metabolizes. If it metabolizes, we can kill it. Axiom number seventeen, paragraph number four."

"Oh, it metabolizes, all right, but you'd better find yourself another axiom, pretty quick."

"Why?"

"Because it not only metabolizes, it *consumes*. There's no sign of the usual protein-carbohydrate-fat metabolism going on here. This baby has an enzyme system that's straight from hell. It bypasses the usual metabolic activities that produce heat and energy and gets right down to basic-basic."

Jenkins swallowed. "What do you mean?"

"It attacks the nuclear structure of whatever matter the creature comes in contact with. There's a partial mass-energy conversion in its rawest form. The creature goes after carbon-bearing substances first, since the C seems to break down more easily than anything else—hence its preference for plant and animal material over non-C stuff. But it can use anything if it has to—"

Jenkins stared at the little biochemist, an image in his mind of the pink creature in the hold, growing larger by the minute as it ate its way through the hydroponics, through the dry stores, through—

"Is there anything it *can't* use?"

"If there is, I haven't found it," Hrunta said sadly. "In fact, I can't see any reason why it couldn't consume this ship and everything in it, right down to the last rivet—"

*   *   *   *   *

They walked down to the hold for another look at their uninvited guest, and almost wished they hadn't.

It had reached the size of a small hippopotamus, although the resemblance ended there. Twenty hours had elapsed since the survey had begun. The *hlorg* had used every minute of it, draining the tanks, engulfing dry stores, devouring walls and floors as it spread out in search of food, leaving trails of eroded metal wherever it went.

It was ugly—ugly in its pink shapelessness, ugly in its slimy half-sentient movements, in its very *purposefulness*. But its ugliness went even deeper, stirring primordial feelings of revulsion and loathing in their minds as they watched it oozing implacably across the hold to another dry-storage bin.

Wally Stone shuddered. "It's *grown*."

"Too fast. Bowman charts it as geometric progression."

Stone scratched his jaw as a lone pink pseudopod pushed out on the floor toward him. Then he leaped forward and stamped on it, severing the strand from the body.

The severed member quivered and lay still for a moment. Then it flowed back to rejoin the body with a wet gurgle.

Stone looked at his half-dissolved shoe.

"Egotropism," Jenkins said. "Bowman played around with that, too. A severed piece will rejoin if it can. If it can't it just takes up independent residence and we have two *hlorgs*."

"What happens to it outside the ship?" Stone wanted to know.

"It falls dormant for several hours, and then splits up into a thousand independent chunks. One of the boys spent half of yesterday out there gathering them up. I tell you, this thing is equipped to *survive*."

"So are we," said Green Doctor Stone grimly. "If we can't outwit this free-flowing gob of obscenity, we deserve anything we get. Let's have a conference."

They met in the pilot room. The Black Doctor was there; so were Bowman and Hrunta. Chambers, the physiologist, was glumly clasping and unclasping his hands in a corner. The geneticist, Piccione, drew symbols on a scratch pad and stared blankly at the wall.

Jenkins was saying: "Of course, these are only preliminary reports, but they serve to outline the problem. This is not just an annoyance any longer, it's a crisis. We'd all better understand that."

The Black Doctor cut him off with a wave of his hand, and glowered at the papers as he read them through minutely. As he sat hunched at the desk with the black cowl of his office hanging down from his shoulders he looked like a squat black judge,

Jenkins thought, a shadow from the Inquisition, a Passer of Spells. But there was no medievalism in Black Doctor Neelsen. In fact, it was for that reason, and only that reason, that the Black Service had come to be the leaders and the whips, the executors and directors of all the manifold operations of Hospital Earth.

*   *   *   *   *

The physicians of the General Practice Patrol were fledglings, newly trained in their specialties, inexperienced in the rigorous discipline of medicine that was required of the directors of permanent Planetary Dispensaries in the heavily populated systems of the Galaxy. On outlying worlds where little was known of the ways of medicine, the temptation was great to substitute faith for knowledge, cant for investigation, nonsense rituals for hard work. But the physicians of the Black Service were always waiting to jerk wandering neophytes back to the scientific disciplines that made the service of Hospital Earth so effective. The Black Doctors would not tolerate sloppiness. "Show me the tissue, Doctor," they would say. "Prove to me that what you say is so. Prove that what you did was valid medicine...." Their laboratories were the morgues and autopsy rooms of a thousand planets, the Temples of Truth from which no physician since the days of Pasteur and Lister could escape for long and retain his position.

The Black Doctors were the pragmatists, the gadflies of Hospital Earth.

For this reason it was surprising to hear Black Doctor Neelsen saying, "Perhaps we are being too scientific, just now. When the creature has exhausted our food stores, it will look elsewhere for food. Perhaps we must cut at the tree and not at the root."

"A frontal attack?" said Jenkins.

"Just so. Its enzyme system is its vulnerability. Enzyme systems operate under specific optimum conditions, right? And every known enzyme system can be inactivated by adverse conditions of one sort or another. A physical approach may tell us how in this case. Meanwhile we will be on emergency rations, and hope that we don't starve to death finding out." The Black

Doctor paused, looking at the men around him. "And in case you are thinking of enlisting help from outside, forget it. I've sent plague-warnings out for Galactic relay. We have this thing isolated, and we're going to keep it that way as long as I command this ship."

They went gloomily back to their laboratories to plan their frontal attack.

That was the night that Hrunta disappeared.

*   *   *   *   *

He was gone when they came to wake him from his sleep period. His bunk had been slept in, but he wasn't in it. In fact, he wasn't anywhere on the ship.

"But he couldn't just vanish!" the Black Doctor burst out when they told him the news. "Maybe he's hiding somewhere. Maybe this business was working on his mind."

Green Doctor Stone took a crew of men to search the ship again, even though he considered it a waste of precious time. He had his private convictions about where Hrunta had gone.

So did every other man on the ship, including Jenkins.

The *hlorg* had stopped eating. Huge and round and wet and ugly, it squatted in the after-hold, quivering gently, without any other sign of life.

Surfeited. Like a fat man after a turkey dinner.

Jenkins reviewed progress with the others. No stone had been left unturned. They had sliced the *hlorg*, and squeezed it. They had boiled it and frozen it. They had dropped chunks of it in acid vats and covered other chunks with desiccants and alkalis. Nothing seemed to bother it.

A cold environment slowed down its activity, true, but it also stimulated the process of fission. Warmed up again, the portions sucked back together again and resumed eating.

Heat was a little more effective, but not much. It stunned the creature for a brief period, but it would not burn. It hissed frightfully and gave off an overpowering stench, and curled up at the edges, but as soon as the heat was turned off it began to recover.

In Hrunta's lab chunks of the *hlorg* sat in a dozen vats on tables and in sinks. Some contained antibiotics, some concentrated acids, some desiccants. In each vat a blob of pink protoplasm wiggled happily, showing no sign of discomfiture. On another table were the remains of Hrunta's (unsuccessful) attempt to prepare an anti-*hlorg* serum.

But no Hrunta.

"He was down there with the thing all day," Bowman said sadly. "He felt it was his responsibility, really. Hrunta thought biochemistry was the answer to all things, of course. Very conscientious man."

"But he was in *bed*."

"He claimed he did his best thinking in bed. Maybe he had a brainstorm and went down to try it out, and—"

"Yes." Jenkins nodded sourly. "And." He walked down the row of vats. "You'd think that at least concentrated sulphuric would dessicate it a little. But it's just formed a crust of coagulated protein around itself, and sits there—"

Bowman peered over his shoulder, his mustache twitching. "But it does dessicate."

"If you use enough long enough."

"How about concentrated hydrochloric?"

"Same thing. Maybe a little more effective, but not enough to count."

"Okay. Next we try combinations. There's got to be *something* the wretched beast can't tolerate—"

There was, of course.

*   *   *   *   *

Green Doctor Stone brought it to Jenkins as he was getting ready to turn in for a sleep period. Jenkins had checked to make sure double guards were posted in the *hlorg's* vicinity, and jolted them with Sleep-Not to keep them on their toes. All the same, he tied a length of stout cord around his ankle just to make sure he didn't do any sleepwalking. He was tying it to the bunk when Stone came in with a pan in his hand and a peculiar look on his face.

"Take a look at this," he said.

Jenkins looked at the sickly brown mass in the tray, and then up at Stone. "Where did you find it?"

"Down in the hold. Our *hlorg* has broken precedent. It's *rejected* something that it ate."

"Yeah. What is it?"

"I don't know. I'm taking it to Neelsen for paraffin sections. But I know what it looks like to me."

"Mm. I know." Jenkins felt sick. Stone headed up to the path lab, leaving the Red Doctor settled in his bunk.

Ten minutes later Jenkins sat bolt upright in the darkness. Frantically he untied himself and slid into his clothes. "Idiot!" he growled to himself. "Seventh son of a seventh son—"

Five minutes later he was staring at the vats in Hrunta's laboratory. He found the one he was looking for. A pink blob of *hlorg* wiggled slowly around the bottom.

Jenkins drew a beaker of distilled water and added it to the fluid in the vat. It hissed and sputtered and sent up quantities of acrid steam. When the steam had cleared away, Jenkins peered in eagerly.

The pink thing in the bottom was turning a sickly violet. It had quit wiggling. As Jenkins watched, the violet color changed to mud grey, then to black. He prodded it with a stirring rod. There was no response.

With a whoop Jenkins buzzed Bowman and Stone. "We've got it!" he shouted to them when they appeared. "Look! Look at it!"

Bowman poked and probed and broke into a wide grin. The piece of *hlorg* was truly and sincerely dead. "It inactivates the enzyme system, and renders the base protoplasm vulnerable to anything that normally attacks it. What are we waiting for?"

They began tearing the laboratory apart, searching for the right bottles. The supply was discouragingly small, but there was some in stock. The three of them raced down the corridor for the hold where the *hlorg* was.

It took them three hours of angry work to exhaust the supply. They whittled chunks off the *hlorg*, tossed them in pans of the deadly fluid. With each slice they stopped momentarily to watch it turn violet, then black, as it died. The *hlorg*, dwindling in size, sensed the attack and slapped frantically at their ankles, sending out angry plumes of wet jelly, but they ducked and dodged and whittled some more. The *hlorg* quivered and gurgled and wept pinkish goo all over the floor, but it grew smaller and weaker with every whack.

"Hrunta must have spotted it and come down here alone," Jenkins panted between slices. "Maybe he slipped, lost his footing, I don't know—"

They continued to work until the supply was exhausted. They had reduced the *hlorg* to a quarter its previous size. "Check the other labs, see if they have some more," said Stone.

"I already have," Bowman said. "They don't. This is it."

"But we haven't got it all killed. There's still—" He pointed to the thing quailing in the corner.

"I know. We're licked, that's all. There isn't any more of the stuff on the ship."

They stopped and looked at each other suddenly. Then Jenkins said: "Oh, yes there is."

There was silence. Bowman looked at Stone, and Stone looked at Bowman. They both looked at Jenkins. "Oh, no. Sorry. I decline." Stone shook his head slowly.

"But we have to! There's no other way. If the enzyme system is inactivated, it's just protoplasm—there's no physiological or biochemical reason—"

"You know what you can do with your physiology and biochemistry," Bowman said succinctly. "You can also count me out." He left them and the hatchway clanged after him.

"Wally?"

"Yeah."

"It'll be months before we get back to Hospital Earth. We know how we can hold it in check until we get there."

"Yeah."

"Well?"

Green Doctor Wally Stone sighed. "Greater love hath no man," he said wearily. "We'd better go tell Neelsen, I guess."

*   *   *   *   *

Black Doctor Turvold Neelsen's answer was a flat, unequivocal no. "It's monstrous and preposterous. I won't stand for it. Nobody will stand for it."

"But you have the proof in your own hands," Jenkins said. "You saw the specimen that the Green Doctor brought you."

Neelsen hunched back angrily. "I saw it."

"And your impression of it? As a pathologist?"

"I fail to see how my impression applies one way or the other—"

"Doctor, sometimes we have to face facts. Remember?"

"All right." Neelsen seemed to curl up into himself still further. "The specimen was stomach."

"Human stomach?"

"Human stomach."

"But the only human on this ship that doesn't have a stomach is Hrunta," said Jenkins.

"So the *hlorg* ate him."

"*Most* of him. Not quite all. It threw out the one part of him it couldn't eat. The part containing a substance that inactivated its enzyme system. Dilute hydrochloric acid, to be specific. We used the entire ship's supply, and cut the *hlorg* down to three-quarters size, but we need a continuous supply to keep it whittled down until we get home. And there's only one good, permanent, reliable source of dilute hydrochloric acid on board this ship—"

The Black Doctor's face was purple. "I said no," he choked. "My answer stands."

The Red Doctor sighed and turned to Green Doctor Stone. "All right, Wally," he said.

*   *   *   *   *

(*From the files of the Medical Disciplinary Board, Hospital Earth, op. cit.*)

I am certain that you can see from the foregoing that a reasonable effort was made by Green Doctor Stone and myself to put the plan in effect peaceably and with full approval of our commander. It was our conviction, however, that the emergency nature of the circumstances required that it be done with or without his approval. Our subsequent success in containing the *hlorg* to at least reasonable and manageable proportions should bear out the wisdom of our decision.

Actually, it has not been as bad as one might think. It has been necessary to confine the crew to their quarters, and to restrain the Black Doctor forcibly, but with liberal use of Happy-O we can occasionally convince ourselves that it is rare beefsteak, and the Green Doctor, our pro-tem cook has concocted several very tasty sauces, such as mushroom, onion, etc. We reduce the *hlorg* to half its size each day, and if thoroughly heated the chunks lie still on the plate for quite some time.

No physical ill effects have been noted, and the period of quarantine is recommended solely to allow the men an adequate period for psychological recovery.

I have only one further recommendation: that the work team from the Grey Service be recalled at once from their assignment on Mauki IV. The problem is decidedly not psychiatric, and it would be one of the tragedies of the ages if our excellent psychiatric service were to succeed in persuading the Maukivi out of their 'delusion'.

After all, Hospital Earth cannot afford to jeopardize a Contract—

(Signed)
Samuel B. Jenkins,
Physician Grade VI
Red Service
GPP Ship *Lancet*
(Attached GSS *Mercy* pro tem)

An Ounce of Cure

Originally Published In *Imaginative Tales*,
November 1955

AN OUNCE OF CURE

The doctor's office was shiny and modern. Behind the desk the doctor smiled down at James Wheatley through thick glasses. "Now, then! What seems to be the trouble?"

Wheatley had been palpitating for five days straight at the prospect of coming here. "I know it's silly," he said. "But I've been having a pain in my toe."

"Indeed!" said the doctor. "Well, now! How long have you had this pain, my man?"

"About six months now, I'd say. Just now and then, you know. It's never really been bad. Until last week. You see—"

"I see," said the doctor. "Getting worse all the time, you say."

Wheatley wiggled the painful toe reflectively. "Well—you might say that. You see, when I first—"

"How old did you say you were, Mr. Wheatley?"

"Fifty-five."

"Fifty-*five*!" The doctor leafed through the medical record on his desk. "But this is incredible. You haven't had a checkup in almost ten years!"

"I guess I haven't," said Wheatley, apologetically. "I'd been feeling pretty well until—"

"*Feeling* well!" The doctor stared in horror. "But my dear fellow, no checkup since January 1963! We aren't in the Middle Ages, you know. This is 1972."

"Well, of course—"

"Of course you may be *feeling* well enough, but that doesn't mean everything is just the way it should be. And now, you see, you're having pains in your toes!"

"One toe," said Wheatley. "The little one on the right. It seemed to me—"

"One toe *today*, perhaps," said the doctor heavily. "But *tomorrow*—" He heaved a sigh. "How about your breathing lately? Been growing short of breath when you hurry upstairs?"

"Well—I *have* been bothered a little."

"I thought so! Heart pound when you run for the subway? Feel tired all day? Pains in your calves when you walk fast?"

"Uh—yes, occasionally, I—" Wheatley looked worried and rubbed his toe on the chair leg.

"You know that fifty-five is a dangerous age," said the doctor gravely. "Do you have a cough? Heartburn after dinner? Prop up on pillows at night? Just as I thought! And no checkup for ten years!" He sighed again.

"I suppose I should have seen to it," Wheatley admitted. "But you see, it's just that my toe—"

"My dear fellow! Your toe is *part* of you. It doesn't just exist down there all by itself. If your *toe* hurts, there must be a *reason*."

Wheatley looked more worried than ever. "There must? I thought—perhaps you could just give me a little something—"

"To stop the pain?" The doctor looked shocked. "Well, of course I could *do* that, but that's not getting at the root of the trouble, is it? That's just treating symptoms. Medieval quackery. Medicine has advanced a long way since your last checkup, my friend. And even treatment has its dangers. Did you know that more people died last year of *aspirin* poisoning than of *cyanide* poisoning?"

Wheatley wiped his forehead. "I—dear me! I never realized—"

"We have to *think* about those things," said the doctor. "Now, the problem here is to find out *why* you have the pain in your toe. It could be inflammatory. Maybe a tumor. Perhaps it could be, uh, functional ... or maybe vascular!"

"Perhaps you could take my blood pressure, or something," Wheatley offered.

"Well, of course I *could*. But that isn't really my field, you know. It wouldn't really *mean* anything, if I did it. But there's nothing to worry about. We have a fine Hypertensive man at the Diagnostic Clinic." The doctor checked the appointment book on his desk. "Now, if we could see you there next Monday morning at nine—"

*   *   *   *   *

"Very interesting X rays," said the young doctor with the red hair. "*Very* interesting. See this shadow in the duodenal cap? See the prolonged emptying time? And I've never seen such beautiful pylorospasm!"

"This is my toe?" asked Wheatley, edging toward the doctors. It seemed he had been waiting for a very long time.

"Toe! Oh, no," said the red-headed doctor. "No, that's the Orthopedic Radiologist's job. I'm a Gastro-Intestinal man, myself. Upper. Dr. Schultz here is Lower." The red-headed doctor turned back to his consultation with Dr. Schultz. Mr. Wheatley rubbed his toe and waited.

Presently another doctor came by. He looked very grave as he sat down beside Wheatley. "Tell me, Mr. Wheatley, have you had an orthodiagram recently?"

"No."

"An EKG?"

"No."

"Fluoroaortogram?"

"I—don't *think* so."

The doctor looked even graver, and walked away, muttering to himself. In a few moments he came back with two more doctors. "—no question in *my* mind that it's cardiomegaly," he was saying, "but Haddonfield should know. He's the best Left Ventricle man in the city. Excellent paper in the AMA Journal last July: 'The Inadequacies of Modern Orthodiagramatic Techniques in Demonstrating Minimal Left Ventricular Hypertrophy.' A brilliant study, simply brilliant! Now *this* patient—" He glanced toward Wheatley, and his voice dropped to a mumble.

Presently two of the men nodded, and one walked over to Wheatley, cautiously, as though afraid he might suddenly vanish. "Now, there's nothing to be worried about, Mr. Wheatley," he said. "We're going to have you fixed up in just no time at all. Just a few more studies. Now, if you could see me in Valve Clinic tomorrow afternoon at three—"

Wheatley nodded. "Nothing serious, I hope?"

"Serious? Oh, no! Dear me, you *mustn't* worry. Everything is going to be all right," the doctor said.

"Well—I—that is, my toe is still bothering me some. It's not nearly as bad, but I wondered if maybe you—"

Dawn broke on the doctor's face. "Give you something for it? Well now, we aren't Therapeutic men, you understand. Always best to let the expert handle the problem in his own field." He paused, stroking his chin for a moment. "Tell you what we'll do. Dr. Epstein is one of the finest Therapeutic men in the city. He could take care of you in a jiffy. We'll see if we can't arrange an appointment with him after you've seen me tomorrow."

Mr. Wheatley was late to Mitral Valve Clinic the next day because he had gone to Aortic Valve Clinic by mistake, but finally he found the right waiting room. A few hours later he was being thumped, photographed, and listened to. Substances were popped into his right arm, and withdrawn from his left arm as he marveled at the brilliance of modern medical techniques. Before they were finished he had been seen by both the Mitral men and the Aortic men, as well as the Great Arteries man and the Peripheral Capillary Bed man.

The Therapeutic man happened to be in Atlantic City at a convention and the Rheumatologist was on vacation, so Wheatley was sent to Functional Clinic instead. "Always have to rule out these things," the doctors agreed. "Wouldn't do much good to give you medicine if your trouble isn't organic, now, would it?" The Psychoneuroticist studied his sex life, while the Psychosociologist examined his social milieu. Then they conferred for a long time.

Three days later he was waiting in the hallway downstairs again. Heads met in a huddle; words and phrases slipped out from time to time as the discussion grew heated.

"—no doubt in my mind that it's a—"

"But we can't ignore the endocrine implications, doctor—"

"You're perfectly right there, of course. Bittenbender at the University might be able to answer the question. No better Pituitary Osmoreceptorologist in the city—"

"—a Tubular Function man should look at those kidneys first. He's fifty-five, you know."

"—has anyone studied his filtration fraction?"

"—might be a peripheral vascular spasticity factor—"

After a while James Wheatley rose from the bench and slipped out the door, limping slightly as he went.

*   *   *   *   *

The room was small and dusky, with heavy Turkish drapes obscuring the dark hallway beyond. A suggestion of incense hung in the air.

In due course a gaunt, swarthy man in mustache and turban appeared through the curtains and bowed solemnly. "You come with a problem?" he asked, in a slight accent.

"As a matter of fact, yes," James Wheatley said hesitantly. "You see, I've been having a pain in my right little toe...."

THE DARK DOOR

Originally Published In *Galaxy Science Fiction*,
December 1953

THE DARK DOOR

1

It was almost dark when he awoke, and lay on the bed, motionless and trembling, his heart sinking in the knowledge that he should never have slept. For almost half a minute, eyes wide with fear, he lay in the silence of the gloomy room, straining to hear some sound, some indication of their presence.

But the only sound was the barely audible hum of his wrist watch and the dismal splatter of raindrops on the cobbled street outside. There was no sound to feed his fear, yet he knew then, without a flicker of doubt, that they were going to kill him.

He shook his head, trying to clear the sleep from his brain as he turned the idea over and over in his mind. He wondered why he hadn't realized it before, long before, back when they had first started this horrible, nerve-wracking cat-and-mouse game. The idea just hadn't occurred to him. But he knew the game-playing was over. They wanted to kill him now. And he knew that ultimately they *would* kill him. There was no way for him to escape.

He sat up on the edge of the bed, painfully, perspiration standing out on his bare back, and he waited, listening. How could he have slept, exposing himself so helplessly? Every ounce of his energy, all the skill and wit and shrewdness at his command were necessary in this cruel hunt; yet he had taken the incredibly terrible chance of sleeping, of losing consciousness, leaving himself wide open and helpless against the attack which he knew was inevitable.

How much had he lost? How close had they come while he slept?

Fearfully, he walked to the window, peered out, and felt his muscles relax a little. The gray, foggy streets were still light. He still had a little time before the terrible night began.

He stumbled across the small, old-fashioned room, sensing that action of some sort was desperately needed. The bathroom was tiny; he stared in the battered, stained reflector unit, shocked at the red-eyed stubble-faced apparition that stared back at him.

This is Harry Scott, he thought, thirty-two years old, and in the prime of life, but not the same Harry Scott who started out on a ridiculous quest so many months ago. This Harry Scott was being hunted like an animal, driven by fear, helpless, and sure to die, unless he could find an escape, somehow. But there were too many of them for him to escape, and they were too clever, and they *knew* he knew too much.

He stepped into the shower-shave unit, trying to relax, to collect his racing thoughts. Above all, he tried to stay the fear that burned through his mind, driving him to panic and desperation. The memory of the last hellish night was too stark to allow relaxation—the growing fear, the silent, desperate hunt through the night; the realization that their numbers were increasing; his frantic search for a hiding place in the New City; and finally his panic-stricken, pell-mell flight down into the alleys and cobbled streets and crumbling frame buildings of the Old City.... Even more horrible, the friends who had turned on him, who turned out to be *like* them.

Back in the bedroom, he lay down again, his body still tense. There were sounds in the building, footsteps moving around on the floor overhead, a door banging somewhere. With every sound, every breath of noise, his muscles tightened still further, freezing him in fear. His own breath was shallow and rapid in his ears as he lay, listening, waiting.

If only something would happen! He wanted to scream, to bang his head against the wall, to run about the room smashing his fist into doors, breaking every piece of furniture. It was the *waiting*, the eternal waiting, and running, waiting some more, feeling the net drawing tighter and tighter as he waited, feeling the measured, unhurried tread behind him, always following, coming closer and closer, as though he were a mouse on a string, twisting and jerking helplessly.

If only they would move, do something he could counter.

But he wasn't even sure any more that he could detect them. And they were so careful never to move into the open.

He jumped up feverishly, moved to the window, and peered between the slats of the dusty, old-fashioned blind at the street below.

An empty street at first, wet, gloomy. He saw no one. Then he caught the flicker of light in an entry several doors down and across the street, as a dark figure sparked a cigarette to life. Harry felt the chill run down his back again. Still there, then, still waiting, a hidden figure, always present, always waiting....

Harry's eyes scanned the rest of the street rapidly. Two three-wheelers rumbled by, their rubber hissing on the wet pavement. One of them carried the blue-and-white of the Old City police, but the car didn't slow up or hesitate as it passed the dark figure in the doorway. They would never help me anyway, Harry thought bitterly. He had tried that before, and met with ridicule and threats. There would be no help from the police in the Old City.

Another figure came around a corner. There was something vaguely familiar about the tall body and broad shoulders as the man walked across the wet street, something Harry faintly recognized from somewhere during the spinning madness of the past few weeks.

The man's eyes turned up toward the window for the briefest instant, then returned steadfastly to the street. Oh, they were sly! You could never spot them looking at you, never for *sure*, but they were always there, always nearby. And there was no one he could trust any longer, no one to whom he could turn.

Not even George Webber.

Swiftly his mind reconsidered that possibility as he watched the figure move down the street. True, Dr. Webber had started him out on this search in the first place. But even Webber would never believe what he had found. Webber was a scientist, a researcher.

What could he do—go to Webber and tell him that there were men alive in the world who were *not* men, who were somehow men and something more?

Could he walk into Dr. Webber's office in the Hoffman Medical Center, walk through the gleaming bright corridors, past the shining metallic doors, and tell Dr. Webber that he had found people alive in the world who could actually see in four dimensions, live in four dimensions, *think* in four dimensions?

Could he explain to Dr. Webber that he knew this simply because in some way he had sensed them, and traced them, and discovered them; that he had not one iota of proof, except that he was being followed by them, hunted by them, even now, in a room in the Old City, waiting for them to strike him down?

He shook his head, almost sobbing. That was what was so horrible. He couldn't tell Webber, because Webber would be certain that he had gone mad, just like the rest. He couldn't tell anyone, he couldn't do anything. He could just wait, and run, and wait—

It was almost dark now and the creaking of the old board house intensified the fear that tore at Harry Scott's mind. Tonight was the night; he was sure of it. Maybe he had been foolish in coming here to the slum area, where the buildings were relatively unguarded, where anybody could come and go as he pleased. But the New City had hardly been safer, even in the swankiest private chamber in the highest building. They had had agents there, too, hunting him, driving home the bitter lesson of fear they had to teach him. Now he was afraid enough; now they were ready to kill him.

Down below he heard a door bang, and he froze, his back against the wall. There were footsteps, quiet voices, barely audible. His whole body shook and his eyes slid around to the window. The figure in the doorway still waited—but the other figure was not visible. He heard the steps on the stair, ascending slowly, steadily, a tread that paced itself with the powerful throbbing of his own pulse.

Then the telephone screamed out—

Harry gasped. The footsteps were on the floor below, moving steadily upward. The telephone rang again and again; the shrill jangling filled the room insistently. He waited until he couldn't wait any longer. His hand fumbled in a pocket and leveled a tiny, dull-gray metal object at the door. With the other hand, he took the receiver from the hook.

"Harry! Is that you?"

His throat was like sandpaper and the words came out in a rasp. "What is it?"

"Harry, this is George—George Webber."

His eyes were glued to the door. "All right. What do you want?"

"You've got to come talk to us, Harry. We've been waiting for weeks now. You promised us. We've *got* to talk to you."

Harry still watched the door, but his breath came easier. The footsteps moved with ridiculous slowness up the stairs, down the hall toward the room.

"What do you want me to do? They've come to kill me."

There was a long pause. "Harry, are you sure?"

"Dead sure."

"Can you make a break for it?"

Harry blinked. "I could try. But it won't do any good."

"Well, at least try, Harry. Get here to the Hoffman Center. We'll help you all we can."

"I'll try." Harry's words were hardly audible as he set the receiver down with a trembling hand.

The room was silent. The footsteps had stopped. A wave of panic passed up Harry's spine; he crossed the room, threw open the door, stared up and down the hall, unbelieving.

The hall was empty. He started down toward the stairs at a dead run, and then, too late, saw the faint golden glow of a Parkinson Field across the dingy corridor. He gasped in fear, and screamed out once as he struck it.

And then, for seconds stretching into hours, he heard his scream echoing and re-echoing down long, bitter miles of hollow corridor.

2

George Webber leaned back in the soft chair, turning a quizzical glance toward the younger man across the room. He lit a long black cigar.

"Well?" His heavy voice boomed out in the small room. "Now that we've got him here, what do you think?"

The younger man glanced uncomfortably through the glass wall panel into the small dark room beyond. In the dimness, he could barely make out the still form on the bed, grotesque with the electrode-vernier apparatus already in place at its temples. Dr. Manelli looked away sharply, and leafed through the thick sheaf of chart papers in his hand.

"I don't know," he said dully. "I just don't know what to think."

The other man's laugh seemed to rise from the depths of his huge chest. His heavy face creased into a thousand wrinkles. Dr. Webber was a large man, his broad shoulders carrying a suggestion of immense power that matched the intensity of his dark, wide-set eyes. He watched Dr. Manelli's discomfort grow, saw the younger doctor's ears grow red, and the almost cruel lines in his face were masked as he laughed still louder.

"Trouble with you, Frank, you just don't have the courage of your convictions."

"Well, I don't see anything so funny about it!" Manelli's eyes were angry. "The man has a suspicious syndrome—so you've followed him, and spied on him for weeks on end, which isn't exactly highest ethical practice in collecting a history. I still can't see how you're justified."

Dr. Webber snorted, tossing his cigar down on the desk with disgust. "The man is insane. That's my justification. He's out of touch with reality. He's wandered into a wild, impossible, fantastic dream world. And we've got to get him out of it, because what he knows, what he's trying to hide from us, is so incredibly dangerous that we don't dare let him go."

The big man stared at Manelli, his dark eyes flashing. "Can't you see that? Or would you rather sit back and let Harry Scott go the way that Paulus and Wineberg and the others went?"

"But to use the Parkinson Field on him—" Dr. Manelli shook his head hopelessly. "He'd offered to come over, George. We didn't need to use it."

"Sure, he offered to come—fine, fine. But supposing he changed his mind on the way? For all we know, he had us figured into his paranoia, too, and never would have come near the Hoffman Center."

Dr. Webber shook his head. "We're not playing a game any more, Frank. Get that straight. I thought it was a game a couple of years ago, when we first started. But it ceased to be a game when men like Paulus and Wineberg walked in sane, healthy men, and came out blubbering idiots. That's no game any more. We're onto something big. And, if Harry Scott can lead us to the core of it, then I can't care too much what happens to Harry Scott."

Dr. Manelli stood up sharply, walked to the window, and looked down over the bright, clean buildings of the Hoffman

Medical Center. Out across the terraced park that surrounded the glassed towers and shining metal of the Center rose the New City, tier upon tier of smooth, functional architecture, a city of dreams built up painfully out of the rubble of the older, ruined city.

"You could kill him," the young man said finally. "The psycho-integrator isn't any standard interrogative technique; it's dangerous and treacherous. You never know for sure just what you're doing when you dig down into a man's brain tissue with those little electrode probes."

"But we can learn the truth about Harry Scott," Dr. Webber broke in. "Six months ago, Harry Scott was working with us, a quiet, affable, pleasant young fellow, extremely intelligent, intensely co-operative. He was just the man we needed to work with us, an engineer who could take our data and case histories, study them, and subject them to a completely nonmedical analysis. Oh, we had to have it done—the problem's been with us for a hundred years now, growing ever since the 1950s and 60s—insanity in the population, growing, spreading without rhyme or reason, insinuating itself into every nook and cranny of our civilized life."

The big man blinked at Manelli. "Harry Scott was the new approach. We were too close to the problem. We needed a nonmedical outsider to take a look, to tell us what we were missing. So Harry Scott walked into the problem, and then abruptly lost contact with us. We finally track him down and find him gone, out of touch with reality, on the same wretched road that all the others went. With Harry, it's paranoia. He's being persecuted; he has the whole world against him, but most important—the factor we don't dare overlook—*he's no longer working on the problem.*"

Manelli shifted uneasily. "I suppose that's right."

"Of course it's right!" Dr. Webber's eyes flashed. "Harry found something in those statistics. Something about the data, or the case histories; or something Harry Scott himself dug up opened a door for him to go through, a door that none of us ever dreamed existed. We don't know what he found on the other side of that door. Oh, we know what he *thinks* he found, all this garbage about people that look normal but walk through walls when nobody's looking, who think around corners instead of in straight-line logic. But what he *really* found there, we don't have any way of telling. We just know that whatever he *really* found is something new, something unsuspected; something so dangerous it can drive an intelligent man into the wildest delusions of paranoid persecution."

A new light appeared in Dr. Manelli's eyes as he faced the other doctor. "Wait a minute," he said softly. "The integrator is an *experimental* instrument, too."

Dr. Webber smiled slyly. "Now you're beginning to think," he said.

"But you'll see only what Scott himself believes. And *he* thinks his story is true."

"Then we'll have to break his story."

"*Break* it?"

"Certainly. For some reason, this delusion of persecution is far safer for Harry Scott than facing what he really found out. What we've got to do is to make this delusion *less* safe than the truth."

The room was silent for a long moment. Manelli looked up, his fingers trembling. "Let's hear it."

"It's very simple. Up to now, Harry Scott has had *delusions* of persecution. But now we're *really* going to persecute Harry Scott, as he's never been persecuted before."

3

At first he thought he was at the bottom of a deep well and he lay quite still, his eyes clamped shut, wondering where he was and how he could possibly have gotten there. He could feel the dampness and chill of the stone floor under him, and nearby he heard the damp, insistent drip of water splashing against stone. He felt his muscles tighten as the dripping sound forced itself against his senses. Then he opened his eyes.

His first impulse was to scream out wildly in unreasoning, suffocating fear. He fought it down, struggling to sit up in the blackness, his whole mind turned in bitter, hopeless hatred at the ones who had hunted him for so long, and now had trapped him.

Why?

Why did they torture him? Why not kill him outright, have done with it? He shuddered, and struggled to his feet, staring about him in horror.

It was not a well, but a small room, circular, with little rivulets of stale water running down the granite walls. The ceiling closed low over his head, and the only source of light came from the single doorway opening into a long, low stone passageway.

Wave after wave of panic rose in Harry's throat. Each time he fought down the urge to scream, to lie down on the ground and cover his face with his hands and scream in helpless fear. How could they have known the horror that lay in his own mind, the horror of darkness, of damp slimy walls and scurrying rodents, of the clinging, stale humidity of dungeon passageways? He himself had seldom recalled it, except in his most hideous dreams, yet he had known such fear as a boy, so many years ago, and now it was all around him. They had known somehow and *used it against him.*

Why?

He sank down on the floor, his head in his hands, trying to think straight, to find some clue in the turmoil bubbling through his mind that would tell him what had happened.

He had started down the hallway from his room, to find Dr. Webber and tell him about the other people—

He stopped short, looked up wide-eyed. *Had* he been going to Dr. Webber? Had he actually decided to go? Perhaps—yes, perhaps he had, though Webber would only laugh at such a ridiculous story. But the not-men who had hunted him would not laugh; to them, it would not be funny. They knew that it was true. And they knew he knew it was true.

But why not kill him? Why this torture? Why this horrible persecution that dug into the depths of his own nightmares to haunt him?

His breath came fast and a chilly sweat broke out on his forehead. *Where* was he? Was this some long forgotten vault in the depths of the Old City? Or was this another place, another world, perhaps, that the not-men, with their impossible powers, had created to torture him?

His eyes sought the end of the hall, saw the turn at the end, saw the light which seemed to come from the end; and then in an instant he was running down the damp passageway, his pulse pounding at his temples, until he could hardly gasp enough breath as he ran. Finally he reached the turn in the corridor where the light was brighter, and he swung around to stare at the source of the light, a huge, burning, smoky torch which hung from the wall.

Even as he looked at it, the torch went out, shutting him into inky blackness. The only sound at first was the desperation of his own breath; then he heard little scurrying sounds around his feet, and screamed involuntarily as something sleek and four-footed jumped at his chest with snapping jaws.

Shuddering, he fought the thing off, his fingers closing on wiry fur as he caught and squeezed. The thing went limp, and suddenly melted in his hands. He heard it splash as it struck the damp ground at his feet.

What were they doing to his mind?

He screamed out in horror, and followed the echoes of his own scream as he ran down the stone corridor, blindly, slipping on the wet stone floor, falling on his knees into inches of brackish water, scraping back to his feet with an uncontrollable convulsion of fear and loathing, only to run more—

The corridor suddenly broke into two and he stopped short. He didn't know how far, or how long, he had run, but it suddenly occurred to him that he was still alive, still safe. Only his mind was under attack, only his mind was afraid, teetering on the edge of control. And this maze of dungeon tunnels—where could such a thing exist, so perfectly outfitted to horrify him, so neatly fitting into his own pattern of childhood fears and terrors; from where could such a *very individual* attack on his sanity have sprung? From nowhere except....

Except from his own mind!

For an instant, he saw a flicker of light, thought he grasped the edge of a concept previously obscure to him. He stared around him, at the mist swirling down the damp, dark corridor, and thought of the rat that had melted in his hand. Suddenly, his mind was afire, searching through his experience with the strange not-men he had learned to detect, trying to remember everything he had learned and deduced about them before they began their brutal persecution.

They were men, and they looked like men, but they were different. They had other properties of mind, other capabilities that men did not have.

They were not-men. They could exist, and co-exist, two people in one frame, one person known, realized by all who saw, the other one concealed except from those who learned how to look. They could use their minds; they could rationalize correctly; they could use their curious four-dimensional knowledge to bring them to answers no three-dimensional man could reach.

But they couldn't project into men's minds!

Carefully, Harry peered down the misty tunnels. They were clever, these creatures, and powerful. Since they had discovered that he knew them, they had done their work of fear and terror on his mind skillfully. But they were limited, too; they couldn't make things happen that were not true—fantasies, illusions....

Yes, this dungeon was an illusion. It *had* to be.

He cursed and started down the right-hand corridor, his heart sinking. There was no such place and he knew it. He was walking in a dream, a fantasy that had no substance, that could do no more than frighten him, drive him insane; yet he must already have lost his mind to be accepting such an illusion.

Why had he delayed? Why hadn't he gone to the Hoffman Center, laid the whole story before Dr. Webber and Dr. Manelli at the very first, told them what he had found? True, they might have thought him insane, but they wouldn't have put him to torture. They might even have believed him enough to investigate what he told them, and then the cat would have been out of the bag. The tale would have been incredible, but at least his mind would have been safe.

He turned down another corridor and walked suddenly into waist-deep water, so cold it numbed his legs. He stopped again to force back the tendrils of unreasoning horror that brushed his mind. Nothing could really harm him. He would merely wait until his mind finally reached a balance again. There might be no end; it might be a ghastly trap, but he would wait.

Strangely, the mist was becoming greenish in color as it swirled toward him in the damp vaulted passageway. His eyes began watering a little and the lining of his nose started to burn. He stopped short, newly alarmed, and stared at the walls, rubbing the tears away to clear his vision. The greenish-yellow haze grew thicker, catching his eyes and burning like a thousand furies, ripping into his throat until he was choking and coughing, as though great knives sliced through his lungs.

He tried to scream, and started running, blindly. Each gasping breath was an agony as the blistering gas dug deeper and deeper into his lungs. Reason departed from him; he was screaming incoherently as he stumbled up a stony ramp, crashed into a wall, spun around and smashed blindly into another. Then something caught at his shirt.

He felt the heavy planks and pounded iron scrollwork of a huge door, and threw himself upon it, wrenching at the old latch until the door swung open with a screech of rusty hinges. He fell forward on his face, and the door swung shut behind him.

He lay face down, panting and sobbing in the stillness.

Coarse hands grasped his collar, jerking him rudely to his feet, and he opened his eyes. Across the dim, vaulted room he could see the shadowy form of a man, a big man, with a broad chest and powerful shoulders, a man whose rich voice Harry almost recognized, but whose face was deep in shadow. As Harry wiped the tears from his tortured eyes, he heard the man's voice rumble out at him:

"Perhaps you've had enough now to change your mind about telling us the truth."

Harry stared, not quite comprehending. "The—the truth?"

The man's voice was harsh, cutting across the room impatiently. "The truth, I said. The problem, you fool, what you saw, what you learned; you know perfectly well what I'm referring to. But we'll swallow no more of this silly four-dimensional superman tale, so don't bother to start it."

"I—I don't understand you. It's—it's true—" Again he tried to peer across the room. "Why are you hunting me like this? What are you trying to do to me?"

"We want the truth. We want to know what you saw."

"But—but *you're* what I saw. You know what I found out. I mean—" He stopped, his face going white. His hand went to his mouth, and he stared still harder. "Who are you?" he whispered.

"The truth!" the man roared. "You'd better be quick, or you'll be back in the corridor."

"*Webber!*"

"Your last chance, Harry."

Without warning, Harry was across the room, flying across the desk, crashing into the big man's chest. With a scream of fury he fought, driving his fists into the powerful chest, wrenching at the thick, flailing arms of the startled man.

"*It's you!*" he screamed. "It's you that's been torturing me. It's you that's been hunting me down all this time, not the other people, you and your crowd of ghouls have been at my throat!"

He threw the big man off balance, dropped heavily on him as he fell back to the ground, glared down into the other's angry brown eyes.

And then, as though he had never been there at all, the big man vanished, and Harry sat back on the floor, his whole body shaking with frustrated sobs as his mind twisted in anguish.

He had been wrong, completely wrong, ever since he had discovered the not-men. Because he had thought *they* had been the ones who hunted and tortured him for so long. And now he knew how far he had been wrong. For the face of the shadowy man, the man behind the nightmare he was living, was the face of Dr. George Webber.

*　　*　　*　　*　　*

"You're a fool," said Dr. Manelli sharply, as he turned away from the sleeping figure on the bed to face the older man. "Of all the ridiculous things, to let him connect you with this!" The young doctor turned abruptly and sank down in a chair, glowering at Dr. Webber. "You haven't gotten to first base yet, but you've just given Scott enough evidence to free himself from integrator control altogether, if he gives it any thought. But I suppose you realize that."

"Nonsense," Dr. Webber retorted. "He had enough information to do that when we first started. I'm no more worried now than I was then. I'm sure he doesn't know enough about the psycho-integrator to be able voluntarily to control the patient-operator relationship to any degree. Oh, no, he's safe enough. But you've missed the whole point of that little interview." Dr. Webber grinned at Manelli.

"I'm afraid I have. It looked to me like useless bravado."

"The persecution, man, the *persecution*! He's shifted his sights! Before that interview, the *not-men* were torturing him, remember? Because they were afraid he would report his findings to me, of course. But now it's *I* that's against him." The grin widened. "You see where that leads?"

"You're talking almost as though you believed this story about a different sort of people among us."

Dr. Webber shrugged. "Perhaps I do."

"Oh, come now, George."

Dr. Webber's eyebrows went up and the grin disappeared from his face.

"Harry Scott believes it, Frank. We mustn't forget that, or miss its significance. Before Harry started this investigation of his, he wouldn't have paid any attention to such nonsense. But he believes it now."

"But Harry Scott is insane. You said it yourself."

"Ah, yes," said Dr. Webber. "Insane. Just like the others who started to get somewhere along those lines of investigation. Try to analyze the growing incidence of insanity in the population and you yourself go insane. You've got to be crazy to be a psychiatrist. It's an old joke, but it isn't very funny any more. And it's too much for coincidence.

"And then consider the nature of the insanity—a full-blown paranoia—oh, it's amazing. A cunning organization of men who are *not*-men, a regular fairy story, all straight from Harry Scott's agile young mind. But now it's *we* who are persecuting him, *and he still believes his fairy tale.*"

"So?"

Dr. Webber's eyes flashed angrily. "It's too neat, Frank. It's clever, and it's powerful, whatever we've run up against. But I think we've got an ace in the hole. We have Harry Scott."

"And you really think he'll lead us somewhere?"

Dr. Webber laughed. "That door I spoke of that Harry peeked through, I think he'll go back to it again. I think he's started to open that door already. And this time I'm going to follow him through."

It seemed incredible, yet Harry Scott knew he had not been mistaken. It had been Dr. Webber's face he had seen, a face no one could forget, an unmistakable face. And that meant that it had been Dr. Webber who had been persecuting him.

But why? He had been going to report to Webber when he had run into that golden field in the rooming-house hallway. And suddenly things had changed.

Harry felt a chill reaching to his fingers and toes. Yes, something had changed, all right. The attack on him had suddenly become butcherous, cruel, sneaking into his mind somehow to use his most dreaded nightmares against him. There was no telling what new horrors might be waiting for him. But he knew that he would lose his mind unless he could find an escape.

He was on his feet, his heart pounding. He had to get out of here, wherever he was. He had to get back to town, back to the city, back to where people were. If he could find a place to hide, a place where he could rest, he could try to think his way out of this ridiculous maze, or at least try to understand it.

He wrenched at the door to the passageway, started through, and smashed face-up against a solid brick wall.

He cried out and jumped back from the wall. Blood trickled from his nose. The door was *walled up*, the mortar dry and hard.

Frantically, he glanced around the room. There were no other doors, only the row of tiny windows around the ceiling of the room, pale, ghostly squares of light.

He pulled the chair over to the windows, peered out through the cobwebbed openings to the corridor beyond.

It was not the same hallway as before, but an old, dirty building corridor, incredibly aged, with bricks sagging away from the walls. At the end he could see stairs, and even the faintest hint of sunlight coming from above.

Wildly, he tore at the masonry of the window, chipping away at the soggy mortar with his fingers until he could squeeze through the opening. He fell to the floor of the corridor outside.

It was much colder and the silence was no longer so intense. He seemed to feel, rather than hear, the surging power, the rumble of many machines, the little, almost palpable vibrations from far above him.

He started in a dead run down the musty corridor to the stairs and began to climb them, almost stumbling over himself in his eagerness.

After several flights, the brick walls gave way to cleaner plastic, and suddenly a brightly lighted corridor stretched before him.

Panting from the climb, Harry ran down the corridor to the end, wrenched open a door, and looked out anxiously.

He was almost stunned by the bright light. At first he couldn't orient himself as he stared down at the metal ramp, the moving strips of glowing metal carrying the throngs of people, sliding along the thoroughfare before him, unaware of him watching, unaware of any change from the usual. The towering buildings before him rose to unbelievable heights, bathed in ever-changing rainbow colors, and he felt his pulse thumping in his temples as he gaped.

He was in the New City, of that there was no doubt. This was the part of the great metropolis which had been built again since the devastating war that had nearly wiped the city from the Earth a decade before. These were the moving streets, the beautiful residential apartments, following the modern neo-functional patterns and participational design which had completely altered the pattern of city living. The Old City still remained, of course—the slums, the tenements, the skid-rows of the metropolis—but this was the teeming heart of the city, a new home for men to live in.

And this was the stronghold where the not-men could be found, too. The thought cut through Harry's mind, sending a tremor up his spine. He had found them here; he had uncovered his first clues here, and discovered them; and even now his mind was filled with the horrible, paralyzing fear he had felt that first night when he had made the discovery. Yet he knew now that he dared not go back where he had come from.

At least he could understand why the not-men might have feared and persecuted him, but he could not understand the horrible assault that Dr. Webber had unleashed. And somehow he found Dr. Webber's attack infinitely more frightening.

He seemed to be safe here, though, at least for the moment.

Quickly he moved down onto the nearest moving sidewalk heading toward the living section of the New City. He knew where he could go there, where he could lock himself in, a place where he could think, possibly find a way to fight off Dr. Webber's attack of nightmares.

He settled back on a bench on the moving sidewalk, watching the city slide past him for several minutes before he noticed the curious shadow-form which seemed to whisk out of his field of vision every time he looked.

They were following him again! He looked around wildly as the sidewalk moved swiftly through the cool evening air. Far above, he could see the shimmering, iridescent screen that still stood to protect the New City from the devastating virus attacks which might again strike down from the skies without warning. Far ahead he could see the magnificent "bridge" formed by the sidewalk crossing over to the apartment area, where the thousands who worked in the New City were returning to their homes.

Someone was still following him.

Presently he heard the sound, so close to his ear he jumped, yet so small he could hardly identify it as a human voice. "What was it you found, Harry? What did you discover? Better tell, better tell."

He saw the rift in the moving sidewalk coming, far ahead, a great, gaping rent in the metal fabric of the swiftly moving escalator, as if a huge blade were slicing it down the middle. Harry's hand went to his mouth, choking back a scream as the hole moved with incredible rapidity down the center of the strip, swallowing up whole rows of the seats, moving straight toward his own.

He glanced in fright over the side just as the sidewalk moved out onto the "bridge," and he gasped as he saw the towering canyons of buildings fall far below, saw the seats tumble end over end, heard the sounds of screaming blend into the roar of air by his ears.

Then the rift screamed by him with a demoniac whine and he sank back onto his bench, gasping as the two cloven halves of the strip clanged back together again.

He stared at the people around him on the strip and they stared back at him, mildly, unperturbed, and returned to their evening papers as the strip passed through the first local station on the other side of the "bridge."

Harry Scott sprang to his feet, moving swiftly across the slower strips for the exit channels. He noted the station stop vaguely, but his only thought now was speed, desperate speed, fear-driven speed to put into action the plan that had suddenly burst in his mind.

He knew that he had reached his limit. He had come to a point beyond which he couldn't fight alone.

Somehow, Webber had burrowed into his brain, laid his mind open to attacks of nightmare and madness that he could never hope to fight. Facing this alone, he would lose his mind. His only hope was to go for help to the ones he feared only slightly less, the ones who had minds capable of fighting back for him.

He crossed under the moveable sidewalks and boarded the one going back into the heart of the city. Somewhere there, he hoped, he would find the help he needed. Somewhere back in that city were men he had discovered who were men and something more.

*   *   *   *   *

Frank Manelli carefully took the blood pressure of the sleeping figure on the bed; then turned to the other man. "He'll be dead soon," he snapped. "Another few minutes now is all it'll take. Just a few more."

"Absurd. There's nothing in these stimuli that can kill him." George Webber sat tense, his eyes fixed on the pale fluctuating screen near the head of the bed.

"His own mind can kill him! He's on the run now; you've broken him loose from his nice safe paranoia. His mind is retreating, running back to some other delusions. It's escaping to the safety his fantasy people can afford him, these not-men he thinks about."

"Yes, yes," agreed Dr. Webber, his eyes eager. "Oh, he's on the run now."

"But what will he do when he finds there aren't any 'not-men' to save him? What will he do then?"

Webber looked up, frowning and grim. "Then we'll know what he found behind the dark door that he opened, that's what."

"No, you're wrong! He'll die. He'll find nothing and the shock will kill him. My God, Webber, you can't tamper with a man's mind like this and hope to save his life! You're obsessed; you've always been obsessed by this impossible search for something in our society, some undiscovered factor to account for the mental illness, the divergent minds, but you can't kill a man to trace it down!"

"It's too neat," said Webber. "He comes back to tell us the truth, and we call him insane. We say he's paranoid, throw him in restraint, place him in an asylum; and we never *know* what he found. The truth is too incredible; when we hear it, it must be insanity we're hearing."

The big doctor laughed, jabbing his thumb at the screen. "This isn't insanity we're seeing. Oh, no, this is the answer we're following. I won't stop now. I've waited too long for this show."

"Well, I say stop it while he's still alive."

Dr. Webber's eyes were deadly. "Get out, Frank," he said softly. "I'm not stopping now."

His eyes returned to the screen, to the bobbing figure that the psycho-integrator traced on the fluorescent background. Twenty years of search had led him here, and now he knew the end was at hand.

5

It was a wild, nightmarish journey. At every step, Harry's senses betrayed him: his wrist watch turned into a brilliant blue-green snake that snapped at his wrist; the air was full of snarling creatures that threatened him at every step. But he fought them off, knowing that they would harm him far less than panic would. He had no idea where to hunt, nor whom to try to reach, but he knew they were there in the New City, and somehow he knew they would help him, if only he could find them.

He got off the moving strip as soon as the lights of the center of the city were clear below, and stepped into the self-operated lift that sped down to ground level. From the elevator, he moved on to one of the long, honeycombed concourses, filled with passing shoppers who stared at the colorful, enticing three-dimensional displays.

At one of the intersections ahead, he spotted a visiphone station, and dropped onto the little seat before the screen. There had been a number, if only he could recall it. But as he started to dial, the silvery screen shattered into a thousand sparkling glass chips, showering the floor with crystal and sparks.

Harry cursed, grabbed the hand instrument, and jangled frantically for the operator. Before she could answer, the instrument grew warm in his hand, then hot and soft, like wax. Slowly, it melted and ran down his arm.

He bolted out into the stream of people, trying desperately to draw some comfort from the crowd around him.

He felt utterly alone; he *had* to contact the not-men who were in the city, warn them, before they spotted him, of the attack he carried with him. If he were leading his pursuer, he could expect no mercy from the ones whose help he sought. He knew the lengths to which they would go to remain undetected in the society around them. Yet he had to find them.

In the distance, he saw a figure waiting, back against one of the show windows. Harry stopped short, ducked into a doorway, and peered out fearfully. Their eyes locked for an instant; then the figure moved on. Harry felt a jolt of horror surge through him. Dr. Webber hunting him in person!

He ducked out of the doorway, turned and ran madly in the opposite direction, searching for an up escalator he could catch. Behind him he heard shots, heard the angry whine of bullets past his ear.

He breathed in great, gasping sobs as he found an almost empty escalator, and bounded up it four steps at a time. Below, he could see Webber coming too, his broad shoulders forcing their way relentlessly through the mill of people.

Panting, Harry reached the top, checked his location against a wall map, and started down the long ramp which led toward the building he had tried to call.

Another shot broke out behind him. The wall alongside powdered away, leaving a gaping hole. On impulse, he leaped into the hole, running through to the rear of the building as the weakened wall swayed and crumbled into a heap of rubble just as Webber reached the place Harry had entered.

Harry breathed a sigh of relief and raced up the stairs of the building to reach a ramp on another level. He turned his eyes toward the tall building at the end of the concourse. There he could hide and relax and try, somehow, to make a contact.

Someone fell into step beside him and took his arm gently but firmly. Harry jerked away, turning terrified eyes to the one who had joined him.

"Quiet," said the man, steering him over toward the edge of the concourse. "Not a sound. You'll be all right."

Harry felt a tremor pass through his mind, the barest touching of mental fingertips, a recognition that sent a surge of eager blood through his heart.

He stopped short, facing the man. "I'm being followed," he gasped. "You can't take me anywhere you don't want Webber to follow, or you'll be in terrible danger."

The stranger shrugged and smiled briefly. "You're not here. You're in a psycho-integrator. It can hurt you, if you let it. But it can't hurt me." He stepped up his pace slightly, and in a moment they turned abruptly into a darkened cul-de-sac.

Suddenly, they were moving *through* the wall of the building into the brilliantly lit lobby of the tall building. Harry gasped, but the stranger led him without a sound toward the elevator, stepped aboard with him, and sped upward, the silence broken only by the whish-whish-whish of the passing floors. Finally they stepped out into a quiet corridor and down through a small office door.

A man sat behind the desk in the office, his face quiet, his eyes very wide and dark. He hardly glanced at Harry, but turned his eyes to the other man.

"Set?" he asked.

"Couldn't miss now."

The man nodded and looked at last at Harry. "You're upset," he murmured. "What's bothering you?"

"Webber," said Harry hoarsely. "He's following me here. He'll spot you. I tried to warn you before I came, but I couldn't."

The man at the desk smiled. "Webber again, eh? Our old friend Webber. That's all right. Webber's at the end of his tether. There's nothing he can do to stop us. He's trying to attack with force, and he fails to realize that time and thought are on our side. The time when force would have succeeded against us is long past. But now there are many of us, almost as many as not."

Harry stared shrewdly at the man behind the desk. "Then why are you so afraid of Webber?" he asked.

"Afraid?"

"You know you are. Long ago you threatened me, if I reported to him. You watched me, played with me. Why are you afraid of him?"

The man sighed. "Webber is premature. We are stalling for time, that's all. We wait. We have grown from so very few, back in the 1940s and 50s, but the time for quiet usurpation of power has not quite arrived. But men like Webber force our hand, discover us, try to expose us."

Harry Scott's face was white, his hands shaking. "And what do you do to them?"

"We—deal with them."

"And those like me?"

The man smiled lopsidedly. "Those like Paulus and Wineberg and the rest—they're happy, really, like little children. But one like you is so much more useful." He pointed almost apologetically to the small screen on his desk.

Harry looked at it, realization dawning. He watched the huge, broad-shouldered figure moving down the hallway toward the door.

"Webber was dangerous to you?"

"Unbelievably dangerous. So dangerous we would use any means to trap him."

Suddenly the door burst open and there stood Webber, a triumphant Webber, face flushed, eyes wide, as he stared at the man behind the desk.

The man smiled back and said, "Come on in, George. We've been waiting for you."

Webber stepped through the door. "Manelli, you fool!"

There was a blinding flash as he crossed the threshold. A faint crackle of sound reached Harry's ears; then the world blacked out....

*   *   *   *   *

It might have been minutes, or hours, or days. The man who had been behind the desk was leaning over Harry, smiling down at him, gently bandaging the trephine wounds at his temples.

"Gently," he said, as Harry tried to sit up. "Don't try to move. You've been through a rough time."

Harry peered up at him. "You're—not Dr. Webber."

"No. I'm Dr. Manelli. Dr. Webber's been called away—an accident. He'll be some time recovering. I'll be taking care of you."

Vaguely, Harry was aware that something was peculiar, something not quite as it should be. The answer slowly dawned on him.

"The statistical analysis!" he exclaimed. "I was supposed to get some data from Dr. Webber about an analysis, something about rising insanity rates."

Dr. Manelli looked blank. "Insanity rates? You must be mistaken. You were brought here for an immunity examination, nothing more. But you can check with Dr. Webber, when he gets back."

6

George Webber sat in the little room, trembling, listening, his eyes wide in the thick, misty darkness. He knew it would be a matter of time now. He couldn't run much farther. He hadn't seen them, true. Oh, they had been very clever, but they thought they were dealing with a fool, and they weren't. He *knew* they'd been following him; he'd known it for a long time now.

It was just as he had been telling the man downstairs the night before: they were everywhere—your neighbor upstairs, the butcher on the corner, your own son or daughter, maybe even the man you were talking to—*everywhere*!

And of course he had to warn as many people as he possibly could before *they* caught him, throttled him off, as they had threatened to if he talked to anyone.

If only the people would *listen* to him when he told them how cleverly it was all planned, how it would only be a matter of months, maybe only weeks or days before the change would happen, and the world would be quietly, silently taken over by the *other* people, the different people who could walk through walls and think in impossibly complex channels. And no one would know the difference, because business would go on as usual.

He shivered, sinking down lower on the bed. If only people would listen to him—

It wouldn't be long now. He had heard the stealthy footsteps on the landing below his room some time ago. This was the night they had chosen to make good their threats, to choke off his dangerous voice once and for all. There were footsteps on the stairs now, growing louder.

Wildly he glanced around the room as the steps moved down the hall toward his door. He rushed to the window, threw up the sash and screamed hoarsely to the silent street below: "Look out! They're here, all around us! They're planning to take over! Look out! Look out!"

The door burst open and there were two men moving toward him, grim-faced, dressed in white; tall, strong men with sad faces and strong arms.

One was saying, "Better come quietly, mister. No need to wake up the whole town."

Meeting of the Board

Originally Published In *If, Worlds of Science Fiction*,
October 1955

MEETING OF THE BOARD

It was going to be a bad day. As he pushed his way nervously through the crowds toward the Exit Strip, Walter Towne turned the dismal prospect over and over in his mind. The potential gloominess of this particular day had descended upon him the instant the morning buzzer had gone off, making it even more tempting than usual just to roll over and forget about it all. Twenty minutes later, the water-douse came to drag him, drenched and gurgling, back to the cruel cold world. He had wolfed down his morning Koffee-Kup with one eye on the clock and one eye on his growing sense of impending crisis. And now, to make things just a trifle worse, he was going to be late again.

He struggled doggedly across the rumbling Exit strip toward the plant entrance. After all, he told himself, why should he be so upset? He *was* Vice President-in-Charge-of-Production of the Robling Titanium Corporation. What could they do to him, really? He had rehearsed *his* part many times, squaring his thin shoulders, looking the union boss straight in the eye and saying, "Now, see here, Torkleson—" But he knew, when the showdown came, that he wouldn't say any such thing. And this was the morning that the showdown would come.

Oh, not because of the *lateness*. Of course Bailey, the shop steward, would take his usual delight in bringing that up. But this seemed hardly worthy of concern this morning. The reports waiting on his desk were what worried him. The sales reports. The promotion-draw reports. The royalty reports. The anticipated dividend reports. Walter shook his head wearily. The shop steward was a goad, annoying, perhaps even infuriating, but tolerable. Torkleson was a different matter.

He pulled his worn overcoat down over frayed shirt sleeves, and tried vainly to straighten the celluloid collar that kept scooting his tie up under his ear. Once off the moving strip, he started up the Robling corridor toward the plant gate. Perhaps he would be fortunate. Maybe the reports would be late. Maybe his secretary's two neurones would fail to synapse this morning, and she'd lose them altogether. And, as long as he was dreaming, maybe Bailey would break his neck on the way to work. He walked quickly past the workers' lounge, glancing in at the groups of men, arguing politics and checking the stock market reports before they changed from their neat gray business suits to their welding dungarees. Running up the stairs to the administrative wing, he paused outside the door to punch the time clock. 8:04. Damn. If only Bailey could be sick—

Bailey was not sick. The administrative offices were humming with frantic activity as Walter glanced down the rows of cubbyholes. In the middle of it all sat Bailey, in his black-and-yellow checkered tattersall, smoking a large cigar. His feet were planted on his desk top, but he hadn't started on his morning Western yet. He was busy glaring, first at the clock, then at Walter.

"Late again, I see," the shop steward growled.

Walter gulped. "Yes, sir. Just four minutes, this time, sir. You know those crowded strips—"

"So it's *just* four minutes now, eh?" Bailey's feet came down with a crash. "After last month's fine production record, you think four minutes doesn't matter, eh? Think just because you're a vice president it's all right to mosey in here whenever you feel like it." He glowered. "Well, this is three times this month you've been late, Towne. That's a demerit for each time, and you know what that means."

"You wouldn't count four minutes as a whole demerit!"

Bailey grinned. "Wouldn't I, now! You just add up your pay envelope on Friday. Ten cents an hour off for each demerit."

Walter sighed and shuffled back to his desk. Oh, well. It could have been worse. They might have fired him like poor Cartwright last month. He'd just *have* to listen to that morning buzzer.

The reports were on his desk. He picked them up warily. Maybe they wouldn't be so bad. He'd had more freedom this last month than before, maybe there'd been a policy change. Maybe Torkleson was gaining confidence in him. Maybe—

The reports were worse than he had ever dreamed.

"*Towne!*"

Walter jumped a foot. Bailey was putting down the visiphone receiver. His grin spread unpleasantly from ear to ear. "What have you been doing lately? Sabotaging the production line?"

"What's the trouble now?"

Bailey jerked a thumb significantly at the ceiling. "The boss wants to see you. And you'd better have the right answers, too. The boss seems to have a lot of questions."

Walter rose slowly from his seat. This was it, then. Torkleson had already seen the reports. He started for the door, his knees shaking.

It hadn't always been like this, he reflected miserably. Time was when things had been very different. It had *meant* something to be vice president of a huge industrial firm like Robling Titanium. A man could have had a fine house of his own, and a 'copter-car, and belong to the Country Club; maybe even have a cottage on a lake somewhere.

Walter could almost remember those days with Robling, before the switchover, before that black day when the exchange of ten little shares of stock had thrown the Robling Titanium Corporation into the hands of strange and unnatural owners.

*   *   *   *   *

The door was of heavy stained oak, with bold letters edged in gold:

TITANIUM WORKERS
OF AMERICA
Amalgamated Locals
Daniel P. Torkleson, Secretary

The secretary flipped down the desk switch and eyed Walter with pity. "Mr. Torkleson will see you."

Walter pushed through the door into the long, handsome office. For an instant he felt a pang of nostalgia—the floor-to-ceiling windows looking out across the long buildings of the Robling plant, the pine paneling, the broad expanse of desk—

"Well? Don't just stand there. Shut the door and come over here." The man behind the desk hoisted his three hundred well-dressed pounds and glared at Walter from under flagrant eyebrows. Torkleson's whole body quivered as he slammed a

sheaf of papers down on the desk. "Just what do you think you're
doing with this company, Towne?"

Walter   swallowed.   "I'm   production   manager   of   the
corporation."

"And just what does the production manager *do* all day?"

Walter reddened. "He organizes the work of the plant,
establishes production lines, works with Promotion and Sales,
integrates Research and Development, operates the planning
machines."

"And you think you do a pretty good job of it, eh? Even asked
for a raise last year!" Torkleson's voice was dangerous.

Walter spread his hands. "I do my best. I've been doing it for
thirty years. I should know what I'm doing."

"*Then how do you explain these reports?*" Torkleson threw the
heap of papers into Walter's arms, and paced up and down
behind the desk. "*Look* at them! Sales at rock bottom. Receipts
impossible. Big orders canceled. The worst reports in seven
years, and you say you know your job!"

"I've been doing everything I could," Walter snapped. "Of
course the reports are bad, they couldn't help but be. We haven't
met a production schedule in over two years. No plant can keep
up production the way the men are working."

Torkleson's face darkened. He leaned forward slowly. "So it's
the *men* now, is it? Go ahead. Tell me what's wrong with the
men."

"Nothing's wrong with the men—if they'd only work. But
they come in when they please, and leave when they please, and
spend half their time changing and the other half on Koffee-Kup.
No company could survive this. But that's only half of it—"
Walter searched through the reports frantically. "This
International Jet Transport account—they dropped us because
we haven't had a new engine in six years. Why? Because
Research and Development hasn't had any money for six years.
What can two starved engineers and a second rate chemist drag
out of an attic laboratory for competition in the titanium
market?" Walter took a deep breath. "I've warned you time and
again. Robling had built up accounts over the years with fine
products and new models. But since the switchover seven years
ago, you and your board have forced me to play the cheap
products for the quick profit in order to give your men their

dividends. Now the bottom's dropped out. We couldn't turn a quick profit on the big, important accounts, so we had to cancel them. If you had let me manage the company the way it should have been run—"

Torkleson had been slowly turning purple. Now he slammed his fist down on the desk. "We should just turn the company back to Management again, eh? Just let you have a free hand to rob us blind again. Well, it won't work, Towne. Not while I'm secretary of this union. We fought long and hard for control of this corporation, just the way all the other unions did. I know. I was through it all." He sat back smugly, his cheeks quivering with emotion. "You might say that I was a national leader in the movement. But I did it only for the men. The men want their dividends. They own the stock, stock is supposed to pay dividends."

"But they're cutting their own throats," Walter wailed. "You can't build a company and make it grow the way I've been forced to run it."

"Details!" Torkleson snorted. "I don't care *how* the dividends come in. That's your job. My job is to report a dividend every six months to the men who own the stock, the men working on the production lines."

Walter nodded bitterly. "And every year the dividend has to be higher than the last, or you and your fat friends are likely to be thrown out of your jobs—right? No more steaks every night. No more private gold-plated Buicks for you boys. No more twenty-room mansions in Westchester. No more big game hunting in the Rockies. No, you don't have to know anything but how to whip a board meeting into a frenzy so they'll vote you into office again each year."

Torkleson's eyes glittered. His voice was very soft. "I've always liked you, Walter. So I'm going to pretend I didn't hear you." He paused, then continued. "But here on my desk is a small bit of white paper. Unless you have my signature on that paper on the first of next month, you are out of a job, on grounds of incompetence. And I will personally see that you go on every White list in the country."

Walter felt the fight go out of him like a dying wind. He knew what the White list meant. No job, anywhere, ever, in management. No chance, ever, to join a union. No more house, no more weekly pay envelope. He spread his hands weakly. "What do you want?" he asked.

"I want a production plan on my desk within twenty-four hours. A plan that will guarantee me a five per cent increase in dividends in the next six months. And you'd better move fast, because I'm not fooling."

*   *   *   *   *

Back in his cubbyhole downstairs, Walter stared hopelessly at the reports. He had known it would come to this sooner or later. They all knew it—Hendricks of Promotion, Pendleton of Sales, the whole managerial staff.

It was wrong, all the way down the line. Walter had fought it tooth and nail since the day Torkleson had installed the moose heads in Walter's old office, and moved him down to the cubbyhole, under Bailey's watchful eye. He had argued, and battled, and pleaded, and lost. He had watched the company deteriorate day by day. Now they blamed him, and threatened his job, and he was helpless to do anything about it.

He stared at the machines, clicking busily against the wall. An idea began to form in his head. Helpless?

Not quite. Not if the others could see it, go along with it. It was a repugnant idea. But there was one thing they could do that even Torkleson and his fat-jowled crew would understand.

They could go on strike.

*   *   *   *   *

"It's ridiculous," the lawyer spluttered, staring at the circle of men in the room. "How can I give you an opinion on the legality of the thing? There isn't any legal precedent that I know of." He mopped his bald head with a large white handkerchief. "There just hasn't *been* a case of a company's management striking against its own labor. It—it isn't done. Oh, there have been lockouts, but this isn't the same thing at all."

Walter nodded. "Well, we couldn't very well lock the men out, they own the plant. We were thinking more of a lock-*in* sort of thing." He turned to Paul Hendricks and the others. "We know how the machines operate. They don't. We also know that the data we keep in the machines is essential to running the business; the machines figure production quotas, organize blueprints, prepare distribution lists, test promotion schemes. It would take an office full of managerial experts to handle even a single phase of the work without the machines."

The man at the window hissed, and Pendleton quickly snapped out the lights. They sat in darkness, hardly daring to breathe. Then: "Okay. Just the man next door coming home."

Pendleton sighed. "You're sure you didn't let them suspect anything, Walter? They wouldn't be watching the house?"

"I don't think so. And you all came alone, at different times." He nodded to the window guard, and turned back to the lawyer. "So we can't be sure of the legal end. You'd have to be on your toes."

"I still don't see how we could work it," Hendricks objected. His heavy face was wrinkled with worry. "Torkleson is no fool, and he has a lot of power in the National Association of Union Stockholders. All he'd need to do is ask for managers, and a dozen companies would throw them to him on loan. They'd be able to figure out the machine system and take over without losing a day."

"Not quite." Walter was grinning. "That's why I spoke of a lock-in. Before we leave, we throw the machines into feedback, every one of them. Lock them into reverberating circuits with a code sequence key. Then all they'll do is buzz and sputter until the feedback is broken with the key. And the key is our secret. It'll tie the Robling office into granny knots, and scabs won't be able to get any more data out of the machines than Torkleson could. With a lawyer to handle injunctions, we've got them strapped."

"For what?" asked the lawyer.

Walter turned on him sharply. "For new contracts. Contracts to let us manage the company the way it should be managed. If they won't do it, they won't get another Titanium product off their production lines for the rest of the year, and their dividends will *really* take a nosedive."

"That means you'll have to beat Torkleson," said Bates. "He'll never go along."

"Then he'll be left behind."

Hendricks stood up, brushing off his dungarees. "I'm with you, Walter. I've taken all of Torkleson that I want to. And I'm sick of the junk we've been trying to sell people."

The others nodded. Walter rubbed his hands together. "All right. Tomorrow we work as usual, until the noon whistle. When we go off for lunch, we throw the machines into lock-step. Then we just don't come back. But the big thing is to keep it quiet until the noon whistle." He turned to the lawyer. "Are you with us, Jeff?"

Jeff Bates shook his head sadly. "I'm with you. I don't know why, you haven't got a leg to stand on. But if you want to commit suicide, that's all right with me." He picked up his briefcase, and started for the door. "I'll have your contract demands by tomorrow," he grinned. "See you at the lynching."

They got down to the details of planning.

*   *   *   *   *

The news hit the afternoon telecasts the following day. Headlines screamed:

MANAGEMENT SABOTAGES ROBLING MACHINES
OFFICE STRIKERS THREATEN LABOR ECONOMY
ROBLING LOCK-IN CREATES PANDEMONIUM

There was a long, indignant statement from Daniel P. Torkleson, condemning Towne and his followers for "flagrant violation of management contracts and illegal fouling of managerial processes." Ben Starkey, President of the Board of American Steel, expressed "shock and regret"; the Amalgamated Buttonhole Makers held a mass meeting in protest, demanding that "the instigators of this unprecedented crime be permanently barred from positions in American Industry."

In Washington, the nation's economists were more cautious in their views. Yes, it *was* an unprecedented action. Yes, there would undoubtedly be repercussions—many industries were having managerial troubles; but as for long term effects, it was difficult to say just at present.

On the Robling production lines the workmen blinked at each other, and at their machines, and wondered vaguely what it was all about.

Yet in all the upheaval, there was very little expression of surprise. Step by step, through the years, economists had been watching with wary eyes the growing movement toward union, control of industry. Even as far back as the '40's and '50's unions, finding themselves oppressed with the administration of growing sums of money—pension funds, welfare funds, medical insurance funds, accruing union dues—had begun investing in corporate stock. It was no news to them that money could make money. And what stock more logical to buy than stock in their own companies?

At first it had been a quiet movement. One by one the smaller firms had tottered, bled drier and drier by increasing production costs, increasing labor demands, and an ever-dwindling margin of profit. One by one they had seen their stocks tottering as they faced bankruptcy, only to be gobbled up by the one ready buyer with plenty of funds to buy with. At first, changes had been small and insignificant: boards of directors shifted; the men were paid higher wages and worked shorter hours; there were tighter management policies; and a little less money was spent on extras like Research and Development.

At first—until that fateful night when Daniel P. Torkleson of TWA and Jake Squill of Amalgamated Buttonhole Makers spent a long evening with beer and cigars in a hotel room, and floated the loan that threw steel to the unions. Oil had followed with hardly a fight, and as the unions began to feel their oats, the changes grew more radical.

Walter Towne remembered those stormy days well. The gradual undercutting of the managerial salaries, the tightening up of inter-union collusion to establish the infamous White list of Recalcitrant Managers. The shift from hourly wage to annual salary for the factory workers, and the change to the other pole for the managerial staff. And then, with creeping malignancy, the hungry howling of the union bosses for more and higher dividends, year after year, moving steadily toward the inevitable crisis.

Until Shop Steward Bailey suddenly found himself in charge of a dozen sputtering machines and an empty office.

*   *   *   *   *

Torkleson was waiting to see the shop steward when he came in next morning. The union boss's office was crowded with TV cameras, newsmen, and puzzled workmen. The floor was littered with piles of ominous-looking paper. Torkleson was shouting into a telephone, and three lawyers were shouting into Torkleson's ear. He spotted Bailey and waved him through the crowd into an inner office room. "Well? Did they get them fixed?"

Bailey spread his hands nervously. "The electronics boys have been at it since yesterday afternoon. Practically had the machines apart on the floor."

"I know that, stupid," Torkleson roared. "I ordered them there. Did they get the machines *fixed?*"

"Uh—well, no, as a matter of fact—"

"Well, *what's holding them up?*"

Bailey's face was a study in misery. "The machines just go in circles. The circuits are locked. They just reverberate."

"Then call American Electronics. Have them send down an expert crew."

Bailey shook his head. "They won't come."

"They *what?*"

"They said thanks, but no thanks. They don't want their fingers in this pie at all."

"Wait until I get O'Gilvy on the phone."

"It won't do any good, sir. They've got their own management troubles. They're scared silly of a sympathy strike."

The door burst open, and a lawyer stuck his head in. "What about those injunctions, Dan?"

"Get them moving," Torkleson howled. "They'll start those machines again, or I'll have them in jail so fast—" He turned back to Bailey. "What about the production lines?"

The shop steward's face lighted. "They slipped up, there. There was one program that hadn't been coded into the machines yet. Just a minor item, but it's a starter. We found it in Towne's desk, blueprints all ready, promotion all planned."

"Good, good," Torkleson breathed. "I have a directors' meeting right now, have to get the workers quieted down a bit. You put the program through, and give those electronics men three more hours to unsnarl this knot, or we throw them out of the union." He started for the door. "What were the blueprints for?"

"Trash cans," said Bailey. "Pure titanium-steel trash cans."

It took Robling Titanium approximately two days to convert its entire production line to titanium-steel trash cans. With the total resources of the giant plant behind the effort, production was phenomenal. In two more days the available markets were glutted. Within two weeks, at a conservative estimate, there would be a titanium-steel trash can for every man, woman, child, and hound dog on the North American continent. The jet engines, structural steels, tubing, and other pre-strike products piled up in the freight yards, their routing slips and order requisitions tied up in the reverberating machines.

But the machines continued to buzz and sputter.

The workers grew restive. From the first day, Towne and Hendricks and all the others had been picketing the plant, until angry crowds of workers had driven them off with shotguns. Then they came back in an old, weatherbeaten 'copter which hovered over the plant entrance carrying a banner with a plaintive message: ROBLING TITANIUM UNFAIR TO MANAGEMENT. Tomatoes were hurled, fists were shaken, but the 'copter remained.

The third day, Jeff Bates was served with an injunction ordering Towne to return to work. It was duly appealed, legal machinery began tying itself in knots, and the strikers still struck. By the fifth day there was a more serious note.

"You're going to have to appear, Walter. We can't dodge this one."

"When?"

"Tomorrow morning. And before a labor-rigged judge, too." The little lawyer paced his office nervously. "I don't like it. Torkleson's getting desperate. The workers are putting pressure on him."

Walter grinned. "Then Pendleton is doing a good job of selling."

"But you haven't got *time*," the lawyer wailed. "They'll have you in jail if you don't start the machines again. They may have you in jail if you *do* start them, too, but that's another bridge. Right now they want those machines going again."

"We'll see," said Walter. "What time tomorrow?"

"Ten o'clock." Bates looked up. "And don't try to skip. You be there, because *I* don't know what to tell them."

Walter was there a half hour early. Torkleson's legal staff glowered from across the room. The judge glowered from the bench. Walter closed his eyes with a little smile as the charges were read: "—breach of contract, malicious mischief, sabotage of the company's machines, conspiring to destroy the livelihood of ten thousand workers. Your Honor, we are preparing briefs to prove further that these men have formed a conspiracy to undermine the economy of the entire nation. We appeal to the spirit of orderly justice—"

Walter yawned as the words went on.

"Of course, if the defendant will waive his appeals against the previous injunctions, and will release the machines that were sabotaged, we will be happy to formally withdraw these charges."

There was a rustle of sound through the courtroom. His Honor turned to Jeff Bates. "Are you counsel for the defendant?"

"Yes, sir." Bates mopped his bald scalp. "The defendant pleads guilty to all counts."

The union lawyer dropped his glasses on the table with a crash. The judge stared. "Mr. Bates, if you plead guilty, you leave me no alternative—"

"—but to send me to jail," said Walter Towne. "Go ahead. Send me to jail. In fact, I *insist* upon going to jail."

The union lawyer's jaw sagged. There was a hurried conference. A recess was pleaded. Telephones buzzed. Then: "Your Honor, the plaintiff desires to withdraw all charges at this time."

"Objection," Bates exclaimed. "We've already pleaded."

"—feel sure that a settlement can be effected out of court—"

The case was thrown out on its ear.

And still the machines sputtered.

*   *   *   *   *

Back at the plant rumor had it that the machines were permanently gutted, and that the plant could never go back into production. Conflicting scuttlebutt suggested that persons high in uniondom had perpetrated the crisis deliberately, bullying Management into the strike for the sole purpose of cutting current dividends and selling stock to themselves cheaply. The rumors grew easier and easier to believe. The workers came to the plants in business suits, it was true, and lounged in the finest of lounges, and read the *Wall Street Journal*, and felt like stockholders. But to face facts, their salaries were not the highest. Deduct union dues, pension fees, medical insurance fees, and sundry other little items which had formerly been paid by well-to-do managements, and very little was left but the semi-annual dividend checks. And now the dividends were tottering.

Production lines slowed. There were daily brawls on the plant floor, in the lounge and locker rooms. Workers began joking about the trash cans; then the humor grew more and more remote. Finally, late in the afternoon of the eighth day, Bailey was once again in Torkleson's office.

"Well? Speak up! What's the beef this time?"

"Sir—the men—I mean, there's been some nasty talk. They're tired of making trash cans. No challenge in it. Anyway, the stock room is full, and the freight yard is full, and the last run of orders we sent out came back because nobody wants any more trash cans." Bailey shook his head. "The men won't swallow it any more. There's—well, there's been talk about having a board meeting."

Torkleson's ruddy cheeks paled. "Board meeting, huh?" He licked his heavy lips. "Now look, Bailey, we've always worked well together. I consider you a good friend of mine. You've got to get things under control. Tell the men we're making progress. Tell them Management is beginning to weaken from its original stand. Tell them we expect to have the strike broken in another few hours. Tell them anything."

He waited until Bailey was gone. Then, with a trembling hand he lifted the visiphone receiver. "Get me Walter Towne," he said.

*   *   *   *   *

"I'm not an unreasonable man," Torkleson was saying miserably, waving his fat paws in the air as he paced back and forth in front of the spokesmen for the striking managers. "Perhaps we were a little demanding, I concede it! Overenthusiastic with our ownership, and all that. But I'm sure we can come to some agreement. A hike in wage scale is certainly within reason. Perhaps we can even arrange for better company houses."

Walter Towne stifled a yawn. "Perhaps you didn't understand us. The men are agitating for a meeting of the board of directors. We want to be at that meeting. That's the only thing we're interested in right now."

"But there wasn't anything about a board meeting in the contract your lawyer presented."

"I know, but you rejected that contract. So we tore it up. Anyway, we've changed our minds."

Torkleson sat down, his heavy cheeks quivering. "Gentlemen, be reasonable! I can guarantee you your jobs, even give you a free hand with the management. So the dividends won't be so large—the men will have to get used to that. That's it, we'll put it through at the next executive conference, give you—"

"The board meeting," Walter said gently. "That'll be enough for us."

The union boss swore and slammed his fist on the desk. "Walk out in front of those men after what you've done? You're fools! Well, I've given you your chance. You'll get your board meeting. But you'd better come armed. Because I know how to handle this kind of board meeting, and if I have anything to say about it, this one will end with a massacre."

*   *   *   *   *

The meeting was held in a huge auditorium in the Robling administration building. Since every member of the union owned stock in the company, every member had the right to vote for members of the board of directors. But in the early days of the switchover, the idea of a board of directors smacked too strongly of the old system of corporate organization to suit the men. The solution had been simple, if a trifle ungainly. Everyone who owned stock in Robling Titanium was automatically a member of the board of directors, with Torkleson as chairman of the board. The stockholders numbered over ten thousand.

They were all present. They were packed in from the wall to the stage, and hanging from the rafters. They overflowed into the corridors. They jammed the lobby. Ten thousand men rose with a howl of anger when Walter Towne walked out on the stage. But they quieted down again as Dan Torkleson started to speak.

It was a masterful display of rabble-rousing. Torkleson paced the stage, his fat body shaking with agitation, pointing a chubby finger again and again at Walter Towne. He pranced and he ranted. He paused at just the right times for thunderous peals of applause.

"This morning in my office we offered to compromise with these jackals," he cried, "and they rejected compromise. Even at the cost of lowering dividends, of taking food from the mouths of your wives and children, we made our generous offers. They were rejected with scorn. These thieves have one desire in mind, my friends, to starve you all, and to destroy your company and your jobs. To every appeal they heartlessly refused to divulge the key to the lock-in. And now this man—the ringleader who keeps the key word buried in secrecy—has the temerity to ask an audience with you. You're angry men; you want to know the man to blame for our hardship."

He pointed to Towne with a flourish. "I give you your man. Do what you want with him."

The hall exploded in angry thunder. The first wave of men rushed onto the stage as Walter stood up. A tomato whizzed past his ear and splattered against the wall. More men clambered up on the stage, shouting and shaking their fists.

Then somebody appeared with a rope.

Walter gave a sharp nod to the side of the stage. Abruptly the roar of the men was drowned in another sound—a soul-rending, teeth-grating, bone-rattling screech. The men froze, jaws sagging, eyes wide, hardly believing their ears. In the instant of silence as the factory whistle died away, Walter grabbed the microphone. "You want the code word to start the machines again? I'll give it to you before I sit down!"

The men stared at him, shuffling, a murmur rising. Torkleson burst to his feet. "It's a trick!" he howled. "Wait 'til you hear their price."

"We have no price, and no demands," said Walter Towne. "We will *give* you the code word, and we ask nothing in return but that you listen for sixty seconds." He glanced back at Torkleson, and then out to the crowd. "You men here are an electing body—right? You own this great plant and company, top to bottom—right? *You should all be rich*, because Robling could make you rich. But not one of you out there is rich. Only the fat ones on this stage are. But I'll tell you how *you* can be rich."

They listened. Not a peep came from the huge hall. Suddenly, Walter Towne was talking their language.

"You think that since you own the company, times have changed. Well, have they? Are you any better off than you were? Of course not. Because you haven't learned yet that oppression by either side leads to misery for both. You haven't learned moderation. And you never will, until you throw out the ones who have fought moderation right down to the last ditch. You know whom I mean. You know who's grown richer and richer since the switchover. Throw him out, and you too can be rich." He paused for a deep breath. "You want the code word to unlock the machines? All right, I'll give it to you."

He swung around to point a long finger at the fat man sitting there. "The code word is TORKLESON!"

*   *   *   *   *

Much later, Walter Towne and Jeff Bates pried the trophies off the wall of the big office. The lawyer shook his head sadly. "Pity about Dan Torkleson. Gruesome affair."

Walter nodded as he struggled down with a moose head. "Yes, a pity, but you know the boys when they get upset."

"I suppose so." The lawyer stopped to rest, panting. "Anyway, with the newly elected board of directors, things will be different for everybody. You took a long gamble."

"Not so long. Not when you knew what they wanted to hear. It just took a little timing."

"Still, I didn't think they'd elect you secretary of the union. It just doesn't figure."

Walter Towne chuckled. "Doesn't it? I don't know. Everything's been a little screwy since the switchover. And in a screwy world like this—" He shrugged, and tossed down the moose head. "*Anything* figures."

Circus

Originally Published In *The Counterfeit Man: More Science Fiction Stories by Alan E. Nourse*, 1963

CIRCUS

"Just suppose," said Morgan, "that I *did* believe you. Just for argument." He glanced up at the man across the restaurant table. "Where would we go from here?"

The man shifted uneasily in his seat. He was silent, staring down at his plate. Not a strange-looking man, Morgan thought. Rather ordinary, in fact. A plain face, nose a little too long, fingers a little too dainty, a suit that doesn't quite seem to fit, but all in all, a perfectly ordinary looking man.

Maybe *too* ordinary, Morgan thought.

Finally the man looked up. His eyes were dark, with a hunted look in their depths that chilled Morgan a little. "Where do we go? I don't know. I've tried to think it out, and I get nowhere. But you've *got* to believe me, Morgan. I'm lost, I mean it. If I can't get help, I don't know where it's going to end."

"I'll tell you where it's going to end," said Morgan. "It's going to end in a hospital. A mental hospital. They'll lock you up and they'll lose the key somewhere." He poured himself another cup of coffee and sipped it, scalding hot. "And that," he added, "will be that."

*   *   *   *   *

The place was dark and almost empty. Overhead, a rotary fan swished patiently. The man across from Morgan ran a hand through his dark hair. "There must be some other way," he said. "There has to be."

"All right, let's start from the beginning again," Morgan said. "Maybe we can pin something down a little better. You say your name is Parks—right?"

The man nodded. "Jefferson Haldeman Parks, if that helps any. Haldeman was my mother's maiden name."

"All right. And you got into town on Friday—right?"

Parks nodded.

"Fine. Now go through the whole story again. What happened first?"

The man thought for a minute. "As I said, first there was a fall. About twenty feet. I didn't break any bones, but I was shaken up and limping. The fall was near the highway going to the George Washington Bridge. I got over to the highway and tried to flag down a ride."

"How did you feel? I mean, was there anything strange that you noticed?"

"*Strange!*" Parks' eyes widened. "I—I was speechless. At first I hadn't noticed too much—I was concerned with the fall, and whether I was hurt or not. I didn't really think about much else until I hobbled up to that highway and saw those cars coming. Then I could hardly believe my eyes. I thought I was crazy. But a car stopped and asked me if I was going into the city, and I knew I wasn't crazy."

Morgan's mouth took a grim line. "You understood the language?"

"Oh, yes. I don't see how I could have, but I did. We talked all the way into New York—nothing very important, but we understood each other. His speech had an odd sound, but—"

Morgan nodded. "I know, I noticed. What did you do when you got to New York?"

"Well, obviously, I needed money. I had gold coin. There had been no way of knowing if it would be useful, but I'd taken it on chance. I tried to use it at a newsstand first, and the man wouldn't touch it. Asked me if I thought I was the U.S. Treasury or something. When he saw that I was serious, he sent me to a money lender, a hock shop, I think he called it. So I found a place—"

"Let me see the coins."

Parks dropped two small gold discs on the table. They were perfectly smooth and perfectly round, tapered by wear to a thin blunt edge. There was no design on them, and no printing. Morgan looked up at the man sharply. "What did you get for these?"

Parks shrugged. "Too little, I suspect. Two dollars for the small one, five for the larger."

"You should have gone to a bank."

"I know that now. I didn't then. Naturally, I assumed that with everything else so similar, principles of business would also be similar."

Morgan sighed and leaned back in his chair. "Well, then what?"

Parks poured some more coffee. His face was very pale, Morgan thought, and his hands trembled as he raised the cup to his lips. Fright? Maybe. Hard to tell. The man put down the cup and rubbed his forehead with the back of his hand. "First, I went to the mayor's office," he said. "I kept trying to think what anyone at home would do in my place. That seemed a good bet. I asked a policeman where it was, and then I went there."

"But you didn't get to see him."

"No. I saw a secretary. She said the mayor was in conference, and that I would have to have an appointment. She let me speak to another man, one of the mayor's assistants."

"And you told him?"

"No. I wanted to see the mayor himself. I thought that was the best thing to do. I waited for a couple of hours, until another assistant came along and told me flatly that the mayor wouldn't see me unless I stated my business first." He drew in a deep breath. "So I stated it. And then I was gently but firmly ushered back into the street again."

"They didn't believe you," said Morgan.

"Not for a minute. They laughed in my face."

Morgan nodded. "I'm beginning to get the pattern. So what did you do next?"

"Next I tried the police. I got the same treatment there, only they weren't so gentle. They wouldn't listen either. They muttered something about cranks and their crazy notions, and when they asked me where I lived, they thought I was—what did they call it?—a wise guy! Told me to get out and not come back with any more wild stories."

"I see," said Morgan.

Jefferson Parks finished his last bite of pie and pushed the plate away. "By then I didn't know quite what to do. I'd been prepared for almost anything excepting this. It was frightening. I tried to rationalize it, and then I quit trying. It wasn't that I attracted attention, or anything like that, quite the contrary. Nobody even looked at me, unless I said something to them. I began to look for things that were *different*, things that I could show them, and say, see, this proves that I'm telling the truth, look at it—" He looked up helplessly.

"And what did you find?"

"Nothing. Oh, little things, insignificant little things. Your calendars, for instance. Naturally, I couldn't understand your frame of reference. And the coinage, you stamp your coins; we don't. And cigarettes. We don't have any such thing as tobacco." The man gave a short laugh. "And your house dogs! We have little animals that look more like rabbits than poodles. But there was nothing any more significant than that. Absolutely nothing."

"Except yourself," Morgan said.

"Ah, yes. I thought that over carefully. I looked for differences, obvious ones. I couldn't find any. You can see that, just looking at me. So I searched for more subtle things. Skin texture, fingerprints, bone structure, body proportion. I still couldn't find anything. Then I went to a doctor."

Morgan's eyebrows lifted. "Good," he said.

Parks shrugged tiredly. "Not really. He examined me. He practically took me apart. I carefully refrained from saying anything about who I was or where I came from; just said I wanted a complete physical examination, and let him go to it. He was thorough, and when he finished he patted me on the back and said, 'Parks, you've got nothing to worry about. You're as fine, strapping a specimen of a healthy human being as I've ever seen.' And that was that." Parks laughed bitterly. "I guess I was supposed to be happy with the verdict, and instead I was ready to knock him down. It was idiotic, it defied reason, it was infuriating."

Morgan nodded sourly. "Because you're not a human being," he said.

"That's right. I'm not a human being at all."

*   *   *   *   *

"How did you happen to pick this planet, or this sun?" Morgan asked curiously. "There must have been a million others to choose from."

Parks unbuttoned his collar and rubbed his stubbled chin unhappily. "I didn't make the choice. Neither did anyone else.

Travel by warp is a little different from travel by the rocket you fiction writers make so much of. With a rocket vehicle you pick your destination, make your calculations, and off you go. The warp is blind flying, strictly blind. We send an unmanned scanner ahead. It probes around more or less hit-or-miss until it locates something, somewhere, that looks habitable. When it spots a likely looking place, we keep a tight beam on it and send through a manned scout." He grinned sourly. "Like me. If it looks good to the scout, he signals back, and they leave the warp anchored for a sort of permanent gateway until we can get a transport beam built. But we can't control the directional and dimensional scope of the warp. There are an infinity of ways it can go, until we have a guide beam transmitting from the other side. Then we can just scan a segment of space with the warp, and the scanner picks up the beam."

He shook his head wearily. "We're new at it, Morgan. We've only tried a few dozen runs. We're not too far ahead of you in technology. We've been using rocket vehicles just like yours for over a century. That's fine for a solar system, but it's not much good for the stars. When the warp principle was discovered, it looked like the answer. But something went wrong, the scanner picked up this planet, and I was coming through, and then something blew. Next thing I knew I was falling. When I tried to make contact again, the scanner was gone!"

"And you found things here the same as back home," said Morgan.

"The same! Your planet and mine are practically twins. Similar cities, similar technology, everything. The people are the same, with precisely the same anatomy and physiology, the same sort of laws, the same institutions, even compatible languages. Can't you see the importance of it? This planet is on the other side of the universe from mine, with the first intelligent life we've yet encountered anywhere. But when I try to tell your people that I'm a native of another star system, *they won't believe me!*"

"Why should they?" asked Morgan. "You look like a human being. You talk like one. You eat like one. You act like one. What you're asking them to believe is utterly incredible."

"*But it's true.*"

Morgan shrugged. "So it's true. I won't argue with you. But as I asked before, even if I *did* believe you, what do you expect *me* to do about it? Why pick *me*, of all the people you've seen?"

There was a desperate light in Parks' eyes. "I was tired, tired of being laughed at, tired of having people looking at me as though I'd lost my wits when I tried to tell them the truth. You were here, you were alone, so I started talking. And then I found out you wrote stories." He looked up eagerly. "I've got to get back, Morgan, somehow. My life is there, my family. And think what it would mean to both of our worlds—contact with another intelligent race! Combine our knowledges, our technologies, and we could explore the galaxy!"

He leaned forward, his thin face intense. "I need money and I need help. I know some of the mathematics of the warp principle, know some of the design, some of the power and wiring principles. You have engineers here, technologists, physicists. They could fill in what I don't know and build a guide beam. But they won't do it if they don't believe me. Your government won't listen to me, they won't appropriate any money."

"Of course they won't. They've got a war or two on their hands, they have public welfare, and atomic bombs, and rockets to the moon to sink their money into." Morgan stared at the man. "But what can *I* do?"

"You can *write*! That's what you can do. You can tell the world about me, you can tell exactly what has happened. I know how public interest can be aroused in my world. It must be the same in yours."

Morgan didn't move. He just stared. "How many people have you talked to?" he asked.

"A dozen, a hundred, maybe a thousand."

"And how many believed you?"

"None."

"You mean *nobody* would believe you?"

"*Not one soul.* Until I talked to you."

And then Morgan was laughing, laughing bitterly, tears rolling down his cheeks. "And I'm the one man who couldn't help you if my life depended on it," he gasped.

"You believe me?"

Morgan nodded sadly. "I believe you. Yes. I think your warp brought you through to a parallel universe of your own planet, not to another star, but I think you're telling the truth."

"Then you *can* help me."

"I'm afraid not."

"Why not?"

"Because I'd be worse than no help at all."

Jefferson Parks gripped the table, his knuckles white. "Why?" he cried hoarsely. "If you believe me, why can't you help me?"

Morgan pointed to the magazine lying on the table. "I write, yes," he said sadly. "Ever read stories like this before?"

Parks picked up the magazine, glanced at the bright cover. "I barely looked at it."

"You should look more closely. I have a story in this issue. The readers thought it was very interesting," Morgan grinned. "Go ahead, look at it."

The stranger from the stars leafed through the magazine, stopped at a page that carried Roger Morgan's name. His eyes caught the first paragraph and he turned white. He set the magazine down with a trembling hand. "I see," he said, and the life was gone out of his voice. He spread the pages viciously, read the lines again.

The paragraph said:

"Just suppose," said Martin, "that I *did* believe you. Just for argument." He glanced up at the man across the table. "Where do we go from here?"

My Friend Bobby

Originally Published In *Orbit No. 3*,
July-August 1954

MY FRIEND BOBBY

My name is Jimmy and I am five years old, and my friend
Bobby is five years old too but he says he thinks he's really more
than five years old because he's already grown up and I'm just a
little boy. We live out in the country because that's where
mommy and daddy live, and every morning daddy takes the car
out of the barn and rides into the city to work, and every night
he comes back to eat supper and to see mommy and Bobby and
me. One time I asked daddy why we don't live in the city like
some people do and he laughed and said you wouldn't really
want to live in the city would you? After all he said you couldn't
have Bobby in the city, so I guess it's better to live in the country
after all.

Anyway daddy says that the city is no place to raise kids
these days. I asked Bobby if I am a kid and he said he guessed so
but I don't think he really knows because Bobby isn't very smart.
But Bobby is my friend even if he doesn't know much and I like
him more than anybody else.

Mommy doesn't like Bobby very much and when I am bad
she makes Bobby go outdoors even when it's cold outside.
Mommy says I shouldn't play with Bobby so much because after
all Bobby is only a dog but I like Bobby. Everyone else is so big,
and when mommy and daddy are home all I can see is their legs
unless I look way up high, and when I do something bad I'm
scared because they're so big and strong. Bobby is strong too but
he isn't any bigger than I am, and he is always nice to me. He
has a long shaggy brown coat and a long pointed nose, and a nice
collar of white fur and people sometimes say to daddy what a
nice collie that is and daddy says yes isn't he and he takes to the
boy so. I don't know what a collie is but I have fun with Bobby all
the time. Sometimes he lets me ride on his back and we talk to
each other and have secrets even though I don't think he is very
smart. I don't know why mommy and daddy don't understand

me when I talk to them the way I talk to Bobby but maybe they just pretend they can't hear me talk that way.

I am always sorry when daddy goes to work in the morning. Daddy is nice to me most times and takes me and Bobby for walks. But mommy never takes me for walks and when we are alone she is busy and she isn't nice to me. Sometimes she says I am a bad boy and makes me stay in my room even when I haven't done anything bad and sometimes she thinks things in her head that she doesn't say to me. I don't know why mommy doesn't like me and Bobby doesn't know either, but we like it best when mommy lets us go outdoors to play in the barn or down by the creek. If I get my feet wet mommy says I am very bad so I stay on the bank and let Bobby go in, but one day when Bobby went into the water just before we went home for supper mommy scolded me and told me I was bad for letting Bobby go into the water and when I told her she hadn't told me not to let Bobby go in she was angry and I could tell that she didn't like me at all that day.

Almost every day I do something that mommy says is bad even when I try specially to be good. Sometimes right after daddy goes away in the morning I know that mommy is angry and is going to spank me sooner or later that day because she is already thinking how she will spank me, but she never says so out loud. Sometimes she pretends that she's not angry and takes me up on her lap and says I'm her nice little boy but all the time I can hear her thinking that she doesn't really like me even when she tries and she doesn't even want to touch me if she can help it. I can hear her wondering why my hair doesn't grow nice like the Bennet twins that live up the road. I don't see how mommy can be saying one thing out loud and something else inside her head at the same time but when I look at her she puts me down and says she's busy and will I get out from underfoot, and then pretty soon I do something that makes her angry and she makes me go to my room or she spanks me. Bobby doesn't like this. Once when she spanked me he growled at mommy, and mommy chased him outdoors with a broom before she sent me to bed. I cried all day that day because it was cold outdoors and I wanted to have Bobby with me.

I wonder why mommy doesn't like me?

*   *   *   *   *

One day I was a bad boy and let Bobby come into the house before mommy told me I could. Bobby hadn't done anything bad but mommy hit him on the back with the broom and hurt him and chased him back outdoors and then she told me I was a very bad boy. I could tell that she was going to spank me and I knew she would hurt me because she was so big, and I ran upstairs and hid in my room. Then mommy stamped her foot hard and said Jimmy you come down here this minute. I didn't answer and then she said if I have to come upstairs and get you I'll whip you until you can't sit down, and I still didn't answer because mommy hurts me when she gets angry like that. Then I heard her coming up the stairs and into my room and she opened the closet door and found me. I said please don't hurt me mommy but she reached down and caught my ear and dragged me out of the closet. I was so scared I bit her hand and she screamed and let go and I ran and locked myself in the bathroom because I knew she would hurt me bad if I didn't. I stayed there all day long and I could hear mommy running the sweeper downstairs and I couldn't see why she wanted to hurt me so much just because I let Bobby come in before she told me I could. But somehow it seemed that mommy was afraid of me even though she was so big and strong. I don't see why anybody as big as mommy should be afraid of me but she was.

When daddy came home that night I heard him talking to mommy, and then he came up to the bathroom and said open the door Jimmy I want to talk to you. I said I want Bobby first so he went down and called Bobby and then I opened the door and came out of the bathroom. Daddy reached down and lifted me high up on his shoulder and took me into my bedroom and just sat there for a long time patting Bobby's head and I couldn't hear what he was thinking very well. Finally he said out loud Jimmy you've got to be good to your mommy and do what she says and not lock yourself up in rooms any more. I said but mommy was going to hurt me and daddy said when you're a bad boy your mommy has to punish you so you'll remember to be good, but she doesn't like to spank you. She only does it because she loves you.

I knew that wasn't true because mommy likes to punish me but I didn't dare say that to daddy. Daddy isn't afraid of me the way mommy is and he is nice to me most times, so I said all right if you say so. Daddy said fine, will you promise to be nice to mommy from now on? I said yes if mommy won't hit Bobby any more with the broom. And daddy said well after all Bobby can be a bad dog just the way you can be a bad boy, can't he? I knew Bobby was never a bad dog on purpose but I said yes I guessed so. Then I wanted to ask daddy why mommy was afraid of me but I didn't dare because I knew daddy liked mommy more than anybody and maybe he would be angry at me for saying things like that about her.

That night I heard mommy and daddy talking down in the living room and I sat on the top step so I could hear them. Bobby sat there too, but I knew he didn't know what they were saying because Bobby isn't very smart and can't understand word-talk like I can. He can only understand think-talk, and he doesn't understand that very well. But now even I couldn't understand what mommy was saying. She was crying and saying Ben I tell you there's something wrong with the child, he knows what I'm *thinking*, I can tell it by the way he looks at me. And daddy said darling, that's ridiculous, how could he possibly know what you're thinking? Mommy said I don't know but he does! Ever since he was a little boy he's known—oh, Ben, it's horrible, I can't do anything with him because he *knows* what I'm going to do before I do it. Then daddy said Carol, you're upset about today and you're making things up. The child is just a little smarter than most kids, there's nothing wrong with that. And mommy said no, there's more to it than that and I can't stand it any longer. We've got to take him to a doctor, I don't even like to look at him. Daddy said you're tired, you're just letting little things get on your nerves. So maybe the boy does look a little strange, you know the doctor said it was just that the fontanelles hadn't closed as soon as they should have and lots of children don't have a good growth of hair before they're six or seven. After all he said he isn't a *bad* looking boy.

Then mommy said that isn't true, he's horrible! I can't bear it, Ben, *please* do something, and daddy said what can I do? I talked to the boy and he was sorry and promised he'd behave himself. And mommy said then there's that dog—it follows him around wherever he goes, and he's simply wicked if the dog isn't around, and daddy said isn't it perfectly normal for a boy to love his dog? Mommy said no, not like this, talking to him all the time, and the dog acting exactly as if he understands—there's something wrong with the child, something horribly wrong.

Then daddy was quiet for a while, and then he said all right, if it will make you feel any better we can have Doctor Grant take another look at him. Maybe he can convince you that there's nothing wrong with the boy, and mommy said please, Ben, anything, I can't stand much more of this.

When I went back to bed and Bobby curled up on the floor, I asked him what were fontanelles, and Bobby just yawned and said he didn't know but he thought I was nice, and he would always take care of me, so I didn't worry any more and went to sleep.

*   *   *   *   *

I have a panda out in the barn and the panda's name is Bobby too and at first Bobby the dog was jealous of Bobby the panda until I told him that the panda was only a make-believe Bobby and he was a real Bobby. Then Bobby liked the panda, and the three of us played out in the barn all day. We decided not to tell mommy and daddy about the panda, and kept it for our own secret. It was a big panda, as big as mommy and daddy, and sometimes I thought maybe I would make the panda hurt mommy but then I knew daddy would be sorry so I didn't.

Bobby and I were playing with Bobby the panda the day the doctor came and mommy called me in and made Bobby stay outside. I didn't like the doctor because he smelled like a dirty old cigar and he had a big red nose with three black hairs coming out of it and he wheezed when he bent down to look at me. Daddy and mommy sat on the couch and the doctor said let me have a look at you young fellow and I said but I'm not sick and the doctor said ha ha, of course you aren't, you're a fine looking boy but just let me listen to your chest for a minute. So he put a cold thing on my chest and stuck some tubes in his ears and listened, and then he looked in my eyes with a bright light and looked into my ears, and then he felt my head all over. He had big hairy hands and I didn't like him touching me but I knew mommy would be angry if I didn't hold still so I let him finish. Then he told daddy some big words that I couldn't understand, but in think-talk he was saying that my head still hadn't closed up right and I didn't have as much hair as you'd expect but otherwise I seemed to be all right. He said I was a good stout looking boy but if they wanted a specialist in to look at me he would arrange it. Daddy asked if that would cost very much and the doctor said yes it probably would and he didn't see any real need for it because my bones were just a little slow in developing, and mommy said have you seen other children like that? The doctor said no but if the boy seems to be normal and intelligent why should she be worrying so? Then mommy told me to go upstairs, and I went but I stopped on the top stair and listened.

When I was gone the doctor said now Carol what is it that's really bothering you? Then mommy told him what she had told daddy, how she thought I knew what she was thinking, and the doctor said to daddy, Ben, have you ever felt any such thing about the boy? Daddy said of course not, sometimes he gives you the feeling that he's smarter than you think he is but all parents have that feeling about their children sometimes. And then mother broke down and her voice got loud and she said he's a monster, I know it, there's something wrong and he's different from us, him and that horrible dog. The doctor said but it's a beautiful collie, and mommy said but he *talks* to it and it *understands* him, and the doctor said now, Carol, let's be reasonable. Mommy said I've been reasonable too long, you men just can't see it at all, don't you think I'd know a normal child if I saw one? And then she cried and cried, and finally she said all right, I know I'm making a fool of myself, maybe I'm just overtired, and the doctor said I'm sure that's the trouble, try to get some rest, and sleep longer at night, and mommy said I can't sleep at night, I just lie there and think.

The doctor said well we'll fix that, enough of this nonsense now, you need your sleep and if you're not sleeping well it's *you* that should be seeing the doctor. He gave her some pills from his bag and then he went away, and pretty soon daddy let Bobby in, and Bobby came upstairs and jumped up and licked my face as if he'd been away for a hundred million years. Later mommy called me down for supper, and she wasn't crying any more, and she and daddy didn't say anything about what they had said to the doctor. Mommy made me a special surprise for dessert, some ice cream with chocolate syrup on top, and after supper we all went for a walk, even though it was cold outside and snowing again. Then daddy said well, I think things will be all right, and mommy said I hope so, but I could tell that she didn't really think so, and she was more afraid of me than ever.

*   *   *   *   *

For a while I thought mommy was really going to be nice to me and Bobby then. She was especially nice when daddy was home but when daddy was away at work sometimes mommy jumped when she saw me looking at her and then sent me outdoors to play and told me not to come in until lunch. I liked that because I knew if I weren't near mommy everything would be all right. When I was with mommy I tried hard not to look at her and I tried not to hear what she was thinking, but lots of times I would see her looking first at me and then at Bobby, and those times I couldn't help hearing what she was thinking because it seemed so loud inside my head that it made my eyes hurt. But I knew mommy would be angry so I pretended I couldn't hear what she was thinking at all.

One day when we were out in the barn playing with Bobby the panda we saw mommy coming down through the snow from the kitchen and Bobby said look out Jimmy mommy is coming and I quick told Bobby the panda to go hide under the hay so mommy couldn't see him. But the panda was so big his whole top and his little pink nose stuck out of the hay. Mommy came in and looked around the barn and said you've been out here for a long time, what have you been doing? I said nothing, and Bobby said nothing too, only in think-talk. And mommy said you are too, you've been doing something naughty, and I said no mommy we haven't done *anything*, and then the panda sneezed and I looked at him and he looked so funny with his nose sticking out of the hay that I laughed out loud.

Mommy looked angry and said well what's so funny, what are you laughing at? I said nothing, because I knew mommy couldn't see the panda, but I couldn't stop laughing because he looked so funny sticking out of the hay. Then mommy got mad and grabbed my ear and shook me until it hurt and said you naughty boy, *don't you lie to me*, what have you been doing out here? She hurt me so much I started to cry and then Bobby snarled at mommy loud and low and curled his lips back over his teeth and snarled some more. And mommy got real white in the face and let go of me and she said get out of here you nasty dog and Bobby snarled louder and then snapped at her. She screamed and she said Jimmy you come in the house this minute and leave that nasty dog outdoors and I said I won't come, I hate you.

Then mommy said Jimmy! You wicked, ugly little monster, and I said I don't care, when I get big I'm going to hurt you and throw you in the wood shed and lock you in until you die and make you eat coconut pudding and Bobby hates you too. And mommy looked terrible and I could feel how much she was afraid of me and I said you just wait, I'll hurt you bad when I get big, and then she turned and ran back to the house. And Bobby wagged his tail and said don't worry, I won't let her hurt you any more and I said Bobby you shouldn't have snapped at her because daddy won't like me when he comes home but Bobby said *I* like you and I won't let anything ever hurt you. I'll always take care of you no matter what. And I said promise? No matter what? And Bobby said I promise. And then we told Bobby the panda to come out but it wasn't much fun playing any more.

After a little while mommy called me and said lunch was ready. She was still white and I said can Bobby come too and she said of course Bobby can come, Bobby's a nice dog, so we went in to eat lunch. Mommy was talking real fast about what fun it was to play in the barn and was I sure I wasn't too cold because it was below zero outside and the radio said a snowstorm was coming, but she didn't say anything about Bobby and me being out in the barn. She was talking so fast I couldn't hear what she was thinking except for little bits while she set my lunch on the table and then she set a bowl of food on the floor for Bobby even though it wasn't Bobby's time to eat and said nice Bobby here's your dinner. Bobby came over and sniffed the bowl and then he looked up at me and said it smells funny and mommy said nice Bobby, it's good hamburger just the way you like it—

And then for just a second I saw what she was thinking and it was terrible because she was thinking that Bobby would soon be dead, and I remembered daddy saying a long time ago that somebody fed bad things to the Bennet's dog and the dog died and I said don't eat it, Bobby, and Bobby snarled at the dish. And then mommy said you tell the dog to eat it and I said no you're bad and you want to hurt Bobby, and then I picked up the dish and threw it at mommy. It missed and smashed on the wall and she screamed and turned and ran out into the other room. She was screaming for daddy and saying I can't stand it, he's a monster, a murderous little monster and we've got to get out of here before he kills us all, he knows what we're thinking, he's horrible, and then she was on the telephone, and she couldn't make the words come out right when she tried to talk.

I was scared and I said come on Bobby let's lock ourselves up in my room and we ran upstairs and locked the door. Mommy was banging things and laughing and crying downstairs and screaming we've got to get out, he'll kill us if we don't, and a while later I heard the car coming up the road fast, and saw daddy run into the house just as it started to snow. Then mommy was screaming please, Ben, we've got to get out of here, he tried to kill me, and the dog is vicious, he bit me when I tried to make him stop.

The next minute daddy was running up the stairs two at a time and I could feel him inside my head for the first time and I knew he was angry. He'd never been this angry before and he rattled the knob and said open this door Jimmy in a loud voice. I said no I won't and he said open the door or I'll break your neck when I get in there and then he kicked the door and kicked it again. The third time the lock broke and the door flew open and daddy stood there panting. His eyes looked terrible and he had a leather belt doubled up in his hand and he said now come out here and his voice was so loud it hurt my ears.

Down below mommy was crying please Ben, take me away, he'll kill us both, he's a monster! I said don't hurt me daddy it was mommy, she was bad to me, and he said I said *come out here* even louder. I was scared then and I said please daddy I'll be good I promise. Then he started for me with the belt and I screamed out Bobby! Don't let him hurt me, Bobby, and Bobby snarled like a wild animal and jumped at daddy and bit his wrist so bad the blood spurted out. Daddy shouted and dropped the belt and kicked at Bobby but Bobby was too quick. He jumped for daddy again and I saw his white teeth flash and heard him snap close to daddy's throat and then Bobby was snarling and snapping and I was excited and I shouted hurt him, Bobby, he's been bad to me too and he wants to hurt me and you've got to stop him.

Then I saw daddy's eyes open wide, and felt something jump in his mind, something that I'd never felt there before and I knew he was understanding my think-talk. I said I want Bobby to hurt you and mommy because you're not nice to me, only Bobby and my panda are nice to me. Go ahead, Bobby, hurt him, bite him again and make him bleed. And then daddy caught Bobby by the neck and threw him across the room and slammed the door shut and dragged something heavy up to block it. In a minute he was running downstairs shouting Carol, *I heard it!* you were right all along—*I felt him, I felt what he was thinking!* And mommy cried please, Ben, take me away, let's leave them and never come back, never, and daddy said it's horrible, he told that dog to kill me and it went right for my throat, the boy is evil and monstrous. Even from downstairs I could feel daddy's fear pounding into my head and then I heard the door banging and looked out the window and saw daddy carrying suitcases out through the snow to the car and then mommy came out running and the car started down the hill and they were gone. Everything downstairs was very quiet. I looked out the window and I couldn't see anything but the big falling snowflakes and the sun going down over the hill.

Now Bobby and I and the panda are all together and I'm glad mommy and daddy are gone. I went to sleep for a little while because my head hurt so but now I'm awake and Bobby is lying across the room licking his feet and I hope mommy and daddy never come back because Bobby will take care of me. Bobby is my friend and he said he'd always take care of me no matter what and he understands my think-talk even if he isn't very smart.

It's beginning to get cold in the house now because nobody has gone down to fix the fire but I don't care about that. Pretty soon I will tell Bobby to push open the door and go down and fix the fire and then I will tell him to get supper for me and then I will stay up all night because mommy and daddy aren't here to make me go to bed. There's just me and Bobby and the panda, and Bobby promised he'd take care of me because he's my friend.

It's getting very cold now, and I'm getting hungry.

THE LINK

ORIGINALLY PUBLISHED IN *IF, WORLDS OF SCIENCE FICTION*,
JUNE 1954

The Link

It was nearly sundown when Ravdin eased the ship down into the last slow arc toward the Earth's surface. Stretching his arms and legs, he tried to relax and ease the tension in his tired muscles. Carefully, he tightened the seat belt for landing; below him he could see the vast, tangled expanse of Jungle-land spreading out to the horizon. Miles ahead was the bright circle of the landing field and the sparkling glow of the city beyond. Ravdin peered to the north of the city, hoping to catch a glimpse of the concert before his ship was swallowed by the brilliant landing lights.

A bell chimed softly in his ear. Ravdin forced his attention back to the landing operation. He was still numb and shaken from the Warp-passage, his mind still muddled by the abrupt and incredible change. Moments before, the sky had been a vast, starry blanket of black velvet; then, abruptly, he had been hovering over the city, sliding down toward warm friendly lights and music. He checked the proper switches, and felt the throbbing purr of the anti-grav motors as the ship slid in toward the landing slot. Tall spires of other ships rose to meet him, circle upon circle of silver needles pointing skyward. A little later they were blotted out as the ship was grappled into the berth from which it had risen days before.

With a sigh, Ravdin eased himself out of the seat, his heart pounding with excitement. Perhaps, he thought, he was too excited, too eager to be home, for his mind was still reeling from the fearful discovery of his journey.

The station was completely empty as Ravdin walked down the ramp to the shuttles. At the desk he checked in with the shiny punch-card robot, and walked swiftly across the polished floor. The wall panels pulsed a somber blue-green, broken sharply by brilliant flashes and overtones of scarlet, reflecting with subtle accuracy the tumult in his own mind. Not a sound was in the air, not a whisper nor sign of human habitation.

Vaguely, uneasiness grew in his mind as he entered the shuttle station. Suddenly, the music caught him, a long, low chord of indescribable beauty, rising and falling in the wind, a distant whisper of life....

The concert, of course. Everyone would be at the concert tonight, and even from two miles away, the beauty of four hundred perfectly harmonized voices was carried on the breeze. Ravdin's uneasiness disappeared; he was eager to discharge his horrible news, get it off his mind and join the others in the great amphitheater set deep in the hillside outside the city. But he knew instinctively that Lord Nehmon, anticipating his return, would not be at the concert.

Riding the shuttle over the edges of Jungle-land toward the shining bright beauty of the city, Ravdin settled back, trying to clear his mind of the shock and horror he had encountered on his journey. The curves and spires of glowing plastic passed him, lighted with a million hues. He realized that his whole life was entangled in the very beauty of this wonderful city. Everything he had ever hoped or dreamed lay sheltered here in the ever-changing rhythm of colors and shapes and sounds. And now, he knew, he would soon see his beloved city burning once again, turning to flames and ashes in a heart-breaking memorial to the age-old fear of his people.

The little shuttle-car settled down softly on the green terrace near the center of the city. The building was a masterpiece of smoothly curving walls and tasteful lines, opening a full side to the south to catch the soft sunlight and warm breezes. Ravdin strode across the deep carpeting of the terrace. There was other music here, different music, a wilder, more intimate fantasy of whirling sound. An oval door opened for him, and he stopped short, staggered for a moment by the overpowering beauty in the vaulted room.

A girl with red hair the color of new flame was dancing with enthralling beauty and abandon, her body moving like ripples of wind to the music which filled the room with its throbbing cry. Her beauty was exquisite, every motion, every flowing turn a symphony of flawless perfection as she danced to the wild music.

"Lord Nehmon!"

The dancer threw back her head sharply, eyes wide, her body frozen in mid-air, and then, abruptly, she was gone, leaving only the barest flickering image of her fiery hair. The music slowed, singing softly, and Ravdin could see the old man waiting in the room. Nehmon rose, his gaunt face and graying hair belying the youthful movement of his body. Smiling, he came forward, clapped Ravdin on the shoulder, and took his hand warmly. "You're too late for the concert—it's a shame. Mischana is the master tonight, and the whole city is there."

Ravdin's throat tightened as he tried to smile. "I had to let you know," he said. "*They're coming*, Nehmon! I saw them, hours ago."

The last overtones of the music broke abruptly, like a glass shattered on stone. The room was deathly still. Lord Nehmon searched the young man's face. Then he turned away, not quite concealing the sadness and pain in his eyes. "You're certain? You couldn't be mistaken?"

"No chance. I found signs of their passing in a dozen places. Then I saw *them*, their whole fleet. There were hundreds. They're coming, I saw them."

"Did they see you?" Nehmon's voice was sharp.

"No, no. The Warp is a wonderful thing. With it I could come and go in the twinkling of an eye. But I could see them in the twinkling of an eye."

"And it couldn't have been anyone else?"

"Could anyone else build ships like the Hunters?"

Nehmon sighed wearily. "No one that we know." He glanced up at the young man. "Sit down, son, sit down. I—I'll just have to rearrange my thinking a little. Where were they? How far?"

"Seven light years," Ravdin said. "Can you imagine it? Just seven, and moving straight this way. *They know where we are*, and they are coming quickly." His eyes filled with fear. "They *couldn't* have found us so soon, unless they too have discovered the Warp and how to use it to travel."

The older man's breath cut off sharply, and there was real alarm in his eyes. "You're right," he said softly. "Six months ago it was eight hundred light years away, in an area completely remote from us. Now just *seven*. In six months they have come so close."

The scout looked up at Nehmon in desperation. "But what can we do? We have only weeks, maybe days, before they're here.

We have no time to plan, no time to prepare for them. What can we do?"

The room was silent. Finally the aged leader stood up, wearily, some fraction of his six hundred years of life showing in his face for the first time in centuries. "We can do once again what we always have done before when the Hunters came," he said sadly. "We can run away."

* * * * *

The bright street below the oval window was empty and quiet. Not a breath of air stirred in the city. Ravdin stared out in bitter silence. "Yes, we can run away. Just as we always have before. After we have worked so hard, accomplished so much here, we must burn the city and flee again." His voice trailed off to silence. He stared at Nehmon, seeking in the old man's face some answer, some reassurance. But he found no answer there, only sadness. "Think of the concerts. It's taken so long, but at last we've come so close to the ultimate goal." He gestured toward the thought-sensitive sounding boards lining the walls, the panels which had made the dancer-illusion possible. "Think of the beauty and peace we've found here."

"I know. How well I know."

"Yet now the Hunters come again, and again we must run away." Ravdin stared at the old man, his eyes suddenly bright. "Nehmon, when I saw those ships I began thinking."

"I've spent many years thinking, my son."

"Not what I've been thinking." Ravdin sat down, clasping his hands in excitement. "The Hunters come and we run away, Nehmon. Think about that for a moment. We run, and we run, and we run. From what? We run from the Hunters. They're hunting *us*, these Hunters. They've never quite found us, because we've always already run. We're clever, we're fortunate, and we have a way of life that they do not, so whenever they have come close to finding us, we have run."

Nehmon nodded slowly. "For thousands of years."

Ravdin's eyes were bright. "Yes, we flee, we cringe, we hide under stones, we break up our lives and uproot our families, running like frightened animals in the shadows of night and secrecy." He gulped a breath, and his eyes sought Nehmon's angrily. "*Why do we run, my lord?*"

Nehmon's eyes widened. "Because we have no choice," he said. "We must run or be killed. You know that. You've seen the records, you've been taught."

"Oh, yes, I know what I've been taught. I've been taught that eons ago our remote ancestors fought the Hunters, and lost, and fled, and were pursued. But why do we keep running? Time after time we've been cornered, and we've turned and fled. *Why?* Even animals know that when they're cornered they must turn and fight."

"We are not animals." Nehmon's voice cut the air like a whiplash.

"But we could fight."

"Animals fight. We do not. We fought once, like animals, and now we must run from the Hunters who continue to fight like animals. So be it. Let the Hunters fight."

Ravdin shook his head. "Do you mean that the Hunters are not men like us?" he said. "That's what you're saying, that they are animals. All right. We kill animals for our food, isn't that true? We kill the tiger-beasts in the Jungle to protect ourselves, why not kill the Hunters to protect ourselves?"

Nehmon sighed, and reached out a hand to the young man. "I'm sorry," he said gently. "It seems logical, but it's false logic. The Hunters are men just like you and me. Their lives are different, their culture is different, but they are men. And human life is sacred, to us, above all else. This is the fundamental basis of our very existence. Without it we would be Hunters, too. If we fight, we are dead even if we live. That's why we must run away now, and always. Because we know that we must not kill men."

* * * * *

On the street below, the night air was suddenly full of voices, chattering, intermingled with whispers of song and occasional brief harmonic flutterings. The footfalls were muted on the polished pavement as the people passed slowly, their voices carrying a hint of puzzled uneasiness.

"The concert's over!" Ravdin walked to the window, feeling a chill pass through him. "So soon, I wonder why?" Eagerly he searched the faces passing in the street for Dana's face, sensing the lurking discord in the quiet talk of the crowd. Suddenly the sound-boards in the room tinkled a carillon of ruby tones in his ear, and she was in the room, rushing into his arms with a happy cry, pressing her soft cheek to his rough chin. "You're back! Oh, I'm so glad, so very glad!" She turned to the old man. "Nehmon, what has happened? The concert was ruined tonight. There was something in the air, everybody felt it. For some reason the people seemed *afraid*."

Ravdin turned away from his bride. "Tell her," he said to the old man.

Dana looked at them, her gray eyes widening in horror. "The Hunters! They've found us?"

Ravdin nodded wordlessly.

Her hands trembled as she sat down, and there were tears in her eyes. "We came so close tonight, so very close. I *felt* the music before it was sung, do you realize that? I *felt* the fear around me, even though no one said a word. It wasn't vague or fuzzy, it was *clear*! The transference was perfect." She turned to face the old man. "It's taken so long to come this far, Nehmon. So much work, so much training to reach a perfect communal concert. We've had only two hundred years here, only *two hundred*! I was just a little girl when we came, I can't even remember before that. Before we came here we were undisturbed for a thousand years, and before that, four thousand. But *two hundred*—we *can't* leave now. Not when we've come so far."

Ravdin nodded. "That's the trouble. They come closer every time. This time they will catch us. Or the next time, or the next. And that will be the end of everything for us, unless we fight them." He paused, watching the last groups dispersing on the street below. "If we only knew, for certain, what we were running from."

There was a startled silence. The girl's breath came in a gasp and her eyes widened as his words sank home. "Ravdin," she said softly, "*have you ever seen a Hunter?*"

Ravdin stared at her, and felt a chill of excitement. Music burst from the sounding-board, odd, wild music, suddenly hopeful. "No," he said, "no, of course not. You know that."

The girl rose from her seat. "Nor have I. Never, not once." She turned to Lord Nehmon. "Have *you*?"

"Never." The old man's voice was harsh.

"Has *anyone* ever seen a Hunter?"

Ravdin's hand trembled. "I—I don't know. None of us living now, no. It's been too long since they last actually found us. I've read—oh, I can't remember. I think my grandfather saw them, or my great-grandfather, somewhere back there. It's been thousands of years."

"Yet we've been tearing ourselves up by the roots, fleeing from planet to planet, running and dying and still running. But suppose we don't need to run anymore?"

He stared at her. "They keep coming. They keep searching for us. What more proof do you need?"

Dana's face glowed with excitement, alive with new vitality, new hope. "Ravdin, can't you see? *They might have changed.* They might not be the same. Things can happen. Look at us, how we've grown since the wars with the Hunters. Think how our philosophy and culture have matured! Oh, Ravdin, you were to be master at a concert next month. Think how the concerts have changed! Even my grandmother can remember when the concerts were just a few performers playing, and everyone else just sitting and *listening*! Can you imagine anything more silly? They hadn't even thought of transference then, they never dreamed what a *real* concert could be! Why, those people had never begun to understand music until they themselves became a part of it. Even we can see these changes, why couldn't the Hunters have grown and changed just as we have?"

Nehmon's voice broke in, almost harshly, as he faced the excited pair. "The Hunters don't have concerts," he said grimly. "You're deluding yourself, Dana. They laugh at our music, they scoff at our arts and twist them into obscene mockeries. They have no concept of beauty in their language. The Hunters are incapable of change."

"And you can be certain of that when *nobody has seen them for thousands of years*?"

Nehmon met her steady eyes, read the strength and determination there. He knew, despairingly, what she was thinking—that he was old, that he couldn't understand, that his mind was channeled now beyond the approach of wisdom. "You mustn't think what you're thinking," he said weakly. "You'd be blind. You wouldn't know, you couldn't have any idea what you would find. If you tried to contact them, you could be lost completely, tortured, killed. If they haven't changed, you wouldn't stand a chance. You'd never come back, Dana."

"But she's right all the same," Ravdin said softly. "You're wrong, my lord. We can't continue this way if we're to survive. Sometime our people must contact them, find the link that was once between us, and forge it strong again. We could do it, Dana and I."

"I could forbid you to go."

Dana looked at her husband, and her eyes were proud. "You could forbid us," she said, facing the old man. "But you could never stop us."

                    *   *   *   *   *

At the edge of the Jungle-land a great beast stood with green-gleaming eyes, licking his fanged jaws as he watched the glowing city, sensing somehow that the mystifying circle of light and motion was soon to become his Jungle-land again. In the city the turmoil bubbled over, as wave after wave of the people made the short safari across the intervening jungle to the circles of their ships. Husbands, wives, fathers, mothers—all carried their small, frail remembrances out to the ships. There was music among them still, but it was a different sort of music, now, an eerie, hopeless music that drifted out of the city in the wind. It caused all but the bravest of the beasts, their hair prickling on their backs, to run in panic through the jungle darkness. It was a melancholy music, carried from thought to thought, from voice to voice as the people of the city wearily prepared themselves once again for the long journey.

To run away. In the darkness of secrecy, to be gone, without a trace, without symbol or vestige of their presence, leaving only the scorched circle of land for the jungle to reclaim, so that no eyes, not even the sharpest, would ever know how long they had stayed, nor where they might have gone.

In the rounded room of his house, Lord Nehmon dispatched the last of his belongings, a few remembrances, nothing more, because the space on the ships must take people, not remembrances, and he knew that the remembrances would bring only pain. All day Nehmon had supervised the loading, the intricate preparation, following plans laid down millennia before. He saw the libraries and records transported, mile upon endless mile of microfilm, carted to the ships prepared to carry them, stored until a new resting place was found. The history of a people was recorded on that film, a people once proud and strong, now equally proud, but dwindling in numbers as toll for the constant roving. A proud people, yet a people who would turn and run without thought, in a panic of age-old fear. They *had* to run, Nehmon knew, if they were to survive.

And with a blaze of anger in his heart, he almost hated the two young people waiting here with him for the last ship to be filled. For these two would not go.

It had been a long and painful night. He had pleaded and begged, tried to persuade them that there was no hope, that the very idea of remaining behind or trying to contact the Hunters was insane. Yet he knew *they* were sane, perhaps unwise, naive, but their decision had been reached, and they would not be shaken.

The day was almost gone as the last ships began to fill. Nehmon turned to Ravdin and Dana, his face lined and tired. "You'll have to go soon," he said. "The city will be burned, of course, as always. You'll be left with food, and with weapons against the jungle. The Hunters will know that we've been here, but they'll not know when, nor where we have gone." He paused. "It will be up to you to see that they don't learn."

Dana shook her head. "We'll tell them nothing, unless it's safe for them to know."

"They'll question you, even torture you."

She smiled calmly. "Perhaps they won't. But as a last resort, we can blank out."

Nehmon's face went white. "You know there is no coming back, once you do that. You would never regain your memory. You must save it for a last resort."

Down below on the street the last groups of people were passing; the last sweet, eerie tones of the concert were rising in the gathering twilight. Soon the last families would have taken their refuge in the ships, waiting for Nehmon to trigger the fire bombs to ignite the beautiful city after the ships started on their voyage. The concerts were over; there would be long years of aimless wandering before another home could be found, another planet safe from the Hunters and their ships. Even then it would be more years before the concerts could again rise from their hearts and throats and minds, generations before they could begin work again toward the climactic expression of their heritage.

Ravdin felt the desolation in the people's minds, saw the utter hopelessness in the old man's face, and suddenly felt the pressure of despair. It was such a slender hope, so frail and so dangerous. He knew of the terrible fight, the war of his people against the Hunters, so many thousand years before. They had risen together, a common people, their home a single planet. And then, the gradual splitting of the nations, his own people living in peace, seeking the growth and beauty of the arts, despising the bitterness and barrenness of hatred and killing—and the Hunters, under an iron heel of militarism, of government for the perpetuation of government, split farther and farther from them. It was an ever-widening split as the Hunters sneered and ridiculed, and then grew to hate Ravdin's people for all the things the Hunters were losing: peace, love, happiness. Ravdin knew of his people's slowly dawning awareness of the sanctity of life, shattered abruptly by the horrible wars, and then the centuries of fear and flight, hiding from the wrath of the Hunters' vengeance. His people had learned much in those long years. They had conquered disease. They had grown in strength as they dwindled in numbers. But now the end could be seen, crystal clear, the end of his people and a ghastly grave.

Nehmon's voice broke the silence. "If you must stay behind, then go now. The city will burn an hour after the count-down."

"We will be safe, outside the city." Dana gripped her husband's hand, trying to transmit to him some part of her strength and confidence. "Wish us the best, Nehmon. If a link can be forged, we will forge it."

"I wish you the best in everything." There were tears in the old man's eyes as he turned and left the room.

*   *   *   *   *

They stood in the Jungle-land, listening to the scurry of frightened animals, and shivering in the cool night air as the bright sparks of the ships' exhausts faded into the black starry sky. A man and a woman alone, speechless, watching, staring with awful longing into the skies as the bright rocket jets dwindled to specks and flickered out.

The city burned. Purple spumes of flame shot high into the air, throwing a ghastly light on the frightened Jungle-land. Spires of flame seemed to be seeking the stars with their fingers as the plastic walls and streets of the city hissed and shriveled, blackening, bubbling into a vanishing memory before their eyes. The flames shot high, carrying with them the last remnants of the city which had stood proud and tall an hour before. Then a silence fell, deathly, like the lifeless silence of a grave. Out of the silence, little whispering sounds of the Jungle-land crept to their ears, first frightened, then curious, then bolder and bolder as the wisps of grass and little animals ventured out and out toward the clearing where the city had stood. Bit by bit the Jungle-land gathered courage, and the clearing slowly, silently, began to disappear.

Days later new sparks of light appeared in the black sky. They grew to larger specks, then to flares, and finally settled to the earth as powerful, flaming jets.

They were squat, misshapen vessels, circling down like vultures, hissing, screeching, landing with a grinding crash in the tall thicket near the place where the city had stood. Ravdin's signal had guided them in, and the Hunters had seen them, standing on a hilltop above the demolished amphitheater. Men had come out of the ships, large men with cold faces and dull eyes, weapons strapped to their trim uniforms. The Hunters had blinked at them, unbelieving, with their weapons held at ready. Ravdin and Dana were seized and led to the flagship.

As they approached it, their hearts sank and they clasped hands to bolster their failing hope.

The leader of the Hunters looked up from his desk as they were thrust into his cabin. Frankle's face was a graven mask as he searched their faces dispassionately. The captives were pale and seemed to cringe from the pale interrogation light. "Chickens!" the Hunter snorted. "We have been hunting down chickens." His eyes turned to one of the guards. "They have been searched?"

"Of course, master."

"And questioned?"

The guard frowned. "Yes, sir. But their language is almost unintelligible."

"You've studied the basic tongues, haven't you?" Frankle's voice was as cold as his eyes.

"Of course, sir, but this is so different."

Frankle stared in contempt at the fair-skinned captives, fixing his eyes on them for a long moment. Finally he said, "Well?"

Ravdin glanced briefly at Dana's white face. His voice seemed weak and high-pitched in comparison to the Hunter's baritone. "You are the leader of the Hunters?"

Frankle regarded him sourly, without replying. His thin face was swarthy, his short-cut gray hair matching the cold gray of his eyes. It was an odd face, completely blank of any thought or emotion, yet capable of shifting to a strange biting slyness in the briefest instant. It was a rich face, a face of inscrutable depth. He pushed his chair back, his eyes watchful. "We know your people were here," he said suddenly. "Now they've gone, and yet you remain behind. There must be a reason for such rashness. Are you sick? Crippled?"

Ravdin shook his head. "We are not sick."

"Then criminals, perhaps? Being punished for rebellious plots?"

"We are not criminals."

The Hunter's fist crashed on the desk. "Then why are you here? *Why?* Are you going to tell me now, or do you propose to waste a few hours of my time first?"

"There is no mystery," Ravdin said softly. "We stayed behind to plead for peace."

"For peace?" Frankle stared in disbelief. Then he shrugged, his face tired. "I might have known. Peace! Where have your people gone?"

Ravdin met him eye for eye. "I can't say."

The Hunter laughed. "Let's be precise, you don't *choose* to say, just now. But perhaps very soon you will wish with all your heart to tell me."

Dana's voice was sharp. "We're telling you the truth. We want peace, nothing more. This constant hunting and running is senseless, exhausting to both of us. We want to make peace with you, to bring our people together again."

Frankle snorted. "You came to us in war, once, long ago. Now you want peace. What would you do, clasp us to your bosom, smother us in your idiotic music? Or have you gone on to greater things?"

Ravdin's face flushed hotly. "Much greater things," he snapped.

Frankle sat down slowly. "No doubt," he said. "Now understand me clearly. Very soon you will be killed. How quickly or slowly you die will depend largely upon the civility of your tongues. A civil tongue answers questions with the right answers. That is my definition of a civil tongue." He sat back coldly. "Now, shall we commence asking questions?"

Dana stepped forward suddenly, her cheeks flushed. "We don't have the words to express ourselves," she said softly. "We can't tell you in words what we have to say, but music is a language even you can understand. We can tell you what we want in music."

Frankle scowled. He knew about the magic of this music, he had heard of the witchcraft these weak chicken-people could weave, of their strange, magic power to steal strong men's minds from them and make them like children before wolves. But he had never heard this music with his own ears. He looked at them, his eyes strangely bright. "You know I cannot listen to your music. It is forbidden, even you should know that. How dare you propose—"

"But this is different music." Dana's eyes widened, and she threw an excited glance at her husband. "Our music is beautiful, wonderful to hear. If you could only hear it—"

"Never." The man hesitated. "Your music is forbidden, poisonous."

Her smile was like sweet wine, a smile that worked into the Hunter's mind like a gentle, lazy drug. "But who is to permit or forbid? After all, you are the leader here, and forbidden pleasures are all the sweeter."

Frankle's eyes were on hers, fascinated. Slowly, with a graceful movement, she drew the gleaming thought-sensitive stone from her clothing. It glowed in the room with a pearly luminescence, and she saw the man's eyes turning to it, drawn as if by magic. Then he looked away, and a cruel smile curled his lips. He motioned toward the stone. "All right," he said mockingly. "Do your worst. Show me your precious music."

Like a tinkle of glass breaking in a well, the stone flashed its fiery light in the room. Little swirls of music seemed to swell from it, blossoming in the silence. Frankle tensed, a chill running up his spine, his eyes drawn back to the gleaming jewel. Suddenly, the music filled the room, rising sweetly like an overpowering wave, filling his mind with strange and wonderful images. The stone shimmered and changed, taking the form of dancing clouds of light, swirling with the music as it rose. Frankle felt his mind groping toward the music, trying desperately to reach into the heart of it, to become part of it.

Ravdin and Dana stood there, trancelike, staring transfixed at the gleaming center of light, forcing their joined minds to create the crashing, majestic chords as the song lifted from the depths of oblivion to the heights of glory in the old, old song of their people.

A song of majesty, and strength, and dignity. A song of love, of aspiration, a song of achievement. A song of peoples driven by ancient fears across the eons of space, seeking only peace, even peace with those who drove them.

Frankle heard the music, and could not comprehend, for his mind could not grasp the meaning, the true overtones of those glorious chords, but he felt the strangeness in the pangs of fear which groped through his mind, cringing from the wonderful strains, dazzled by the dancing light. He stared wide-eyed and trembling at the couple across the room, and for an instant it seemed that he was stripped naked. For a fleeting moment the authority was gone from his face; gone too was the cruelty, the avarice, the sardonic mockery. For the briefest moment his cold gray eyes grew incredibly tender with a sudden ancient, long-forgotten longing, crying at last to be heard.

And then, with a scream of rage he was stumbling into the midst of the light, lashing out wildly at the heart of its shimmering brilliance. His huge hand caught the hypnotic stone and swept it into crashing, ear-splitting cacophony against the cold steel bulkhead. He stood rigid, his whole body shaking, eyes blazing with fear and anger and hatred as he turned on Ravdin and Dana. His voice was a raging storm of bitterness drowning out the dying strains of the music.

"Spies! You thought you could steal my mind away, make me forget my duty and listen to your rotten, poisonous noise! Well, you failed, do you hear? I didn't hear it, I didn't listen, *I didn't*! I'll hunt you down as my fathers hunted you down, I'll bring my people their vengeance and glory, and your foul music will be dead!"

He turned to the guards, wildly, his hands still trembling. "Take them out! Whip them, burn them, do anything! But find out where their people have gone. Find out! Music! We'll take the music out of them, once and for all."

*   *   *   *   *

The inquisition had been horrible. Their minds had had no concept of such horror, such relentless, racking pain. The blazing lights, the questions screaming in their ears, Frankle's vicious eyes burning in frustration, and their own screams, rising with each question they would not answer until their throats were scorched and they could no longer scream. Finally they reached the limit they could endure, and muttered together the hoarse words that could deliver them. Not words that Frankle could hear, but words to bring deliverance, to blank out their minds like a wet sponge over slate. The hypnotic key clicked into the lock of their minds; their screams died in their brains. Frankle stared at them, and knew instantly what they had done, a technique of memory obliteration known and dreaded for so many thousands of years that history could not remember. As his captives stood mindless before him, he let out one hoarse, agonized scream of frustration and defeat.

But strangely enough he did not kill them. He left them on a cold stone ledge, blinking dumbly at each other as the ships of his fleet rose one by one and vanished like fireflies in the dark night sky. Naked, they sat alone on the planet of the Jungleland. They knew no words, no music, nothing. And they did not even know that in the departing ships a seed had been planted. For Frankle *had* heard the music. He had grasped the beauty of his enemies for that brief instant, and in that instant they had become less his enemies. A tiny seed of doubt had been planted. The seed would grow.

The two sat dumbly, shivering. Far in the distance, a beast roared against the heavy night, and a light rain began to fall. They sat naked, the rain soaking their skin and hair. Then one of them grunted, and moved into the dry darkness of the cave. Deep within him some instinct spoke, warning him to fear the roar of the animal.

Blinking dully, the woman crept into the cave after him. Three thoughts alone filled their empty minds. Not thoughts of Nehmon and his people; to them, Nehmon had never existed, forgotten as completely as if he had never been. No thoughts of the Hunters, either, nor of their unheard-of mercy in leaving them their lives—lives of memoryless oblivion, like animals in this green Jungle-land, but lives nonetheless.

Only three thoughts filled their minds:

It was raining.

They were hungry.

The Saber-tooth was prowling tonight.

They never knew that the link had been forged.

IMAGE OF THE GODS

ORIGINALLY PUBLISHED IN *ORBIT NO. 4,*
SEPTEMBER-OCTOBER 1954

IMAGE OF THE GODS

It was nearly winter when the ship arrived. Pete Farnam never knew if the timing had been planned that way or not. It might have been coincidence that it came just when the colony was predicting its first real bumper crop of all time. When it was all over, Pete and Mario and the rest tried to figure it out, but none of them ever knew for sure just *what* had happened back on Earth, or *when* it had actually happened. There was too little information to go on, and practically none that they could trust. All Pete Farnam really knew, that day, was that this was the wrong year for a ship from Earth to land on Baron IV.

Pete was out on the plantation when it landed. As usual, his sprayer had gotten clogged; tarring should have been started earlier, before it got so cold that the stuff clung to the nozzle and hardened before the spray could settle into the dusty soil. The summer past had been the colony's finest in the fourteen years he'd been there, a warm, still summer with plenty of rain to keep the dirt down and let the *taaro* get well rooted and grow up tall and gray against the purple sky. But now the *taaro* was harvested. It was waiting, compressed and crated, ready for shipment, and the heavy black clouds were scudding nervously across the sky, faster with every passing day. Two days ago Pete had asked Mario to see about firing up the little furnaces the Dusties had built to help them fight the winter. All that remained now was tarring the fields, and then buckling down beneath the wind shields before the first winter storms struck.

Pete was trying to get the nozzle of the tar sprayer cleaned out when Mario's jeep came roaring down the rutted road from the village in a cloud of dust. In the back seat a couple of Dusties were bouncing up and down like happy five-year-olds. The brakes squealed and Mario bellowed at him from the road. "Pete! The ship's in! Better get hopping!"

Pete nodded and started to close up the sprayer. One of the Dusties tumbled out of the jeep and scampered across the field to give him a hand. It was an inexpert hand to say the least, but the Dusties seemed so proud of the little they were able to learn about mechanized farming that nobody had the heart to shoo them away. Pete watched the fuzzy brown creature get its paws thoroughly gummed up with tar before he pulled him loose and sent him back to the jeep with a whack on the backside. He finished the job himself, grabbed his coat from the back of the sprayer, and pulled himself into the front seat of the jeep.

Mario started the little car back down the road. The young colonist's face was coated with dust, emphasizing the lines of worry around his eyes. "I don't like it, Pete. There isn't any ship due this year."

"When did it land?"

"About twenty minutes ago. Won't be cool for a while yet."

Pete laughed. "Maybe Old Schooner is just getting lonesome to swap tall stories with us. Maybe he's even bringing us a locker of T-bones. Who knows?"

"Maybe," said Mario without conviction.

Pete looked at him, and shrugged. "Why complain if they're early? Maybe they've found some new way to keep our fields from blowing away on us every winter." He stared across at the heavy windbreaks between the fields—long, ragged structures built in hope of outwitting the vicious winds that howled across the land during the long winter. Pete picked bits of tar from his beard, and wiped the dirt from his forehead with the back of his hand. "This tarring is mean," he said wearily. "Glad to take a break."

"Maybe Cap Schooner will know something about the rumors we've been hearing," Mario said gloomily.

Pete looked at him sharply. "About Earth?"

Mario nodded. "Schooner's a pretty good guy, I guess. I mean, he'd tell us if anything was *really* wrong back home, wouldn't he?"

Pete nodded, and snapped his fingers. One of the Dusties hopped over into his lap and began gawking happily at the broad fields as the jeep jogged along. Pete stroked the creature's soft brown fur with his tar-caked fingers. "Maybe someday these little guys will show us where *they* go for the winter," he said. "They must have it down to a science."

Somehow the idea was funny, and both men roared. If the Dusties had *anything* down to a science, nobody knew what.

Mario grinned and tweaked the creature's tail. "They sure do beat the winter, though," he said.

"So do we. Only we have to do it the human way. These fellas grew up in the climate." Pete lapsed into silence as the village came into view. The ship had landed quite a way out, resting on its skids on the long shallow groove the colonists had bulldozed out for it years before, the first year they had arrived on Baron IV. Slowly Pete turned Mario's words over in his mind, allowing himself to worry a little. There *had* been rumors of trouble back on Earth, persistent rumors he had taken care to soft-pedal, as mayor of the colony. There were other things, too, like the old newspapers and magazines that had been brought in by the lad from Baron II, and the rare radio message they could pick up through their atmospheric disturbance. Maybe something *was* going wrong back home. But somehow political upheavals on Earth seemed remote to these hardened colonists. Captain Schooner's visits were always welcome, but they were few and far between. The colony was small; one ship every three years could supply it, and even then the *taaro* crates wouldn't half fill up the storage holds. There were other colonies far closer to home that sent back more *taaro* in one year than Baron IV could grow in ten.

But when a ship did come down, it was a time of high excitement. It meant fresh food from Earth, meat from the frozen lockers, maybe even a little candy and salt. And always for Pete a landing meant a long evening of palaver with the captain about things back home and things on Baron IV.

Pete smiled to himself as he thought of it. He could remember Earth, of course, with a kind of vague nostalgia, but Baron IV was home to him now and he knew he would never leave it. He had too many hopes invested there, too many years of heartache and desperate hard work, too much deep satisfaction in having cut a niche for himself on this dusty, hostile world, ever to think much about Earth any more.

Mario stopped in front of the offices, and one of the Dusties hopped out ahead of Pete. The creature strode across the rough gravel to the door, pulling tar off his fingers just as he had seen Pete do. Pete followed him to the door, and then stopped, frowning. There should have been a babble of voices inside, with Captain Schooner's loud laugh roaring above the excitement.

But Pete could hear nothing. A chill of uneasiness ran through him; he pushed open the door and walked inside. A dozen of his friends looked up silently, avoiding the eyes of the uniformed stranger in the center of the room. When he saw the man, Pete Farnam knew something was wrong indeed.

It wasn't Captain Schooner. It was a man he'd never seen before.

*   *   *   *   *

The Dustie ran across the room in front of Pete and hopped up on the desk as though he owned it, throwing his hands on his hips and staring at the stranger curiously. Pete took off his cap and parka and dropped them on a chair. "Well," he said. "This is a surprise. We weren't expecting a ship so soon."

The man inclined his head stiffly and glanced down at the paper he held in his hand. "You're Peter Farnam, I suppose? Mayor of this colony?"

"That's right. And you?"

"Varga is the name," the captain said shortly. "Earth Security and Supply." He nodded toward the small, frail-looking man in civilian clothes, sitting beside him. "This is Rupert Nathan, of the Colonial Service. You'll be seeing a great deal of him." He held out a small wallet of papers. "Our credentials, Farnam. Be so good as to examine them."

Pete glanced around the room. John Tegan and Hank Mario were watching him uneasily. Mary Turner was following the proceedings with her sharp little eyes, missing nothing, and Mel Dorfman stood like a rock, his heavy face curiously expressionless as he watched the visitors. Pete reached out for the papers, flipped through them, and handed them back with a long look at Captain Varga.

He was younger than Captain Schooner, with sandy hair and pale eyes that looked up at Pete from a soft baby face. Clean-shaven, his whole person seemed immaculate as he leaned back calmly in the chair. His civilian companion, however, had indecision written in every line of his pink face. His hands fluttered nervously, and he avoided the colonist's eyes.

Pete turned to the captain. "The papers say you're our official supply ship," he said. "You're early, but an Earth ship is always good news." He clucked at the Dustie, who was about to go after one of the shiny buttons on the captain's blouse. The little brown creature hopped over and settled on Pete's knee. "We've been used to seeing Captain Schooner."

The captain and Nathan exchanged glances. "Captain Schooner has retired from Security Service," the captain said shortly. "You won't be seeing him again. But we have a cargo for your colony. You may send these people over to the ship to start unloading now, if you wish—" his eye swept the circle of windburned faces—"while Nathan and I discuss certain matters with you here."

Nobody moved for a moment. Then Pete nodded to Mario. "Take the boys out to unload, Jack. We'll see you back here in an hour or so."

"Pete, are you sure—"

"Don't worry. Take Mel and Hank along to lend a hand." Pete turned back to Captain Varga. "Suppose we go inside to more comfortable quarters," he said. "We're always glad to have word from Earth."

They passed through a dark, smelly corridor into Pete's personal quarters. For a colony house, if wasn't bad—good plastic chairs, a hand-made rug on the floor, even one of Mary Turner's paintings on the wall, and several of the weird, stylized carvings the Dusties had done for Pete. But the place smelled of tar and sweat, and Captain Varga's nose wrinkled in distaste. Nathan drew out a large silk handkerchief and wiped his pink hands, touching his nose daintily.

The Dustie hopped into the room ahead of them and settled into the biggest, most comfortable chair. Pete snapped his fingers sharply, and the brown creature jumped down again like a naughty child and climbed up on Pete's knee. The captain glanced at the chair with disgust and sat down in another. "Do you actually let those horrid creatures have the run of your house?" he asked.

"Why not?" Pete said. "We have the run of their planet. They're quite harmless, really. And quite clean."

The captain sniffed. "Nasty things. Might find a use for the furs, though. They look quite soft."

"We don't kill Dusties," said Pete coolly. "They're friendly, and intelligent too, in a childish sort of way." He looked at the captain and Nathan, and decided not to put on the coffee pot. "Now what's the trouble?"

"No trouble at all," the captain said, "except the trouble you choose to make. You have your year's *taaro* ready for shipping?"

"Of course."

The captain took out a small pencil on a chain and began to twirl it. "How much, to be exact?"

"Twenty thousand, Earth weight."

"Tons?"

Pete shook his head. "Hundredweight."

The captain raised his eyebrows. "I see. And there are—" he consulted the papers in his hand—"roughly two hundred and twenty colonists here on Baron IV. Is that right?"

"That's right."

"Seventy-four men, eighty-one women, and fifty-nine children, to be exact?"

"I'd have to look it up. Margaret Singman had twins the other night."

"Well, don't be ridiculous," snapped the captain. "On a planet the size of Baron IV, with seventy-four men, you should be producing a dozen times the *taaro* you stated. We'll consider that your quota for a starter, at least. You have ample seed, according to my records. I should think, with the proper equipment—"

"Now wait a minute," Pete said softly. "We're fighting a climate here, captain. You should know that. We have only a two-planting season, and the 'proper equipment,' as you call it, doesn't operate too well out here. It has a way of clogging up with dust in the summer, and rusting in the winter."

"Really," said Captain Varga. "As I was saying, with the proper equipment, you could cultivate a great deal more land than you seem to be using. This would give you the necessary heavier yield. Wouldn't you say so, Nathan?"

The little nervous man nodded. "Certainly, captain. With the proper organization of labor."

"That's nonsense," Pete said, suddenly angry. "Nobody can get that kind of yield from this planet. The ground won't give it, and the men won't grow it."

The captain gave him a long look. "Really?" he said. "I think you're wrong. I think the men will grow it."

Pete stood up slowly. "What are you trying to say? This business about quotas and organization of labor—"

"You didn't read our credentials as we instructed you, Farnam. Mr. Nathan is the official governor of the colony on Baron IV, as of now. You'll find him most co-operative, I'm sure, but he's answerable directly to me in all matters. My job is administration of the entire Baron system. Clear enough?"

Pete's eyes were dark. "I think you'd better draw me a picture," he said tightly. "A very clear picture."

"Very well. Baron IV is not paying for its upkeep. *Taaro*, after all, is not the most necessary of crops in the universe. It has value, but not very much value, all things considered. If the production of *taaro* here is not increased sharply, it may be necessary to close down the colony altogether."

"You're a liar," said Pete shortly. "The Colonization Board makes no production demands on the colonies. Nor does it farm out systems for personal exploitation."

The captain smiled. "The Colonization Board, as you call it, has undergone a slight reorganization," he said.

"*Reorganization!* It's a top-level board in the Earth Government! Nothing could reorganize it but a wholesale—" He broke off, his jaw sagging as the implication sank in.

"You're rather out on a limb, you see," said the captain coolly. "Poor communications and all that. The fact is that the entire Earth Government has undergone a slight reorganization also."

*   *   *   *   *

The Dustie knew that something had happened.

Pete didn't know how he knew. The Dusties couldn't talk, couldn't make *any* noise, as far as Pete knew. But they always seemed to know when something unusual was happening. It was wrong, really, to consider them unintelligent animals. There are other sorts of intelligence than human, and other sorts of communication, and other sorts of culture. The Baron IV colonists had never understood the queer perceptive sense that the Dusties seemed to possess, any more than they knew how many Dusties there were, or what they ate, or where on the planet they lived. All they knew was that when they landed on Baron IV, the Dusties were there.

At first the creatures had been very timid. For weeks the men and women, busy with their building, had paid little attention to the skittering brown forms that crept down from the rocky hills to watch them with big, curious eyes. They were about half the size of men, and strangely humanoid in appearance, not in the sense that a monkey is humanoid (for they did *not* resemble monkeys) but in some way the colonists could not quite pin down. It may have been the way they walked around on their long, fragile hind legs, the way they stroked their pointed chins as they sat and watched and listened with their pointed ears lifted alertly, watching with soft gray eyes, or the way they handled objects with their little four-fingered hands. They were so remarkably human-like in their elfin way that the colonists couldn't help but be drawn to the creatures.

That whole first summer, when the colonists were building the village and the landing groove for the ships, the Dusties were among them, trying pathetically to help, so eager for friendship that even occasional rebuffs failed to drive them away. They *liked* the colony. They seemed, somehow, to savor the atmosphere, moving about like solemn, fuzzy overseers as the work progressed through the summer. Pete Farnam thought that they had even tried to warn the people about the winter. But the colonists couldn't understand, of course. Not until later. The Dusties became a standing joke, and were tolerated with considerable amusement—until the winter struck.

It had come with almost unbelievable ferocity. The houses had not been completed when the first hurricanes came, and they were smashed into toothpicks. The winds came, vicious winds full of dust and sleet and ice, wild erratic twisting gales that ripped the village to shreds, tearing off the topsoil that had been broken and fertilized—merciless, never-ending winds that wailed and screamed the planet's protest. The winds drove sand and dirt and ice into the heart of the generators, and the heating units corroded and jammed and went dead. The jeeps and tractors and bulldozers were scored and rusted. The people began dying by the dozens as they huddled down in the pitiful little pits they had dug to try to keep the winds away.

Few of them were still conscious when the Dusties had come silently, in the blizzard, eyes closed tight against the blast, to drag the people up into the hills, into caves and hollows that still showed the fresh marks of carving tools. They had brought food—what kind of food nobody knew, for the colony's food had been destroyed by the first blast of the hurricane—but whatever it was it had kept them alive. And somehow, the colonists had survived the winter which seemed never to end. There were frozen legs and ruined eyes; there was pneumonia so swift and virulent that even the antibiotics they managed to salvage could not stop it; there was near-starvation—but they were kept alive, until the winds began to die, and they walked out of their holes in the ground to see the ruins of their first village.

From that winter on, nobody considered the Dusties funny any more. What had motivated them no one knew, but the colony owed them their lives. The Dusties tried to help the people rebuild. They showed them how to build windshields that would keep houses intact and anchored to the ground when the winds came again. They built little furnaces out of dirt and rock which defied the winds and gave great heat. They showed the colonists a dozen things they needed to know for life on the rugged planet. The colonists in turn tried to teach the Dusties something about Earth, and how the colonists had lived, and why they had come. But there was a barrier of intelligence that could not be crossed. The Dusties learned simple things, but only slowly and imperfectly. They seemed content to take on their mock overseer's role, moving in and about the village, approving or disapproving, but always trying to help. Some became personal pets, though "pet" was the wrong word, because it was more of a strange personal friendship limited by utter lack of communication, than any animal-and-master relationship. The colonists made sure that the Dusties were granted the respect due them as rightful masters of Baron IV. And somehow the Dusties perceived this attitude, and were so grateful for the acceptance and friendship that there seemed nothing they wouldn't do for the colonists.

There had been many discussions about them. "You'd think they'd resent our moving in on them," Jack Mario had said one day. "After all, we *are* usurpers. And they treat us like kings. Have you noticed the way they mimic us? I saw one chewing tobacco the other day. He hated the stuff, but he chewed away, and spat like a trooper."

One of the Dusties had been sitting on Pete's knee when Captain Varga had been talking, and he had known that something terrible was wrong. Now he sat on the desk in the office, moving uneasily back and forth as Pete looked up at Mario's dark face, and then across at John Tegan and Mel Dorfman. John's face was dark with anger as he ran his fingers through the heavy gray beard that fell to his chest. Mel sat stunned, shaking his head helplessly. Mario was unable to restrain himself. His face was bitter as he stomped across the room, then returned to shake his fist under Pete's nose. "But did you see him?" he choked. "Governor of the colony! What does he know about growing *taaro* in this kind of soil? Did you see those hands? Soft, dainty, pink! How could a man with hands like that govern a colony?"

Pete looked over at John Tegan. "Well, John?"

The big man looked up, his eyes hollow under craggy brows. "It's below the belt, Pete. But if the government's been overthrown, then the captain is right. It leaves us out on a limb."

Pete shook his head. "*I* can't give him an answer," he said. "The answer has got to come from the colony. All I can do is speak for the colony."

Tegan stared at the floor. "We're an Earth colony," he said softly. "I know that. I was born in New York. I lived there for many years. But Earth isn't my home any more. This is." He looked at Pete. "I built it, and so did you. All of us built it, even when things were getting stormy back home. Maybe that's why we came, maybe somehow we saw the handwriting on the wall."

"But when did it happen?" Mel burst out suddenly. "How could *anything* so big happen so fast?"

"Speed was the secret," Pete said gloomily. "It was quick, it was well organized, and the government was unstable. We're just caught in the edge of it. Pity the ones living there, now. But the new government considers the colonies as areas for exploitation instead of development."

"Well, they can't do it," Mario cried. "This is *our* land, *our* home. Nobody can tell us what to grow in our fields."

Pete's fist slammed down on the desk. "Well, how are you going to stop them? The law of the land is sitting out there in that ship. Tomorrow morning he's coming back here to install his fat little friend as governor. He has guns and soldiers on that ship to back him up. What are you going to do about it?"

"Fight it," Mario said.

"How?"

Jack Mario looked around the room. "There are only a dozen men on that ship," he said softly. "We've got seventy-four. When Varga comes back to the village tomorrow, we tell him to take his friend back to the ship and shove off. We give him five minutes to get turned around, and if he doesn't, we start shooting."

"Just one little thing," said Pete quietly. "What about the supplies? Even if we fought them off and won, what about the food, the clothing, the replacement parts for the machines?"

"We don't need machinery to farm this land," said Mario eagerly. "There's food here, food we can live on; the Dusties showed us that the first winter. And we can farm the land for our own use and let the machinery rust. There's nothing they can bring us from Earth that we can't do without."

"We couldn't get away with it!" Mel Dorfman shook his head bitterly. "You're asking us to cut ourselves off from Earth completely. But they'd never let us. They'd send ships to bomb us out."

"We could hide, and rebuild after they had finished."

Pete Farnam sighed. "They'd never leave us alone, Jack. Didn't you see that captain? His kind of mind can't stand opposition. We'd just be a thorn in the side of the new Earth Government. They don't want *any* free colonies."

"Well, let's give them one." Mario sat down tiredly, snapping his fingers at the Dustie. "Furs!" he snarled. He looked up, his dark eyes burning. "It's no good, Pete. We can't let them get away with it. Produce for them, yes. Try to raise the yield for them, yes. But not a governor. If they insist on that we can throw them out, and keep them out."

"I don't think so. They'd kill every one of us first."

John Tegan sat up, and looked Pete Farnam straight in the eye. "In that case, Peter, it might just be better if they did."

Pete stared at him for a moment and slowly stood up. "All right," he said. "Call a general colony meeting. We'll see what the women think. Then we'll make our plans."

*   *   *   *   *

The ship's jeep skidded to a halt in a cloud of dust. Captain Varga peered through the windshield. Then he stood up, staring at the three men blocking the road at the edge of the village. The little pink-faced man at his side turned white when he saw their faces, and his fingers began to tremble. Each of the men had a gun.

"You'd better clear the road," the captain snapped. "We're driving through."

Pete Farnam stepped forward. He pointed to Nathan. "Take your friend there back to the ship. Leave him there. We don't want him here."

Nathan turned to Varga. "I told you," he said viciously. "Too big for their boots. Go on through."

The captain laughed and gunned the motor, started straight for the men blocking the road. Then Jack Mario shot a hole in his front tire. The jeep lurched to a stop. Captain Varga stood up, glaring at the men. "Farnam, step out here," he said.

"You heard us," Pete said, without moving. "Crops, yes. We'll try to increase our yield. But no overseer. Leave him here and we'll kill him."

"Once more," said the captain, "clear the way. This man is your new governor. He will be regarded as the official agent of the Earth Government until the final production capacity of this colony is determined. Now clear out."

The men didn't move. Without another word, the captain threw the jeep into reverse, jerked back in a curve, and started the jeep, flat tire and all, back toward the ship in a billow of dust.

Abruptly the village exploded into activity. Four men took up places behind the row of windbreaks beyond the first row of cabins. Pete turned and ran back into the village. He found John Tegan commandeering a squad of ten dirty-faced men. "Are the women and children all out?" he shouted.

"All taken care of." Tegan spat tobacco juice, and wiped his mouth with the back of his hand.

"Where's Mel?"

"Left flank. He'll try to move in behind them. Gonna be tough, Pete, they've got good weapons."

"What about the boys last night?"

John was checking the bolt on his ancient rifle. "Hank and Ringo? Just got back an hour ago. If Varga wants to get his surface planes into action, he's going to have to dismantle them and rebuild them outside. The boys jammed up the launching ports for good." He spat again. "Don't worry, Pete. This is going to be a ground fight."

"Okay." Pete held out his hand to the old man. "This may be it. And if we turn them back, there's bound to be more later."

"There's a lot of planet to hide on," said Tegan. "They may come back, but after a while they'll go again."

Pete nodded. "I just hope we'll still be here when they do."

They waited. It seemed like hours. Pete moved from post to post among the men, heavy-faced men he had known all his life, it seemed. They waited with whatever weapons they had available—pistols, home-made revolvers, ortho-guns, an occasional rifle, even knives and clubs. Pete's heart sank. They were bitter men, but they were a mob with no organization, no training for fighting. They would be facing a dozen of Security's best-disciplined shock troops, armed with the latest weapons from Earth's electronics laboratories. The colonists didn't stand a chance.

Pete got his rifle and made his way up the rise of ground overlooking the right flank of the village. Squinting, he could spot the cloud of dust rising up near the glistening ship, moving toward the village. And then, for the first time, he realized that he hadn't seen any Dusties all day.

It puzzled him. They had been in the village in abundance an hour before dawn, while the plans were being laid out. He glanced around, hoping to see one of the fuzzy brown forms at his elbow, but he saw nothing. And then, as he stared at the cloud of dust coming across the valley, he thought he saw the ground moving.

He blinked, and rubbed his eyes. With a gasp he dragged out his binoculars and peered down at the valley floor. There were thousands of them, hundreds of thousands, their brown bodies moving slowly out from the hills surrounding the village, converging into a broad, liquid column between the village and the ship. Even as he watched, the column grew thicker, like a heavy blanket being drawn across the road, a multitude of Dusties lining up.

Pete's hair prickled on the back of his neck. They knew so little about the creatures, so *very* little. As he watched the brown carpet rolling out, he tried to think. Could there be a weapon in their hands, could they somehow have perceived the evil that came from the ship, somehow sensed the desperation in the men's voices as they had laid their plans? Pete stared, a sinking feeling in the pit of his stomach. They were there in the road, thousands upon thousands of them, standing there, waiting—for what?

Three columns of dust were coming from the road now. Through the glasses Pete could see the jeeps, filled with men in their gleaming gray uniforms, crash helmets tight about their heads, blasters glistening in the pale light. They moved in deadly convoy along the rutted road, closer and closer to the crowd of Dusties overflowing the road.

The Dusties just stood there. They didn't move. They didn't shift, or turn. They just waited.

The captain's car was first in line. He pulled up before the line with a screech of brakes, and stared at the sea of creatures before him. "Get out of there!" he shouted.

The Dusties didn't move.

The captain turned to his men. "Fire into them," he snapped. "Clear a path."

There was a blaze of fire, and a half a dozen Dusties slid to the ground, convulsing. Pete felt a chill pass through him, staring in disbelief. The Dusties had a weapon, he kept telling himself, they *must* have a weapon, something the colonists had never dreamed of. The guns came up again, and another volley echoed across the valley, and a dozen more Dusties fell to the ground. For every one that fell, another moved stolidly into its place.

With a curse the captain sat down in the seat, gunned the motor, and started forward. The jeep struck the fallen bodies, rolled over them, and plunged straight into the wall of Dusties. Still they didn't move. The car slowed and stopped, mired down. The other cars picked up momentum and plunged into the brown river of creatures. They too ground to a stop.

The captain started roaring at his men. "Cut them down! We're going to get through here!" Blasters began roaring into the faces of the Dusties, and as they fell the jeeps moved forward a few feet until more of the creatures blocked their path.

Pete heard a cry below him, and saw Jack Mario standing in the road, gun on the ground, hands out in front of him, staring in horror as the Dusties kept moving into the fire. "Do you see what they're doing!" he screamed. "They'll be slaughtered, every one of them!" And then he was running down the road, shouting at them to stop, and so were Pete and Tegan and the rest of the men.

Something hit Pete in the shoulder as he ran. He spun around and fell into the dusty road. A dozen Dusties closed in around him, lifted him up bodily, and started back through the village with him. He tried to struggle, but vaguely he saw that the other men were being carried back also, while the river of brown creatures held the jeeps at bay. The Dusties were hurrying, half carrying and half dragging him back through the village and up a long ravine into the hills beyond. At last they set Pete on his feet again, plucking urgently at his shirt sleeve as they hurried him along.

He followed them willingly, then, with the rest of the colonists at his heels. He didn't know what the Dusties were doing, but he knew they were trying to save him. Finally they reached a cave, a great cleft in the rock that Pete knew for certain had not been there when he had led exploring parties through these hills years before. It was a huge opening, and already a dozen of the men were there, waiting, dazed by what they had witnessed down in the valley, while more were stumbling up the rocky incline, tugged along by the fuzzy brown creatures.

Inside the cavern, steps led down the side of the rock, deep into the dark coolness of the earth. Down and down they went, until they suddenly found themselves in a mammoth room lit by blazing torches. Pete stopped and stared at his friends who had already arrived. Jack Mario was sitting on the floor, his face in his hands, sobbing. Tegan was sitting, too, blinking at Pete as if he were a stranger, and Dorfman was trembling like a leaf. Pete stared about him through the dim light, and then looked where Tegan was pointing at the end of the room.

He couldn't see it clearly, at first. Finally, he made out a raised platform with four steps leading up. A torch lighted either side of a dais at the top, and between the torches, rising high into the gloom, stood a statue.

It was a beautifully carved thing, hewn from the heavy granite that made up the core of this planet, with the same curious styling as other carving the Dusties had done. The design was intricate, the lines carefully turned and polished. At first Pete thought it was a statue of a Dustie, but when he moved forward and squinted in the dim light, he suddenly realized that it was something else indeed. And in that moment he realized why they were there and why the Dusties had done this incredible thing to protect them.

The statue was weirdly beautiful, the work of a dedicated master sculptor. It was a figure, standing with five-fingered hands on hips, head raised high. Not a portrait, but an image seen through other eyes than human, standing high in the room with the lights burning reverently at its feet.

Unmistakably it was the statue of a man.

*   *   *   *   *

They heard the bombs, much later. The granite roof and floor of the cavern trembled, and the men and women stared at each other, helpless and sick as they huddled in that great hall. But presently the bombing stopped. Later, when they stumbled out of that grotto into the late afternoon light, the ship was gone.

They knew it would be back. Possibly it would bring back search parties to hunt down the rebels in the hills; perhaps it would just wait and again bomb out the new village when it rose. But searching parties would never find their quarry, and the village would rise again and again, if necessary.

And in the end, somehow, Pete knew that the colonists would find a way to survive here and live free as they had always lived. It might be a bitter struggle, but no matter how hard the fight, there would be one strange and wonderful thing they could count on.

No matter what they had to do, he knew the Dusties would help them.

SECOND SIGHT

ORIGINALLY PUBLISHED IN *FANTASTIC UNIVERSE*,
APRIL 1956

Second Sight

(Note: The following excerpts from Amy Ballantine's journal have never actually been written down at any time before. Her account of impressions and events has been kept in organized fashion in her mind for at least nine years (even she is not certain when she started), but it must be understood that certain inaccuracies in transcription could not possibly have been avoided in the excerpting attempted here. *The Editor*.)

*   *   *   *   *

Tuesday, 16 May. Lambertson got back from Boston about two this afternoon. He was tired; I don't think I've ever seen Lambertson so tired. It was more than just exhaustion, too. Maybe anger? Frustration? I couldn't be sure. It seemed more like *defeat* than anything else, and he went straight from the 'copter to his office without even stopping off at the lab at all.

It's good to have him back, though! Not that I haven't had a nice enough rest. With Lambertson gone, Dakin took over the reins for the week, but Dakin doesn't really count, poor man. It's such a temptation to twist him up and get him all confused that I didn't do any real *work* all week. With Lambertson back I'll have to get down to the grind again, but I'm still glad he's here. I never thought I'd miss him so, for such a short time away.

But I wish he'd gotten a rest, if he ever rests! And I wish I knew why he went to Boston in the first place. Certainly he didn't *want* to go. I wanted to read him and find out, but I don't think I'm supposed to know yet. Lambertson didn't want to talk. He didn't even tell me he was back, even though he knew I'd catch him five miles down the road. (I can do that now, with Lambertson. Distance doesn't seem to make so much difference any more if I just ignore it.)

So all I got was bits and snatches on the surface of his mind. Something about me, and Dr. Custer; and a nasty little man called Aarons or Barrons or something. I've heard of him somewhere, but I can't pin it down right now. I'll have to dig that out later, I guess.

But if he saw Dr. Custer, *why doesn't he tell me about it?*

*   *   *   *   *

Wednesday, 17 May. It was *Aarons* that he saw in Boston, and now I'm sure that something's going wrong. I know that man. I remember him from a long time ago, back when I was still at Bairdsley, long before I came here to the Study Center. He was the consulting psychiatrist, and I don't think I could ever forget him, even if I tried!

That's why I'm sure something very unpleasant is going on.

Lambertson saw Dr. Custer, too, but the directors sent him to Boston because Aarons wanted to talk to him. I wasn't supposed to know anything about it, but Lambertson came down to dinner last night. He wouldn't even look at me, the skunk. I fixed *him*. I told him I was going to peek, and then I read him in a flash, before he could shift his mind to Boston traffic or something. (He knows I can't stand traffic.)

I only picked up a little, but it was enough. There was something very unpleasant that Aarons had said that I couldn't quite get. They were in his office. Lambertson had said, "I don't think she's ready for it, and I'd never try to talk her into it, at this point. Why can't you people get it through your heads that she's a *child*, and a human being, not some kind of laboratory animal? That's been the trouble all along. Everybody has been so eager to *grab*, and nobody has given her a wretched thing in return."

Aarons was smooth. Very sad and reproachful. I got a clear picture of him—short, balding, mean little eyes in a smug, self-righteous little face. "Michael, after all she's twenty-three years old. She's certainly out of diapers by now."

"But she's only had two years of training aimed at teaching *her* anything."

"Well, there's no reason that *that* should stop, is there? Be reasonable, Michael. We certainly agree that you've done a wonderful job with the girl, and naturally you're sensitive about others working with her. But when you consider that public taxes are footing the bill—"

"I'm sensitive about others exploiting her, that's all. I tell you, I won't push her. And I wouldn't let her come up here, even if she agreed to do it. She shouldn't be tampered with for another year or two at least." Lambertson was angry and bitter. Now, three days later, he was still angry.

"And you're certain that your concern is entirely— professional?" (Whatever Aarons meant, it wasn't nice. Lambertson caught it, and oh, my! Chart slapping down on the table, door slamming, swearing—from mild, patient Lambertson, can you imagine? And then later, no more anger, just disgust and defeat. That was what hit me when he came back yesterday. He couldn't hide it, no matter how he tried.)

Well, no wonder he was tired. I remember Aarons all right. He wasn't so interested in me, back in those days. *Wild one*, he called me. *We haven't the time or the people to handle anything like this in a public institution. We have to handle her the way we'd handle any other defective. She may be a* plus-*defective instead of a* minus-*defective, but she's as crippled as if she were deaf and blind.*

Good old Aarons. That was years ago, when I was barely thirteen. Before Dr. Custer got interested and started ophthalmoscoping me and testing me, before I'd ever heard of Lambertson or the Study Center. For that matter, before anybody had done anything but feed me and treat me like some kind of peculiar animal or something.

Well, I'm glad it was Lambertson that went to Boston and not me, for Aarons' sake. And if Aarons tries to come down here to work with me, he's going to be wasting his time, because I'll lead him all around Robin Hood's Barn and get him so confused he'll wish he'd stayed home. But I can't help but wonder, just the same. *Am* I a cripple like Aarons said? Does being psi-high mean that? *I* don't think so, but what does Lambertson think? Sometimes when I try to read Lambertson I'm the one that gets confused. I wish I could tell what he *really* thinks.

*   *   *   *   *

Wednesday night. I asked Lambertson tonight what Dr. Custer had said. "He wants to see you next week," he told me. "But Amy, he didn't make any promises. He wasn't even hopeful."

"But his letter! He said the studies showed that there wasn't any anatomical defect."

Lambertson leaned back and lit his pipe, shaking his head at me. He's aged ten years this past week. Everybody thinks so. He's lost weight, and he looks as if he hasn't slept at all. "Custer's afraid that it isn't a question of anatomy, Amy."

"But what is it, then, for heaven's sake?"

"He doesn't know. He says it's not very scientific, but it may just be that what you don't use, you lose."

"Oh, but that's silly." I chewed my lip.

"Granted."

"But he thinks that there's a chance?"

"Of course there's a chance. And you know he'll do everything he can. It's just that neither of us wants you to get your hopes up."

It wasn't much, but it was something. Lambertson looked so beat. I didn't have the heart to ask him what Aarons wanted, even though I know he'd like to get it off his chest. Maybe tomorrow will be better.

I spent the day with Charlie Dakin in the lab, and did a little work for a change. I've been disgustingly lazy, and poor Charlie thinks it's all his fault. Charlie reads like twenty-point type ninety per cent of the time, and I'm afraid he knows it. I can tell just exactly when he stops paying attention to business and starts paying attention to *me*, and then all of a sudden he realizes I'm reading him, and it flusters him for the rest of the day. I wonder why? Does he really think I'm shocked? Or surprised? Or *insulted*? Poor Charlie!

I guess I must be good enough looking. I can read it from almost every fellow that comes near me. I wonder why? I mean, why me and not Marjorie over in the Main Office? She's a sweet girl, but she never gets a second look from the guys. There must be some fine differential point I'm missing somewhere, but I don't think I'll ever understand it.

I'm not going to press Lambertson, but I *hope* he opens up tomorrow. He's got me scared silly by now. He has a lot of authority around here, but other people are paying the bills, and when he's frightened about something, it can't help but frighten me.

*   *   *   *   *

Thursday, 18 May. We went back to reaction testing in the lab with Lambertson today. That study is almost finished, as much as anything I work on is ever finished, which isn't very much. This test had two goals: to clock my stimulus-response pattern in comparison to normals, and to find out just exactly *when* I pick up any given thought-signal from the person I'm reading. It isn't a matter of developing speed. I'm already so fast to respond that it doesn't mean too much from anybody else's standpoint, and I certainly don't need any training there. But where along the line do I pick up a thought impulse? Do I catch it at its inception? Do I pick up the thought formulation, or just the final crystalized pattern? Lambertson thinks I'm with it right from the start, and that some training in those lines would be worth my time.

Of course, we didn't find out, not even with the ingenious little random-firing device that Dakin designed for the study. With this gadget, neither Lambertson nor I know what impulse the box is going to throw at him. He just throws a switch and it starts coming. He catches it, reacts, I catch it from him and react, and we compare reaction times. This afternoon it had us driving up a hill, and sent a ten-ton truck rolling down on us out of control. I had my flasher on two seconds before Lambertson did, of course, but our reaction times are standardized, so when we corrected for my extra speed, we knew that I must have caught the impulse about 0.07 seconds after he did.

Crude, of course, not nearly fast enough, and we can't reproduce on a stable basis. Lambertson says that's as close as we can get without cortical probes. And that's where I put my foot down. I may have a gold mine in this head of mine, but nobody is going to put burr-holes through my skull in order to tap it. Not for a while yet.

That's unfair, of course, because it sounds as if Lambertson were trying to force me into something, and he isn't. I've read him about that, and I know he wouldn't allow it. *Let's learn everything else we can learn without it first,* he says. *Later, if you want to go along with it, maybe. But right now you're not competent to decide for yourself.*

He may be right, but why not? Why does he keep acting as if I'm a child? *Am* I, really? With everything (and I mean *everything*) coming into my mind for the past twenty-three years, haven't I learned enough to make decisions for myself? Lambertson says of course everything has been coming in, it's just that I don't know what to do with it all. But somewhere along the line I have to reach a maturation point of some kind.

It scares me, sometimes, because I can't find an answer to it and the answer might be perfectly horrible. I don't know where it may end. What's worse, I don't know what point it has reached *right now.* How much difference is there between my mind and Lambertson's? I'm psi-high, and he isn't—granted. But is there more to it than that? People like Aarons think so. They think it's a difference between *human* function and something else.

And that scares me because it *just isn't true.* I'm as human as anybody else. But somehow it seems that I'm the one who has to prove it. I wonder if I ever will. That's why Dr. Custer has to help me. Everything hangs on that. I'm to go up to Boston next week, for final studies and testing.

If Dr. Custer can do something, what a difference that will make! Maybe then I could get out of this whole frightening mess, put it behind me and forget about it. With just the psi alone, I don't think I ever can.

*   *   *   *   *

Friday, 19 May. Today Lambertson broke down and told me what it was that Aarons had been proposing. It was worse than I thought it would be. The man had hit on the one thing I'd been afraid of for so long.

"He wants you to work against normals," Lambertson said. "He's swallowed the latency hypothesis whole. He thinks that everybody must have a latent psi potential, and that all that is needed to drag it into the open is a powerful stimulus from someone with full-blown psi powers."

"Well?" I said. "Do you think so?"

"Who knows?" Lambertson slammed his pencil down on the desk angrily. "No, I don't think so, but what does that mean? Not a thing. It certainly doesn't mean I'm right. Nobody knows the answer, not me, nor Aarons, nor anybody. And Aarons wants to use you to find out."

I nodded slowly. "I see. So I'm to be used as a sort of refined electrical stimulator," I said. "Well, I guess you know what you can tell Aarons."

He was silent, and I couldn't read him. Then he looked up. "Amy, I'm not sure we can tell him that."

I stared at him. "You mean you think he could *force* me?"

"He says you're a public charge, that as long as you have to be supported and cared for, they have the right to use your faculties. He's right on the first point. You *are* a public charge. You have to be sheltered and protected. If you wandered so much as a mile outside these walls you'd never survive, and you know it."

I sat stunned. "But Dr. Custer—"

"Dr. Custer is trying to help. But he hasn't succeeded so far. If he can, then it will be a different story. But I can't stall much longer, Amy. Aarons has a powerful argument. You're psi-high. You're the first full-fledged, wide-open, free-wheeling psi-high that's ever appeared in human history. The *first*. Others in the past have shown potential, maybe, but nothing they could ever learn to control. You've got control, you're fully developed. You're *here*, and you're *the only one there is*."

"So I happened to be unlucky," I snapped. "My genes got mixed up."

"That's not true, and you know it," Lambertson said. "We know your chromosomes better than your face. They're the same as anyone else's. There's no gene difference, none at all. When you're gone, you'll be *gone*, and there's no reason to think that your children will have any more psi potential than Charlie Dakin has."

Something was building up in me then that I couldn't control any longer. "You think I should go along with Aarons," I said dully.

He hesitated. "I'm afraid you're going to have to, sooner or later. Aarons has some latents up in Boston. He's certain that they're latents. He's talked to the directors down here. He's convinced them that you could work with his people, draw them out. You could open the door to a whole new world for human beings."

I lost my temper then. It wasn't just Aarons, or Lambertson, or Dakin, or any of the others. It was *all* of them, dozens of them, compounded year upon year upon year. "Now listen to me for a minute," I said. "Have any of you ever considered what *I* wanted in this thing? *Ever?* Have any of you given that one single thought, just once, one time when you were so sick of thinking great thoughts for humanity that you let another thought leak through? Have you ever thought about what kind of a shuffle I've had since all this started? Well, you'd better think about it. *Right now.*"

"Amy, you know I don't want to push you."

"Listen to me, Lambertson. My folks got rid of me fast when they found out about me. Did you know that? They hated me because I *scared* them! It didn't hurt me too much, because I thought I knew *why* they hated me, I could understand it, and I went off to Bairdsley without even crying. They were going to come see me every week, but do you know how often they managed to make it? *Not once* after I was off their hands. And then at Bairdsley Aarons examined me and decided that I was a cripple. He didn't know anything about me then, but he thought psi was a *defect*. And that was as far as it went. I did what Aarons wanted me to do at Bairdsley. Never what *I* wanted, just what *they* wanted, years and years of what *they* wanted. And then you came along, and I came to the Study Center and did what *you* wanted."

It hurt him, and I knew it. I guess that was what I wanted, to hurt him and to hurt everybody. He was shaking his head, staring at me. "Amy, be fair. I've tried, you know how hard I've tried."

"Tried what? To train me? Yes, but why? To give me better use of my psi faculties? Yes, but why? Did you do it for *me*? Is that really why you did it? Or was that just another phoney front, like all the rest of them, in order to use me, to make me a little more valuable to have around?"

He slapped my face so hard it jolted me. I could feel the awful pain and hurt in his mind as he stared at me, and I sensed the stinging in his palm that matched the burning in my cheek. And then something fell away in his mind, and I saw something I had never seen before.

He loved me, that man. Incredible, isn't it? He *loved* me. Me, who couldn't call him anything but Lambertson, who couldn't imagine calling him Michael, to say nothing of Mike—just Lambertson, who did this, or Lambertson who thought that.

But he could never tell me. He had decided that. I was too helpless. I needed him too much. I needed love, but not the kind of love Lambertson wanted to give, so that kind of love had to be hidden, concealed, *suppressed*. I needed the deepest imaginable understanding, but it had to be utterly unselfish understanding, anything else would be taking advantage of me, so a barrier had to be built—a barrier that I should never penetrate and that he should never be tempted to break down.

Lambertson had done that. For me. It was all there, suddenly, so overwhelming it made me gasp from the impact. I wanted to throw my arms around him; instead I sat down in the chair, shaking my head helplessly. I hated myself then. I had hated myself before, but never like this.

"If I could only go somewhere," I said. "Someplace where nobody knew me, where I could just live by myself for a while, and shut the doors, and shut out the thoughts, and *pretend* for a while, just pretend that I'm perfectly normal."

"I wish you could," Lambertson said. "But you can't. You know that. Not unless Custer can really help."

We sat there for a while. Then I said, "Let Aarons come down. Let him bring anybody he wants with him. I'll do what he wants. Until I see Custer."

That hurt, too, but it was different. It hurt both of us together, not separately any more. And somehow it didn't hurt so much that way.

*   *   *   *   *

Monday, 22 May. Aarons drove down from Boston this morning with a girl named Mary Bolton, and we went to work.

I think I'm beginning to understand how a dog can tell when someone wants to kick him and doesn't quite dare. I could feel the back of my neck prickle when that man walked into the conference room. I was hoping he might have changed since the last time I saw him. He hadn't, but I had. I wasn't afraid of him any more, just awfully tired of him after he'd been here about ten minutes.

But that girl! I wonder what sort of story he'd told her? She couldn't have been more than sixteen, and she was terrorized. At first I thought it was *Aarons* she was afraid of, but that wasn't so. It was *me*.

It took us all morning just to get around that. The poor girl could hardly make herself talk. She was shaking all over when they arrived. We took a walk around the grounds, alone, and I read her bit by bit—a feeler here, a planted suggestion there, just getting her used to the idea and trying to reassure her. After a while she was smiling. She thought the lagoon was lovely, and by the time we got back to the main building she was laughing, talking about herself, beginning to relax.

Then I gave her a full blast, quickly, only a moment or two. *Don't be afraid—I hate him, yes, but I won't hurt you for anything. Let me come in, don't fight me. We've got to work as a team.*

It shook her. She turned white and almost passed out for a moment. Then she nodded, slowly. "I see," she said. "It feels as if it's way inside, *deep* inside."

"That's right. It won't hurt. I promise."

She nodded again. "Let's go back, now. I think I'm ready to try."

We went to work.

I was as blind as she was, at first. There was nothing there, at first, not even a flicker of brightness. Then, probing deeper, something responded, only a hint, a suggestion of something powerful, deep and hidden—but where? What was her strength? Where was she weak? I couldn't tell.

We started on dice, crude, of course, but as good a tool as any. Dice are no good for measuring anything, but that was why I was there. I was the measuring instrument. The dice were only reactors. Sensitive enough, two balsam cubes, tossed from a box with only gravity to work against. I showed her first, picked up her mind as the dice popped out, led her through it. *Take one at a time, the red one first. Work on it, see? Now we try both. Once more—watch it! All right, now.*

She sat frozen in the chair. She was trying; the sweat stood out on her forehead. Aarons sat tense, smoking, his fingers twitching as he watched the red and green cubes bounce on the white backdrop. Lambertson watched too, but his eyes were on the girl, not on the cubes.

It was hard work. Bit by bit she began to grab; whatever I had felt in her mind seemed to leap up. I probed her, amplifying it, trying to draw it out. It was like wading through knee-deep mud—sticky, sluggish, resisting. I could feel her excitement growing, and bit by bit I released my grip, easing her out, baiting her.

"All right," I said. "That's enough."

She turned to me, wide-eyed. "I—I did it."

Aarons was on his feet, breathing heavily. "It worked?"

"It worked. Not very well, but it's there. All she needs is time, and help, and patience."

"But it worked! Lambertson! Do you know what that means? It means I was right! It means others can have it, just like she has it!" He rubbed his hands together. "We can arrange a full-time lab for it, and work on three or four latents simultaneously. It's a wide-open door, Michael! Can't you see what it means?"

Lambertson nodded, and gave me a long look. "Yes, I think I do."

"I'll start arrangements tomorrow."

"Not tomorrow. You'll have to wait until next week."

"Why?"

"Because Amy would prefer to wait, that's why."

Aarons looked at him, and then at me, peevishly. Finally he shrugged. "If you insist."

"We'll talk about it next week," I said. I was so tired I could hardly look up at him. I stood up, and smiled at my girl. Poor kid, I thought. So excited and eager about it now. And not one idea in the world of what she was walking into.

Certainly Aarons would never be able to tell her.

* * * * *

Later, when they were gone, Lambertson and I walked down toward the lagoon. It was a lovely cool evening; the ducks were down at the water's edge. Every year there was a mother duck herding a line of ducklings down the shore and into the water. They never seemed to go where she wanted them to, and she would fuss and chatter, waddling back time and again to prod the reluctant ones out into the pool.

We stood by the water's edge in silence for a long time. Then Lambertson kissed me. It was the first time he had ever done that.

"We could go away," I whispered in his ear. "We could run out on Aarons and the Study Center and everyone, just go away somewhere."

He shook his head slowly. "Amy, don't."

"We could! I'll see Dr. Custer, and he'll tell me he can help, I *know* he will. I won't *need* the Study Center any more, or any other place, or anybody but you."

He didn't answer, and I knew there wasn't anything he could answer. Not then.

*   *   *   *   *

Friday, 26 May. Yesterday we went to Boston to see Dr. Custer, and now it looks as if it's all over. Now even I can't pretend that there's anything more to be done.

Next week Aarons will come down, and I'll go to work with him just the way he has it planned. He thinks we have three years of work ahead of us before anything can be published, before he can really be sure we have brought a latent into full use of his psi potential. Maybe so, I don't know. Maybe in three years I'll find some way to make myself care one way or the other. But I'll do it, anyway, because there's nothing else to do.

There was no anatomical defect—Dr. Custer was right about that. The eyes are perfect, beautiful gray eyes, he says, and the optic nerves and auditory nerves are perfectly functional. The defect isn't there. It's deeper. Too deep ever to change it.

What you no longer use, you lose, was what he said, apologizing because he couldn't explain it any better. It's like a price tag, perhaps. Long ago, before I knew anything at all, the psi was so strong it started compensating, bringing in more and more from *other* minds—such a wealth of rich, clear, interpreted visual and auditory impressions that there was never any need for my own. And because of that, certain hookups never got hooked up. That's only a theory, of course, but there isn't any other way to explain it.

But am I wrong to hate it? More than anything else in the world I want to *see* Lambertson, *see* him smile and light his pipe, *hear* him laugh. I want to know what color *really* is, what music *really* sounds like unfiltered through somebody else's ears.

I want to see a sunset, just once. Just once I want to see that mother duck take her ducklings down to the water. But I never will. Instead, I see and hear things nobody else can, and the fact that I am stone blind and stone deaf shouldn't make any difference. After all, I've always been that way.

Maybe next week I'll ask Aarons what he thinks about it. It should be interesting to hear what he says.

And Now a Message . . .
By Greg Fowlkes

A short Story from the upcoming Book
- Back Road to the Stars

And Now A Message . . .

For the third time that night Jack Olsen was about to nod off over the copy of *Statistical Information Theory* that he was attempting to read. Giving it up as a bad effort, he shut the book and looked out the window of the control room at the giant bowl of the Arecibo radio telescope. Theoretically he was running the huge instrument, but in reality all the controlling was being done by the computers in the room around him. For six months he had been working eight hour shifts every night, and his job had consisted of the five minutes a shift that it took to enter the coordinates to be examined on the control console. Other than that, he was on hand only for the off chance that the monitoring programs would recognize some pattern in the radio noise, in which case an alarm would sound. So far, in the six months, it hadn't happened.

He walked over to the coffee machine in the hopes that a cup would revive him enough so that he could continue his studies. He never made it, for as if to prove the lie of his earlier thoughts, the alarm sounded. For a moment Jack was frozen, the alarm beating raucously in his ears, then he pulled himself together and flicked off the switch on the bell. With the room returned to the relative quiet of the whoosh of the cooling fans on the equipment, Jack sat down at the console and keyed in an enquiry. Within seconds the computer had replied that it was receiving a strong periodic signal on the 42 centimeter band. Further questioning showed that it was not a program malfunction but a genuine signal.

Jack picked up the phone and dialed his boss's number. It was three in the morning, but his instructions had been clear. If anything was received that could possibly be an intelligent signal, he was supposed to contact his superior immediately.

Despite the long drive through the mountains in the cool Puerto Rican night, Professor Kraft showed up with his eyes still sleepy. Shuffling over to the coffee pot by the window he poured himself a large mug before he said anything. "You'd better have something good to get me up at this hour."

"I think so," Jack said, aware that his boss's irritation was only feigned. "I've been checking with the computer since I called you. It shows a strong periodic signal with a sharp pulse every fifty milliseconds. It runs on like that for about two and a half minutes before the signal fades below the background."

"Any chance that it might be a pulsar?" Kraft asked, referring to the radio signals of rapidly rotating neutron stars. "That's within the range of periods for them. When the first one was discovered, they thought that they had received intelligent signals."

"I thought of that, so I checked the record of the broad band receiver." Jack brought out a long strip of graph paper and pointed to the evenly spaced patterns of peaks on it. "Where the narrow band shows only a single repetitive pulse, the wide band gives us this fine structure. It's far too regular to be a pulsar and much too detailed. It's more like some sort of timing signal or spacer. And in between the pulses there is another signal. It's not as repetitive as the main pulse. That's why the program doesn't bring it out. But there definitely is some sort of transmission in between. It's weaker, but I think that we can write a processing program to pick it out from the noise."

Kraft looked at the trace in his hand thoughtfully. "I hate to make snap judgements. You can be suckered in too easily that way. But it does look like some kind of artificial signal. We'll get the team working on it in the morning. Have you received any additional signals?"

"No. I've kept the dish tracking the source, but all we get on 42 cm. is background noise. It's like there was a moment of freak atmospheric conditions that opened a window, and then it shut again. Just like you get with shortwave sometimes because of the ionosphere."

"Well, we should be grateful for what we've got. I don't think I can sleep anymore tonight, so I'll keep you company. I'd like to be here if we get any more messages from our friends out there," he said, pointing with his cup towards the star filled sky that loomed over the radio telescope's antenna.

"Frustrating, isn't it?" Prof. Kraft remarked to the team of graduate students and post doctoral fellows that were working under him on the interstellar communications project. And frustrating it had been. For six months they had continuously monitored the sky searching for signs of life finally to be rewarded by a two minute snippet of extraterrestrial conversation.

Now, another six months later, they had still made no sense of the signal, nor had they received any further transmissions from that part of the sky, though they had concentrated their efforts in that direction.

"Rumors have leaked out about our discovery, and I've been getting requests for the data. I'd sure hate to have someone else steal our thunder by deciphering the signal, but if we don't make some progress soon, we're going to have to release it." He looked around the table at the young faces of his assistants. At the moment they didn't look nearly as bright and intelligent as he knew they were.

"Why don't I summarize what we've found so far in hopes that it will give us some new ideas?"

"First, we've got this repetitive pattern of pulses every twentieth of a second as regular as clockwork. So regular, in fact, that we can't decide whether they serve as breaks in the message or were just put there to attract our attention. Remember, it was these pulses that were first recognized by the computer."

"But the pulses aren't the real message. That lays in the spaces in between. We've been able to deduce that the messages are digitized and the computer has been able to enhance them so that we have a fairly error free record of them. There is some repetitive structure to them, and they do vary in some sort of progression, but beyond that, we haven't been able to get the least notion of what they mean. Anyone have something to add?"

Bill Warden, one of the post docs, spoke up. "Well, we've tried mathematical analysis on the signals and have gotten zero results. It has already been assumed that any sort of interstellar communications would be based on sort of easily recognizable mathematical progression. Like one, two three. Something like that to show that they were rational. From there you can always build up more complicated concepts."

"With this message we don't have that, which leads us to one of two assumptions. One, we have only a fragment of a broadcast, and from a very advanced lesson at that. If that's the case, I don't see much hope of our being able to decipher the message until we can receive more signals to give us a broader base to work from."

"The other alternative is that they, whoever they are, just don't think like us. Their minds work in some fashion so that this mess we have makes sense to them. If so, I don't see any hope at all. Their minds may just be too foreign for us to hold a dialog with them."

"Thank you for that optimistic note," Prof. Kraft said wryly. "For the first time mankind has received a message from another species and we can't tell whether it is a cure for cancer, a means of achieving universal peace, or a recipe for sauerbratten. Any comments?"

"If it's sauerbratten, where do we go for a tablespoon of powdered bandersnatch egg?" quipped one of the grad students. They all laughed at the joke more than it deserved. Six months of unrewarded work had left them all a little giddy. After the giggles and comments had died down, Jack Olsen coughed, trying to get their attention.

"You've got something useful to say, Jack?" Kraft asked. "You might as well tell us. I don't think anyone else has anything useful to add," he said, pointedly looking at the wisecracker.

"I've been thinking about the signal, and I remember something that I said to you the night it came in. I don't know if you recall, but I called the pulses timing signals. Now there is one type of common transmission that has the same kind of pulses, and that's television. They use the pulses to synchronize the frames. It's possible that the message in between each pulse is a picture, and the whole transmission is meant to be viewed in sequence."

"How long have you been sitting on this while the rest of us were beating our brains out?" Kraft asked.

"It just came to me," Jack said, his face flushed. "I should have thought of it earlier, but like Bill said, we've all been conditioned to look for something like one plus one equals two."

"I think that we should all have seen it," Kraft said. "It makes as much sense as anything else that's been suggested. Do you think that you can get us a picture?"

"If it's there, I should be able to pick it out using the computer," Jack answered.

"Good. Then, since it was your idea, you're in charge. Dragoon anything or anybody that you need to help you."

Five days later they were all gathered around the conference room table again, but this time there was a TV set and a video recorder on a cart at its end. From the nervous stubbing of cigarette butts and fingers drumming on the table, it was obvious that all the members of the team were in a state of anticipation.

"It took some time to figure out exactly how the signal was put together," Jack began. "After all, we didn't know how many lines there were in each frame or how many bits made up each unit of picture. In the end, I had to have the computer run through all the likely possibilities for one of the frames. It took a lot of computer time, but I've finally got some recognizable pictures."

"It turns out that the original broadcast was in color. That threw us for a while, but we finally psyched it out. The aliens must have eyes structurally different from ours; there are only two colors, not three in the signal. Which colors they are is anybody's guess. They might be ultraviolet and infrared for all we can tell. Arbitrarily, I've assigned them red and bluish green, so keep that in mind. Also, because the video recorder uses thirty frames a second instead of the twenty in the transmission, it was necessary to compress the program a bit. This means that everything you'll be seeing has been speeded up about fifty percent.

"I guess you're all more interested in seeing the tape than in listening to me." A snort from Prof. Kraft indicated agreement. Jack flicked off the lights and started the tape. For a minute the screen showed only snow, then a face became recognizable. It was a sickly chartreuse, and there was no nose between the two large, oval eyes, but it was recognizable as a face. The figures movements were quick and jerky like an old silent movie, the result of the difference in frame speed, and the picture left a lot to be desired in clarity, the product of interstellar noise, but it was a picture, the first of an alien race.

As the tape played, a weird, sings song voice came from the speaker sounding something like a Chinese chipmunk. "I forgot to mention that there was also an audio track along with the signal. Again, it's only a reconstruction and may not bear much resemblance to the original, but then, we'll never know," Jack commented. They had determined that the source of the transmission was at least several dozen light years away. It would take twice that number of years to send a message and receive a reply, by which time they would all be dead.

They continued to watch the tape. The camera had drawn back to show the alien from the waist up revealing rounded shoulders and a pair of six fingered hands. Apparently he was standing behind a low lectern or a table of some sort. The fuzzy picture and camera angle made it hard to tell which. As he, or her, or it, spoke, the alien pointed at a chart or poster suspended on the backdrop. A pattern of red and blue that hurt the eye with violent contrasts seemed to be some sort of text. The voice continued as the picture disappeared in a sea of snow and then it broke into static. The transmission had ended.

"You've done a fine job, Jack," Prof. Kraft said after they had played the tape through a half dozen times. "It's actually far better than I thought it would be, and I think we can accept any of the shortcomings that you mentioned."

"So, we've got a face and body of what certainly is a rational creature. He seemed to be giving us a lesson or lecture of some sort, though I for one don't have the faintest idea of what he was talking about. We have an idea of what they look like which I am sure will give the biologists a lot to speculate on, so I guess that we should be thankful for small favors, but I still don't see how we're going to learn any more about them without receiving further signals."

"I wouldn't hold out much hope of that," Jack interjected. "I think that it's clear now that the signal we picked up was not meant for interstellar communication. Any such signal would have been designed with much greater noise immunity. We were able to receive it only because of an accident of atmospheric conditions. It was actually just a local TV broadcast. As we haven't received anything since, those conditions must be rare."

"So," Kraft said, "we have a message of great potential import, that at the very least could provide us with insights on a totally alien culture, and no way to decipher it."

"I've got an idea," Bill said. "We've all been looking at the problem from the point of view of hardware and computer programs. That's natural because of our backgrounds, but now that we have what amounts to an artifact, maybe we should call in a specialist. We need someone who is trained in resurrecting a culture from its fragments. I suggest that we show the tape to some archeologists and get their opinions."

Convincing an archeologist to look at the tape was harder than it had sounded. Most of them were more interested in ancient rather than alien civilizations. Jack suspected that they felt out of their depth with the computers and electronics. With some pressure and pleading, a group finally agreed to view the tape, but after the showing, only one evinced any interest in following up on it.

A visiting lecturer from Norway, she was reputed to have a good background in languages, though Jack lacked the knowledge to judge her qualifications. However, as she was young, blond, and attractive, he was quite willing to spend the time required to familiarize her with the tape and the equipment they had used to come up with it. Together, they spent hours viewing the tape, studying it frame by frame attempting to pick out the slightest piece of information.

The project team had been assembled in the conference room, and this time it was the archeologist's turn to address them. For three weeks Cristina Peterson had been studying the tape almost constantly, and now she was ready to give her opinion. With the exception of Jack, who had been working closely with her, they were all, even Prof. Kraft, eagerly awaiting the report. There had been a great deal of speculation about what her findings would be.

"First," she began, "before I get your hopes up, I want to say that I have not been able to get a word for word translation of the voice on the tape. The sample of speech is just too brief for that to be possible. If the scene had contained more action, I might have been more successful, but we were not that fortunate. I have, however, been able to form a hypothesis based on the spoken word as well as visual clues such as facial expression, setting, and so on."

"An important point to remember is that the aliens, despite certain differences in appearance, are not too dissimilar from ourselves. They are bipedal, intelligent, and possess opposable thumbs. They have binocular vision and a form of color perception as well. Brain size is about the same in relationship to total body size as in humans, and I would be greatly surprised if they were much larger or smaller than ourselves. That much can be guessed on the basis of physiology from the picture and the nature of the signal. From this information, I think that we can draw the conclusion that their planet is, within limits, earthlike."

"Probably more relevant is their state of culture. They obviously have a technology and one that is recognizable in terms of our own. That we can receive their signals is proof of that. Also, they speak, they wear clothing, we can even guess at the purpose of some of the objects visible in the tape. I might add that this is more than we can do for some of the artifacts of primitive human cultures. In some ways we have more in common with the aliens than we do with the Tasadi or Bushman."

"I want you to bear in mind that these beings are not greatly different from ourselves. If we are to properly analyze the contents of the message, we must remember that they are influenced by the same drives and forces as humans." There was an uneasy shifting in their seats on the part of the team members as they took in the meaning of her statement.

"If we accept this premise, and replace the alien with a human, we can make an educated guess as to what we are seen on the tape. I'll run it again for you so that you can make the substitution." Jack tapped the switch, and for the next minute and a half they watched the now familiar scene replay itself.

"Before I give my own opinion, would anyone else like to make a guess?" Cristina asked.

Kraft looked around the room, but it appeared as though no one had the courage to be the first to put his own views forward. To break the silence he said, "It's only a guess, but to start the discussion, I'd say that the alien might be a lecturer. He's obviously standing at some sort of podium or speaker's table."

"He seems a little too impassioned for a lecturer, at least in the physical sciences," one of the grad students remarked. "I've never seen you that excited before a class." Kraft smiled at the reference to his own low keyed classroom delivery.

"Maybe it's a political science class. They get more aroused."

Bill Warden broke in, "Why a class? It looks to me more like he's a politician trying to persuade the voters. He must be up for reelection. The sign in back could be an election poster." That brought a couple of laughs and a few less than serious comments.

"We've all had a crack at it," Prof. Kraft said. "You obviously have your own interpretation, and I think that we've been kept in suspense long enough. From the look on Jack's face, it must be a good one. Let's hear it now. After all, the communication between two species is one of the most important events in human history."

She smiled at the jibe. "All your suggestions are plausible, but I've spent more time analyzing the tape than you have. I'll play it again for you and point out the features that have led me to my interpretation."

"The first thing that caught my attention was the fact that the word 'gratach' was mentioned fourteen times, an unusually high incidence in such a brief speech. Furthermore, at least four of those times the speaker pointed to the symbols on the chart behind him. I think that we can assume that 'gratach' is a name, and the symbols form the written version."

"Now here's something that I want you to see." She froze the picture on the television. "Note the artifacts on the table, a bowl filled with a substance and a box or container. There appears to be some writing on the box, but the resolution of the picture isn't good enough to allow us to make it out. However," she said as the tape began to roll again, "as the alien points to the box and says 'gratach' it is likely that the symbols again spell out the name in the chart behind the alien. Note, too, the expression on his face. Despite the lack of a nose, the face is surprisingly human, and if that expression was on a human face, it would be one of approval or pleasure."

"I think that if you put all the clues together, you can come to only one conclusion. Dr. Warden was not far off when he suggested a political campaign. The speaker is definitely trying to persuade his audience, but it is the package, not himself, that he is trying to sell."

"Oh, god," Kraft sputtered. "You can't mean it. The first communication from another planet and it's only . . ."

"Yes, I'm afraid so," Cristina said. "The first and only signal received from another world is nothing more than a breakfast food commercial."

Also From Resurrected Press
SCIENCE FICTION AUTHORS RESURRECTED

FYFE RESURRECTED - THE STORIES OF H. B. FYFE
Stories from the Golden Age of Science Fiction by the author of D-99. dealing with the interaction of humans and aliens on far off worlds in ways that were as creative as they were imaginative.

SCHMITZ RESURRECTED - SELECTED STORIES OF JAMES H. SCHMITZ
Includes "An Incident on Route 12", "Watch the Sky", "The Other Likeness", "The Star Hyacinths", "Oneness", "The Winds of Time", "Ham Sandwich" and "Gone Fishing".

SHECKLY RESURRECTED - THE EARLY STORIES OF ROBERT SHECKLEY
Resurrected Press has collected some of the best of these from the 50's including "Warrior Race", "The Leech", "Watchbird", "Warm", "Diplomatic Immunity", "The Hour of Battle", "Besides Still Waters", "Keep Your Shape", "One Man's Poison", 'Ask a Foolish Question", "Cost of Living", "Death Wish Forever".

DICK RESURRECTED - THE EARLY STORIES OF PHILIP K. DICK
Early stories from the author of the novels that inspired "Blade Runner," "Total Recall," and "A Scanner Darkly".

HAMILTON RESURRECTED - CLASSIC STORIES OF EDMOND HAMILTON
Edmond Hamilton was one of the most popular writers during the 30's and 40's, the period that saw the first flowering of modern science fiction.

SMITH RESURRECTED - SELECTED STORIES OF EVELYN E. SMITH ton
During an era when women rarely appeared in science fiction magazines, Evelyn E. Smith appeared regularly in the pages of Galaxy and Fantastic Universe. Resurrected Press is proud to return these stories to print.

OTHER CLASSIC SCIENCE FICTION NOVELS

TALENTS, INCORPORATED - BY MURRAY LEINSTER
When a Mekinese fleet conquers his home planet, Captain Bors turns to Talents, Incorporated for help using their collection of individuals with unusual abilities to defeat the enemy and save the galaxy.

THE PIRATES OF ERSATZ - BY MURRAY LEINSTER
Bran Hodden just wanted to be an electronic engineer and marry a delightful girl. But when he's framed by the powers on Walden he's forced to turn back to his family's trade, piracy. Also published as The Pirates of Zan.

EMPIRE - BY CLIFFORD SIMAK
Spencer Chambers and Interplanetary Power owned the Solar System because they controlled the source of power. It fell to Russell Page and Harry Wilson to challenge that control if they had to cross the universe to do it.

NIGHT OF THE LONG KNIVES - THE CREATURE FROM THE CLEVELAND DEPTHS - BY FRITZ LEIBER
Two classic novellas set in the not too distant future from a classic master of science fiction.

ARMAGEDDON - 2419 A.D. - THE AIR LORDS OF HAN - BY PHILLIP FRANCIS NOWLAN
The two novels that introduced the world to that intrepid hero of the 25th Century, Buck Rogers. Buck Rogers must save the world from the clutches of the insidious Han.

Resurrected Press Fiction by Randall Garrett

Anything You Can Do...

What do you do when an alien with exceptional physical abilities crash lands on Earth and leaves a path of death and destruction in its wake? You use biological modification to create an enhanced human able to match the alien in strength and speed. But is the result still human?

Unwise Child

After two unsuccessful and seemingly random attempts on his life in the space of as many hours, Michael Raphael Gabriel finds himself called on to act as engineering officer on a new type of spacecraft designed for one mission only, to carry a giant computer to a distant destination before it can destroy the Earth. But once under way he discovers there is a murderer on board and the computer has gone crazy.

By Randall Garrett and Laurence Janifer

Pagan Passions

The Gods and Goddesses of the Ancient Greece and Rome have returned to rule Earth. William Forrester, a mortal teacher, dedicated to the pleasures of the mind, finds himself caught up in the power struggles of the immortals and seduced by the pleasures of the flesh.

The Fictional Detective
by Greg Fowlkes

Who killed Ezekial O. Handler?

A beautiful dame, a hard-boiled private eye — and a dead body.

It started like any other case. When a famous writer dies in a mysterious car crash, private detective Frank Slade is called in to find answers, but all he finds is more questions. Who killed Ezekial Handler? Who is Janet Nielsen and why is she so interested in finding out? Who is leaving the neatly typed clues? And as Slade tries to find answers to these questions he starts to wonder if the ultimate answer will threaten his very existence.

Read about it in
The Fictional Detective

Visit www.thefictionaldetective.com

About Resurrected Press

A division of Intrepid Ink, LLC, Resurrected Press is dedicated to bringing high quality, vintage books back into publication. See our entire catalogue and find out more at www.ResurrectedPress.com.

About Intrepid Ink, LLC

Intrepid Ink, LLC provides full publishing services to authors of fiction and non-fiction books, eBooks and websites. From editing to formatting, from publishing to marketing, Intrepid Ink gets your creative works into the hands of the people who want to read them. Find out more at www.IntrepidInk.com.

www.ingramcontent.com/pod-product-compliance
Lightning Source LLC
Chambersburg PA
CBHW071156250626
47159CB00001B/117